ZANE GREY

WILDERNESS TREK

HarperPaperbacks
A Division of HarperCollins*Publishers*

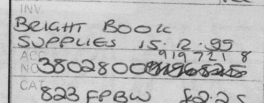
This is a work of fiction, the characters, incidents, and
dialogues are products of the author's imagination and
are not be construed as real. Any resemblance to actual
events or persons, living or dead, is entirely coincidental.

HarperPaperbacks *A Division of* HarperCollins*Publishers*
10 East 53rd Street, New York, N.Y. 10022

Copyright 1944 by Zane Grey, Inc.
Copyright © renewed 1972 by Zane Grey, Inc.
All rights reserved. No part of this book may be used
or reproduced in any manner whatsoever without written permission of the publisher, except in the case of
brief quotations embodied in critical articles and re-
views. For information address HarperCollins*Publishers*,
10 East 53rd Street, New York, N.Y. 10022.

Cover photo courtesy of Culver Pictures

First HarperPaperbacks printing: September 1991

Printed in the United States of America

HarperPaperbacks and colophon are trademarks of
HarperCollins*Publishers*

10 9 8 7 6 5 4 3 2

CHAPTER 1

ACROSS the blue Tasman Sea, smooth and heaving on that last day, the American adventurers eagerly watched the Australian horizon line grow bold and rugged.

"Red, it's land—land," said Sterl, his gray eyes dim from watching and remembrance of other land like that, from which he must forever be an exile. "The mate told me that was Sidney Heads over there."

"Shore, pard, I seen it long ago," replied Red. "This heah sea gettin' level an' that sight just about saved my life....Sterl, no more ridin' ships for Red Krehl."

"But Red, I begged you not to come," replied Hazelton.

"What kind of talk is thet? Do you think I'd ever let you go to hell alone? Pard, this heah Australia begins to loom up kinda big, at thet. But it's English— an' whoever heerd of an English gurl lookin' at a cowboy?"

"Red, someday you'll get enough girl to do you for good and all, as I got."

"Shore I can stand a lot, Sterl....Say, if I'd had a bottle on this ship I wouldn't be near daid now.... Sterl, let's have one orful drunk before we hunt for jobs."

"Sounds good, but it's not sense."

"But we never had no sense nohow," protested Red. "You takin' the blame for thet gunplay! An' me fool enough to let you!"

This time Sterling Hazelton did not reprove his friend.—The pang was still there in his breast.—Nan Halbert had loved him as well as his cousin, Ross Haight—Ross, lovable and sweet-tempered except in his cups, the only child of an ailing father with lands and herds to bequeath—Ross, who had shot a man who certainly deserved it. Sterl had taken upon himself that guilt, which to him was not guilt. His family had been gone so long that he hardly remembered them, except his schoolteacher mother who had loved and taught him. There had been only Nan. And what could he have done for her, compared with what Ross could do? It all rolled back in poignant memory to the scene where Ross had confronted him and Red that last night.

"But Sterl!" he had rung out, "Nan will believe

you killed this man!...And everybody else. How can I *stand* that?"

"For her sake! She loves you best.... Go straight, Ross.... Good-by!"

And Sterl had raced away into the blackness of the Arizona night, followed by the loyal Red.

"Red, you remember the package that Ross forced upon you to give me?" Hazelton said suddenly.

"Shore I remember," replied Red, looking up with interest. "I had a hunch it was money...."

"Yes—money. Ten thousand dollars!"

"Holy mavericks!" ejaculated Red, astounded. "Where'd Ross get it?"

"Must have told his father. Red, I'm asking you to take half of this money and go back home."

"Yeah! The hell you air?" retorted Red.

"Yes, pard, I'm begging you."

"An' why for?" queried Red. " 'Cause you don't want me with you?"

"No—no. It'd be grand to have you—but for your sake!"

"Wal, if it's for my sake don't insult me no more. Would you leave me if you was me an' I you? Honest Injun, Sterl? Wal, what's eatin' you then?"

"All right, I apologize. Stay with me, Red. God knows I'll need you.... Boy, we're getting somewhere. Look. There's a big ship steaming along under the left wall, from the west."

"Gosh, they shore look grand. I never seen ships atall till we got to Frisco.... This Sydney must be a real man-sized burg, huh?"

"Big city, Red, and I'm going to take you out of it *muy pronto*."

"Suits me, pard. But what air we gonna do? We don't know nuthin' but hosses, guns an' cattle."

"I read that Australia is going to be a big cattle country."

"If thet's a fact we're ridin' pretty," returned Red, with satisfaction.

They lapsed into one of their frequent silences while the ship sailed on, her yards and booms creaking. Soon the mile-wide gateway to Australia offered the sailing ship a lonely entrance. Australia's far-famed harbor opened up to Sterl's sight, a long curving bay with many arms cutting into the land. Miles inland, around a broad turn where ships rode at anchor, the city of Sydney stood revealed, foreign and stately, gray-walled, red-roofed.

While Sterl and Red packed their bags, the ship eased alongside a dock, and tied up. From the dock, they were led into a shed, and after a brief examination were free. One of the stevedores directed them to an inn, where soon they had a room.

It was early in the afternoon. Krehl voted for seeing the sights. But Sterl disapproved, for that meant looking upon drink.

"Pard, we must get our bearings and rustle for the open range," he said.

Whereupon they set out to ask two cardinally important questions—where was the cattle country and how could they get there?

"Outback," replied more than one person, waving a hand, that like an Indian's gesture signified vague and remote distance. At last a big man looked them up and down and smiled when he asked, "Yankees?"

"Yes. It must be written all over us," admitted Sterl, with an answering smile.

"Are you drovers?"

"Drovers?" echoed Sterl.

"Horsemen—drivers of cattle."

"Oh! You bet. Plain Arizona and Texas cowboys. We eat up hard work. Where can we get jobs?"

"Any station owner will hire you. But I advise you to go to Queensland. Big cattle mustering there."

"Where and how far?" queried Sterl, eagerly.

"Five hundred miles up the coast and inland three or four hundred more. Board the freighter 'Merryvale' down at the dock. Sails at six today. Brisbane, is your stop. Good luck, cowboys."

Sterl led his comrade down the waterfront to where the big freighter was tied up in the center of busy shipping activities and bought passage to Brisbane. Next morning they awoke to find the sea calm, with the steamer tearing along not five miles out from a picturesque shoreline. And as the partners leaned over the rail of this steamer, to gaze at a white-wreathed shoreline, extending for leagues on leagues to north and south, at the rolling green ridges rising on and upward to the high ranges, Sterl felt that beyond these calling, dim mountains there might await him the greatest adventure of his life.

"Dog-gone-it!" Red was drawling. "I wanta be

mad as hell, but I jest cain't. Gosh, pard, it's grand country! I hate to knuckle to it, but even Texas cain't beat thet!"

The sailors were friendly and talkative. On the second afternoon, the skipper, a fine old seadog, invited them to come up on the bridge. Sterl took advantage of the opportunity to tell him their plans.

"Boys, you've a fine opening, if you can stand the heat, the dust, the drought, the blacks, the floods, the fires, besides harder work than galley slaves," he said.

"Captain, driving cattle on the Texas plain wasn't just a picnic," replied Sterl.

"You'll think so, after droving upcountry here."

"Boss, I reckon we've been up agin' all you said 'cept the blacks. Jest what air these blacks?" inquired Red, deeply interested.

"The natives of Australia. Aborigines."

"You mean niggers?"

"Some people call them niggers. They're not negroes. But they are black as coal."

"Bad medicine, mebbe?" inquired Red.

"Cannibals. They eat you."

"Boss," said Red, "I've had my fill of fightin' greasers, rustlers, robbers an' redskins on the Texas trails, but gosh! all of them put together cain't be as wuss as black men—cannibals who eat you."

"Captain," said Sterl, "you're sure putting the wind up us, as you Australians say. But tell us a little about cattle, and ranches—you call them stations."

"I've only a general bit of knowledge," returned

the skipper. "There are stations up and down New South Wales, and eastern and central Queensland. Gradually cattlemen are working outback. I've heard of the terrible times they had. No drovers have yet gone into the unknown interior—called the Never-never Land by the few explorers who did not leave their bones to be picked by the black men."

"Pard, thet's kinda hard to believe," said Red, shaking his head. "No places I ever heerd about was as bad as they was painted."

"You are in for an adventure at any rate," went on the skipper. "There's some big movement on from Brisbane. We have consignments of flour, harness, wagons, on board that prove it."

The "Merryvale" docked at dawn. After breakfast Sterl and Red labored ashore, dragging their burdens of baggage, curious and eager as boys half their age. Brisbane did not impress them with its bigness, but it sparkled under a bright sun, and appeared alive and bustling.

They found a hotel, and sallied forth on the second lap of their adventure. They were directed to a merchandise store which was filling orders for a company of drovers making ready to leave Downsville in Central Queensland for points unknown.

Sterl got hold of the manager, a weather-beaten man who had seen service in the open.

"Is there any chance for jobs outback?" he asked.

"Chance? Young man, they'll welcome you with open arms. Report is that the drovers can't find men enough to start. Bing Slyter is here with his teamsters. He's one of the drovers and he's buying supplies for the Danns. I'll find him for you."

In a moment they faced a big man whose wide shoulders made his height appear moderate. If he was an Australian cattleman, Sterl thought, he surely liked the type. Slyter had a strong face cast in bronze, a square chin, and eyes that pierced like daggers.

"Good day, young men," he said, in a voice that matched his size. "Watson here tells me you're American cowboys looking for jobs."

"Yes, sir. I'm Sterling Hazelton, from Arizona, and this is Red Krehl, from Texas. I'm twenty-five and he's a year younger. We were born to the saddle and have driven cattle all our lives. We rode the Chisholm Trail for three years. That's our recommendation."

"It's enough, after looking you over," returned Slyter, in booming gladness. "We Australians have heard of the Chisholm Trail. You drove mobs of cattle across Texas north to new markets in Kansas?"

"Yes, sir. Five hundred miles of hard going. Sand, bad rivers, buffalo stampedes, electric storms, hail-stones, Indians and rustlers."

"Rustlers? We call them bushrangers. Cattle thieves just beginning to make themselves felt. I'll give you jobs. What wages do you ask?"

"Whatever you want to pay will satisfy us," replied Sterl. "We want hard riding in a new country."

"Settled: If it's hard riding you want you'll get it. We drovers are undertaking the greatest trek in Australian history. Seven or eight thousand cattle three thousand miles across the Never-never!"

"Mr. Slyter," burst out Sterl, "such a drive is unheard of. Three thousand Texas longhorns made hell on earth for a dozen cowboys. But this herd— this mob, as you call it—across that Never-never Land, if it's unknown and as terrible as they say.... Why, man, the drive is impossible."

"Hazelton, we can do it, and you're going to be a great help. I was discouraged before I left home. But my daughter Leslie said: 'Dad, don't give up. You'll find men!' Leslie's a grand kid."

"You're taking your family on this trek?" queried Sterl, aghast.

"Yes. And there'll be at least one other family."

"You Australians don't lack nerve," smiled Sterl. "Do you need money to outfit?"

"No, sir. But we need to know what to buy."

"Buy rifles, and all the ammunition you can afford. Tents, blankets, and mosquito nets, clothes, extra boots, socks, some tools, a medicine kit, bandages, gloves—a dozen pairs, some bottles of whisky, and about a ton, more or less, of tobacco. That goes farthest with the blacks. You needn't stint on account of room. We'll have wagons and drays."

"But, Mr. Slyter," exclaimed Sterl, in amaze, "we don't want to stock a store!"

"Boys," laughed the drover, "this great trek will take two years. Two years droving across the Never-

never Land to the Kimberleys!"

"It *will* be never!" cried Sterl, staggered at the import.

"*Whoopee!*" yelled Red.

*T**HE** remainder of that stimulating day Sterl and Red spent in the big merchandise store, making purchases for a two-years' trip beyond the frontier. Investment in English saddles, two fine English rifles to supplement Sterl's Winchester .44 and thousands of cartridges broke the ice of old accustomed frugality, and introduced an orgy of spending.

It took a dray to transport their outfit to the yard on the outskirts of town, to which they had been directed. Late in the afternoon they had all their purchases stowed away in the front of one of the big new wagons, with their baggage on top, and the woolen blankets spread. Before that, however, they had changed their traveling clothes to the worn and comfortable garb of cowboys. Sterl had not felt so good for weeks. It was all settled. No turning back! That time of contending tides of trouble was past. He would be happy, presently, and forget.

They had scraped acquaintance with one of Slyter's teamsters, a hulking, craggy-visaged chap some years their senior, who announced that his name was Roland Tewksbury Jones. Red's reaction to that cognomen was characteristic.

"Yeah? Have a cigar," he said, producing one with a grand flourish. "My handle is Red. Seein' as how I couldn't remember yore turrible name I'll call you Rol, for short. On the Texas trails I knowed a lot of Joneses, in particular Buffalo Jones, Dirty Face Jones and Wrong-Wheel Jones."

Roland evinced a calm speculation as to what manner of man this Yankee cowboy was. He accepted Sterl's invitation to have dinner with them, and invited them to go to a pub for a drink. Returning to their wagon, they found a fire blazing and the other teamsters busily loading the supplies. Spreading their canvas and blankets under the wagon, as they had done thousands of times, the cowboys turned in. Sterl slept infinitely sounder out in the open, on the hard ground, than he had for two months, on soft beds. Indeed, the sun was shining brightly when the cowboys awoke. Teamsters were leading horses out of the paddock; others were tying tarpaulins over the wagons. Jones addressed Red: "You have time for breakfast if you move as fast as you said you did in Texas."

Returning to the outfit, Sterl saw that they were about ready to start, two teams to a wagon. He had an appreciative eye for the powerful horses. He found a seat beside the driver, while Red propped himself up behind. Inquiry about Mr. Slyter elicited the information that the head drover had left at daylight in his light two-horse rig. Jones took up the reins and led the procession of drays and wagons out into the road.

Soon the town was left behind. A few farms and gardens lined the road for several miles. Then the yellow grass-centered road led into a jungle of green and gold and bronze. They had ten days or more to drive, mostly on a level road, said Jones, with good camp sites, plenty of water and grass, meat for the killing, mosquitoes in millions, and bad snakes.

"Bad snakes?" echoed Sterl, in dismay. He happened to be not over-afraid of snakes, and he had stepped on many a rattler, to jump out of his boots, but the information was not welcome.

"Say, Rol, I heahed you," interposed Red, who feared neither man nor beast nor savage, but was in mortal terror of snakes. "Thet's orful bad news. What kind of snakes?"

Sterl sensed Jones's rising to the occasion. "Black and brown snakes most common, and grow to eight feet. Hit you hard and are not too poisonous. Tiger snakes mean and aggressive. If you hear a sharp hiss turn to stone right where you are. Death adders are the most dangerous. They are short, thick, sluggish beggars and rank poison. The pythons and boas are not so plentiful. But you meet them. They grow to twenty feet and can give you quite a hug."

"Aw, is thet all?" queried Red, who evidently was impressively scared, despite his natural skepticism.

The thick golden-green grass grew as high as the flanks of a horse; cabbage trees and a stunted brushy palm stood up conspicuously; and the gum trees, or eucalyptus, grew in profusion. Shell-barked and smooth, some of them resembled the bronze and opal sycamores of America, and others beeches and laurels. Here and there stood up a lofty spotted gum, branchless for a hundred feet, and then spreading great, curved limbs above the other trees to terminate in fine, thin-leaved, steely-green foliage.

As they penetrated inland, birds began to attract Sterl. A crow with a dismal and guttural caw took him back to the creek bottoms of Texas. Another crow, black with white spotted wings, Jones called Australia's commonest bird, the magpie. It appeared curious and friendly, and had a melodious note that grew upon Sterl. It was deep and rich—a lovely sound—*cur-ra-wong—cur-ra-wong*.

"See you like birds. So do I," said Jones to Sterl. "Australians ought to, for we have hundreds of wonderful kinds. The lyre-bird in the bush can imitate any song or sound he hears. Leslie Slyter loves them. She knows where they stay, too. Perhaps she'll take you at daybreak to hear them."

Here Red Krehl pricked up his ears to attention. Anything in the world that could be relegated in the slightest to femininity, Red clasped to his breast.

Presently the road led out of the jungle into a big area of ground cleared of all except the largest trees. On a knoll stood a house made of corrugated iron. Jones called it a cattle station. Sterl looked for cattle in vain. Red said: "Shines out like a dollar in a fog."

Grass and brush densely covered the undulating hills. Sterl concluded that Australian cattle were equally browsers and grazers. The road wound to and fro between the hills, keeping to a level, eventually to enter thick bush again. Sterl made the acquaintance of flocks of colored parrots—galahs the driver called them—that flew swiftly as bullets across the road; and then a flock of white cockatoos that squawked in loud protest at the invasion of their domain. When they sailed above the wagon, wide wings spread, Sterl caught a faint tinge of yellow. When they crossed the first brook, a clear swift little stream that passed on gleaming and glancing under the wide-spreading foliage, a blue heron and a white crane took lumbering flight.

They came into a wide valley, rich in wavy grass, and studded with bunches of cattle and horses. "Ha! Some hosses," quoth Red. As Jones slowed up along a bank higher than the wagon bed, Sterl heard solid thumping thuds, then a swish of grass, and Red's stentorian, "WHOOPEE!"

He wheeled in time to see three great, strange, furry animals leaping clear over the wagon. They had long ears and enormous tails. He recognized them in the middle of their prodigious leap, but could not remember their names. They cleared the road, to bound away as if on springs.

"Whoa!" yelled Red. "What'n'll was thet? ... Did you see what I see? Lord! there ain't no such critters!"

"Kangaroos," said the teamster. "And that biggest one is an old man roo all right."

"Oh, what a sight!" exclaimed Sterl. "Kangaroos—of course.... One of them almost red. Jones, it struck me they sprang off their tails."

"Kangaroos do use their tails. Wait till you get smacked with one."

The trio of queer beasts stopped some hundred rods off and sat up to gaze at the wagon.

"Air they good to eat?" queried the practical Red.

"We like kangaroo meat when we can't get beef or turkey or fowl. But that isn't often."

"What's that?" shouted Sterl, suddenly, espying a small gray animal hopping across the road.

"Wallaby. A small species of kangaroo."

More interesting miles, that seemed swift, brought them to an open flat crossed by a stream bordered with full-foliaged yellow-blossoming trees, which Jones called wattles. Jones made a halt here to rest and water the horses, and to let the other wagons catch up. Red began to make friends with the other teamsters, always an easy task for the friendly, loquacious cowboy. They appeared to belong to a larger, brawnier type than the American outdoor men, and certainly were different from the lean, lithe, narrow-hipped, cowboy. They built a fire and set about making tea "boiling the billy," Jones called it. Sterl sampled the beverage and being strange even to American tea he said: "Now I savvy why you English are so strong."

"I should smile," drawled Red, making a wry face. "I shore could ride days on thet drink."

Under a huge gum tree, in another green valley, on the bank of a creek, Jones drove into a cleared space and called a halt for camp.

"Wal, Rol, what air there for me an' my pard to do?" queried the genial Red.

"That depends. What *can* you Yankees do?" replied Jones, simply, as if really asking for information.

Red cocked a blazing blue eye at the teamster and drawled: "Wal, it'd take a lot less time if you'd ask what we cain't do. Outside of possessin' all the cowboy traits such as ridin', ropin', shootin', we can hunt, butcher, cook, bake sour-dough biscuits an' cake, shoe hosses, mend saddle cinches, plait ropes, chop wood, build fires in wet weather, bandage wounds an' mend broken bones, smoke, drink, play poker, an' fight."

"You forgot one thing, I've observed, Red, and that is—you can talk," replied Jones, still sober-faced as a judge.

"Yeah? . . . But fun aside, what mought we do?"

"Anything you can lay a hand to," answered the driver, cheerily.

One by one the other wagons rolled up. These teamsters were efficient and long used to camp tasks. The one who evidently was cook knew his business.

"Easy when you have everything," he said to Sterl. "But when we get out on trek, with nothing but meat and tea, and damper, then no cook is good."

After supper Sterl got out his rifle and, loading it, strolled away from camp along the edge of the creek. The sun was setting gold, lighting the shiny-barked gums and burnishing the long green leaves. He came upon a giant tree fern where high over his head the graceful lacy leaves drooped down. The great gum was by far the most magnificent tree Sterl had ever seen. It stood over two hundred feet high, with no branches for half that distance; then they spread wide, as large in themselves as ordinary trees. The color was a pale green with round pieces of red-brown bark sloughing off.

All at once Sterl's keen eye caught the movement of something. It was a small, round, furry animal, gray in color, with blunt head and tiny ears. It was clinging to a branch, peering comically down at him, afraid. Then Sterl espied another one, farther up, another far out on the same branch, and at last a fourth, swinging upon a swaying tip. Sterl yelled lustily for Red and Jones.

"Look, Red! Jones, what are those queer little animals?"

"Koala bears," said the teamster, "Queensland bush alive with them."

"Pard, pass me yore gun," said Red.

"Ump-umm, you bloodthirsty cowboy!... They look tame."

"They are tame," rejoined Jones. "Friendly little

fellows. Leslie has some for pets."

Night made the campfire pleasant. The teamsters, through for the day, sat around smoking and talking. Campfires in Australia seemed to have the same cheer, the same opal hearts and flying sparks, the same drawing together of kindred spirits, that they had on the ranges of America. But the great Southern Cross, an aloof and marvelous constellation, proved to Sterl that he was an exile. A dismal chorus of wild barks sounded from the darkness.

"Dingoes," said a teamster.

"Dingoes. Haw! Haw!" laughed Red, "Another funny one."

"Wild dogs. They overrun Australia. Hunt in packs. When hungry, which is often, they're dangerous."

"Listen," said Sterl, "Isn't that a dismal sound? Not a yelp in it. Nor any of that long, wailing sharp cry of the coyote which we range riders love so well."

"A little too cool tonight to be bothered with mosquitoes," remarked Jones. "We'll run into some farther outback. They can bite through two pairs of socks."

"Gee!" said Red. "But thet's nothin' atall, Rol. We have muskeeters in Texas—wal, I heahed about one cowboy who was alone when a flock of 'em flew down on him. Smoke an' fire didn't help none. By golly, he had to crawl under a copper kettle thet the cook had. Wal, the sons-of-guns bored through the kettle. The cowboy took his gun an' riveted their bills on the inside. An' damn me if them skeeters didn't fly away with the kettle!"

Red's listeners remained mute under the onslaught of that story, no doubt beginning a reversal of serious acceptance of all the cowboy said. Sterl followed Red toward their tent.

The crackling of fire without awoke him. Dark, moving shadows on the yellow tent wall told that the teamsters were stirring.

He parted the tent flaps and went out to find it dark as pitch beyond the blazing fires, air cold, stars like great white lanterns through the branches, active teamsters whistling as they hitched up the teams, fragrance of ham and tea wafting strong.

"Morning, Hazelton," was Jones's cheery greeting. "Was just going to yell that cowboy call, 'Come and get it!'...We'll have a good early start." Sterl could not recall when he had faced a day with such exuberance.

A long gradual ascent through thick bush offered no view, but the melodious carol of magpies, the squall of the cockatoos, the sweet songs of thrush, were worth the early rising. Topping a long ascent Jones drove out of the bush into the open. "Kangaroo Flat," said the teamster. "Thirty miles. Good road. We'll camp at the other end tonight."

"Aw, thet's fine....Holy Mackeli, pard, air you seein' what I see?" exclaimed Red.

Sterl was indeed, and quite speechless. A soft hazed valley, so long that the far end appeared lost in purple vagueness, stretched out beneath them, like a sea burnished with golden fire. It was so fresh, so pure, so marvelously vivid in sunrise tones! The enchanted distances struck Sterl anew. Australia was prodigal with its endless leagues. As the sun came up above the low bushland a wave of flame stirred the long grass and spread on and on. The cool air blew sweet and odorous into his face, reminding him of the purple sage uplands of Utah.

Down on a level again their view was restricted to space near at hand. A band of dingoes gave them a parting chorus where the bush met the flat. Rabbits began to scurry through the short gray-green grass and run ahead along the road, and they increased in numbers until there appeared to be thousands.

"One of Australia's great pests," said Jones.

"Yeah? Wal, in thet case I gotta take some pegs," replied Red, and he proceeded to raise the small calibre rifle and to shoot at running targets. This little rifle and full store of cartridges had been gifts from Sterl. Red did not hit any of the rabbits. Deadly with a handgun, as were so many cowboys, he shot only indifferently well with a rifle. Sterl's unerring aim, however, applied to both weapons.

Kangaroos made their appearance, sticking their heads out of the grass, long ears erect, standing at gaze watching the wagon go by, or hopping along ahead with their awkward yet easy gait. In some places they slowed the trotting team to a walk.

The sky was dotted with waterfowl. Jones explained there were watercourses through the flat, and a small lake in the center, where birds congregated by the thousands.

Sterl's quick eye caught a broken column of smoke rising from the bushland in the rear.

"By golly! Red, look at that!"

"Shore I was wonderin'. How about it, Rol?"

"Black men signaling across the flat. Look over here. They know all about us twenty miles ahead. The aborigines talk with smoke."

"All the same Indian stuff," ejaculated Red.

"Stanley Dann, who's mustering this big trek, says the abos will be our worst obstacle," volunteered Jones.

"Has Dann make a trek before?"

"No. This will be new to all the drovers."

"Do they believe there's safety in numbers?"

"That is one reason for the large muster of men and cattle."

"Like our wagon trains crossing the Great Plains. But driving cattle is a different thing. The Texas trail drivers found out that ten or twelve cowboys and up to three thousand head of longhorns moved faster, had fewer stampedes and lost fewer cattle than a greater number."

After a short rest the cavalcade proceeded onward across the rippling sea of colored grass. Herons were not new to Sterl, but white ibis, spoonbills, egrets, jaribu, and other wading fowl afforded him lasting wonder and appreciation. The storks particularly caught his eye. Their number seemed incredible. They were mostly gray in color, huge cranelike birds, tall as a man; they had red on their heads, and huge bills. Sterl exchanged places with Red, and drowsy from excessive looking, went to sleep. He was awakened by yells. Sitting up he found Red waving wildly.

"Ostriches!...Black ostriches!" yelled Red, beside himself..."Whoever'd thunk it?...Dog-gone my pictures!...Sterl, wake up. You're missin' somethin'.'"

Sterl did not need Red's extended arm to sight a line of huge black bird creatures, long-necked and long-legged, racing across the road.

"Emu," said the teamster, laconically. "You run over them outback."

"As I'm a born sinner heah comes a bunch of hosses!" exclaimed Red, pointing. On the range Red had been noted, even among hawk-eyed riders and *vaqueros*, for his keen sight.

"Brumbies," declared Jones.

"What?—What you say?" shouted Red. "If they're not wild hosses, I'll eat 'em."

"Wild, surely. But they're brumbies," said the Australian.

Red emitted a disgusted snort. "Brumbies! Who in the hell ever heahed of callin' wild hosses such an orful name?"

"Red, it is a silly name," responded Jones, with his rare grin. "I suggest we have an interchange and understanding of names, so you won't have to lick me."

"Wal, I reckon I couldn't lick you, at thet," retorted Red, quick as a flash to meet friendliness.

"You're an orful big chap, Rol, an' could probably beat hell out of me pronto. So I'll take you up."

"What does pronto mean?"

"Quick. Right now.... I heahed you say 'pad.' In my country a pad is what you put under a saddle. What is it heah?"

"A pad is a path through the bush. A narrow single track."

"Ahuh. But thet's a trail, Rol. Say, you're gonna have fun ediccatin' us. Sterl heah had a mother who was a schoolteacher, an' he's one smart *hombre*."

The sun slanted toward the far horizon, the brightness changed to gold and rose. It was some time short of twilight when Jones hauled up at the edge of the bush, which had beckoned for so many hours. A bare spot on the bank of a narrow slow-moving stream attested to many campfires.

"Look!" interposed Sterl, pointing at forms across the stream. They were natives, of course, but a first actual sight was disconcerting.

"Black man, with gin and lubra, and some kids," said Jones.

"Holy Mackeli!" ejaculated Red. "They look human—but—"

Sterl's comrade, with his usual perspicuity, had hit it. The group of natives stood just at the edge of the bush. Sterl saw six figures out in the open, but he had a glimpse of others. The man was exceedingly tall, thin, black as coal, almost naked. He held a spear upright, and it stood far above his shaggy head. A scant beard fuzzed the lower part of his face. His big, bold, somber eyes glared a moment, then with a long stride he went back into the bush. The women lingered curiously. The older, the "gin," was hideous to behold. The lubra, a young girl, appeared sturdy and voluptuous. Both were naked except for short grass skirts. The children were wholly nude. A harsh voice sent them scurrying into the bush.

"Gosh! I'd hate to meet thet long-laiged *hombre* in the dark," said Red.

"Hope some of them come around our campfire," added Sterl, with zest.

He had his wish. After supper, about dusk, the black man appeared, a towering unreal figure. He did not have the long spear. The cook gave him something to eat; and the native, making quick despatch of that, accosted Jones in a low voice.

"Him sit down alonga fire," replied Jones, pointing to Sterl.

The black man slowly approached the fire, then stood motionless on the edge of the circle of light. Presently he came up to Sterl.

"Tobac?" he asked, in low deep voice.

"Yes," replied Sterl, and offered what he had taken the precaution to get from his pack. At the exchange Sterl caught a good look at the native's hands, to find them surprisingly supple and shapely. He next caught a strong body odor, which was unpleasant.

"Sit down, chief," said Sterl, making appropriate signs. The black man, folding his long legs under him, appeared to sit on them. A cigar Sterl had given him was evidently a new one on the native. But as Sterl was smoking one, he quickly caught on. Sterl, adopting the method cowboys always used when plains Indians visited the campfires, manifested a silent dignity. The black man was old—no one could have told how old. There was gray in his shaggy locks, and his visage was a map of lines that portrayed the havoc of elemental strife. Sterl divined thought and feeling in this savage, and he felt intensely curious.

Jones left the other teamsters, to come over and speak to the native.

"Any black fella close up?" he asked.

"Might be," was the terse reply.

"Me watchem smokes all alonga bush."

But the aborigine returned silence to that remark. Presently he arose and stalked away in the gloom.

"Queer duck," said Red, reflectively.

"He sure interested me," replied Sterl. "All except the smell of him. Rol, do all these blacks smell that bad?"

"Some worse, some not at all. It's something they grease themselves with."

On the fifth day, they reached the blue hills that had beckoned to Sterl. The wagon road wound into a region of numerous creeks and fertile valleys where parrots and parakeets abounded. They passed by one station that day and through one little sleepy hamlet of a few houses and a store, with outlying paddocks where Sterl espied some fine horses. Camp that night offered a new experience to the cowboys. The cook was out of beef, and Jones took them hunting. They did not have to go far to find kangaroo, or shoot often. The meat had a flavor that Sterl thought would grow on him, and Red avowed it was equal to porterhouse steak or buffalo rump.

Two noons later Jones drove out of the jungle to the edge of a long slope that afforded view of Slyter's valley.

"That road goes on to Downsville," said Jones, pointing, "a good few miles. This road leads to Slyter's station. Water and grass for a reasonable sized mob of cattle. But Bing has big ideas."

Presently Slyter's gray-walled, tin-roofed house came into sight, picturesquely located on a green bench with a background of huge eucalyptus trees, and half hidden in a bower of golden wattle. The hills on each side spread wider and wider, to where the valley opened into the range, and numberless cattle dotted the grassy land.

Along the brook, farther down, bare-poled fences of corrals came into sight, and then a long, low, log barn, with a roof of earth and green grass and yellow flowers, instead of the ugly galvanized iron.

"Home!" sang out Jones. "Eight days' drive! Not so bad. If we just didn't have that impossible trek to face!"

"Wal, Rollie Tewksbury Jones!" declared Red, gayly. "You air human after all. Fust time I've heahed you croak."

Sterl leaped down to stretch his cramped legs.

Red called for him to pick out a camp site up from the low ground a little, while he helped the teamsters unhitch. Sterl walked on, intending to find a place for the tent under those yellow-blooming wattles. He heard rapid footfalls coming from somewhere. As he passed the corner of the barn, his face turned the other way, trying to locate whoever was running, someone collided violently with him, almost upsetting him.

He turned to see that this individual had been knocked almost flat. He thought that it was a boy because of the boots and blue pants. But a cloud of chestnut hair, tossed aside, disclosed the tanned face and flashing, hazel eyes of a girl. She raised herself, hands propped on the ground, to lean back and look up at him. Spots of red came into her clear cheeks. Lips of the same hue curled in a smile, disclosing even, white teeth.

"Oh, miss! I'm sorry," burst out Sterl, in dismay. "I wasn't looking....You ran plump into me."

"Rath-thur!" she replied, "Dad always said I'd run into something some day. I did....I'm Leslie."

*T*HE girl leaped erect, showing herself to be above medium height, lithe and strong, yet with a rounded form no boy's garb could hide.

"You're Dad's Yankee cowboy—not the red-headed one?"

"I'm Sterl Hazelton," returned Sterl, "Glad to meet you, Miss Leslie."

"Thanks. I'm glad, too. Dad has been home four days, and I could hardly wait." She looked up at him with wonderful clear eyes that took him in from head to foot.

"I came up here to find a place for our tent. All right to put it there, under this tree?"

"Of course. But we have a spare room in the house."

"No, thank you. Red and I couldn't sleep indoors."

"Let us go down. I want to meet Red. Did you have a good trek outback?"

"It was simply great. I never looked so hard and long before."

"Oh, how nice! You're going to like Australia?"

"I do already. And Red can't hide from me how he likes it, too."

It chanced that they came upon Red when his back was turned, as he was lifting bags out of the wagon.

"Red, a lady to meet you." Sterl saw him start, grow rigid, then slowly turn, to disclose a flushing, amazed face. "Miss Slyter, this is my pard, Red Krehl. . . . Red, our boss's daughter, Miss Leslie."

At this juncture Slyter, stalwart and vital in his range garb, stamped down upon them. "Roland, you made a fine drive. So, cowboys, here you are. Welcome to Australia's outback! We saw you coming, and I sent Leslie to meet you. How are you, and did you like the short ride out?"

"Mr. Slyter, I never had a finer ride in my life," averred Sterl.

"Boss, it shore was grand," added Red. "But short? Umpumm. It was orful long. I see right heah we gotta get so we can savvy each other's lingo."

"That will come in time, Krehl. I'm just back from Downsville. Allan Hathaway leaves tomorrow with six drovers and a mob of fifteen hundred cattle. Woolcott has mustered twelve hundred and will follow. Stanley and Eric Dann go next day with ten drovers and thirty-five hundred head. We are to catch up with them. Ormiston has three drovers and eight hundred head. He wants to drove with us. I don't know Ormiston and I'm not keen about joining him. But what can I do? Stanley Dann is our leader. Our own mob is about mustered. Now all that's left to do is pack and start."

"Oh, Dad! I'm on pins and needles!" cried Leslie, jumping up and down, and clapping her hands.

"Slyter, how many riders—drovers have you?" queried Sterl.

"Four, not counting you cowboys. Here's Leslie, who's as good as any drover. I'll drive our covered wagon and Bill Williams, our cook, will drive one dray. Roland, you'll have the other."

"Seven riders, counting Miss Leslie," pondered Sterl.

"I see you think that's not enough," spoke up Slyter. "Hazelton, it'll have to do. I can't hire any more in this country."

"Boss, how about yore *remuda*?" interposed Red, anxiously.

"Remuda?"

"Excoose me, boss. Thet's Texas lingo for hosses. How many hosses will you take?"

"We've mustered the best of my stock. About a hundred. The rest I've sold in Downsville."

"Dad has the finest horses in Queensland," interrupted Leslie.

"Well, men, I'm glad to get that off my mind,"
concluded Slyter, with a laugh. "Roland, send Bill up
to get supper. Hazelton, you boys come up when
you've unpacked. Leslie, let's go back to Mum."

Sterl labored up the grassy bench, conscious of
a queer little sensation of pleasure, the origin of
which he thought he had better not analyze. He
dropped the heavy canvas roll in the likeliest spot,
and sat down in the golden glow from the wattle.
The adventure he had fallen upon seemed unbelievable. But here was this golden-green valley, with purple sunset-gilded ranges in the distance; there was
bowlegged Red staggering up the gentle slope with
his burdens. He reached Sterl, wiped the sweat from
his red face, and said:

"Queer deal, eh pard?"

"I should snicker to snort, as you say sometimes."

"Pard, I've a hunch these fine Australian men
have no idee what they're up agin'. They're takin'
their familees. Leastways Slyter is, an' this Stanley
Dann. One fine *hombre*, accordin' to Jones. Takin'
his only daughter, too. Beryl Dann. Wal, it'd be hard
enough an' tough enough for us without a couple of
girls.... This Leslie kid. About sixteen, I'd say. But a
woman, an' full of all a woman has to make men
trouble."

Just before dusk, they were called to supper.
They entered a big plain living room, where a fire
burned in a rude stone fireplace, and a long table
with steaming, savory foods invited keen relish. Mrs.

Slyter was a buxom, pleasant woman. Leslie inherited her fine physique. However, when the girl came in, Sterl hardly recognized her in a dress. Her frank, winning gaiety offset the mother's silence. Red brought a smile to Mrs. Slyter's face, however, by saying that such a supper would be something to remember when he was hungry way out on the Never-never.

"Boys, in the morning first thing I want you to look over the horses," said Slyter. "After that we'll ride over to town. Dann is keen to talk with you."

"Miss Leslie, what was thet you said about yore Dad's hosses?" asked Red.

"Dad breeds the finest stock in Australia," she replied. "That's where his heart is. And mine, too. The chief reason Dad wants to cross the Never-never is because he has learned that in the far northwest, in the country of the Kimberleys, there is a perfect climate, grass and water beyond a drover's dreams."

"Sounds sweet. What air the Kimberleys?"

"Mountain ranges. Stanley Dann's brother Eric has seen them. He says they are paradise. He trekked to the Kimberleys several years ago. But that trek did not cross the Never-never."

"I savvy. Then thet three-thousand-mile drive we're undertakin' is jest a short cut?"

"It is, really. The whole idea thrills me through and through."

"Shore. I can see why for a boy. But for a girl—"

"I'm tired of that Downsville school. Then I

couldn't let Mum and Dad go without me."

"Yeah? But can you ride, Miss Leslie?" went on Red, drawling, quizzically.

"Please don't call me miss....Ride? I'll give you a go any day, Mister Cowboy."

"Please don't call me mister.... 'Course I wouldn't race you. No girl in the world could beat a Texas cowboy."

"I wouldn't risk any guesses or wagers," said Sterl.

"You'd better not. My horses are the finest in Queensland. We'll miss the races this fall. I'm sorry about that. All the fun we ever have here is racing."

"Yore hosses. You mean yore Dad's?" inquired Red.

"No, my own. I have ten. I'm just waiting to show you!"

When the cowboys said good night and walked toward their camp, Red inquired: "Pard, did you look Leslie over tonight?"

"I saw her, but I didn't look twice."

"Shore a fine looker in thet blue dress. She was born on a hoss all right. Did you notice she was a little less free with you than with me?"

"No, pard, I didn't."

"Wal, she was. But thet isn't goin' to keep me from takin' my chance. Aw, I don't entertain no big hope of cuttin' you out. I never could win any girl when you was around."

"Red, you can have them all," declared Sterl.

At day-break they were off for the paddock,

laden with saddles, bridles and blankets. Another barn marked the opening to the level valley. Cattle were bawling, horses whistling, thrushes singing. A heavy dew glistened upon grass and brush. Down the lane, riders mounted bareback were riving a string of horses into a corral.

Presently Sterl and Red were perched upon the top bar of the corral fence, as they had been perhaps thousands of times on western ranches, directing keen and experienced eyes at the drove of dusty, shaggy horses. They proved to be fat, full of fire and dash, superb in every requirement. They came of a rangier, heavier, more powerful stock that the ordinary western horses, and in these particulars were markedly superior to the plains cayuse.

"Gosh-durn-it! I never seen their beat. Did we have to come way out heah to see English stock beat the socks off ours?" said Red.

"But, Red, good horses have to have speed and stamina," returned Sterl, weakly.

"Hell, you can see thet in every line. Hosses gotta be the same all over. We never knowed any but ornery-eyed, kickin', bitin' cayuses."

"Red, I remember a few that you couldn't call that. Baldy, Whiteface, Spot—and you couldn't forget Dusty—that broke his heart and died on his feet for you."

"Shet up! I wasn't meanin' a hoss in a thousand. Lord, could I forget the day Dusty outrun them Comanches?"

Jones sauntered over, accompanied by a brawny young man whom he introduced as Larry. "Boss's orders are for you each to pick out five horses. Hurry now!"

"Wal, Rol, they look so darn good I don't see any sense in pickin' atall. But it's fun ... Sterl, toss you for first pick."

Red won, and his choice was the very black that Sterl had set his heart on. Still in a moment, he burst out with enthusiasm, "There's a chestnut. Gosh, what a hoss! I pick him...."

"Here's a sorrel for me. I'll name him after you, Red. But I don't see a black like that one you beat me to."

Leslie's rich contralto rang out from behind. "What's that about a black?"

"Hello. I wondered about you," replied Sterl.

"Mawnin', Leslie," drawled Red. "I kinda like you better in them ridin' togs. Not so dangerous lookin' to a pore cowboy.... Looks like you been ridin' some, at thet."

Indeed she did, thought Sterl, and could not recall any ranch girl who equaled her. Leather worn thin, shiny metal, spurs that showed bits of horsehair, ragged trousers stuffed in high boots, gray blouse and colorful scarf, her chestnut hair in a braid down her back—these charmed Sterl, entirely aside from her gold-tan cheeks with their spots of red, her curved lips, like cherries, and her flashing eyes.

"Red got first pick on me," explained Sterl. "Snitched that black."

"Not too bad, you cowboys," returned Leslie, her glance taking in their choice.

"You Yankees are the queerest talking people!" said Leslie when the cowboys had finished their horse-choosing contest. "But I believe you'll be good cobbers. Come now, I'll show you some real Australian horses."

Sterl had prepared himself for a treat to a horse lover's eyes, but when he looked through the fence of a corral adjoining the shed he could hardly credit his sight. He beheld the finest horses he had ever seen in one bunch in his whole range experience. These were not shaggy, dusty, range-free animals, but well-groomed, sleek and shiny thoroughbreds in the pink of condition.

"Leslie—who takes such grand care of these horses?" gasped Sterl.

"I do—a little. But Friday does most of it. He's my black man. Dad sent him up town.... You might *say* something."

"I can't, child," returned Sterl, feelingly. "Horses have been the most important things in my life. And these of yours! But are they really yours, Leslie?"

"Indeed they are. Mine! I haven't anything else. Hardly a new dress to my name. A few books."

"Leslie, haven't you any beaus?" asked Sterl lightly.

"I had. But Dad shut down on them lately," replied the girl, seriously. "Not that I cared much. Only I've been lonesome."

"Wal, young lady," drawled Red, "you ain't gonna be so lonesome from now on, if my hunch is correct."

"That black horse—" spoke up Sterl, pointing to a noble, rangy beast.

"That's King. He's five years old. Bred from Dad's great dam. King has won all his races the last two years. Oh, he's swift! He threw me last race. But we won."

"So you were up on him? Well!" rejoined Sterl, in wonder and admiration.

"Yes, I can ride him. But Dad says no more. At least not in races. He's too strong. Has a mouth like iron. And once running against other horses, he's terrific."

"I'll have to put my hands on him," said Sterl.

"You're going to ride him, cowboy," replied the girl. "Let's go inside the paddock."

Red had straddled the top bar of the fence, and his silence was eloquent. Leslie led the way inside. She called and whistled. All the horses threw up their heads, and some of them started for her. Then they trooped forward, fine heads up, manes flying. Still they halted some yards from the fence, eager, whinnying, but not trustful of the strangers.

"Come up heah, pard," called Red. "They're skeered of you. Instinct! They know you're a hard-ridin' *hombre* from Arizonie."

Leslie walked away from the fence somewhat, and coaxed. A spotted iron-gray animal, clean-cut in build, was the first to come to the girl.

"Jester," she called to him, and got hold of his mane to lead him back to the fence. "One of my best. He's tricky—full of the devil, but fast, tireless. . . . Red, would you like to have him on the trek? It would please me. I think you'd be clever enough to match him."

"Would I?—Aw, Leslie, that's too good of you. Why, he took my eye fust thing. But I oughtn't take him!"

"Done! He's yours. Get down and make friends with him."

Red complied with alacrity. Sterl watched as he saw the cowboy's lean brown hand, slow and sure, creep out to touch the arching, glossy neck. "Jester, you dog-gone lucky hoss! Why, I'm the kindest rider that ever threw his laig over a saddle."

"King, come here," called Leslie to the magnificent black. But it was a beautiful bay that approached at the girl's bidding. "Lady Jane, you know I'm going to ride you this morning, now don't you?" She petted the sniffing muzzle, and laid her cheek against the trim black mane. Then most of the others except King came begging for her favor. She introduced them to the cowboys as if they were persons of rank—Duke, a great rangy sorrel, almost red, pride and power in every line; Duchess, a long-tailed white mare, an aristocrat whose name was felicitous; Lord Chester, a trim gray stallion, hard to overlook even in that band.

The black still hung behind; Leslie had to go for him. Closer at hand, his magnificent physical qualities appeared more striking.

"King," said Leslie, impressively, "this is an American cowboy, Sterl Hazelton, who is going to ride you—*ride* you, I said, you big devil—on our great trek."

Sterl had feared this very thing. "Leslie, don't ask me to take him—your favorite!" he protested.

"But he's not my favorite! I don't love him—well, not so much—since he threw me. Please, Sterl!"

"I only wanted to be coaxed," rejoined Sterl, lamely. "Thanks, Leslie. It's just too good to be true. . . . I had a horse once. . . ."

"Lead him out," said Leslie, then with surprising ease she leaped upon the bare back of Lady Jane. Red followed with Jester, and Sterl gently urged the black to join them.

"King, let's look each other over," said Sterl, as he let go of the mane and squared away in front of the horse. King threw up his noble head, and his black eyes had a piercing curiosity. But he was not in the least afraid. Sterl put out a confident hand to rub his nose.

"Saddle up, boys," said Leslie, slipping off. "Let's get this trip to town over. I don't mind showing you to the girls, because they'll be left behind, except Beryl Dann. And I just hate to present you to her."

Sterl did not voice his surprise, but Red blurted out. "An' 'cause why, Leslie?"

"I'll be jealous," laughed the girl, frankly. "I'd

like you both for my cavaliers. Oh, Beryl is lovely, even if she is spoiled and proud. Her father is lord of the manor, so to speak."

In short order they were mounted in the unfamiliar English saddles, and ready to ride away. King pranced a little. Sterl sensed his tremendous, latent power.

One branch of the road turned back past the house; the other, which Leslie took, crossed the creek and wound up the slope into the bush. Wattle trees sent a golden shade down upon them, singing *cur-ra-wongs* followed them.

"Bell magpies," said Leslie. "I love them almost as well as the kookaburras. That reminds me. Dad won't let me take all my pets."

They rode on. Thick bush began to thin out; another mile brought open country, green rolling hills and vales that looked overgrazed. Presently Sterl saw horses and cattle, and columns of smoke, and at length a big white house with great tin water tanks under the eaves. He had not observed this around Slyter's house, but he had grasped that most of these Australian station owners had to catch their water in the dry season. This was the Dann station, just outside of town.

"There she is—Beryl," said Leslie, and waving a gauntleted hand she called. Sterl saw a fair-faced, fair-haired girl, distinguished by grace even in what was evidently the workaday dress of the moment.

"Pard, don't you reckon I oughta pull leather oot

of heah?" said Red, in perturbation.

"I should smile you should," returned Sterl. "And me too!"

"Stand to your colors, men," retorted Leslie. Presently Sterl was doffing his sombrero, and gallantly bowing to a handsome girl, some years Leslie's senior, whose poise permitted graciousness, yet hid curiosity.

Sterl made a pleasant little speech and Red cut in with his southern drawl, "Wal, Miss Dann, I shore am glad to meet another Australian girl. My pard heah, Sterl an' me, have been sorta worried over this long trek an' thought of backin' out. But not no more."

Beryl Dann was neither too dignified nor too grown up not to be pleased and flattered by what Sterl divined was an extraordinary speech to her.

As Sterl rode on with Leslie, he observed without looking back that Red did not accompany them.

"Did you like her?" queried Leslie, a dark flash of her hazel eyes on Sterl. She was a woman; still Sterl could not react to the situation with playful duplicity, as one impulse prompted him to.

"Yes, of course," he said, frankly. "Pretty and gracious, if a little haughty. I wonder—has she lived out here long?"

"Yes. The Danns have been here all of five years. But Beryl went to school in Sydney. She visits there often. She's lovely! All the young men court her.... Didn't you fall in love with her at first sight?"

"My child, I did not."

"Don't call me child," she flashed, quickly. "I'm grown up. Old enough to get married!"

"You don't say. I wouldn't have thought it," replied Sterl, teasingly.

"Yes. Dad thought so. He wanted to give me to a station man over here. But I wouldn't. . . . Red has not escaped Beryl—that's obvious. Look back."

Sterl did so, to see the cowboy still leaning over his saddle gazing down upon the fair-haired girl.

"Sterl, I like Red," went on Leslie, confidentially. "But I'd never let him see it. I don't know cowboys, of course, But I know young men who are devils after women. And he's one. I could feel it. . . . But I guess you're different. Sterl, I'm crazy to take this trek. But I'm frightened. There will be twenty young men with us. I know how they can be, even trekking in to Brisbane. Eight days! My mother, Stanley Dann's sister, Beryl and I the only women! . . ."

"Leslie, your fathers never should take you."

"But I *want* to go. Beryl does, too. It means new homes, new friends, new lives. . . . Sterl, I hope you'll be a big brother to me. Will you?"

"Thank you. I'll try," responded Sterl, sincerely. The girl's frank wistfulness touched him deeply. "But I'm a stranger. I might be what Red calls no good atall."

"You might be, but I don't believe it. . . . I like you, Sterl. I'm not afraid of you. Mum says I'm a hoyden. But I'm sensitive. These outback men court you on sight—hug and kiss you—or try to. Outback it's a fight for love, women, cattle—for life it-self."

"Leslie, it's much like that on the western ranges where I come from. I understand a little how a young girl feels."

"You are going to be a comfort, Sterl," she said, happily. "Here we are, right in town. And there comes Red, putting Jester to a canter.... There's where I went to school.... Oh, I forgot something I wanted to tell you. Do you remember Dad mentioning a drover, Ashley Ormiston?"

"Yes. He is the man Mr. Dann wants your dad to throw in with."

"Sterl, I don't like the idea at all. Mr. Ormiston is new to Downsville. You'll meet him today, so I don't need to describe him. But he has been very much in evidence since the races. I met him that day, and to be honest I was fascinated. Sterl, he—he insulted me that very first night. I've tried to avoid him ever since."

"Have you told your father?" queried Sterl.

"I dare not," she replied, simply.

At that moment Red caught up with them.

"Let's tie up here," Leslie said, halting. "Now boys, you hunt up Dad. He'll be somewhere, waiting for you. Stanley Dann wants to meet you. Be good. Don't drink—or forget you're my cowboys."

They turned a corner to reach a point opposite a large store, in front of which had collected a crowd, mostly men, all trying to get out of the way of a conflict of some kind. Then Sterl saw a white man kick an aborigine into the street. He heard a woman cry out that it was Slyter's black man, Friday.

Sterl stepped out of the crowd and off from the pavement. Then a white man, agile and powerful, leaped into the street to kick the black viciously, knocking him flat.

Striding over, Sterl placed a hard hand against the aggressor and shoved him back, far from gently.

The man straightened up. He was a dark-browed, handsome fellow of about thirty, garbed as a drover.

"What business—of yours?" he panted, hoarsely.

"I just thought you'd kicked that black enough," declared Sterl, deliberately.

"Who are—you?" demanded the other, his dark eyes burning. Sterl caught a strong odor of whisky.

"No matter. I'm a newcomer."

"Damned, meddling, Yankee blighter," shouted the Australian, and with a back-handed sweep he struck Sterl a blow across the mouth that staggered him.

Recovering his balance, Sterl leaped forward, and gave his antagonist a sudden blow low down, then swung his right fist hard and fierce at those malignant eyes, and felled him like a bullock under the ax.

Red lined up alongside his comrade. The buzzing circle crowded into the street. Sterl, to his dismay, espied Leslie's pale face. Then her father dragged her back and strode out, accompanied by a tawny-haired giant, leonine in build and mein.

Slyter gazed at the prostrate man, who was stirring, and from him to the black.

"Friday! Who hit you?"

"Boss, that one fella," replied the black, and pointed to his brutal attacker.

"Dann, it's Ash Ormiston!" ejaculated Slyter.

"I see. Looks as if a horse kicked him....Here you, what does this mean?" boomed the giant, wheeling upon Sterl.

Red intervened, cool and wary. "Watch thet *hombre*, pard. He might have a gun."

"Krehl!" exclaimed Slyter. "Did you slug Ormiston?"

"No. Sterl did thet. But I'd have liked to."

"Stanley, these are my two American cowboys, Krehl and Hazelton."

"Drunk and rowing, eh?" queried Dann.

Sterl confronted Dann, and he was not in a humor to be conciliatory.

"No, I'm not drunk," he rang out. "It's your countryman who is that. I came upon him kicking this black man, Friday. Kicking him in the face and chest! I interfered. He called me a damned, meddling Yankee blighter and hit me. Then I soaked him."

"Friday, what you do alonga Ormiston?" asked Slyter, gruffly.

"Black fella tellum bimeby," replied Friday, and stalked into the crowd, where Sterl saw Leslie try to stop him and fail.

Meanwhile Ormiston staggered to his unsteady feet, one of his eyes beginning to puff.

"Where's that —— Yankee who hit me?" he bit out.

Dann laid a restraining hand on him. "Man, you're drunk."

Sterl confronted him. "Go for your gun if you've got one."

Ormiston violently threw Dann off.

Dann waved the crowd back. "Get off the street!" he roared.

CHAPTER 4

IF ORMISTON had a gun concealed on his person, he made no move to draw it. Sterl's hand dropped back to his side.

"I'll not exchange shots—with a Yankee tramp," panted Ormiston.

"No. But you're not above kicking a poor black when he's down," replied Sterl.

Red again slouched over to Sterl's side. "Haw! Haw!" His hard, mirthless laugh rang with scorn. "Orful particular, ain't you, Mr. Ormiston, about who you throw a gun on? Wal, you got some sense, at thet."

"Dann, you're magistrate here!" shouted Ormiston. "Order these Yankees out of town."

"You're drunk, I told you," replied Dann. "You started a fight, then failed to go through with it."

"No, I didn't. I only kicked that snooping black. This Yankee started it. . . . I'll not engage in a gun fight with a foreign adventurer," replied Ormiston in hoarse haste.

"Mister, why don't you pull thet gun I see inside yore coat?" drawled Red.

"Dann, order these Yankees to leave," repeated Ormiston, stridently.

"No. You're making a fool of yourself," declared Dann. "Slyter has hired these cowboys to help him on the trek."

"Slyter, is that true—you're taking these cowboys?"

"Yes, I've hired them."

"Will you discharge them?"

"No, I certainly will not."

"Then I refuse to take my drovers and my mob of cattle on Dann's trek."

"Ormiston, I don't care a damn what you do," said Slyter.

Ormiston made a forceful and passionate gesture, then shouldered his way through the crowd to disappear. Slyter lost no time in getting to Sterl and Red and dragged them with him across the pavement into a store. Dann strode after them. And there the four men faced each other.

"Gentlemen, I'm terribly sorry," began Sterl, "It's just too bad that I had to mess up your plans at the last moment. But I couldn't stand for such dirty, low-down brutality."

"Pard," drawled Red, coolly rolling a cigarette.

"If you hadn't been so damn quick I'd have busted Ormiston myself."

Dann stroked his golden beard with a massive hand, and his penetrating eyes studied the cowboys.

"It was unfortunate," he began, "Ormiston had been drinking. But I'll swear the black absolutely did not deserve that kicking. Friday is the best native I ever knew. He's honest, loyal, devoted to Leslie, who was good to his gin when she lay dying."

Red eased forward a step, in his slow way. "Mr. Dann, I'd like to ask you, without meanin' offense, if there ain't Englishmen heah an' there who's jest no good atall?"

Dann let out a deep laugh that was convincing. "There are, cowboy, and you can lay to that."

"Wal, I'm glad to heah you admit it. If ever I met a low-down *hombre* thet Ormiston is one. Mebbe it wouldn't have been so easy to see through him but for the drink. No, Ormiston is jest no good atall— an' he come damn near bein' a daid one."

"Tell me, Hazelton," spoke up Dann, his amber eyes full of little, dancing glints, "if Ormiston had moved to draw his revolver—what would you have done?"

"I'd have killed the fool," declared Sterl.

"Indeed!—Did you see that Ormiston was armed?"

"No. But I knew it.... Now, Slyter, I think the thing for Red and me to do is to leave town at once."

"You will do nothing of the kind," rejoined Slyter, stoutly.

"Boys, it's not to be thought of," added Dann. "Ormiston was bluffing. He won't quit us. Like all of us he sees a way to wealth. And we need him with us. The more drovers, the more cattle, the better our chances for success.

"Mr. Dann, I see the necessity for you. But if Red and I go—we'll clash with Ormiston."

"Listen, you young gamecocks," went on Dann, persuasively. "Outback there will be too much clash with the elements and the blacks for us drovers to fight among ourselves. We'll all be brothers before we reach the Never-never. Isn't that so, Bing?"

"It has been proved by other treks," replied Slyter, earnestly. "If you boys are concerned about me or Leslie—just forget that and take the risk."

"Boss, we'll never throw you down," said Red.

"We will go," added Sterl, and his tone was a pledge. "But have you ever driven cattle into a hard wilderness, months on end, against all the hard knocks a desolate country can deal you?"

"No, Hazelton, we have never been on a real trek," Dann replied. "But my brother Eric has. He slights the hardships either because he is callous, unfeeling, or because he doesn't want me to know. In fact, Eric has failed after several starts in Queensland."

"Do you want my advice?"

Dann nodded his leonine head. "Indeed yes! It's too late now, even if I would back out. Hazelton, perhaps Providence sent you rangemen to help us. To get down to fundamentals, tell us just what kind of range you have driven mobs of cattle over—how far—what kind of obstacles—how you worked."

"That's easy, gentlemen, and you can believe what I tell you," replied Sterl. "Some years ago, just after the Civil War, Texas was overrun with millions of longhorn cattle. The ranchers had no home market. A rancher named Jesse Chisholm conceived the idea of driving herds of cattle from southern Texas across the plains to Kansas. Chisholm started out with over three thousand head of cattle and twelve riders. He made it—five hundred miles—in something over ninety days, losing four cowboys and two thousand head of cattle. But he sold what was left at a huge profit. His Chisholm Trail inaugurated trail driving in Texas.

"As for hardships—in that early day fifty million buffalo ranged from the Gulf to the Dakotas. For years stampedes of buffalo were the worst obstacles the trail drivers had to overcome. Next to that were the attacks and raids of savage Indians. There were rivers to ford, some of them big and wide, often in flood. In dry years there were long drives from water to water. Thunderstorms often stampeded herds. Dust storms, sandstorms were terrible to drive against. In the fall and winter, the Del Norte, the freezing gale that blew out of a clear sky, was something the riders hated and feared. Lastly there came rustling—the era of the cattle thieves, which is in its heyday right now."

"Wonderful! Wonderful!" exclaimed Dann, his eyes shining. "Jesse Chisholm was a man after my heart. A savior of Texas, yes?"

"Indeed he saved Texas and built the cattle empire."

Red emitted a cloud of smoke, and drawled: "Boss, I rode for Jesse once. He was a great *hombre*. Harder than the hinges on the gates of hell! Sometime I'll tell you stories about him, one thing special, his jingle-bob brand, thet was so famous."

"Boys, I'll enjoy your stories, when time permits," boomed the drover. "I thank the good Lord for sending you to Australia! Hazelton, one thing more. How did you drive your mobs?"

"We rounded them up into a great triangle, with the apex pointing in the direction we had to go. 'Pointing the herd,' that was called. Two of the nerviest cowboys had the lead at the point. The mass of cattle would follow the leads. Two cowboys on each side at the center of the herd, the rest at the broad base where stragglers and deserters—'drags' we called them—had to be watched and driven."

"Were you one of those cowboys who rode at the head?" queried Dann.

"No, but Red was, always. I was a good hand after the drags."

"Shake hands with me, cowboys," bellowed Dann, "Slyter, I'll order my drovers to start my mob tomorrow, positively. I'll tell Ormiston to go or stay, as he chooses.... Meet us soon out on the trek. Goodby."

Sterl became aware that the store was full of inquisitive people. He and Red were the cynosure of all eyes. Red enjoyed such attention, but Sterl hated it, especially, as had happened so often, when he had just engaged in a fight. He shivered when he thought how closely he had come to shooting Ormiston. He had hoped Australia had not bred the type of bad men among whom he had been compelled to work.

Leslie met him outside with her arms full of packages. Sterl and Red promptly relieved her of them. After one look at Leslie's white face and eyes blazing almost black, Sterl felt too dismayed to speak. She had witnessed his encounter with Ormiston. As she walked along between him and Red, she had a hand on Sterl's arm. They came to a point opposite the horses.

"Heah we air, Jester, agonna make a pack hoss out of you fust thing," spoke up Red, and Sterl knew that the cowboy was talking to ease the situation.

"Leslie, have you finished your buying?" asked Sterl.

"Not quite. But I'll not stay longer—in town," she replied in thick unsteady tone. She mounted her horse as Sterl remembered seeing Comanches mount. "Let me have some of the parcels."

Handing these to her, Sterl looked up into her face.

"Leslie—you were there?" he asked.

"Yes. I saw it—all."

"I'm sorry. Bad luck like that always hounds me."

"Who said it was bad luck?" she retorted. "But Sterl—you jumped at that chance to hit Ormiston—on my account?"

"Well—Friday's first—and then yours. Still I'd have interfered if I'd never heard of either of you. I'm built that way, Leslie."

"You're built greatly, then....A thrill hardly does justice to what I felt—when you hit him....But, afterward—when it looked like shooting—I nearly fainted."

"So that's why you're so pale?" rejoined Sterl, endeavoring to speak lightly, as he mounted. Red rode a tactful distance ahead.

"Am I pale?" she asked.

"Not so much now. But a few minutes back you were white as a sheet."

"Sterl, I ran into Ormiston."

"And what did he say?"

"I don't remember everything. One thing, though, was what you called him."

"That's not calculated to make Ormiston love me any better."

"Do you think he'll make good his threat not to go on the trek?"

"I do not," said the girl, positively. "Ash Ormiston couldn't be kept from going. I wouldn't say wholly because he's so keen after Beryl Dann and me."

"Beryl too? Well!...He's what Red would call an enterprising gent."

"He's deep, Sterl. I distrust his attitude toward the trek."

"Leslie, what had he against your black man?"

"He had enough. I should have told you that.... Once when Mum and Dad were in town, Ormiston found me in my hammock. He made violent love to me. I was scared, Sterl. He . . . I . . . I fought him—and Friday ran up with his spear. It was all I could do to keep him from killing Ormiston."

"Is Friday going on the trek?"

"Dad wants him. To track lost horses. The blacks are marvelous trackers. But Friday says no. Maybe you can persuade him, Sterl. A black never forgets a wrong or fails to return a service."

"I sure will try. What a lot I could learn!"

They rode on at a canter and halted at the paddock. "Come up later for tea—oh, yes, and to see my pets," said Leslie, as they dismounted and gathered up her bundles.

Left to his own devices, Sterl went among his string of horses, which Roland had tethered in the shed, and while he set about the slow and pleasing task of making friends with them, he mused over the momentous journey from Brisbane. He could no more keep things from happening to him than he could stop breathing. But he recalled only one man, out of the many rustlers and hard characters who had crossed his trail, who had incited as quick a hatred in him, as had this man Ormiston. If possible, he must keep out of the man's way. Offsetting that was the inspiring personality of Stanley Dann. Here was a man. And Sterl did not pass by the fair-haired Beryl, with her dark-blue eyes and the proud poise of her head. Leslie was appealing in many ways, but the charm she had, which he found vaguely sweet and disquieting, was the fact of his apparent appeal to her, of which she was wholly unconscious. Well, he was in the open again, already in contact with raw nature, about to ride out on this incredible trek. That was all left him in life—this strenuous action of the natural man. Sterl discounted any lasting relation with these good white folk who needed him.

When he returned to the tent, Sterl found Red sitting before the flap, profoundly thoughtful and solemn. He had not even heard Sterl's approach.

"Pard, did you heah anythin'?" he asked, almost in a whisper.

"Hear?—When?"

"Jest about a minnit ago—mebbe longer. I don't know. I'm dotty....Did I have any drinks uptown?"

"You sure didn't."

"Gosh, I'm shore I've got the willies....Sterl, I was in the tent heah, when somebody busted out in a laugh—snortinest hoss laugh you ever heahed. 'Who'n'hell's laughin' at me?' I said, an' I was mad. Wal, Pard, you never in yore life heahed such a loud brayin'-ass laugh. When the smart alec got through I come out to bust him. Seen nobody. Then I seen a big brown an' white bird, sittin' right there on thet branch. Stuck his haid on one side an' looked out of his devilish black eyes at me, as if to say, 'Heah's one of them Yankee blighters'....If thet bird didn't give me thet hoss-laugh, then yore pard has gone plumb stark ravin' crazy."

"Let's go up and ask Leslie."

On the way up the path under the wattles they met her. Red burst into the narrative of his perplexing experience. Leslie burst into uncontrollable mirth.

"Oh—Oh! It was—Jack," she choked out.

"Jack who?"

"My pet kookaburra—Oh, Red!—my laughing jackass!"

"Wal, I figgered he was a laughin' hyena, all right! But thet pet kooka somethin'—thet has me beat."

"Jack is our most famous bird. He is a kind of giant kingfisher. I'm taking him on the trek, but I can't take my little bears. It breaks my heart—Come in to tea." At the door Leslie whispered to Sterl. "I didn't tell Mum about what happened uptown."

Slyter had not returned, nor did his wife expect him. "I'm too terribly busy to chat," she said, after serving them, and drinking a cup of tea. "Les, I wanted Friday to carry things down to the wagon. Have you seen him?"

"I'll find him, Mum."

"Mrs. Slyter," said Sterl when the party settled down. "I'd like a look at your wagon while it's empty. We must make a boat out of it, so that it can be floated across the rivers."

"How thoughtful of you! That had not occurred to Bingham."

"We'll fix up a little room in the front of your wagon, behind the seat," went on Sterl. "I've done that before. A wagon can be made really comfortable, considering all your baggage...."

Suddenly they were interrupted by a discordant, concatenated, rollicking laugh from outside.

"Jack saucing other kookaburras," declared Leslie. "Come and see him."

They went outdoors. The black man Friday stood under one of the gum trees, looking up into the branches, and holding out a queer stick with a white oval end. In his other hand he held out a long spear.

"Friday has his wommera—the stick he uses to throw his spear"—said Leslie, gravely. "That doesn't look so good for Ormiston."

Just then a large brown and white bird fluttered down from the tree to alight on the black's spear. "There's Jack," cried Leslie. He was a rather short bird, built heavily forward, with a big head and strong bill.

Sterl's attention shifted to the black man. He was well over six feet tall, slender, muscular, black as ebony. He wore a crude garment around his loins. His dark visage held an inscrutable dignity.

Sterl went up to Friday, tapped him on his deep breast and asked, "Friday no hurt bad?" The native understood, for he grinned and shook his head.

"Leslie, you ask him to go with us on the trek."

"Friday, white man wantum you go with him, far, far that way," said Leslie, making a slow gesture which indicated immeasurable distance toward the outback. Friday fastened great, black unfathomable eyes upon Sterl.

"White man come from far country, away cross big water," said Sterl, pointing toward the east, and speaking as if to an Indian. "He need Friday—track horse—kill meat—fight—tell where pads go."

"Black fella go alonga you," replied Friday.

Leslie clapped her hands. "Good-o! I was sure he'd go, if you asked him," she cried. "Dad will be happy!"

Red slouched over to Friday and handed him a cigar.

"You close up, boss?" asked the black, looking from one to the other.

"Shore, Friday," replied Red.

"You um fadder?"

"Fadder? Hell no!...Gosh, do I look thet old? Him my brudder, Friday."

"Black fella im brudder your brudder," declared Friday, loftily, and stalked away.

CHAPTER 5

***I**T TURNED* out that Leslie's freeing of her native bear pets was merely a matter of saying good-by to them, for they were not confined. They lived in the trees of a small eucalyptus grove back of the house. Sterl enjoyed the sensation of holding some of them, of feeling their sharp strong, abnormally large claws cling to his coat. The one that pleased Sterl most was a mother that carried her baby in a pouch. The little one had his head stuck out, and his bright black eyes said that he wanted to see all there was to see.

Gently but firmly Leslie drew the little bear from the pouch and placed it on the mother's back, where it stuck like a burr and appeared perfectly comfortable. Sterl never saw a prettier animal sight, and said so emphatically.

"Marsupials!" said Leslie; "All sorts of them down under, from kangaroos to a little blind mole no longer than my finger."

"Well I'm a son of a gun!" exclaimed Red, "What's a marsupial?"

This started Leslie on a lecture concerning Australian mammals and birds. When she finished with marsupials, which carry their babies in a pouch, and came to the unbelievable platypus which wears fur, suckles its young, lays eggs and has a bill like a duck and web feet fastened on backward, she stretched Red's credulity to the breaking point.

"How can you stand there, a sweet pictoor of honest girlhood, and be such an orful liar? How about thet liar bird Jones said you could show us?—the wonderfulest bird in Australia!"

"Righto! Boys, if you'll get up early, I'll promise you shall hear a lyrebird, and maybe see one."

"It's a date, Leslie, tomorrow mawnin'. Right heah. Hey, pard?"

"You bet," said Sterl, "And now let's get to work making that wagon."

The wagon, which Slyter intended for his womenfolk and all their personal effects, was big and sturdy, with wide-tired wheels, high sides, and a roomy canvas top stretched over hoops. Sterl examined it carefully.

"How about in water an' sand?" queried Red, dubiously.

"In deep water she'll float—when we fix her. Red, dig up a couple of chisels and hammers while I get something to calk these seams."

In short order they had the wagon bed so that it would not leak. Then, while Red began the same job on the other wagon, Sterl devoted himself to fixing up some approach to a prairie-schooner tent dwelling. Sterl had Leslie designate the bags and trunks which would be needed en route; with these he packed the forward half of the wagon bed two feet deep. Then he transformed the rear half into a bed-room.

Slyter arrived with the dray, and climbed off the driver's seat to begin unhitching. His face was dark, his brow lined and pondering.

"Roland, pack all the flour on top of this load and tie on a cover," said Slyter. "Hazelton, how's the work progressing?"

"We're about done. Hope nothing more came off uptown?"

"Testy day. Just my personal business.... You'll be interested in this. Ormiston sobered up and tried to get back into our good graces. Stanley Dann accepted his apologies."

"Then Ormiston will go on the trek?"

"Yes. He said to tell you he had been half drunk, and would speak to you when opportunity afforded. But he asked *me* if you cowboys had any references!"

"I was surprised that you did not ask for any."

"I didn't need any. Nor did Stanley Dann. Ormiston was trying to sow seeds of discord."

"Thank you, Slyter. I'm sure you'll never regret
your kindness."

"Hathaway and Woolcott left about midday,"
went on Slyter. "Some of their drovers were drunk.
The Danns are all ready to leave at dawn. We'll start
tomorrow sometime."

"How about waterholes?"

"No fear. We've had a good few rains lately.
There'll be plenty of water—maybe too much—and
grass all the way out of Queensland. Stanley Dann
and his brother Eric had another hot argument. Eric
was one of the drovers who made that Gulf trek. He
wants to stick to that route. But Stanley argues we
should leave it beyond the Diamantina River and
head northwest more directly across the Never-
never. I agree with him."

It was dim gray morning when, keeping their
engagement with Leslie, the Americans mounted the
shadowy aisle leading up to the house.

They found her waiting with Friday. "Aren't you
ashamed? You're late.... Come. Don't talk. Don't
make the slightest sound."

They followed Friday, a shadow in the gray
gloom. The east was brightening. Presently, Friday
glided noiselessly into the bush. Gradually it grew
lighter. Soft mist hung low under the pale-trunked
trees. They came to a glade that led down into a
ravine where water tinkled. It opened out wide upon

a scene of veiled enchantment. Small trees, pyramid shape, pointed up to the brightening sky, and shone as white as if covered by frost. Great fern trees spread long, lacy, exquisite leaves from a symmetrical head almost to the ground. Huge eucalyptus sent marble-like pillars aloft. Their fragrance attacked Sterl's nostrils with an acute, strangling sensation. A bell-like note struck lingeringly upon his ear. Friday halted. As he lifted his hand with the gesture of an Indian, Sterl heard the lovely call of a thrush near at hand. Leslie put her lips right on Sterl's ear. "It is the lyre-bird!" Then it seemed to Sterl that his tingling ears caught the songs of other birds, intermingled with that of the thrush. Suddenly a bursting *cur-ra-wong, cur-ra-wong* shot through Sterl. Could that, too, be the lyrebird? The note was repeated again and again, so full of wild melody that it made Sterl ache. It was followed by *caw, caw, caw*, the most dismal and raucous note of a crow.

"Don't you understand, boys?" whispered Leslie, bending her head between them. "The lyrebird is a mocker. He can imitate any sound."

That sweet concatenation of various bird notes was disrupted by what seemed to be the bawling of a cow.

From off in the woods sounded a mournful, rich note, like the dong of a bell.

"Another!" Oh, but we're lucky!" whispered Leslie.

Across a little leafy glade, Sterl noticed low foliage move and part to admit a dark brown bird, half the size of a hen turkey. It had a sleek, delicate head. As it stepped daintily out from under the foliage, its tail, erect and exquisite, described the perfect shape of a lyre. Long, slender fernlike feathers rose and spread from the two central feathers—broad, dark velvety brown, barred in shiny white or gray, with graceful curling tips that bowed and dipped as it passed out of sight into the bush.

"Wal," said Red, "yore lyrebird has our mockers skinned to a frazzle."

"That must mean something!" returned Leslie, giggling. "Come. We'll be late and Dad will row. Let's run."

When they went into breakfast, Roland and Larry were leaving, sober as judges. Bill Williams, the cook, was banging pots and pans with unnecessary force. Slyter looked as if he were going to a funeral, and his wife was weeping. Leslie's smile vanished. She served the cowboys, who made short work of that meal.

"Boss, what's the order for today?" queried Sterl, shortly.

"Drake's mustering for the trek," replied Slyter, gruffly.

Leslie followed them out. "I'll catch up somewhere. I'd go with you now, but Mum.... Ride King and Jester, won't you?"

Sterl found difficulty in expressing his sympathy. The girl was brave, though deeply affected by her mother's grief. It really was a terrible thing to do— this forsaking a comfortable home in a beautiful valley, to ride out into the unknown and forbidding wilderness.

King surprised Sterl with his willingness to be saddled and bridled. He knew he was leaving the paddock, and liked it. Sterl tied on the slicker and canteen, and slipped into his worn leather chaps, conscious of a quickening of his pulse. He took up his rifle and walked around in front of the horse. "Are you gun shy, King?" The black apparently knew a rifle and, showing no fear, stood without a quiver while Sterl shoved it into the saddle sheath.

"Say, air you a mud hen, thet you go duckin' jest 'cause I've got a gun?" Red was complaining to his horse.

In another moment they were in the unfamiliar English saddles. Joining Larry, they rode out into the open valley. Ahead of them, about a mile out in the widening valley, a herd of grazing horses, and beyond them Slyter's cattle, added the last link to the certainty of the trek.

Waiting this side of the horses were three riders, superbly mounted. Their garb, and the trappings of the horses, appeared markedly different from those of the Americans. Sterl had made up his mind about these riders of Slyter's; still he gave each a keen scrutiny. Drake was middle-aged, honest and forcible of aspect, strong of build. The other two, Benson and Heald, were sturdy young men not out of their teens, and sat their saddles as if used to them.

"Drake, we have Slyter's orders to report to you," added Sterl, after the introductions.

"I've sent Monkton on ahead to let down the bars," replied Drake. "We fenced the valley ahead there where it narrows. I'll join him. You men bring up the rear."

"No particular formation?"

"Just let the mob graze along at a walk. We'll keep right on till Slyter halts us, probably at Blue Gum."

Drake said no more, and rode away to the left, accompanied by Heald, while Benson trotted off to the right.

"Huh! Short an' sweet. All in the day's work," complained Red.

"Red, you ought to be in front," said Sterl, "but, no doubt, that'll come in time."

In another moment Sterl was alone. He lighted a cigarette. King pranced a little and wanted to go. Sterl patted the arched neck, and fell at once into his old habit of talking to his horse. "King, we don't know each other yet. But if you're as good as you look, we'll be pards. Take it easy. I see you're too well trained to graze with a bridle on. You can unlearn that, King."

He was to ride across a whole unknown continent, from which journey, even if he survived it, he would never return. Sterl faced the east. And he could not keep back a farewell whisper: "Good-by, Nan.... Good-by!" which seemed final and irrevocable.

When he turned back again, prompted by the keen King, the long line of cattle was on the move. The great trek had begun. The valley was filled with a rich, thick, amber light. Fleecy white clouds sailed above the green line of bush. The gold of wattles and the scarlet of eucalyptus stood out vividly even in the brilliance of the sun-drenched foliage. A faint and failing column of smoke rose above the forsaken farmhouse, that seemed to have gone to sleep among the wattles. A glancing gleam of tranquil, reed-bordered pond caught Sterl's sight. All this pastoral beauty, this land of flowers and grass and blossoming trees, this land of milk and honey, was being abandoned for the chimera of the pioneer!

*F*IRST camp! A huge dead gum tree, bleached and gnarled, marking a sunset-flushed stream; outcropping rock and jungle beyond; to the right lanes of open country opening into the bush. Cattle and horses made for the creek and spread along its low bank for a mile. When they had drunk their fill some of the cattle fell again to grazing, while many of them lay down to rest. The horses, which had fed all day behind the cattle, trooped back to their grazing. In Sterl's judgment both would require little night guarding on such pasture as that.

He watered King, then rode down the creek into camp. Pungent wood smoke brought back other camp scenes. But no other camp site he could remember had possessed such an imposing landmark as the great dead blue gum tree. On its spreading branches Sterl identified herons, parrots, a hawk perched on a topmost tip, kookaburras low down. The wagons were spaced conveniently, though not close together. Locating his own, Sterl dismounted to strip King and let him go. He was unrolling his tent when Leslie approached.

"Well, so here you are? I wondered if you'd ever catch up," said Sterl.

"I hadn't the heart to leave Mum today. I...I would have been all right, but for her."

"Why you're all right anyhow, Leslie. Don't look back—don't think back!... Our first camp's a dandy. ...Where're Friday and your Dad?"

"Friday walked all the way. I rode a little. Mum came out of it all at once. Dad is all fit. He and Drake just had a drop from a bottle....And here come Red and Larry."

Sterl with Leslie crossed over to the center of camp, where Friday was carrying water. Slyter, after rummaging under the seat of his wagon, brought a book to Leslie.

"Les, one of your jobs is keeping our journal. Record date, distance trekked, weather, incident, everything."

"Whew! what a job!" exclaimed Leslie. "But I'll love it....How far today?"

"A long trek. Sixteen miles?" said Slyter, dubiously.

"And then some," interposed Sterl. "Ask Red.

He's a wonderful judge of distance. . . . Now, boss, how about night guard?"

"Three changes. Two men on for three hours each. Eight to eleven, eleven to two, two till five. Which watch would you and Krehl like?"

"The late one, boss. We're used to the wee small hours."

"You'll have our black man, Friday. Hazelton, you'll find him a tower of help."

The thud of horses' hoofs awoke Sterl before Larry called into the tent: "Two o'clock, boys. Roll out."

Ready to go, the cowboys repaired to the fire for the tea Larry had poured for them. It was scalding hot and strong as acid. The band of horses was huddled between camp and the mob of cattle. They were quiet, only a few grazing. The cattle had bedded down.

"What'll we do, Sterl? Circle or stand guard?"

"Circle, Red, till we get the lay of the herd."

Red rode on into the bright starlight, and the cold wind brought back the smoke of his cigarette. Sterl turned to walk his horse in the other direction. Old sensorial habits reasserted themselves—the keen ear, the keen eye, the keen nose and the feel of air, wind, cold. The cattle and the horses were quiet. Strange, discordant barks of dingoes lent unreality to the wild. Wide-winged birds or flying foxes passed over his head with silky swish.

In half an hour Sterl heard Red's horse before

he sighted it, a moving, ghostly white in the brilliant gloom.

"Fine setup, pard," said Red. "A lazy cowboy job!"

"All well on my side. Go halfway round and stand watch."

"Air kinda penetratin', pard. I reckon I'll mosey to an' fro," returned Red, and rode on.

When Sterl reached the end of a half circle, came the voice of Friday, "Cheeky black fella close up," he said, and vanished.

Sterl swept his gaze in wary half circles. Farther outback, this night watch might be a perilous duty. But nothing happened. Friday did not return, although Sterl had a feeling that the black was close. Slowly, mysteriously, the dreaming darkest hour passed.

At the first faint lighting in the east the cattle began to stir. Sterl circled around to meet Red. "Mawnin'," said that worthy. "J'ever see such a tame bunch of cattle? How'd you make out?"

"Just killed time. This sort of work will spoil us. It's after five. Let's ride in."

Breakfast was awaiting them. Two of the wagons were already hitched up. Leslie stood by the fire, drinking tea. Larry came riding up, leading three saddled horses, one of which was Duchess, Leslie's favorite.

Red saw the girl swing up into her saddle with one hand, and said, "Pard, I gotta hand it to thet kid. If Beryl is like her, wal, it's all day with me."

When they rode out on fresh horses the sun had just burst over the eastern bush, and the downs were as if aflame. Drake had the mob ready. Leslie and Larry were driving the straggling horses. Red loped across the wide flank to take up his position on the far right. Friday came along with giant strides, carrying his spears and wommera in his left hand and a boomerang in the other. Leslie rode loping back to turn on the line even with Sterl. Then the four rear riders, pressing forward, drove the horses upon the heels of the cattle, and the day's drive was on. The bustle and hurry before the start seemed to come to an abrupt end in the slow, natural walk of grazing cattle and horses.

Three times before afternoon, Leslie rode over to Sterl on some pretext or other, the last of which was an offer to share the bit of lunch she had brought.

"No thanks, Leslie. A cowboy learns to go without. And on this trek in particular, I'm going to emulate your black men."

"I suppose you cowboys live without fun, food or—love?" she queried, flippantly.

"We do indeed."

"Like hob you do," she flashed. "Oh, well, maybe *you* do. This is the third time you've snubbed me so far today. You're an old crosspatch."

Sterl laughed, though he felt a little nettled. The girl interrupted the even, almost unconscious ebb and flow of his sensorial perceptions.

"I've been called worse than that, by sentimental

young ladies," replied Sterl, satirically. "Would you expect me to babble poetry to you or listen to your silly chatter?"

"Oh-h!" cried Leslie, outraged, reddening from neck to brow. And she wheeled her horse to lope far along the line toward Red.

"That should hold her awhile," murmured Sterl, regretfully. "Too bad I've got to be mean to her! But...."

Slyter halted for camp at the foot of a ridge running out like a spur from the rougher bushland. Manifestly a stream came from around that ridge. It was no later than midafternoon with the sun still warm. A short trek, Sterl thought. Cattle and horses made for the stream, which turned out to be a river that could not be forded with wagons at this point.

Sterl was pitching his tent when Red and Leslie rode in. The girl rode by him as if he had not been there.

Red slid out of his saddle in his old inimitable way, and with slap on flank, sent his horse scampering.

"Aboat ten miles, I'd say," he drawled. "Slick camp an' a hefty river.... Say, pard, what'n'll did you do to the kid? Leslie was all broke up."

"She bothers me, Red."

"Ahuh. I savvy. I'm feared she likes you an' hasn't no idee atall about it."

Sterl remained silent, revolving in mind a realization prompted by Red's talk—that he had felt a distinct throb of pleasure. This would never do!

The cowboys finished their chores, then strolled over to Slyter. Leslie sat near, writing in her journal.

On impulse, Sterl turned to the girl. "Leslie, where is Friday?" As she did not appear to hear, he asked her again. Then she looked up. "Please do not annoy me, Mr. Hazelton. I'm composing poetry," she said coldly.

7

*T*HE late afternoon hour arrived at length when Slyter caught up with the Dann brothers and their partners. From here the drovers would push on together to the end.

Slyter led his mob to the left and hauled up on the wide curve of a stream. In the center, half a mile from Slyter, the Dann encampment, with its ten wagons and drays, its canvas tents bright against the green, its blue smokes and active figures, made an imposing sight, to Sterl's eyes like a plains caravan. Farther to the right showed the camp of Hathaway and Woolcott. Hundreds of horses grazed in between. Across the river flamed the enormous mob of cattle which the drovers had evidently thrown together—

twice as much stock as Sterl had ever seen at one time.

With Slyter's mob and *remuda* placed to rest and graze, the drivers made toward camp by divers routes. Sterl arrived first. The black horse, King, had completed his conquest over the cowboy. They had taken to each other. King recognized a gentle, firm and expert master; Sterl reluctantly crowned the black for spirit, tirelessness and speed, and for remarkable power in the water. After a first ford over slippery rocks Sterl had iron shoes put on him, and that made him invincible.

While Sterl was unrolling the tent, Red and Leslie rode in. Exposure and sun had given the girl a golden tan, which magnified her charm. After that tiff the second day out, she had persistently ignored Sterl.

"Pile off, Red, and go through the motions," called Sterl, and soon his comrade was helping, markedly reticent for him.

"Well, what's on your chest?" queried Sterl.

"Wal, this nice long easy drive is over. It'll be hell from now on. Sterl, what you think?—Leslie has commissioned me to beg you to forgive her for bein' catty."

"Yeah?—Red, you can tell Leslie to ask me herself. I was deliberately rude to her. And I'm sorry. She's worried, now that we've caught up with the big outfit."

"Shore is. An' so'm I. But once I get mad, I'll be good-o, as Leslie says."

"Righto, as Leslie says."

Before sundown of that important day, supper had been disposed of, and Slyter had striden off to visit Dann, accompanied by Drake, and calling upon Sterl and Red to follow.

"Boss, take Red, and let me stay in camp," suggested Sterl.

"No. I may need you. Stanley will ask for you. As for Ormiston—the sooner you meet him the better. I ask you to meet him."

"Thanks, Slyter. I'll come."

"Dad, please let me come with the boys? I want to see Beryl," entreated Leslie.

"Of course, my dear. I'd forgotten you."

"Red, you run along with Leslie," put in Sterl. "I want to shave. Be with you in a jiffy."

Beside the grandest monarch of all these eucalyptus trees, he came upon the wagon and camp of Dann's sister and his daughter Beryl. Leslie was talking excitedly with the girl, while Red stood, sombrero in hand, listening. Sterl was introduced and greeted cordially. Beryl wore boy's garb, more attractive and not so worn as Leslie's.

"Doesn't it seem long since we all met, way back there in Downsville?" she asked. "I nearly died of homesickness for days. But now it's not too bad. I intend to be a drover, like Leslie."

"Wal," interposed Red, "we shore need another trail driver."

"How queerly you cowboys carry your pistols!" exclaimed Beryl, indicating the low-hanging sheaths, well down the right thighs. "Dad's drovers stick them in their hip pockets, or under a belt."

"Wal, Miss Dann," drawled Red, "you see us cowboys gotta throw a gun quick sometimes, an' it needs to be handy."

"Where do you throw it?" she asked, curiously.

"Aw, at jack rabbits, or any ole varmint thet happens along."

"Miss Beryl, Red is teasing you," chimed in Sterl. "To throw a gun means to jerk it out, quickly—like this."

"How strange! ... Oh, so you can shoot quickly at your antagonists?"

"Exactly. And the cowboy who throws his quickest has the best chance to survive. Please excuse us, Miss Beryl. Our boss wants us in on the conference over there."

A little group of men stood in a half circle back of Stanley Dann, who sat before a box doing duty as a table. Here the cowboys met the leader's partners. Eric Dann, the younger of the two brothers, was short and strongly built, with rather stern, dark features. Hathaway was tall and florid, apparently under fifty years. Woolcott appeared fully sixty, a bearded man, with deep-set eyes and gloomy mein.

"All of you have a look at this map," spoke up Dann, indicating a paper on the box. "Eric drew it from memory. And of course it isn't accurate as to distance or points. Still, it will give you a general idea of the country at the headwaters of the rivers that run into the Gulf of Carpentaria.... This line marks the road we're on, and which we can trek fairly well.

This dark line, way up in Queensland, is the Diamantina River, an important obstacle. This open space represents the Never-never—some two thousand miles across, perhaps. Beyond to the northwest, are the Kimberleys, our destination—please God! You observe that they run northwest.... Hello, Ormiston, you're just in time to give your opinion.... Well, my brother wants to follow this old wagon trek beyond the headwaters of the Diamantina River and the Warburton, on north across the Gulf rivers, and then west to Wyndham and the Kimberleys. There's no telling how much farther this route will be, probably a thousand miles. Too far! And just as hard; its only good feature is that it has been traveled. Striking west beyond the Diamantina to the Warburton, following that to its headwaters, and *then* striking straight west again, will be a short cut and save us, Lord only knows how much! I call for a vote from each man present except Drake. And I include these American cowboys, with your permission, because they have had extensive experience in droving cattle."

The vote ended in a deadlock, Slyter, Sterl and Red arraying themselves upon Stanley Dann's side; the others standing by Eric. The leader showed no feeling whatsoever, but Eric Dann and Ormiston argued vigorously for the longer and once-traveled route.

Sterl listened and bent piercing eyes upon this quartet, and at length his deductions were clear-cut, and he would have sworn by them. Eric Dann feared to take the great trek into the unknown. Ormiston had some personal reason for standing by Eric Dann, and he had influenced Hathaway and Woolcott.

"Very well. It hangs fire for the present," concluded Stanley Dann. "Perhaps the months to come will bring at least one of you gentlemen to reason."

If Ormiston tried to conceal his satisfaction he failed to hide it from Sterl.

"Hazelton," said Stanley Dann, "I'm curious to know what you think, if you'll commit yourself."

"Are there black men all over this Never-never Land?" countered Sterl.

"Yes, according to our few explorers."

"If they can be propitiated, perhaps we could learn from them, as the pathfinders in my country have learned from the Indians."

"Good idea!" boomed the leader.

"These niggers are a mean, lying, unscrupulous race," put in Ormiston, contemptuously.

"Perhaps because of the treatment white men have given them," spoke up Slyter.

Ormiston for the moment let well enough alone. Sterl espied Leslie and Beryl, accompanied by a frank-featured blond young giant, nearing the group. He accosted Red.

"Krehl, good day. Glad to see you again," he said, agreeably, as he extended a hand.

"Howdy yoreself," drawled Red, with guile meeting guile. And he shook hands.

"Sorry you are on the wrong side of the fence. But you're a stranger in Australia. I venture to predict you're too experienced an outdoor man to be long deceived by mirages."

"Hell no. I cain't be deceived forever. But this heah country is so grand, I jest don't believe in your Never-never."

"It's a fact, however, and I hope you don't learn from bitter experience."

"Yeah? Wal, you're orful kind."

At this juncture, Leslie with her companions came up to Slyter and Dann. Sterl knew absolutely that Ormiston had timed for their benefit whatever he meant to do, and he burned under his cool exterior.

"Hello, Hazelton," called the drover, in pleasant and resounding tones. "I've wanted to meet you again, to tell you I regret the unpleasantness of our meeting at Downsville."

"I'm sure you regret it, Ormiston," replied Sterl, ignoring the proffered hand, and his piercing gaze met the drover's dark, veiled eyes.

"I didn't regret it because I booted that black," rejoined Ormiston, slowly withdrawing his hand.

"That was perfectly obvious," retorted Sterl, not without contempt.

"Why do *you* think I regret it?" flashed the drover.

"Because you ran into the wrong man and got shown up," flashed Sterl, just as quickly.

"No. I regretted it because I was drunk."

"Drunk or sober you'd be about the same, Ormiston."

Slyter had approached to within a few steps, and Dann, with the girls hanging to him, startled and dismayed, halted beside him, while the others stood back.

"Nonsense," burst out Ormiston. "No man is responsible when he's drunk."

"Righto. That's why you gave yourself away," retorted Sterl.

Ormiston threw up his hands with a gesture indicating the hopelessness of placating this hard-headed American. But under the surface was a mastered fury.

"Cowboy, I approached you to express my regret—to apologize—to prevent discord!"

"If you're so keen on preventing discord, why did you excite it and foment it between our leader and his other partner?" Sterling's tone was contemptuous. As he ended he completed his few slow steps to one side. To any westerner it would have been plain that Sterl wanted to get Ormiston out of line with the others. But the drover did not show that he realized that.

"I'm not exciting discord," returned Ormiston, hotly. "I come from North Queensland. I know something of the Gulf country. Eric Dann is right and Stanley Dann is wrong. It's the safer route."

"Ormiston, how do you *know* it's safer?" queried Sterl, sharply.

"Eric Dann knows. Hathaway and Woolcott are convinced of it. That's enough."

"Not by a damn sight! Not enough for you to

split this outfit," declared Sterl, deliberately.

"You insolent, cocksure Yankee...."

"*Careful!*" interrupted Sterl. "Ormiston, you're not on the level. You've got something up your sleeve. You'll never get away with it."

Ormiston wheeled to the other men. "Dann, you heard him. This intolerable riffraff—this Yankee...."

"Ormiston, you started this," boomed the leader, as the drover choked. "It's between you and him."

"Miss Dann—I appeal to you," went on Ormiston, his voice shaking. "Your father has been—taken in by this—this interloper. Won't you speak up for me?"

"Dad! It's an outrage," cried Beryl, white of face and angry of eye. "Will you permit this crude, lowbred American to insult Ashley so vilely—to threaten him?"

"Girl, go to your tent," ordered Dann, sternly. "If you must take sides you should take mine. Go—it's no place for you!"

"But Dad!" cried the spirited girl. "It *is*. We're all in it!"

"Yes, and it appears I shouldn't have brought you. At least try not to make it harder."

Beryl bent a withering glance upon Sterl. "Mr. Cowboy, do not speak to me again."

"Suits me fine, Miss Dann," replied Sterl curtly. "I'm bound to help and defend your father. Certainly not to concern myself with a girl who's been made a fool of by a coward and a cheat!"

Miss Dann gave Sterl a stinging slap on his cheek.

Then she drew back, gasping, as if realizing to what limit her temper had led her. With red burning out the white of her face, she ran toward her wagon. Ormiston wheeled to three waiting men, evidently his drovers, and stormed away with them, violently gesticulating.

Sterl watched them intently for a moment, then turned away toward Slyter's camp. Stanley Dann called him to wait, but Sterl hurried on. Red did not catch up with him until he had almost reached the tent. Then both discovered that Stanley Dann, Slyter and Leslie had followed them.

"Hazelton, don't run away from me when I call you," complained Dann, as he caught up.

"I'm sorry, boss. I lost my temper."

"Then you fooled me, because I thought you deliberately invited a quarrel with Ormiston."

"Oh, he couldn't rouse my temper. It was Miss Beryl. I shouldn't have spoken as I did to her."

They found seats on a log; except Leslie, who significantly stood close to Sterl, her youthful face grave, her hazel eyes, darkly dilated, fastened upon him.

"Les, you better run over to Mum," said Slyter.

"Not much, Dad. If Beryl is going to share the fights, and everything else, I am too."

"Good-o, Leslie," declared Dann, heartily. "You stay here. I'm going to need all the championship possible. . . . Hazelton, you spoke right from the shoulder. Man to man! I can't understand why Ormiston stood it. What concerns me is this. Have you any justification for the serious insinuations and open accusations you visited upon Ormiston?"

"Boss, they're all a matter of instinct. I've been years on the frontier. I have met hundreds of bad men. I have had to suspect some of them, outguess them, be too quick for them—or get shot myself. Ormiston might have fooled me for awhile, if it had not been for the accident of his kicking Friday. But not for long! He's playing a deep game—what, I can't figure out—yet."

"Hazelton, you impress me," pondered the leader. "I had only one feeling. You were opposing him in my interest. It seems incredible—what you insinuated about him. Yet you might possess some insight denied to me and my partners. This trek looms appallingly. That does not change me—frighten me in the least. But now I begin to see opposition, intrigue, perhaps treachery, blood and death."

"Boss, you can be sure of all of them," rejoined Sterl, earnestly. "And you can be as sure that my opposition to Ormiston is on your behalf."

Dann nodded his shaggy golden mane like a sleepy lion.

"Krehl, suppose you give me your view, unbiased by your friend's," he said, presently.

"Well, boss, when Ormiston rushed me like a bull, I wouldn't have risked my precious right hand on his mug, like Sterl did. I'd jest have bored him, had a coupla drinks of red likker, an' forgot all about him. We say Ormiston is no good. You give him the benefit of the doubt, an' leave it to me an' Sterl to find him out."

"Reason, intelligence, courage," boomed the drover. "These I respect above all other qualities. You have my consent. Go slow. Be sure. That's all I ask. Slyter, can you add anything to that?"

"No, Stanley. That says all."

"Yes, and nothing shall deter us....Hazelton, I was surprised and sorry indeed at the way Beryl took Ormiston's part. She is a headstrong, passionate child. Beryl has been pleading with me to make the trek by way of the Gulf."

Silent acceptance of that statement attested to its significance. Red dropped his gaze to the ground, and Sterl saw his lean brown hand clutch until the knuckles shone white.

"Not that it influences me in the least," continued Dann, rising.

Slyter arose also, shaking his head. "As if droving a mob of eight thousand cattle wasn't enough!"

Leslie walked a few steps with him, then returned.

"Dog-gone you, cain't you leave me an' Sterl alone atall?" complained Red, but a child could see that he did not mean that.

Leslie looked from him to Sterl with troubled, grateful eyes.

"Boys," she said, breathing hard, "if Beryl is in it, so am I. And she *is*! She's on Ash Ormiston's side. He has been making love to her all along. Besides I know her. She had all the boys at home in love with her. She likes it. Cedric, that boy today. He came on this trek solely because of Beryl. Ormiston—Oh, he is two-faced! Neither her father nor my Dad can see that."

"Wal, my dear, *we* can see it," returned Red, persuasively. "I'm not as all-fired stuck on Beryl as I was, at thet. But let's give her a chance."

"Sterl...won't you see me...later?" implored Leslie. "I know you've been angry with me for days. I deserve it. I'm sorry. I told Red to tell you I'd been a cat. Sterl, I couldn't bear to have you despise me longer."

"Leslie, how silly! I never despised you!" replied Sterl, with a smile. "I'll come to see you later."

A light illumined her troubled face. She wheeled to bound away like a deer.

"Pard, shore you see how it is with Leslie?" queried Red.

"I'm afraid I do," reluctantly admitted Sterl.

"Red, what's Ormiston's game?"

"Easy to say, far as the girls air concerned. Shore, he didn't mean marriage with her. But he might with Beryl. If Dann gets to the Kimberleys with half his cattle he'll be rich, an' richer pronto."

"It's a cinch he'll never end this trek with us."

"I've a hunch he doesn't mean to."

Sterl gave Red a searching gaze, comprehending, and indicative of swiftly revolving thoughts. "We're up against the deepest, hardest game we ever struck. Listen, let's try a trick that has worked before. Tip off Slyter and Stanley Dann that you and I will pretend

to quarrel—fall out—and you'll drink and hobnob
with Ormiston's drivers, in order to spy on Ormiston."

"Thet'll queer me with Beryl. Not thet I care
about it now."

"No, it'll make a hero out of you, if through this
you save her father."

"Dog-gone!" ejaculated Red, his face lighting.
"You always could outfigger me. Settled, pard, an' the
cairds air stacked. Tomorrow night you an' me will
have a helluva fight, savvy? Only be careful where
an' how you sock me."

"Righto. There's Friday. Red, I'm going to try to
make that black understand our game."

"Go ahaid. Another good idee. I'll tell Slyter, an'
then talk to Leslie a bit."

Friday and Sterl stood on the brink of the river.
"Friday, you sit down alonga me," said Sterl. "Me bad
here. Trouble," he went on, touching his forehead.
With a map drawn in the sand, in the argot which
Friday understood, he set forth the difference of opin-
ion regarding routes to the Kimberleys.

"Me savvy," replied the black, and tracing the
gulf-line on the sand he shook his head vehemently,
then tracing a line along the big river and across the
big land he nodded just as vehemently.

"Good, Friday," rejoined Sterl, strongly stirred.
"You know country up alonga here?"

The aborigine shook his head. "Might be black
fella tellum."

"Friday get black fella tell?"

"Might be. Some black fella good—some bad."

"Some white fella bad," went on Sterl, intensely. "Ormiston bad. Him wanta go this way. No good. Him make some white fella afraid. Savvy, Friday?"

The native nodded. He encouraged Sterl greatly. If he understood, then it did not matter that he could talk only a little.

"Ormiston bad along missy," continued Sterl. "Alonga big boss missy, too. Friday, watchum all time. Me watchum all time. Savvy, Friday?"

The aborigine nodded his black head instantly, with the mein of an Indian chief damning an enemy to destruction. "Friday savvy. Friday watchum. Friday no afraid!"

Sterl forgot to call for Leslie, but when she stole upon him it was certain that she had not forgotten, and that with the moonlight on her rippling hair, and sweet grave face, she was lovely.

"I waited and waited, but you didn't come," she said, taking his arm and leaning on him.

"Leslie, the talk I just had with Friday would make anyone forget. I'm sorry."

He looked down upon her with stirring of his pulse. In another year Leslie would be a beautiful woman, and irresistible.

"You've forgiven me?"

"Really, Leslie, I didn't have anything to forgive."

"Oh, but I think you had. I don't know what was the matter with me that day. Or *now*, for that matter. Today has been a little too much for your cowgirl.

Red told me about cowgirls. Oh, he's the finest, strangest boy I ever knew. I adore him, Sterl."

"Well, I'm not so sure I'll allow you to adore Red," rejoined Sterl. "And see here, Leslie, now that we've made up, and you're my charge on this trek . . ."

"How did you guess I longed for that?" she interposed frankly.

"I didn't. But as you seemed upset this afternoon and put such store on my friendship, why I decided to sort of boss you."

"I need it. Since we got to this camp, and I saw Ormiston again—I'm just scared out of my wits. Silly of me!"

"Well, outside of Ormiston, I reckon there's plenty to be scared about. Ormiston, though—you needn't fear him personally, any more. Keep out of his way. Always ride within sight of us. Never lose sight of me in a jam of any kind. Don't go to Dann's camp unless with us or your dad."

"Dad would take me, and forget me. Sterl, won't you please let me be with you often like this? I couldn't have slept tonight if you hadn't."

"Yes, you can be with me all you want," promised Sterl, helpless in the current. "But Red and I must go to bed early. Remember I have to ride herd after two o'clock. That means you're slated for bed right now."

"Oh, you darling," she cried, happily, and kissing him soundly she ran toward her wagon.

8

SLYTER wanted to keep his mob of cattle intact, so that it would not be lost in the larger mob. It was inevitable, Sterl told him, that sooner or later there would be only one mob. All the cattle except Woolcott's were unbranded.

Stanley Dann had foreseen this contingency, and his idea was to count the stock of each partner, as accurately as possible, and when they arrived at their destination let him take his percentage.

Discussion of this detail was held at the end of the next day's trek, in a widening part of the valley, where the stream formed a large pool. Ormiston objected to the idea of percentage; and when Stanley Dann put it to a vote, Red Krehl sided with Ormiston.

"Red Krehl, I'm ashamed of you," Leslie burst

out, when Red approached the Slyter campfire that night.

"You air. Wal, thet's turrible," drawled Red, in a voice which would have angered anyone.

"I saw you, after we halted today. You were with Ormiston's drovers. Very jolly! And after that conference at Dann's you were basking in Beryl's smiles. She has won you over for Ormiston."

"Les, you're a sweet kid, but kinda hot-haided an' dotty."

"I'm nothing of the kind."

"Me an' Sterl don't agree on some things."

"Oh, you've been drinking! Drink changes men. I ran from Ormiston when he'd been drinking."

"You'd better run from me, pronto, or I'll spank the daylights out of you."

"You—you!..." Leslie was too amazed and furious to find words. She looked around to see how her parents took this offense. Mrs. Slyter called for Leslie to leave the campfire. Leslie found her voice, and her dignity. "Mr. Krehl, some things are evident, and one is that you're no gentleman. You leave my campfire, or I will!"

Red did not show up at Slyter's camp next morning until time to drive the herd across the stream. The wagons crossed only hub deep at a bar below camp. But the cattle were put to the deep water. The take-off was steep, and many of the steers leaped, to go under. Splashing, cracking horns, bawling, the mob swam across the river, waded out. The horses, following in the deep trough which the cattle had cut into the bank, trooped down to take their own plunge.

It was well Sterl had an oilskin cover over his rifle as King went in, up to his neck. The black loved the water. Leslie came last. She bestrode Duke, who hated a wetting but showed that he could not be left behind. He pranced, he reared.

"Come on, Les," called Sterl cheerily. "Give him the steel."

"Okay," trilled the girl, spirited and sure, and Sterl smiled at the thought that she was absorbing American dialect. She spurred the big sorrel, and he plunged to go clear under. She kept her seat. The sorrel came up with a snort and swam powerfully across.

At last the sun rose high enough to be warm, and to dry wet garments. At noon it was hot. By the almost imperceptible increase in temperature and the changing nature of the verdure, Sterl became aware of the tropics. He saw strange trees and flowering shrubs along with those he already knew. No mile passed that he did not observe a beautifully plumaged bird that was new.

Leslie rode over to offer Sterl a wet biscuit. She had recovered from her shyness, or else in the broad sunlight and mounted on a horse that would jump at a touch, she had something of audacity. Presently he chased her back toward her station. Her eyes were flashing back and her hat swinging.

He would play square with this kid, he thought, but he had grown more aware of her captivating charm and freshness as the nights and days passed. He had no illusion about any cowboy, even himself. Yet he was disgusted with himself for being wooed so easily from a lamentable love affair. He should hate all women.

Sunset had come and passed when the main mob ceased to move, indicating that the drovers on the right had halted for camp. Slyter loped in behind his comrades. By the wagon Red sat his horse, waiting.

"Pard," he said, low-voiced, as Sterl halted close, "I'll eat with thet other outfit tonight. Meet you at the big campfire after supper. Spring the dodge then."

"Depends on how mean you get," replied Sterl, with a mirthless laugh. "Red, honest Injun, I don't like the dodge."

"Hell no! But, pard, it's for them, an' us too," returned Red, sharply. "It's our deal an' I've stacked the cairds. Play the game, you!" And Red rode away at a swinging canter. Darkness descended and the cook pounded a kettle to call all to supper.

Stanley Dann's community campfire blazed brightly in the center of a circle of bronzed faces. Dann had barbecued a beef. It hung revolving over a pit full of red-hot coals. Sterl appeared purposely late, his soft step inaudible as he came up behind Ormiston to hear him say, "But Leslie, my sweet girl, surely you cannot hold that against me?"

Sterl smothered an impulse to kick the man with all his might. Probably Red's arrival, more than his restraint, checked the precipitation of an issue that was bound to come. There were two drovers with Red, trying to hold him back, as he wrestled good-naturedly with them, and broke out in loud, lazy voice: "Dog-gone-it, fellers. Lemme be. Wasser masser with you? I'm a ladies' man—I am—an' I've been some punkins in my day."

His companions let him go, and kept back out of the circle of light. Sterl nerved himself for the prearranged split. Red shouldered Ormiston aside, to bend over Leslie.

"Les, I been huntin' you all over this heah dog-gone camp," said Red, with a gallant bow.

"I've been here, Red," replied Leslie, quickly, evidently glad to welcome him, drunk or sober. "Come, sit down."

"You shore air my sweet lil' girl frien'," returned Red.

What his next move might have been did not transpire, for Ormiston confronted him belligerently. Sterl's alert eye had caught the drover scrutininzing Red, doubtless for the gun usually in plain sight. To-night it was absent. Ormiston shoved Red violently. "You drunken Yankee pup! This is an Australian girl, not one of your trail drabs to mouth over!"

Sterl did not risk Red's reaction to that. He leaped between them, facing Ormiston. "Careful, you fool!" he called, piercingly. "Haven't you any sense? Krehl has killed men for less."

"He's drunk," rejoined the drover. "His familiarity with Leslie is insufferable."

"Yeah, it is, and I'll handle him," retorted Sterl.

"Here, men," boomed Dann, striding over. "Can't we have one little hour free from work and fighting?"

"Boss, there'll not be any fight," returned Sterl. "And Ormiston is not to blame this time, for more than one of his two-faced cracks—It's Red."

"Boss, I wasn't huntin' trouble," interposed Red, sulkily. "Shore I've had a couple drinks. But Whassar masser with thet? I ain't drunk. I jest say a playful word to Leslie, an' I gets insulted by Ormiston heah, an' then my pard. Dog-gone it, thet's too much."

"Red, I'm disgusted with you," declared Sterl, angrily. "This is the second time. I *warned* you."

"What'n'll do I care? You make me sick with yore preachin'. I ain't agonna stand it no more."

"Cowboy, you'd gone to hell long ago but for me."

"Shore. But I'm on my way again. We'll all be on our way, if we stick to the big boss's idee, an' trek off into thet Never-never."

Sterl simulated a man working himself into a rage. Laying a powerful left hand on Red's collar he jerked him so hard that the cowboy's head shot forward and back. "Why you double-crossing lowdown greaser!" raged Sterl. "You fail us for a few drinks!"

"Wal, it shore looks like I got the decidin' vote," rang out the cowboy, with convincing elation.

Sterl let out a fierce cry of wrath. And he knocked Red flat. Despite his promise not to hit too hard, he feared he had done so.

Beryl Dann leaped up to run and drop upon her

knees beside Red. "Oh, he's terribly hurt!" She glanced up at Sterl, face and eyes flaming in the light. "You!—*You* are the discord—the villain on this trek!"

Sterl bowed scornfully and left the campfire for his own tent. Lighting a cigarette Sterl settled down to smoke and think and listen, when rapid footfalls told that someone was coming. He turned round to see Leslie running out of the darkness. At that moment she appeared most distractingly pretty and desirable.

"Can't you ever walk, like a lady should?" queried Sterl, gruffly.

"I can—but not in—the dark—with Ormiston at large," she panted.

"After you again?"

"Yes, he is. Barefaced as—as anything."

"You have encouraged him."

"I—have not!"

"Leslie, I don't believe you," returned Sterl, quite brutally. Somehow that little incident beside Dann's campfire had roused unreasonable jealousy.

A dark wave of color changed the paleness of her face.

"Sterl, I lied to Mum—and Dad about Ormiston. I was scared. But I'd not lie to you."

"Very well then, I apologize!"

"Sterl, Red said something today . . . that *I* didn't know it and *you* didn't know it—but I—I was your girl."

"The rattlebrain! Leslie, don't let him bamboozle you."

"What's bamboozle?"

"Make a little fool of you."

"Oh! then it isn't—true?" she whispered, plaintively.

"Of course it's true, in a way, for this trek," he replied, trying to keep from putting his arm around her, rather than carefully choosing his words.

"Then I can be happy, in spite of your brutality to Red," she rejoined most earnestly, hanging to his arm and devouring his face with eyes of wonder and sorrow. "Why didn't you hit Ormiston instead of your friend?"

"I was angry, Leslie. What happened after I left?"

"Beryl has a tender heart for anyone hurt. And Red was hurt. She bent over him and almost cried. I bent over him, too, and I could see that Red was not only hurt but glorying in it. Then it happened. Ormiston dragged us away. He was perfectly white in the face. Why, the madman thinks he can have us both! Then poor dear Red sat up, his hand to his face, and said: 'Leslie, tell thet pard of mine thet I'll get even for the sock he gave me.' Others were coming, so I ran off."

"Leslie," flashed Sterl, "You're no kid any more, despite what Red says. You've got to be a woman— to use your wits to help us—to be cunning. Listen, can I trust you?"

She looked up wonderingly. "Yes, Sterl."

"That fight with Red was all pretense. Red wasn't

drunk. Our plan is for him to make it look like he's split with me—to hobnob with those drovers, and find out what the hombre has up his sleeve! I'm confiding in you because I won't have you believing me a brute."

"Who thought you a brute? Oh, so Red wasn't drunk? How glad I am! Will Beryl be in the secret?"

"No indeed! Only your Dad, Stanley Dann, and you."

"So that was it," mused the girl.

"That was what?"

"Beryl's sweetness toward Red. The cat! Ormiston has twisted her round his little finger, and now she thinks Red has gone over to Ormiston's side."

"Righto, Leslie. Now you hide those perfectly human feeling and practice deceit yourself. Be a ninny. Be the little softy who looks up to the proud Miss Dann. But be cunning, and find out through her all that is possible about Ormiston."

"So that's my part? Ohhh! But it's for Dad, for Mum, for Mr. Dann, for *you*. Yes, I can do it."

"Good-o! Run! Here comes Red. From the way he walks, I'd gamble he's mad!"

Red stalked into the firelight, his eyes like daggers, his hand to his mouth. He removed it to expose a swollen lip.

"Wal, you—liar!" he said. "You promised not to sock me hard, an' look what you did!"

"I'm sorry, pard," replied Sterl, stifling a laugh. "Honestly, I didn't mean to. When I swung, you dumbhead, you ducked into it."

"Pard, I heah somebody comin'. Let's go in our tent an' hit the hay. Then I'll talk."

Sterl had to strain his eyes to make out Friday's prone form under the low-drooping wattle branches. Somehow he had come to liken the black to a watchdog. He felt how infinitely keener the aborigine was than any white man, and most likely far keener than any Indian scout he had ever known.

Thirty-one days later—according to Leslie's journal on the twenty-ninth of June—after a prodigious trek through a jungle pass, Stanley Dann called a halt for a rest and repairs to equipment and drovers and mob.

Ormiston, with the two partners and drovers whom he dominated, broke out of the pass into the open, after a three-mile trek which took more than half a day. The Danns followed on his heels. Slyter's cattle and riders found the grass and brush trampled, the tree ferns and sassafras knocked down, the creek banks cut into lanes, making it an easy trek except for the grades.

An hour's rest on the flat of his back, a bath, a shave, a change of clothes, restored Sterl to some semblance of his former self. He had a short talk with Slyter, cheerful and energetic again. Mrs. Slyter appeared none the worse for the long wagon rides and the many camps with their incessant tasks. But Leslie showed the wear of six weeks and more of hard riding.

"Howdy, ragamuffin," said Sterl, coming at her call.

"I am, aren't I?" she replied, ruefully, surveying herself. "I've two other suits, but I'll mend these rags and make them go as far as possible. How spic and span you look! Very handsome, Sterl!"

"That goes for you, Les," he rejoined, heartily. "How prettily you tan!"

"Flatterer! I've had to ride myself nearly to death to extract that compliment from you. Oh, what a trek! Sterl, you must help me with my journal."

"Sure will. Let's see." It was then that Sterl discovered they had trekked thirty-one days through these mountain ranges for an aggregate of only one hundred and seventy-eight miles. "Not so good."

"My journal? You don't help me!"

"I was referring to our trek, not your journal. It's very neat. Only there's so little. I saw Beryl's journal the other night. It has yours skinned to a frazzle."

"Yeah? She writes in the wagon. And Red helps her at night. That was another thing which made Ormiston jealous."

"Well, add a long footnote here. I can remember the important things. Of course you would record your loss of Duchess."

"Oh, Sterl, that broke my heart."

"She'll trail us, if she wasn't crippled or stolen by blacks. Put this down. Slyter lost two horses, and some twenty-odd head of cattle. Bad crossing at the ford you called Wattle Rapids. Flooded a wagon there, but no damage. Visited by only few blacks.

Growing unfriendly. Mosquitoes terrible at the Forks.
Big tree ferns. Grand mountain-ash trees. Bad going
last few days. Short treks. Wagons need of repairs
and grease. Leslie about stripped to rags and lost
say five pounds."

"Umpumm, cowyboy! I don't record that!"

Supper, as usual on short day treks, came
early—this time, as had happened often, without Red
in attendance. Members of Slyter's group were always
too hungry to mind the sameness of fare. Beef, al-
ternated with game, was the prime factor. Damper,
tea, dried fruits and beans were the other essentials,
and on occasion Bill, the cook, managed some surprising pastry. Cowboys, Sterl realized, drank too
much coffee, sometimes ten cups a day. Sterl and
Red had learned to like tea, but they confined drinking it to two meals a day.

"We haven't talked with Stanley for ten days,"
said Slyter after supper, "Come along with me, Hazelton."

The Dann camp was bustling. One wagon had
been jacked up, while the hubs were being greased;
hammers rapped vigorously on another, which had
been partly unpacked; tents were in process of erec-
tion; a brawny drover was splitting firewood. Red sat
on the ground beside a hammock, in which Beryl lay,
writing in her journal.

Dann, the blond, golden-bearded giant, greeted
Slyter and Sterl in booming welcome.

"Heard my order that we hold up here a week?"
he queried.

"Yes. Heald brought it. I'm glad. A good few days will put us right again. Sterl agrees."

"Just had words with Ormiston. He disagrees. Says one day is rest enough. I told him he had my order. He replied that he'd go on with Woolcott and Hathaway. At that I put my foot down. He left in high dudgeon."

"Why does he try to block everything?" Sterl queried, "Why? Any fool would know the cattle need rest. Let's ask Red."

Sterl called over the happily engaged cowboy, informed him of Ormiston's defection and asked if he could throw any light on it.

"Boss, I cain't give any reason for Ormiston's angle, except he's a mean cuss."

"Immaterial to me whether he does or not. He'd surely wait for us to catch up."

Dann and Slyter withdrew, leaving Red, accompanied by Sterl, to return to Beryl. She received Sterl with a rather distant hauteur. If anything, Beryl had gained on the trek, in a golden tan, in a little weight, and certainly in beauty. Sterl took advantage of the moment to tell her so. Her answering pleasure betrayed the vain jewel of her soul. Even if she hated a man she could not help responding to a tribute to her beauty.

Sterl returned to Slyter's camp, for he had an engagement with Leslie to climb to the saddle of the ridge and view the country. Letting her carry his rifle, he secured a long stout stick, and they set out. Along their route, knee-high grass had not been trampled, and Sterl kept an eye out for snakes. Presently a movement of grass and a sibilant hiss startled them into jumping back. Then with the long stick Sterl located the snake. Jones had informed Sterl that this species was very poisonous and during the mating season would attack a man.

"Isn't he pretty? Tan, almost gold, with dark bars. Hasn't got a triangular shaped head as our bad snakes have."

"Step back, Sterl. Let me shoot his head off," demanded Leslie, who manifestly was not sentimental over snakes.

"Umpumm. What for? He might be a gentleman like our rattler, who won't strike you unless you step on him."

"This tiger is no gentleman. You're very tender-hearted over *snakes*, aren't you?" said Leslie, with a subtlety into which Sterl thought he had better not inquire. As they surmounted the ridge, they looked down into the magnificent mountain pass through which they had come. From behind the sun shone golden and red. In places the shining ribbon of stream wound through verdure. On the far flat, flame trees were mounds of burning foliage, and the wedge-shaped sassafras trees glistened as with golden frost. But most striking of all was a waterfall which Sterl had not seen on the way through, a lacy, downward-smoking cascade leaping fall after fall in golden glory from the mountainside.

"Sterl, not there—here!" cried Leslie, tugging to wheel him around. "That is pretty—reminds me of home. But this purple land we are trekking into...."

From the height where they stood the glistening, grassy slope with tufts of flowers like bits of fire, descended gradually to the camp, where tents and canvas wagon tops shone white, columns of blue smoke curled and great gum trees towered, their smooth trunks opal-hued, up to the immense spread and sweep of hoary branches, their leaves thin glints of green against the golden sky.

These spreading gums were like pillars of a wide portal opening down into a softly colored vale, from which swells of land, covered with flowering trees, rose and fell away into a plain spotted with flame—trees and wattles, which lured the gaze on over timbered ridges, on and on with dimming gold into the luminous purple that intensified and darkened until it blended with the never ending vastness.

He became aware that Leslie was pressing close to his side, clinging to him, gazing up with darkly shining eyes.

"My Australia!" she murmured. "Isn't it glorious? Don't you love it? Aren't you glad you came?"

"Yes Leslie—yes," he said, his emotion naturally shifting to the sense of her beauty and nearness.

"You will never leave Australia?"

"No child—never," he replied, with sadness in his voice.

"You are my dearest friend?"

"I hope so. I'm trying hard to be—your friend."

"And my big brother?"

Suddenly there came a convulsion within his

breast, a hot gush of blood that swiftly followed his surrender to her sweetness, to her appeal. "Not your big brother, Leslie!" he said, thickly, as he clasped her tight. "You're a woman—sweet. No man could resist....And you torment me." He kissed her passionately, again and again until her cool quivering lips grew hot and responsive—again and again! until she lay relaxed and acquiescent on his breast.

"My God! Now I've done it," he exclaimed, remorsefully.

"*Sterl!*" She drew back to gaze up with wondering eyes and flaming face. Then with a cry she turned and fled down the slope.

"Cowboy, that's what Australia has done to you," he said and bent to pick up his rifle.

CHAPTER 9

DAY after day the great trek crept across the wilderness that Leslie had called the purple land. Day after day the smoke signals of the aborigines arose and drifted away over the horizon. Friday grew mysterious and reticent, answering queries with a puzzling: "Might be." Sterl, grown wise from his long experience with the American Indians, knew better than to question the black about his people.

Stanley Dann had no fear of blacks or endless trek or flood or heat or drought. As the difficulties imperceptibly increased so did his cheer and courage and faith. On Sundays he held a short religious service which all were importuned to attend. Sterl noted, as the spell of the wilderness worked upon the minds of the trekkers, that the attendance gradually de-

creased. Faith had not failed Stanley Dann, but it had
lost its hold on the others, who retrograded toward
the primitive.

Sterl saw all this, understood it only vaguely.
Ormiston had already succumbed to this backward
step in evolution. Red would succumb to it unless a
genuine love for Beryl Dann proved too strong for
this life in the raw. All the drovers were being affected, and Sterl felt that not many of them would
turn out gods.

Beryl responded slowly but surely to this urge.
And in her, its first effect was a growth of her natural
instinct for acquisition of admirers. Every night at
Dann's camp a half dozen or more young drovers
vied with Ormiston and Red for her smiles. Red
played his game differently from his rivals. He confined his efforts to serving Beryl, so that the girl
seemed to rely upon him while being piqued that he
was not at her feet. Ormiston's inordinate jealousy
grew.

Leslie, being the youngest in the trek, and a girl
of red blood and spirit, traveled more rapidly than
the rest of them in her relegation to the physical. For
weeks after that sunset hour in the gateway of the
pass, she had avoided being alone with Sterl. But her
shyness gradually fell away from her, and as the trek
went on through austere days and nights of time and
distance, she warmed anew to him.

But Sterl had never transgressed again, as at that
mad and unrestrained sunset climax, though there
were times when he desired it almost overwhelm-

ingly. Nevertheless love had come to him once more. Yet he never let himself dwell upon a future. For many of Stanley Dann's troop, and very possibly for him, there would be none.

"Plenty smoke," said Friday one afternoon when camp had been made on a dry stream bed, with only a few waterholes.

Sterl and Slyter, together at the campfire when Friday spoke, scanned the horizon where at the moment all was clear.

"Friday, what you mean?" queried Slyter, anxiously. "We come far." He held up three fingers. "Moons—three moons. Plenty smokes. No black man. All same alonga tomorrow?"

"Black fella close up. Plenty black fella. Come more. Bimeby no more smokes. Spear cattle—steal!"

"How long, Friday? When?"

"Mebbe soon—mebbe bimeby."

Slyter looked apprehensively at Sterl, and threw up his hands.

"Let's go tell Stanley."

They found their leader, as had happened before, patiently listening to Ormiston. Sterl's keen eyes noted a graying of Dann's hair over his temples.

Slyter broke the news. Dann stroked his golden beard.

"At last, eh? We are grateful for this long respite," he said, his eyes lighting as if with good news.

"I asked Friday what do? He said, 'Watchum close up! Killum!'" concluded Slyter.

"Well! For a black to advise that!" exclaimed the leader, ponderingly. "But I do not advise bloodshed."

"I do," declared Ormiston, bluntly. "If we don't, this nigger mob will grow beyond our power to cope with it. They will hang on our trek, spearing cattle at a distance."

Sterl wondered what was working in this man's mind to influence him thus. But it seemed wise advice. "Boss, I agree with Ormiston," he spoke up.

"What's your opinion, Slyter?" asked Dann.

"If the blacks spear our cattle and menace us, then I say kill."

Dann nodded his huge head in sad realization. "We will take things as they come. Merge all the cattle into one mob...."

"I told you I'd not agree to that," interrupted Ormiston.

"Don't regard it as my order. I ask you to help me to that extent," returned the leader, with patient persuasion.

"Ormiston, listen," interposed Sterl. "I've had to do with a good many cattle drives, treks you call them. After a stampede or a flood or a terrible storm, things that are bound to happen to us, cattle can never be driven separately again."

"That I do not believe."

"Yeah? All right," snapped Sterl, "what you believe doesn't count so damn much on this trek!"

Ormiston gazed away across the purple distance, his square jaw set, his eyes smoldering, his mein one of relentless opposition.

"Our differences are not the important issue now," he said finally. "That is this danger of blacks." And without looking at his partners he stalked away.

"Slyter, we'll put double guards on watch tonight. Merge your cattle with my mob," ordered Dann.

Before dusk fell this order had been carried out. Ormiston's mob, including Woolcott's and Hathaway's, grazed across the stream bed a mile distant.

Supper at Slyter's camp was late that night, and Red Krehl the last rider to come in. He sat crosslegged between Leslie and Sterl. His dry, droll humor was lacking. It gave Sterl concern, but Leslie betrayed no sign that she noticed it. However, after supper, she teased him about Beryl.

"Les, you're a cold, fishy, soulless girl, no good atall," finally retaliated Red.

"Fishy? I don't know about that. Sterl, should I box his ears?"

"Well, fishy is okay if he means angelfish."

"Red, do you mean I'm an angelfish?"

"I should snicker I don't. Back in Texas there's a little catfish. And can he sting?"

"Red, I'd rather have you in a fighting mood. Three times before this you've been the way you are tonight—and something has happened."

"Wal ..." Ormiston ordered me out of his camp just before I rode in heah."

"What for?" asked Sterl, sharply.

"I ain't shore. Beryl has been kinda sweet to me lately, in front of Ormiston. It ain't foolin' me none.

But it's got him. Another thing. Her Dad makes no bones about likin' me. Ormiston hates thet. I reckon he sees I'm someone to worry about."

"You are, Red. But I've a hunch your attention to Beryl has kept you from getting a line on Ormiston."

"Mebbe it has. All the same, shore as you're knee-high to a grasshopper, Beryl will give him away yet, or let out somethin' thet I can savvy."

"Is Beryl in love with him?" asked Sterl.

"Hell, yes," replied Red, gloomily.

"Les, what do you think?"

"Hell, yes," repeated Leslie, imitating Red's laconic disgust. "Beryl has had a lot of love affairs. But this one is worse."

"You're both wrong," rejoined Sterl. "Beryl is fascinated by a no-good, snaky man. She's a natural-born flirt. But I think she has depth. Wait till she's had real hell!"

Friday loomed out of the shadow. He carried his wommera and bundle of long spears. "Plenty black fella close up. Corroboree!"

"Listen!" cried Leslie.

On the instant a wild dog howled. It seemed a mournful and monstrous sound, accentuating the white-starred, melancholy night. Then a low, weird chanting of many savage voices, almost drowned by the native dogs baying the dingoes, rose high on the still air into a piercing wail, to die away.

"Bimeby plenty black fella. Spear cattle—steal ebrytink," volunteered Friday.

"Will these black men try to kill us?" queried Sterl.

"Might be, bimeby. Watchum close."

Slyter came to the fire, holding up a hand for silence. The howling, the barking, the chanting, transcended any wild sound Sterl had ever heard. The staccato concatenated barks of coyotes, the lonely mourn of bloodthirsty wolves, the roo-roo-rooooo of mating buffalo, the stamping, yelling war dance of the Indians—were hardly to be compared to this Australian bushland chant. Sterl entertained a queer thought that the incalculable difference might be cannibalism.

"Cowboys, how does that strike you?" asked Slyter, grimly. "Daughter, would you like to be home again? Mum has her hands clapped over her ears."

The girl gave him a wan, brave smile. "No. We're on the trek. We'll fight."

"Righto!" ejaculated Slyter. "Les, you have a rifle. If you see a black man spear a horse—kill him!"

It struck Sterl significantly that Slyter thought of his horses, not his cattle.

"Get some sleep," he concluded. "Don't risk your tent tonight. Black men seldom or ever attack before dawn, but sleep under your wagon."

The cowboys piled packs and bundles outside of the wheels of their wagon. Then they crept under to stretch out on their blankets without removing coat or boots. Friday lay just outside of the wheels. When they rolled out, dressed to ride, rifles in hand,

Larry was saddling horses. Drake and his three drovers drinking tea.

"How was the guard?" asked Sterl.

"Mob quiet. Horses resting. No sign of blacks.
But we heard them on and off. Look sharp just before
and at daylight."

"Boys," said Larry, when they reached the herd,
"I'll drove the far end."

Sterl passed Dann's horses, patrolled by one
rider, and a mile farther down came upon another
horseman, who turned out to be Cedric. He had been
on guard for an hour and reported all well. Sterl rode
back.

At intervals low blasts of the corroboree waved
out across the plain. The campfires of the aborigines
still glimmered. Dogs and dingoes had ceased their
howling. Sterl recalled the first time he had stood
guard on the Texas range when Comanches were
expected to raid. They had done it, too, matchless
and fleet riders, swooping down upon the *remuda* to
stampede it and drive off horses, leaving one dead
Indian on the ground, victim of his rifle. He was sixteen years old then and that was his first blood spill-
ing.

Every half hour or thereabouts he rode back to
have a word with Red. The only time he accosted
Friday the black held up his hand, "Bimeby!"

Now the chanting of the aborigines ceased, and
the corroboree fires glimmered fainter and fainter to
die out. The cattle slept. The silence seemed uncanny. The first streaks of gray in the east heralded

a rumble of hoofs, like distant thunder. The mob of cattle belonging to Ormiston and his companions was on the run. Sterl galloped over to Red. Friday joined them.

"They're runnin', pard, but not stampeded," said Red, his lean head bent, his ear to the east.

"Slowing down, Red," returned Sterl, straining his hearing. "Friday, what happen alonga there?"

"Black fella spearum cattle," was the reply.

"Not so bad, thet. But a stampede of this unholy mob would be orful," declared Red. "Listen, Sterl, they're rollin' again, back the other way."

"Saw a gun flash!" cried Sterl, and then a dull report reached them.

"Wal, the ball's opened," said Red, coolly. "Take yore pardners."

Flashes and reports came from several points, widely separated.

"Aw, hell! Our cattle are wakin' up, pard. Heah comes Larry."

The young drover came tearing up, to haul his mount back onto sliding haunches. "Boys, our mob— is about to—break," he panted.

"Umpumm, Larry," replied Red. "They're jest oneasy."

Sterl calculated that a thousand or more cattle were in motion, less than a third of Ormiston's mob. The rumble of hoofs began to diminish in volume as the gunshots became desultory. But the lowing of Dann's mob, the cracking of horns, caused Sterl great concern, in spite of Red's assurance. The center of disturbance appeared to be back along the sector from which Larry had just come.

"Sterl, I'll go with Larry," said Red, wheeling Jester. "Jest in case. If we don't get back pronto come arunnin'."

Presently, when he halted King to listen, Sterl found that the dull trampling from across the flat was dying out, and that the ominous restlessness of Dann's mob was doing likewise. A rapid thud of hoofs proved to be Red, riding back.

"Lost my matches. Gimme some," said the cowboy, as he reined in beside Sterl. Lighting a cigarette relieved Sterl. "They was movin' out up there, but easy to stop. This mob of Dann's fooled me. They've been so tame, you know, not atall like longhorns, thet I reckoned it'd take a hell of a lot to stampede them. But umpumm!—Say, I'll bet two pesos we'll be interested in what came off over there."

"Yes. All quiet now, though. And it's daylight."

At sunrise they rode back to camp. Slyter listened intently to Larry's report, which plainly relieved him. They had just finished breakfast when Cedric dashed up to inform Slyter that Dann wanted him and the cowboys at once.

"What has happened?" queried Slyter.

"Trouble with the blacks at Ormiston's camp," replied Cedric, then loped away.

Slyter himself was the only one who showed surprise. Dominated by Stanley Dann, he just could not believe in calamity.

"That's bad. I wonder who. . . . Boys, come on."

"Friday, run alonga me," said Sterl to the black.

At the larger camp, Stanley Dann and Eric, with Cedric and another drover, were mounted, waiting for them. Beryl was watching them with big troubled eyes.

"Bingham," spoke up the giant, calmly, "Ormiston just sent word that Woolcott had been speared by the blacks."

"Woolcott! Cedric didn't tell us—I thought— Stanley, this is terrible. When—what? ..."

"No other word. I daresay if Ormiston had wanted us he'd have said so. But by all means I should go."

"We all should go," rejoined Slyter.

"Wal, I should smile," drawled Red, in a peculiar tone that only Sterl understood.

The tall Hathaway, bewhiskered now and no longer florid, met Dann's group as they reined in near the wagons.

"A terrible tragedy, Stanley," he said, huskily. "Woolcott insisted on doing guard duty, in spite of Ormiston's advice. The blacks attacked at dawn this morning.... Killed Woolcott and his horse!"

"Where is he?" asked Dann.

Hathaway led them beyond the campfire, to a quartet of men beside a wagon. Ormiston, haggard of face, turned to meet the visitors. Two of the group had shovels, and had evidently just dug a grave.

"Dann, it's a gruesome business I'd hoped to spare you," said Ormiston, not without harshness. "Woolcott heard the blacks, and he went on guard.

I advised him particularly to stay in. But he went—and got killed."

Woolcott lay limp as a sack, with a spear through his middle. Only the side of his gray visage was exposed, but it was enough to show the convulsions of torture that had attended his death.

"Where's his horse?" asked Dann.

"Out there," replied Ormiston, with a motion of his hand toward a low ridge. "We have the saddle and bridle. This won't delay us, Stanley. We'll bury Woolcott, mark his grave, and catch up with you."

"Bury him without any service?"

"You needn't wait to do that. If you wish I'll read a Psalm out of his Bible, and bury it with him."

"I'd like that. We can do no less."

"Wait, boss," called Sterl, "I want to see just what this black man spear work looks like." He slipped out of his saddle, and motioned Friday to come from behind the horses.

"Me too," drawled Red, coolly, as he swung his long leg and stepped down.

Sterl, stepping slowly out from the horses, made it a point to be looking at Ormiston when the drover espied Friday. Evil and forceful as Ormiston undoubtedly was, he was not great. Sterl had seen a hundred outlaws and rustlers who could have hidden what this man failed to hide—a fleeting glimpse of fear.

Friday stepped close to Woolcott's prostrate body, and with sinewy black hand, wonderful in its familiarity with that aboriginal weapon, laid hold of the spear.

Ormiston burst out: "All blacks look the same to me!" And with murder in his protruding eyes he pulled a gun. Sterl, ready and quick as light, shot it out of Ormiston's hand.

The horses, snorting, plunging, kept the riders busy for a moment. Friday backed away. Sterl stepped back a little, smoking gun extended, lining up the shocked Ormiston with his drovers, Bedford and Jack. Red was at Sterl's side. Stanley Dann bellowed an order from behind.

"Ormiston, you and I will have real trouble over Friday yet," rang out Sterl. The bullet had evidently hit the gun, to send it spinning away. Ormiston held his slung hand with his left.

"Next time you throw your gun, do it at me," added Sterl, scornfully. "You'd have killed this black man."

"Yes—I would—and I'll do it—yet," shouted Ormiston, now purple in the face.

"Ormiston, you're blacker at heart than Friday is outside."

Stanley urged his big charger near to the belligerents.

"What revolt is this?" he demanded.

Sterl explained in few words. Ormiston contended that sight of the black had incited him to frenzy.

"Let that do," boomed the leader. "Isn't Woolcott's death lesson enough? We must squash this dissension amongst us. Ormiston, I blame you most. Back to camp, all!"

Dann, with Slyter and his brother Cedric, rode away. "Mosey along, pard," said Red, curtly, "but don't turn yore back."

Sterl had not taken two backward steps before he bumped into King. The cowboys mounted and soon overtook the long-striding Friday. Slowing down to accommodate the black, they rode a beeline for their own camp.

"Sorry, boss," said Sterl to Slyter. "I'm always deepening those furrows in your brow. But you must have seen that Ormiston would have shot Friday. Anyway you heard him say so."

"I heard," declared Slyter. "I tried to convince Stanley that Ormiston has always meant to murder my black."

Leslie bounced out from somewhere. "Dad! You heard what?" she cried, flashing-eyed and keen, not to be denied.

"Oh, Lord!" groaned her father.

"Leslie, put this down in your little book," said Sterl, and he made a concise report of the incident.

She flamed even more readily than usual. "He would have shot Friday!" Then she swore, the first time Sterl had ever heard her use a word of the profanity so prevalent in camp. When her father looked shocked and helpless, Leslie went on, "The louse! The dirty low-down *hombre!*"

"Haw! Haw! Haw!" rang out Red's laugh. "Les, you're shore learning to talk cowboy!"

"Boss," spoke up Sterl, while he fastened the cinches on his rangy sorrel. "Red and I will start out on the trek. But after Ormiston is on the move, we'll go back there with Friday to look over the ground. Red and I can read tracks. And if it's too much for us, maybe Friday can see something. We'll catch up pronto."

A few pieces of lumber lay scattered about Woolcott's grave. Sterl had Friday carry stones to cover it. Then they erected a makeshift cross. That done, they set out on foot, leading their horses. Half a mile out on the grassy flat, at the edge of rising, sandy ground, Friday located a dead horse.

It was a bay, lying on its side, with a spear sticking up high. "Look heah," said Red, presently, pointing to a slash of dried blood running from the ear on the under side of the head.

The black had pulled out the long spear and was scrutinizing it.

"Boss," he said to Sterl, "killum horse like white man." And Friday made one of his impressive gestures back toward Woolcott's grave.

"How, Friday?" queried Sterl.

The black fitted the bloody spear to his wommera, and made ready as if to throw.

"No wommera. No black fella spearum white man! No black fella killum horse!"

"By Gawd!" ejaculated Red, not in horror, but in confirmation of something that had been sensed.

"How then?" cried Sterl.

"Spear pushum in white man. Pushum in horse.

No black fella do!" And Friday took the long spear, to shove it deliberately into the horse.

"Heah, help me turn this hoss over," said Red. The three of them managed it, not without dint of effort. Red thrust his bare hand into the bloody ear. Suddenly he grew tense.

"Shot!" hissed the cowboy. Then again he bent over to move his hand. "Got my finger in a bullet hole. Somebody shoved a gun in this hoss's ear an' shot him! Look heah!" As he pulled out his hand there were black stains merged with blood on his forefinger. "Powder! Burnt powder!"

Red wiped his hand on the sand and grass, then completed the job with his handkerchief. He stood up, and searching his pocket for tobacco and matches sat down to roll a cigarette.

Sterl addressed the watchful black. "Friday, look—see tracks—black fella tracks all around?" Sterl himself could not see a single one except Friday's. Naturally there were boottracks all around, in every sandy spot. Then he sat down heavily.

"*Murder!*"

"Pard, as shore as Gawd made little apples!" replied Red. "Hell, we shouldn't be surprised. We knowed it all the time—only we was afraid to think!"

Red let out as if in relief a long string of vile names—the worst that the western range afforded.

"Why—why?" queried Sterl, passionately.

"What the hell why?" flashed Red, getting up. "It *is*! We don't care why!"

"Could we prove murder to these drovers, if we fetched them back here?"

"Mebbe, if they'd come. But Dann wouldn't come. Pard, I'm afraid he's leanin' to a belief we Yankees air too hardhearted an' suspicious."

"Red, you're figuring we'd better look out for our own scalps, and let these drovers find things out?"

"I reckon I am, pard, though I ain't had time to figger much."

"Maybe you're right, Red. There's Leslie to think of—and Beryl. And Ormiston's a tiger!"

"Leslie is yore lookout, pard, an' Beryl is mine."

Friday interrupted to say: "Boss, no black fella tracks alonga here."

They followed Friday farther into the bush, past dead campfires, merely a few charred sticks crossed, and then to a trampled, blackened, sandy patch where a large fire had burned. A steer's skull marked the spot where there had been an aboriginal feast. What amazed Sterl was the completeness of it. No hide nor hoofs left!—Only a few bones divested of their marrow! From that spot foot tracks of a horde of natives led on in the direction of the trek.

*T*HAT day's trek, owing to the larger mob of cattle becoming infused with the excitement which dominated Ormiston's, proved to be the longest so far. At camp, Sterl had little inclination and not much opportunity to add to Slyter's worries by telling him that Woolcott had been murdered. But Slyter confided in Sterl and Red that he had learned from the Danns of Ormiston's claiming Woolcott's fifteen hundred head of cattle for a gambling debt. Sterl was staggered, and the fluent Red for the moment rendered speechless.

"Hathaway verified it," went on Slyter. "Told me Ormiston, Woolcott, and those drovers Bedford and Jack, gambled every night."

When Slyter went about his tasks Red came out

of his dumb spell. "Pard, thet ain't so. It's another of
Ormiston's —— —— lies. Hathaway might believe
it. He always went to bed with the chickens. For
months, almost, either I have seen Ormiston with
Beryl, or I have been with Jack, an' Bedford. Cairds
was never mentioned to me an' you know I had a
roll thet would have choked a cow."

That night Leslie, in picking up a bundle of firewood, neglected to put on her gloves, and was severely bitten by a red-back spider. She made light of
it, especially after Friday returned to paste some herb
concoction of his own upon the swelling hand. Sterl
had found a better remedy for snakebite than whisky.
He plied the girl with coffee, and walked her up and
down for hours, keeping her awake until she fell
asleep in his arms from exhaustion. Then he carried
her to the wagon and laid her on her bed.

Then when they called Red to ride herd, it was
to discover that he was ill with chills and fever, the
like of which had never before befallen that cowboy.
But he refused to stay in bed. By breakfast time, he
was so ill he could not sit his horse. Stanley Dann
declared that his ailment was intestinal and came
from something he had eaten. Red swore and asked
for whisky. He traveled that day on the dray, high on
top of the great load of flour sacks, where he went
to sleep.

Leslie should not have ridden at all, but neither
her father nor Sterl could dissuade her. "Shucks," she
said. "I'm all right I won't give in to thet pesky old red-
back!" She was absorbing the cowboy vocabulary.

Sterl rode close to her that day, during which she fell twice out of her saddle. But she did not lose her sense of humor.

"Red said I'm gonna be a genuine cowgirl, didn't he?" she said when she slid out of her saddle the second time. "Dog-gone it, Sterl, if I fall off again treat me to some of that—that medicine you gave me back at Purple Land camp."

Two days of laborious travel followed. Before sunset of the first, the expedition stalled on the banks of a considerable stream with steep banks. Even when the mob, driven across in advance, had trampled out crude roads, it required eight horses to drag each wagon across. Leslie was still too weak to brave the treacherous current and Sterl, mounted on King, carried her across in his arms. Mid-current, she looked up and said softly:

"I'd like to ride all the rest of the way like this."

"Yeah? Three thousand miles?" responded Sterl. And he registered this little occurrence as one of the dangerous incidents—if not misfortunes—that were multiplying.

A dry camp that afternoon awakened Sterl anew to the alarming probability that lack of water headed Stanley Dann's list of obstacles to the trek. Friday anticipated a native corroboree that night, and it was forthcoming, with its accompaniment of dingo choruses and dog howls. Dann's order was to let the aborigines alone, unless they stole into camp to attack. Morning disclosed no evidence that the blacks had killed cattle, but Slyter shrewdly declared that their leader could have found out had he put Friday and the cowboys to hunting tracks.

All day the smoke signals rose far ahead, the sun burned hotter, the tiny flies swarmed invisibly around the riders' and drovers' heads. At dusk flying foxes, like vampire bats, swished and whirred over the camps; opossums and porcupines had to be thrust out of the way. Every piece of firewood hid a horde of ants, and as they crawled frantically away, Bill the cook scooped them back into the fire with a shovel.

Then there was a large insect which came out of decayed wood—blue-black, over an inch long— which was not a biter like the fierce ants, but decidedly more annoying in the vile odor it gave off when discovered. Snakes, too, became more common in the bush. Sterl espied a death adder under his lifted foot and stepped on it before he could jump. After that he and Red did not take off their chaps at the end of the day's trek; and Sterl cut down an extra pair of his for Leslie to wear. The girl's extraordinary delight in them was equaled by the picturesque exaggeration of her charm.

For weeks after Woolcott's death Ormiston had kept mostly to his camp. He had even somewhat neglected Beryl, a circumstance Red had made the most of. Stanley Dann remarked that Ormiston had taken the Woolcott tragedy very grievously. Dann had been gratified by the drover's throwing his cattle in with the main mob. The strained relation was certainly no worse, if it had not grown better. But Sterl was not deceived by Ormiston. Red had abandoned his plan of intimacy with Ormiston's drovers. He bided his time. He still clung to his belief that Beryl Dann would be instrumental in exposing Ormiston in his true colors.

One night, Red returned to camp rather earlier than usual, and his look prepared Sterl for a disclosure.

"Pard, I jest happened to heah somethin'," he whispered, impressively, leaning his falcon-shaped red head to Sterl. "I was after a bucket of water for Beryl, kinda under cover of the bank where the brook was clean. Ormiston with Jack an' Bedford came along above. I heahed low voices, kinda sharp, before they got to me. Then, right above Ormiston spit out: 'No, I told you. Not till we get to the haidwaters of the Diamantina.'"

Sterl echoed his last four words. "Red, what do you figure from that?"

"Wal, it's plain as print so far. Whatever Ormiston has in mind it's to come off thar. I figure that those two *hombres* want to pull off the deal sooner."

"You used to have brains. Cain't you help me figgerin' what the hell?"

"I'll try. Suppose I analyze this. Then you give me your old cowboy American slant."

"Hop to it, pard."

"Ormiston wants to be a partner of Stanley Dann's after the trek. Or to get control of a big mob of cattle, and marry Beryl. He is working his deal so that when he threatens to split out from this drive, Dann will give almost anything to keep him. Ormiston's drovers want a showdown for their labors or a speed-up of the break."

"You ain't calculatin' anythin' atall on our idee thet Woolcott was murdered?"

"That is a stickler, I admit, but I am trying to find a more credible motive for those other Australians."

"Pard, listen to a little plain sense from a Texas *hombre* who's knowed a thousand bad eggs....Ormiston is a drover, mebbe, a cattleman, mebbe. He's after cattle, all he can steal!...It's a cinch he killed Woolcott, or had one of his outfit do it. Woolcott probably bucked. Wanted to go back to Dann. An' he got Woolcott's cattle, didn't he? The gamblin' debt can be discounted. Ormiston is workin' to persuade some of Dann's riders to side with him. I know thet. They jest damn near approached me! Wal, muss thet all up an' figger. Ormiston has control of three thousand haid. He'll get hold of more, by hook or crook. An' he'll split with Dann at the haidwaters of thet river, take Beryl with him by persuasion or force, an' light out for some place he is figgerin' on....Thet, my son, is what Old Dudley Texas says!"

"All same just another bloody rustler!"

"All same jest another bloody cow thief, like hundreds we've knowed an' some we've hanged."

"Stanley Dann will never believe that until too late."

"Reckon not. But we might talk Slyter into findin'

out he was alive.... Queer deal, ain't it?"

"Queer—sure!" returned Sterl.

"Red, we can't let it go on—come to a head."

"We jest can," retorted Red. "For the present."

"Somethin' will happen one of these days, jest like thet crack of Ormiston's I heahed today, an' always there's the chance Beryl will put us wise to Ormiston. I'm layin' low, Sterl. We've been in some tough places. This is shore the toughest. Let's not let it get the best of us."

"Red Krehl, did I have to come way out here to Australia to appreciate you?" demanded Sterl.

"You sense things beyond my powers.... But, old-timer, I swear I'll rise to this thing as you have risen. And I'll take a long hitch in my patience."

*T*HE trek plodded on, day after day. And more and more Sterl felt himself back to the level of the unconscious savage as represented so strikingly in the black man Friday, who had mental processes it was true, but was almost wholly guided by his instincts and his emotions. It was a good thing, he reflected. It made for survival. Thrown against the background of the live and inanimate forces of the earth, man had to go back. He discussed his mood sometimes with his companions of his campfires. Slyter laughed, "We call it 'gone bush.' I would say it denoted weak mentality!" Leslie gave proof to his theory by flashing, "Sterl, you make me think. And I don't *want* to think!" Stanley Dann said, "Undoubtedly a trek like this, would be a throwback for most

white men; unless they found their strength in God."
Well, he himself had a job to do—to deal with Ormiston. When that was finished, he could revert to
the savage!

Stanley Dann eventually arrived at the conclusion that any one of several streams they had crossed
might have been Cooper Creek, famed in the annals
of exploration. But he admitted that he had expected
a goodly stream of running water. Long ago, Sterl
thought, Dann should have been warned by a sun
growing almost imperceptibly hotter that water
would grow scarcer. Still, always in the blue distance,
mountain ranges lent hope. Through this bush, the
endless monotony of which wore so strangely on the
trekkers that desert country would have been welcome, they never made an average of five miles a
day. Dry camps occurred more and more often; two-
day stays at waterholes further added to the delay.

In October the expedition at last worked out of
that "Always-always-all-same-land," as Red Krehl
named it, to the gradual slope of open grass leading
down to what appeared to be a boundless valley to
the west with purple mountains to the north. Water
would come down out of them. A thread of darker
green promised a river or stream. They were three
days in reaching it—none too soon to save the cattle.

The mob got out of hand; its rush dammed the
stream. Many of the cattle drowned; others were
mired in the mud; a few were trampled to death. The
horses fared badly, though not to the point of loss.

"Make camp for days," was Stanley Dann's order,

when mob and *remuda* had been droved out upon the green. The night watch was omitted. Horses and cattle and trekkers rested from nightfall until sunrise.

Day disclosed the loveliest site for a camp, the freest from flies and insects, the richest in color and music of innumerable birds, the liveliest in game that the drovers had experienced. But ill luck still dogged the trek. Next morning, Larry reported that horses were missing from the *remuda*.

"Sterl," said Slyter, "I suppose that you, being a cowboy, can track a horse?"

"Used to be pretty good," said Sterl. He got his rifle, and started.

But he only lost himself in the deep bush, and continued to be lost for three days. Afterward, he looked back on this adventure with mixed feelings of chagrin and of glory in the experience. The chagrin rose from the fact that in an obscure stretch of jungle he mistook the faint tracks of a band of cassowaries for those of King's shod hoofs, nor realized it until he came upon a flock of these great, awkward, ostrichlike birds staring at him with protruding, solemn eyes.

The rest, he remembered afterward only in snatches.

An open space where foliage and a cascade of the stream caught an exquisite, diffused golden light breaking through blue rifts in the green dome overhead. Tiny flying insects, like sparks from a fire, vied with wide-winged butterflies in a fascinated fluttering over a pool that mirrored them, and the great opal-hued branches above, and the network of huge-leafed vines, and the spears of lacy foliage. Flycatchers, birds, too beautiful to be murderers, were feeding upon the darting, winged insects.

A splash in a pool, and a movement of something live, distracted Sterl's attention from the tree tent he was examining. He saw a strange animal slide or crawl out on the bank. It had a squatty body that might have resembled a flat pig, but for the thick fur on its back. It had a long head, which took the shape, when Sterl located the eyes, of an abnormal and monstrous bill of a duck. Sterl stared, disputing his own eyesight. But the thing was an animal and alive. It had front feet with long cruel claws. Its back feet and tail were hidden in the grass. All of a sudden Sterl realized that he was staring at the strangest creature in this strange Australia, perhaps in the world, no less than Leslie's much-vaunted duck-billed platypus.

Morning after a cool, wet night on the ground. Light ahead and open sky prepared Sterl for a change in the topography of the bush. And a low hum of falling water was the voice of a waterfall. Out from under giant trees he stepped to the brink of a precipice and to a blue sun-streaked abyss that brought him to a standstill.

The sun, gloriously red and blazing, appeared again to be in the wrong place! Sterl had to reconcile himself that this burst of morning light came from the east. Yet no matter how badly a man was lost he dared not deny the sunrise. The abyss at his feet had the extraordinary beauty, if not the colossal dimensions, of the Arizona canyons he had known from boyhood. Up from his right sounded a low, thunderous roar. By craning his neck he saw where the stream leaped off, turning from shining green to lacy white. It fell a thousand feet, struck a ledge of broken wall, cascaded over and through huge rocks, to leap from a second precipice, from which purple depths no murmur arose. Walls opposite where Sterl stood, rust-stained and lichened, dropped down precipitously into shadow. On his own side, the sun tipped the ramparts with rose and gold, and blazed the great wall halfway down.

A bird, so beautiful in appearance and astounding in action that it halted him in his tracks. The spot was open to a little sunlight, carpeted with fine brown needles like those from a pine tree. The bird espied Sterl, but that did not change its strange and playful antics. It was bright with many colors, not quite so large as an American robin or meadow-lark. This fairy creature of the bush skipped and hopped around so friskily that Sterl had to look sharp and long to perceive all its lovely hue; but the most pronounced was a golden yellow. There was brown, too, marked with white, and a lovely sheen of greenish-olive, like that on a hummingbird, and the under part appeared to be gray. Its exquisite daintiness and sprightliness gave the bird some elfin quality, some spirit of the lonely bush. It seemed to Sterl that the lovely creature's dancing movements were a sort of playing with leaves and twigs. It saw him, assuredly, out of bright dark eyes, and was not afraid. It might have been the incarnation of joy and life in that bush-land. Then again he remembered Leslie's lecture on Australian wild life. It was the golden bowerbird.

At noon of the third day, Sterl felt his powers waning. He needed a long rest. Gathering a store of wood for several fires, he lay down in an open space near water and almost at once went to sleep.

He was roused by a voice and a hand shaking his shoulder. A black visage, beaded with sweat, bent over him.

"Friday!" cried Sterl, in a husky voice, and he struggled to sit up. "You found—me?"

"Yes, boss. Black fella tinkit boss sit down quick."

"No. Boss fool!"

Friday had his wommera and spears in one hand, a small bag in the other. "Meat," he said, and opened it for Sterl. Inside were thick strips of beef, cooked and salted, some hard damper, and a quantity of dried fruit. When had meat ever tasted so good!

"How far camp, Friday?" Sterl asked, between periods of mastication.

"Close up." And the black made circles with his finger in the mat of brown needles, to indicate how Sterl had traveled round and round.

"Horses close up alonga water," volunteered Friday. "Black fella findum." This was such a relief to Sterl that it assuaged his mortification.

So at ten o'clock that night Sterl limped behind

Friday into sight of a welcome campfire, where Slyter and his wife, Leslie and Red and Larry, kept a vigil that had only to be seen to realize their anxiety. The moment was more poignant than Sterl would have anticipated. Red, the sharp-eared fox, heard them coming, and as he saw them emerge from the gloom he let out his stentorian, *"Whoopee!"* Slyter burst out in agitation that surprised Sterl: "It's Sterl! Bless our black man!" Leslie flew at Sterl, met him before he reached the fire, enveloped him with eager arms, crying out indistinguishable, broken words.

CHAPTER

12

*T*HE late October halt, after Sterl had come safely out of the jungle, seemed more than ordinarily marked by pleasant relations among the trekkers. But there was one exception. Sterl, going to the stream for a bucket of water, encountered Ormiston and Beryl some rods away from the camp. The girl had a hand on Ormiston's shoulder, who stood leaning against the log and facing Sterl. She had not seen the cowboy.

"Hazelton," spoke up Ormiston, "I'd never be afraid of being tracked by you!"

Sterl passed on without a word, though he flashed a searching glance at the drover. He heard Beryl ask: "Ash, whatever made you say that?" If Ormiston replied to that query Sterl did not hear.

Back in camp Sterl related the incident to Red.
The cowboy swore long and loud. "Thet's what's on
the ——'s mind. He's gonna slope sooner or later."

"Righto. But since he's secretive and close-
mouthed, as we know, why did he make that crack?"

"Pard, it was a slip."

"Yeah? There's going to be a reason for us to
track him!"

"Beryl had a hand on Ormiston's shoulder,"
added Sterl, casually.

"Hell, thet ain't nothin'," returned the cowboy,
gloomily.

"No? Well, spring it, pard!" shot back Sterl.

Red appeared bitter and ashamed, but he did
not avoid Sterl's gaze. "I've seen Beryl in his arms—
an' kissin' him back to beat hell."

"Where?"

"By thet big tree where you jest met them. You
see since the Danns throwed together with Ormiston
an' Hathaway in one camp, Beryl an' Ormiston have
been thick as hops. I got sore an' jealous, an' I
sneaked up on them at night. An' I'm gonna keep on
doin' it."

"Red, has Beryl ever kissed you?" asked Sterl,
seriously.

"Want me to kiss an' tell?"

"Nonsense! This is different. Red, has she?"

"Wal, yes, a coupla times," admitted Red. "Not
the devourin' kind she gave Ormiston. All the same
it was enough to make me leave home. Sterl, don't
blame the girl. Hell, you know girls, an' what this wild

livin' does to them. Ormiston is a handsome cuss."

"Yes. But I can't forgive Beryl," returned Sterl, with passion. "Listen, pard, I can pick a quarrel with Ormiston. Any day. It'd be a fight. And he'd be out of the way. Lord knows, that might save the Danns."

"Righto, Sterl," rejoined Red, cool of voice and dark of brow. "But shore as Gawd made little apples, if either of us bored Ormiston it'd queer us with these drovers. Let him hang himself. I'll go on spyin'. If Beryl doesn't give him away, he will himself."

Stanley Dann had decided to break camp at dawn next day and continue the trek; and he called a conference at his campfire. All the invited were present except Larry, Cedric and Henley, the latter one of Ormiston's drovers, who were on guard with the mob. Stanley Dann got up from his table with a paper in his hand, his eagle eyes alight, his goldness, his magnificence and virtility, impressively outstanding.

"Well, here we are, family and partners and drovers," he began, in his rich resounding voice, "at this pleasant camp, and it is an occasion to thank God, to take stock of the present, and renew hope for the future. We are one hundred and fifty-seven days and nearly six hundred miles on our great trek. Barring the tragic loss of our partner, Woolcott, we have been wonderfully blessed and guided by Providence. We have lost only fourteen horses—a remarkable showing—and two hundred head of cattle, including, of course, those we used for beef. Let me say this company upholds the prestige of Australians as meat eaters!"

Dann consulted the paper in his hand, and went on: "We have consumed one fourth of our flour. Too much, but it cannot be put down to extravagance or wastefulness. Tea—an abundance left. Also salt and sugar. One fifth of our stock of dried fruits is gone, and that is our worst showing. There is a ton or more of tinned goods left. In view of our good luck so far, I think it well to have everyone present say how he feels about the trek. Now, Sister Emily, will you be the first to speak out?"

One by one all the women—Miss Dann, a spinster of forty, Mrs. Slyter of the weather-beaten face, Leslie with her wonderful eyes flashing, Beryl whose beauty graced the occasion—expressed their hope for the future, their determination not to turn back. The tall Hathaway had a tribute for their leader. Slyter spoke brief, eloquent words about their progress and the surety of success. Eric Dann said: "It has been far better than I believed possible. I have been wavering on my plan to stick to the old Gulf trek."

Stanley Dann let out a roar of approval and called lustily upon Ormiston.

"Friends, I have not yet recovered from the loss of our partner Woolcott," he said, in a deep voice. "But still I see our marvelous success—so far. I may be hard put to make a decision when we come to the headwaters of the Diamantina. Yet there should be one voice of warning. It is absolutely certain that this incredible good luck will not last."

Red Krehl nudged Sterl as if to confirm the thought that formed in Sterl's mind.

"Hazelton, you, being an American trail driver, long versed in this business of cattle and horses and men against the cruel and rugged ranges, you should have something unforgettable and inspiring to say to us novices at the game."

"I hope I have," rang out Sterl. "Stanley Dann, you are the great leader to make this great trek. On to the Kimberleys! No heat, no drought, no flood, no desert—*no man can stop us!*"

Of all those who had spoken thus far only Sterl appeared to strike fire from their leader. Then he called to Red:

"You—cowboy!"

"Dog-gone-it, boss," drawled Red, "I had a helluva nifty speech, but I've clean forgot it. I've the same hunch as my pard heah. We cain't be licked. The thing's too big. It means too much to Australia. Fork yore hosses, an' ride!"

Four weeks later Sterl and Red discussing the situation as they rode herd, were divided between a suspicion that Ormiston plotted to go on with Eric and Hathaway, if he could engineer the split with Stanley, in order to get possession of all their stock, or cut off from all of his partners and drove on alone to some unknown destination. The former was Red's opinion, the latter Sterl's.

*   *   *

All this time, they had been traversing an increasingly dry country with a blazing brassy sky by day and a pitiless, starlit sky by night. Several series of two- and three-day treks without water marked the approach to the Diamantina River. The cattle did not suffer dangerously from thirst until the last arid spell. Then with two hot dry days and no prospect of relief, the adventurers faced their most serious predicament.

That second night all the drovers rode herd. Sterl had observed the absence of game and bird life, always an indication of the lack of water. Friday encouraged Sterl with a hopeful, "Might be water close up." But close up for the black could have a wide range. A full moon was rising. The cattle were restless, bawling, milling; Sterl approached Red.

"Pard, what do you say to my riding ahead on a scout? If I find anything wet around twenty miles, I'll advise Dann to trek clear through tomorrow and tomorrow night."

"Wal, it's a hell of a good idee," declared the cowboy. "Go ahaid. Thet is, if you reckon you can find yore way back!"

Red had never ceased to plague Sterl about getting lost. "Say, you could joke on your grandmother's grave!" retorted Sterl. "I've a notion to bat you one!"

"I reckon we're workin' out on a plateau," said Red, changing the subject. "Not one stream bed today. Rustle, pard!"

Sterl turned away toward the *remuda* to change horses. He wanted to save King. The horses had been in need of water, but always after dark, when the dew was wet on the grass, they had slaked acute thirst. Sterl transferred saddle and bridle to the big rangy sorrel, an animal he had not yet been able to tire. Then he set out, taking his direction from the Southern Cross.

Heat still radiated from the ground. But the night was pleasant. For two weeks and more the trek had been through open country. The heave of the land suggested a last mighty roll toward the interminable level of the interior. Sterl rode through bleached grass, silver in the moonlight. Stunted gum trees reared spectral heads; there were dark clumps of mulga scrub and bare moon-blanched spaces, across which rabbits scurried. When at length the glimmer of campfires failed to pierce the blackness, Sterl halted his horse for a moment.

Two hours of steady riding brought Sterl to the edge of an escarpment which fortunately presented no steep drop from the level. Declivities always meant difficulties for the trail driver, especially when they were not discovered until too late.

The void beneath him appeared majestic in its immensity. Apparently land and sky never met. Far below, a shining ribbon of a river catching the moonlight, made his heart leap. This could not be sand or a strip of grass or rock. It was water, and surely the long-hoped-for Diamantina River. But how far? In that rarefied atmosphere, under a soaring full moon, it might be a few miles away, and it could be a score.

But surely it was within reach of a twenty-four-hour trek.

At daybreak, the drovers came riding in by threes to get breakfast. Sterl lost no time in telling Slyter the good news. He and Red accompanied him to Dann's camp.

"Boss, I rode ahead last night. Found water," announced Sterl, bluntly.

"You did? Good-o, Hazelton," boomed Stanley Dann.

"It's a big river. Surely the Diamantina. I couldn't . tell how far. Twenty miles, maybe less."

"Twenty miles? Two days' trek!" ejaculated Eric Dann, disheartened. "We'll have a big loss."

Ormiston cursed roundly apparently venting his rage on Sterl, as if he could be blamed for a dire calamity. Sterl did not deign to notice him, and addressed their leader: "We can make it in one trek."

Ormiston headed a furious opposition, in which, however, Stanley Dann did not concur. Sterl endeavored to convince the disgruntled and almost hopeless drovers, silencing all except Ormiston.

"You're a disorganizer," flashed Sterl, steely and cold. "You're *glad* of anything that hinders us! You shut up, or I'll shut you up."

Ormiston took the threat sullenly.

"How should we make this long trek to water?" inquired Stanley Dann.

"Take it slow all day, ease the mob along careful during the hottest hours. Then, after sunset push them. When the dew falls they can travel without breaking down."

"You heard Hazelton," thundered Dann. "His plan is sound. Wagons go ahead and make camp! Trek through to water!"

On Sterl's return to Slyter's camp Red appeared supremely elated. "Pard, did you see Beryl?"

"No. Was she there?"

"Sure she was. All eyes. Jest as if she never seen you before. Sterl, she'd like you if it wasn't for Ormiston. Mebbe she does anyhow. But she's scared of that geezer."

"Red, will that showdown with him ever come?"

"It'll come! Be shore you have eyes in the back of yore haid."

Leslie was at her morning chore of feeding her pets. Jack, the kookaburra, was jealous of new birds and Cocky squalled from the top of the wagon.

Sterl told her of his trip during the night and his report to Dann. "You go with the wagons," he concluded.

"Umpumm. I'm good for twenty-four hours."

"But I'd rather you'd take it easy whenever possible. You go with your Dad!"

"Are *you* my boss, Sterl Hazelton?" she retorted, rebelliously.

"Not yet. But considering the remote possibility of my becoming that—and your cantankerous disposition—don't you think it'd be a good idea to get some practice?"

Her smooth nut-brown face slowly grew suffused

with a coursing red blood, and her wide eyes fell. She was tongue-tied. Her breast was swelling. And she fled, leaving her pets in noisy clamor.

They rode back to Dann. "Boss, something I forgot to tell you," said Sterl. "When you reach the river be sure to drive the cattle to either side of the trek for camp, because this mob are liable to stampede when they smell water."

At sunset that day Sterl sat astride King on the rim of the plateau, not far from where he had seen the valley by moonlight. Close at hand the front of the great mob of cattle, like a dust-clouded flood, was pouring wearily over the brink. As Sterl had hoped and predicted, they had ended the day's trek with something to spare. Down grade, in the night, with the dew falling, the beasts could plod and sway on until the scent of water energized them. And then if they were at all like cattle of the western ranges they might stampede. Sterl had seen ten thousand buffalo pile into a river, to enact a spectacle he had never forgotten. If the mob and *remuda* had belonged solely to him he could not have taken their safety and well-being more to heart.

The cowboys rode together down the slope as red dusk mantled the scene. Then as night fell they drifted apart, yet within calling distance. Friday for once had ridden on a wagon. Larry was ahead, at the left of the mob, and Drake behind Sterl. The moon came up to lighten the shadows.

Down grade, through thick grass, dew laden, the

mob labored and the trekkers followed. By midnight the slope had begun to level out. Kangaroos, wallibies, rabbits, emus were roused from their beds, to scamper away. King jumped out of his tracks more than once at the hiss of a snake. The tedium wore on Sterl. There was nothing to do but sit his saddle. King did not need direction or urge. He had become like a shepherd dog. Often Sterl fell asleep for a few moments. Two nights without rest or sleep reminded him of the Texas cattle trail when the rivers were up.

At daybreak, Sterl huddled in his saddle, half asleep, his eyes closed, his mind almost a blank. A yell from Red, however, the old Comanche war whoop, brought him erect and startled. Red was waving his sombrero and pointing toward the river—nearby, marked by a line of timber.

"Look, pard! Leslie ridin' down on us hell-bent for election! Larry's meetin' her."

CHAPTER 13

*L*ESLIE pulled Lady Jane to a halt beside Sterl. The horse was dripping water in little streams. Leslie was wet to her waist. Her eyes glowed dark with excitement.

"Girl, you didn't swim that river for fun?" demanded Sterl.

"Dad sent—me," panted Leslie.

"We couldn't cross. River too deep—with steep banks. Dad said we'd have a job. Stanley Dann's orders are to hold the mob on this side—to drove them that way—two miles up—where the banks are not so steep."

"Leslie, you should have met us five miles out, at least," rejoined Sterl, seriously. "These cattle are thirsty. They're tired and cross. If they smell water...."

"*When* they smell it," interrupted Red. "Rustle, Sterl. We gotta be quick. Come, Larry. We'll try to turn the leaders upstream."

Urging King into a gallop to the rear, Sterl, with Leslie racing beside him, yelled Dann's orders to the drovers in a warning voice.

Between the larger mob and Ormiston's there were four drovers, two on each side, far up the wide lane. The cattle still plodded along with heads down, as if every step would be their last. Sterl caught their hot odor. He rode over to the partners, with Drake and Leslie at his heels.

"We've orders from Dann. Cattle must be bunched and turned upstream. River deep. High banks. Get your drovers out from between."

Ormiston added a dark frown to his forbidding expression. "We won't have our mob mixing with Dann's."

"You can't help it," declared Sterl, curtly.

"That's what you say, Mr. Cowboy. We will keep them separated."

"Hathaway, you have some sense, if this man hasn't," barked Sterl. "The cattle are parched. When they smell water they can't be held or turned. They'll stampede!"

Roland came galloping up, red-faced, sweating, calling on Ormiston to drove his mob to the east.

"Mind your own business," shouted Ormiston.

"You will like hell!" returned Sterl. "Rollie, ride

through and warn Dann's drovers to rustle out of
there. Back this way!"

Sterl wheeled King and was away like the wind.
Leslie and Drake came along. Halfway round the big-
ger mob, Sterl waved the drovers on that side to ride
up toward the front. They strung out after Drake.
Soon Sterl, accompanied by Leslie, came up with
Larry and Red.

"Stubborn as mules!" shouted Red.

"No wonder. But we've got to push them.

"Ormiston doesn't know cattle. He said he
wouldn't let his mob mix with Dann's."

"This's gonna be about as funny as death for
them drovers between!"

Sterl stood up in his stirrups to gaze across the
mob. "They're riding out. The last two of Ormiston's
men. But that fellow up front . . ."

"We cain't wait, pard," yelled Red, pulling his
gun. "Leslie, keep back a little."

Then Red rode up to the herd, gun high over his
head, to yell and shout. Larry took his cue and followed suit. Cedric and Drake, with the drovers farther
back, let loose with guns and lungs.

The front of the great mob, like the sharp end
of a wedge, roused, lunged, headed away from a direct line toward the river. That relieved Sterl exceedingly. The turn was not enough, but it had
started. Cattle, like sheep, blindly follow the leaders.
The trampling of many hoofs, the knocking of horns,
the increase in hoarse bawling, indicated the start of
the milling that Sterl was so keen to accomplish.

Something like a current ran all the way back to the rear. Then he looked ahead. They had the apex of the mob quartering away from a direct line to the river. But the river took a bend to the eastward, and looked less than two miles away!

Suddenly from the far side of the herd sounded a trampling roar that drowned yells and gunshots. Sterl's piercing yell was a whisper in his ears. He had heard that kind of roar. Icy chills chased up his spine. Ormiston's mob was charging straight ahead to meet the milling front of that vast wedge of cattle!

Then Sterl espied the one drover trapped in the swiftly narrowing space. The man saw his peril, but made the mistake of dashing to the fore, hoping to get out of the closing gap. His calculation, however, did not allow for the curving front of the larger mob, and the speed of the smaller one. He was headed off, hemmed in. A moment later there was a terrific impact—a head-on collision of these two fronts. Sterl saw the white horse and its rider go down in a sea of horns, heads, dust. A rattling crash of Ormiston's mob, colliding with Dann's all down the line, drowned the trample of hoofs. Still, only the head of Dann's mob, and the far edge, appeared to be affected. A smashup like that did not necessarily mean a stampede. Sterl thought derisively of the bullheaded Ormiston. If the mob stampeded, he was the one who would suffer most. His branded cattle would be the first to tumble over the river embankment. It would serve him right, thought Sterl, but what a pity so many cattle must be drowned and trampled!

Then it came to him that Ormiston's mob, to windward, had caught the fatal scent. After three days of heat and dust, without a drink, they smelled the river and were off, hell-bent. Water! If they had the scent in their dry nostrils, Dann's herd would catch it soon.

But despite Sterl's readiness for the inevitable shock, when Dann's mob leaped into swift action and an appalling thunder boomed and the ground shook as if in earthquake, he screamed with all his might and never heard his own voice. Mushrooming yellow clouds of dust rolled back over the mob, moving as one animal, covering them, swallowing them up.

Sterl's quick eyes were the first to see that a spur of the herd had shot out below him, between him and the other riders, and swung wide in a swift, enveloping sweep. Red and Larry had gone on; but Leslie! They were cutting her off. Sterl had to get to her in quick time. With the thought, he had King racing down the line. Lady Jane was fast. Sterl had no fear that she could not outrun the wildest of cattle. But being a mare of great spirit she might act up at the crucial moment.

This was the first time that Sterl had ever extended King. Fleet? He was like the wind. Fortunately Leslie saw him coming, and then saw the spur of cattle. She did not lose her head. Quick as a flash she jerked Lady Jane away from that frightful, oncoming rush of hoofs, heads, horns. Plunging under the surprise and pain of the spurs, Lady Jane leaped like an arrow from a bow.

At this juncture King caught up with her. Sterl pointed to Leslie's stirrups. She was quick to grasp his meaning—to slip her feet almost out, and ride on her toes, so that in case Sterl saw fit he could lift her out of the saddle. Sterl's terror left him. The girl could ride and she could be trusted.

Sterl urged King to the fore again, with the object of turning the leaders of that spur to the right. The black, magnificent in action, drove right to the front. A lean, rangy steer, red-eyed and wild, led that mutiny. Sterl drew and fired. The great steer plunged, to plow the earth. The others overran him, leaped and swerved. Larry and Red came up with flaming guns. The drovers behind were lost in dust. The three turned that spur back and in less than a quarter of a mile the mutineers had joined the main mob. To the left, scarcely farther than that, Sterl saw the timber belt and the shining river. It was wide, and the opposite bank looked steep and high. Farther upstream, it appeared to slope gradually. As the mob was headed quarteringly up the river there was some hope that a major catastrophe had been averted. All that could possibly be done by Sterl and his comrades and the drovers sweeping from behind, had been accomplished—and it was a good job that saved thousands of cattle.

Sterl, never forgetting Leslie, gazed back to espy her trotting Lady Jane at a goodly distance behind. Red was riding ahead toward a ridge under which the stampede was rolling. Sterl, and all the others, joined him on this vantage point.

Just under the watchers swept a mighty torrent of beef, indistinct through the streaming dust. Following that flood forward, Sterl's sight came to the front of the mob. It swept on, swallowing up the green, headed for the bend of the river!

The vanguard rolled out of sight, to reappear in splitting around trees, to plunge over the bank in one long cascade that hit the water with a tremendous splash. The bank had a drop of twenty feet. There ensued a threshing melee. The foremost had no chance to rise under the shock of following lines. But presently out of the spouting, muddy splashes heads of swimming cattle appeared. They milled around in bewilderment while the ghastly downpour of heavy bodies continued. Some struck out for the opposite shore. The roar lessened in volume, changed into another sound—the long-drawn bawl of frenzied cattle.

The imperturbable Red was the first to recover. He lighted a cigarette.

"Not too bad! Gawd A'mighty shore is on Stanley Dann's side! I wouldn't have given a handful of Mexican pesos for thet herd. An' lo an' behold heah they air, most of them, swimmin' acrost, wadin' out."

"Men," ejaculated Drake, "a bridge of cattle saved our mob!"

"Yes! And that bridge was Ormiston's! He wasn't going to let his mob mix with Dann's!"

"Haw! Haw!" rolled out Red in caustic mirth, "Wal, fellers, Ormiston's cattle got the start! An' am I tickled!"

Again Sterl surveyed the river. "Let me have Larry, Red and Cedric. There's a good many crazy cattle swimming downstream. And in the middle there's an unholy mess milling around. We'll turn them upstream. Some of them are going to drown, Drake. You see that. Take the rest of the men and rustle up to where the cattle can wade out."

"Fellers, I see Ormiston's outfit up there," interposed Red, pointing his cigarette. "Trailin' up his mob! I'd like to heah him when he sees thet animal bridge of cattle wearin' his brand."

Presently Sterl found a ravine that opened at the edge of the water. "Leslie, this will be work. Won't you go back to camp?"

"Of course, if you say so. But mayn't I help? Sterl, you are always trying to save me from—from everything. I want to 'take my medicine,' as Red calls it."

"Righto," declared Sterl, heartily. "You've got more sense than I have. And I've more sentiment than you."

"So you say, cowboy."

They reached the river where the ravine ended level with the water. "Load your guns, boys," advised Sterl, suiting action to words. "Shooting in front of a steer or cow will save swimming your horses."

King did not need to be urged into the river, as did the other horses. Red called the black a duck. Sterl surveyed the wide channel where just above them thousands of cattle were swimming.

"Red, I don't like this," he called. "It's a long swim. If a horse gave out it'd be good night for the horse. Leslie, stick close to me."

They headed up the river, in the face of as remarkable a conglomeration of animals as Sterl had ever seen. Yells and shots of their riders, soon had all the stragglers headed in the right direction. Sterl made a hasty judgment that there were five thousand cattle in the river. A long string were wading out above. The danger point appeared to be less than a quarter of a mile beyond—a mass of cattle twisting, plunging, in an intricate tangle.

"Sterl, look on the bank," shrieked Leslie.

Then Sterl espied Ormiston, with Hathaway and his drovers on the shore above the yellow, trampled slope which the cattle had cut through the bank. Below them stretched a long line of dead and dying cattle—the bridge of death. Ormiston, on foot, raged to and fro, flinging his arms, stamping. Sterl cupped his hands around his mouth and yelled in stentorian voice: "HEY, YOU DUMBHEAD! KILL THE DYING CATTLE!" Ormiston heard, for he roared curses back. Some of the drovers with Ormiston heeded Sterl's humane suggestion, and began to shoot. Sterl made for a strip of sandy bank, beyond the bend and on the far side. King gave a huge heave, and then appeared to breathe normally again. Sterl rode to a point even with the upper edge of the mob, and surveyed the scene. The river was full of cattle so closely packed that steers and cows would lunge up on others, and sink them. Across, nearer the other side, Red and his two comrades had their contingent of stragglers headed out. On second glance Sterl saw that the dozen or more drovers strung out behind the great mob, shooting, yelling, making splashes, had turned the tide in that quarter. The rear and center areas of cattle were headed across, but could not make much headway owing to the eddying mass of animals in midstream.

Sterl clucked to King, and soon he was swimming gallantly to join the other horses. Red, mounted on Jester, had untied his lasso. Cedric and Larry, who followed him closely, had exchanged their guns for ropes. When he reached the center of the milling mob, Red whirled the loop around his head, with the old, trenchant cry: "*Ki-yi! Yippi-yip!*" and let it fly to rope a big steer around the horns. Turning Jester toward the bank, Red literally dragged that steer out of the wheeling circle. It made a break. And a break like that was a crucial thing for a herd of stampeded cattle. Larry and Cedric followed suit. Then one steer and cow and another and another got into those openings, until the wheel of twisting horns and snouts broke and a stream of cattle, like oil, flowed away from the mob. In less time than it had taken for Red and his followers to break the milling mass, the whole mob was on the move across the river.

Sterl experienced a vast relief when he, the last of the drovers to mount the far bank of the Diamantina and go through the trampled muddy belt of brush and timber, saw the great mob quietly grazing as if no untoward event had come to pass.

"This cain't be the place to ford the wagons," observed Red when Sterl caught up.

"Farther up," returned Sterl. "I see low banks and bars. It'll take time, but be easy. It's afternoon already and Dann will hardly order us to cross to-day."

They recrossed the river without incident, to be met by Leslie. Stanley Dann called them over to where the leaders stood grouped. Ormiston, despite his tan, showed an unusual pallor. Sterl felt that this queer composite of fool and villain would have blamed the stampede upon his partners and their drovers, if there had been any possible excuse.

"Men, it is our first major disaster," boomed Stanley Dann. "That stampede could not have been avoided. I commend you all for heroic work——Hazelton particularly, with Krehl, and Larry and Cedric. You saved the main mob twice, first when you turned the head up this way, and secondly when you got them out of that animated whirlpool. I never saw the like."

"Thanks, boss. Thet last was jest a little mill. All in the day's ride," said Red.

"Dann, we lost one man," added Sterl.

"Yes. Ormiston's drover, Henry Ward. He was warned. But he was overbold or befuddled. Poor fellow!"

"Who warned him?" queried Sterl, bluntly.

"Why, Ormiston sent a drover, he said," returned the leader.

"Ormiston did nothing of the kind," denied Sterl. "When we rode around to the rear of the herd, to give your orders, Ormiston grew furious. He said he wouldn't let his mob mix with yours. I told him he couldn't help it. He told me to mind my own business. It was Drake who sent Roland Jones to ride between your mob and Ormiston's to warn the drovers to come out. Roland, back me up here."

"Yes, sir. Hazelton is right," replied Jones, frankly.

"Ormiston, this report hardly agrees with what you said," declared Dann. "If it is true, you are responsible for Ward's death."

"What do I care for these lie-mongers?" stormed Ormiston, his bold eyes popping. "I gave you my version. Believe it or not!"

Roland Jones thrust forward a reddening visage. "See here, Mr. Ormiston, don't you call me a liar."

"Bah, you big lout! What are you going to do about it?"

"Men, the situation is bad enough already," said Stanley Dann, calmly. "I'll not permit fighting. We've had a trying day, and we're upset."

They all heeded the patient leader's wisdom, except Ormiston. Not improbably he saw opportunity to flay without risk to himself, or else at times his temper was ungovernable.

"Dann, these riffraff drovers of yours haven't a pound to their names. They can't pay for the loss of my cattle. I demand that of you!"

"Very well. I'll be glad to make up for your loss. It was my gain. Your cattle saved mine," boomed the leader.

Red Krehl let out a sibilant hiss. Ormiston's rolling eyes lighted avariciously. Sterl interrupted his reply to Dann. He spurred King into a jump to confront the drover.

"Ormiston, you go to hell!" said Sterl, with a stinging cold contempt that a whole volley of epithets could never have equaled. For once Ormiston's ready retort failed. With a gesture to his lieutenants, Bedford and Jack, he wheeled his horse and rode toward camp.

"Pard, Dann's gonna ask you to make a count of the daid cattle," whispered Red. "An' you lie like a trooper."

Sterl made no reply, though he received that suggestion most sympathetically. He turned to Leslie.

"Les, it'll be a dirty bloody mess. Don't go."

"Why not, Sterl?"

"*Why?* Heavens, you're a girl! Not a hard, callous, blood-spilling man, used to death!"

"Yeah?" she said, flippant on cracking ice and airing her cowboy vocabulary, "Well, I've a hunch there'll be another bloody death around here pronto—and I'll be tickled pink."

Stanley Dann rode along the hoof-torn slant of recently plowed earth, gazing down at the mashed bloody bodies of cattle, at the grotesque horned heads pointing to the sky, mouths open, tongues sticking out, staring dead eyes.

"Sterl, what is your count?" he asked, tersely.

"Boss, I'd rather not say," replied Sterl, with a deprecatory spread of his hands. "I'm only fair on the count. Red has always been the most accurate and reliable counter of stock we ever had on our ranges."

"Very well, Red. I'm sure you could have no higher recommendation. I'll rely upon you. How many?"

"Wal, boss, I'm shore surprised," returned Red, with an air of perfect sincerity, "I was afeared we'd lost a damn sight more'n we really have. Thet water was shallow all along heah. I seen the cattle pitchin' up the mud. But they're layin' only about three deep heah. Yes sir! We're darned lucky. I been countin' all along, an' my tally is just three hundred an' thirteen. Preecislee. An' I'll gamble on thet."

"Is it possible?" boomed the drover, elated. "I am poor in calculation. I thought we had lost a thousand head."

"No indeedee, boss," returned Red, emphatically. "You take my tally. I'm kinda proud of my gift."

"Righto. It's settled. How fortunate we are, after all! I have been blessed with my faith in divine guidance!"

GUARD duty was split that night, half the drovers riding herd from dark till midnight, and the other half from then till sunrise. It was a needless precaution, for, as Sterl told Slyter, the cattle were almost too tired to graze.

Next morning Friday greeted Sterl with an enigmatic: "Black fella close up."

"Bad black fella, Friday?"

"Might be some. Plenty black fella."

"How do you know?" queried Sterl, curiously.

"Lubra tellum."

Sterl told Slyter, who burst out that it was about time. "Except once," he went on, "we've had no trouble with abos. And we expected that to be the worst of our troubles."

"All same splenty bimeby," put in Friday with his air of mystery.

"What're the orders, Slyter?" asked Sterl.

"Transport wagons over the river."

"Wal, it'll be one sweet job. Whereabouts?" asked Red.

"Somewhat above where we droved the mob yesterday."

"Look aheah, boss. Thet's an orful place. No ford atall. We oughta go up the river a ways. This is just a big pond. It's towards the end of the dry season, and shore as shootin' this river ain't runnin'. I'll bet we could find shallow fords."

"Dann's orders, Red. And he's mad this morning."

"Mad? Good heavens! Fust time or I'll eat my sombrero. Gosh, I'm glad he's human, ain't you, Sterl? What about?"

"I'm not certain, but I think it's Ormiston."

"Slyter, does Dann really expect to get across today with this outfit?" asked Sterl, skeptically.

"By noon, he says!"

By a half hour after sunrise Dann had all the wagons packed. They started, with Slyter's *remuda* following in charge of Larry and the cowboys. Dann, who drove the leading wagon, halted on the bank of the river some distance above where the stampede had crossed the day before. He sent for Sterl, who found him arguing with Eric. Ormiston stood by, taciturn and brooding.

"Hazelton," boomed the leader. "This is the

place where we're going to cross. Eric is against my judgment. Ormiston swears he'll drove his mob back to this side. Will you take charge?"

"Yes, sir. It can't all be done today," answered Sterl, earnestly. "But all goods must be crossed before dark because the abos will be here by night. It's a pack job. Give me twenty riders. Five changes of horses. We'll empty the wagons and drays. Each rider will carry over what he can carry safely and keep dry. Provisions to go first."

"Men," boomed the leader, "you all heard Hazelton. Take orders from him. Let's unhitch and get at it!"

"Dann, I want a word in edgewise," demanded Ormiston.

"Ashley, I heard you. No more! I forgot to tell you that I ordered your brand burned on three hundred odd of my cattle, as soon as we cross."

Red had already made for Roland's wagon, and dismounted there to begin unloading. Sterl joined him. Leslie was putting her pets into cages, much to their vociferous disgust.

"Sterl, I've a hunch Stanley Dann will ride roughshod over our friend Ormiston one of these days," said the cowboy.

"You haven't a corner on all the hunches," retorted Sterl. "I had that figured long ago. Beryl now is the last connecting link."

"Bet yore life, pard. An' I'll bust thet!"

"All right. Go over to Beryl and tell her I sent

you to pack her and her treasures across the river. Savvy?"

"Dog-gone yore pictoors!" ejaculated Red, rapturously. "I never thought of thet. Watch me!" And he strode away.

When again Sterl encountered Red, never had he seen that cowboy in such a transport.

"Pard, bless yore heart, Beryl's jest about eatin' out of my hand," whispered Red, huskily. "She'd been cryin'. I reckon her Dad must have hopped her. What do you think she said—'Sterl is a big help to Dad. He'd be a good sort if he wasn't hipped over thet chestnut-haired kid!' Beryl wanted to know how I'd get her across, an' I said I'd pack her in my arms if she was afraid to ride. She said thet would make her look a little coward, which she swore she was. An' she said she'd ride if I came along close to her. I reckon I'll take her and Miss Dann together."

"Righto. I'll send Friday across to watch the stuff."

In short order Sterl had twenty riders, not including Leslie and himself, swimming their horses across the river with packs in front and on their shoulders. Friday grasped King's long tail and held on, to be dragged over. On the return, Sterl met Ormiston and Hathaway in midstream, and farther on, the Danns.

It required twenty trips for each rider to unload Slyter's wagon to the extent where it would be safe to ferry it across. Then ten men lifted the half-loaded wagon-bed off the wheels, carried it down to the river and set it in the water. It floated. It was a boat. It did not leak. With the use of long ropes and a team of horses on the far bank the start was made. There was no mishap. The heavy wheels, dragged along by ropes, gave a good deal more trouble. But they were soon across and up the bank. In a few more minutes the wagon was set up and reloaded. Leslie was as happy as her birds, and they squawked their glee.

"You were fine, kid," complimented Sterl. "That'll do for you. This hot sun will dry you pronto."

"Plenty smokes, boss," said Friday, who sat in the shade whittling on a new boomerang. Sterl saw them far off on the horizon.

"Watchum close, Friday."

This fording supplies and belongings across the Diamantina began as a colorful, noisy, mirthful, splashing procession. But by noontide the labor ceased to be fun. By midafternoon the riders were sagging in their saddles, soaked with sweat and water, dirty, unkempt. The other drays and wagons were not calked; they had to be fully unloaded. That was a harder job. Sunset found the drovers with most of their outfit on the right bank of the river, but half a dozen wagons, with harness and tools, were still left behind.

As the cowboys rode herd that night, big fires burned on the other shore, and hordes of blacks murdered silence with their corroboree over the dead cattle.

"Gosh, what a fiesta, pard," said Red. "If them cannibals don't eat themselves to death they'll foller us till hell freezes over, an' thet ain't gonna be soon in this heah hot country."

With all hands, and the partners doing their share, the toilsome job of crossing was completed by midafternoon. Ormiston, reversing himself, chose to stay on Dann's side of the river. The leader ordered one day's halt in the new camp, to rest and dry things out. He said to Sterl, "Hazelton, I know more about cattle rushes and crossing rivers, thanks to you."

Sterl wondered why Eric Dann did not remember this river, though on his former trek he had undoubtedly crossed it—surely farther up. He strolled out in the open late that day, to take a "look-see," as the Indians used to call it, and stretch his cramped and bruised legs. Across the river he saw hundreds of blacks, like a swarm of ants, noisy and wild.

Sterl was impressed by the river-bottom valley. Despite the heat and the dry season, grass was abundant and luxuriant. Waterfowl swept by in flocks, and the sandbars were dotted with white and blue herons. When he went to bed, which was early after dark, he heard them flying overhead, uttering dismal croaks.

Next day the sky was black with buzzards, flocks of which spiraled down to share the feast with the aborigines. Kangaroos, wallabies, emus, rabbits were more abundant than at any other camp for weeks. They were tame and approached to within a few rods of the wagons. Parrots and cockatoos colored the gum trees along the riverbanks.

At this Diamantina camp Leslie noted in her journal, "Flies something terrible!" And so they were.

Used as Sterl had gotten to the invisible little demons and the whirling dervishes, here they drove him crazy if he did not cover his face. In the heat, that was vastly uncomfortable. But it was the trekkers' misfortune to fall afoul of a bigger and meaner fly—a bold black green-winged fellow that could bite through shirts. Red had been the first to discover this species, to which Slyter could not give a name. Friday said: "Bite like hellum."

Off again, roughly following the old trail of some former trek up the Diamantina. Travel was slow, but easy. Red had been right in his opinion that the river had gone dry. Two miles above the first camp the trekkers could have crossed without wetting their feet.

Ten days along this river bed of waterholes and dry stretches tallied about a hundred miles, not good going to the cowboys, but satisfactory to their serene leader. The grass did not fail. In some deep cuts verdure of tropical luxuriance marked further advance toward eternal summer. But when the sun grew hot and the myriads of flies appeared, the trek became a matter of grim endurance. Sterl covered his face with his scarf and let King or Sorrel or Duke or Baldy graze along behind the *remuda* at will. Hours on end without one word spoken! Friday stalking along carrying his weapons, tireless on bare feet, ever watching the telltale smoke signals on the horizon! Red, slumped in his saddle or riding sidewise, smoking innumerable cigarettes, lost in his unthinking enchantment! The wagons rolling along, creeping like white-spotted snakes, far to the fore! The mob of cattle grazing on contentedly! The drovers, lost in habit now, nailed to their saddles, indifferent to leagues and distances!

Sterl marveled at Leslie Slyter. She rode with the drovers all the way. So sun-browned now that the contrast made her hair golden. She was the most wide-awake, though she sometimes took catnaps as they trekked on. How many many times Sterl saw her face flash in his direction! Ever she turned to him, to see if he was there, absorbed in her dream.

The long, hot days wore on to the solemn starry nights, packed with dread of the unknown and the possible, separated from unreality and dream by the howls of wild dogs and the strange wailing chant of the aborigines. The waterholes in the Diamantina failed gradually. But the myriads of birds and hordes of beasts multiplied because there were fewer watering places for them. One night, at a camp Leslie had named "Oleander," Sterl strolled with her to the bank of the river, where it was narrow and the bed full of water. When dusk fell and the endless string of kangaroos silhouetted black against the gold of the horizon had passed by, there began a corroboree of the aborigines on the opposite bank. It was the closest these natives had been to a camp. By the light of their bonfires Sterl and Leslie could see the wild ceremony.

The cat-eyed Red came along the bank, walking as easily as if it had been day. He dropped down on

a log beside them, indulged in a little cowboy per-
siflage, before he came to the point, "I been spyin'
as usual. Hasn't been much good lately, till tonight.
But I always keep sayin' it'll come some day. An' we
got nothin' but time on our hands. Gosh, Leslie, *what*
date is it, anyhow?"

"My journal says December fourth."

"Jumpin' Jehoshaphat!" ejaculated Red. "Near
Christmas!"

"Maybe it'll please you to know that this Christmas I can remember *last* Christmas—and be far happier," said Sterl.

"Please me? Wal! All I can think of now is Gawd
bless Leslie!"

"Me! Why should God bless me?" inquired Leslie. Intuitively she divined that she had taken the
place of another woman.

Red gave her no satisfaction. Then seriously:
"Sterl, I was snoopin' about early after supper, an' I
heahed Ormiston talkin' low to Bedford. Near as I
can remember heah's their talk word for word. Ormiston first: "Tom, I tell you I won't go any farther
with Dann than the forks of this river.' An' Bedford
asked, 'Why not?' An' Ormiston said: 'Because I don't
know the country across toward the Warburton
River. It's two hundred odd miles from the head of
the Diamantina through the mountains to my station.
If the rains don't come we'll lose all my cattle.' An'
Bedford said: 'Why not go on with Dann till we make
sure of Hathaway's mob? An' also till the rains do
come?

"'I'll have his mob an' some of Dann's—you can lay to thet,' says Ormiston.

"'In thet case it's all right. Jack an' Morse have been kickin'. They want to make sure of more cattle. They came in on this because of a stake worth while—somethin' thet they could end this bush-rangin' on.' Then Ormiston stopped him for fear somebody was listenin'. He left, an' I seen him later with Beryl. How do you figger it?"

Sterl's speech flowed like running water. "Ormiston and his drovers have been rustling, in a two-bit way, until this Dann trek. Now they're playing for big stakes. Ormiston is the boss. He fooled the Danns. His drovers are all in it, aiming to lead some of Dann's men to their side. Old Stuff. You remember how cheap, easygoing cowboys used to fall. How many have we seen hanged? They murdered Woolcott, got his mob. They have Hathaway's, and will do for him, sure as I know rustlers. Ormiston has a range somewhere over the mountains east of the head of the Diamantina. The pot will boil over up at the forks of this river. Ormiston means to get more cattle by hook or crook and then shake us. Damn it, the thing looms bad!"

"Pard, I should snicker to snort. We've never met its equal, let alone its beat. Bet you haven't figgered Beryl. Where's she comin' in?"

"Thunder and blazes! I forgot Beryl."

"Yeah. But I haven't. An' I say she's the pivot on which this deal turns. Ormiston's outfit haven't that hunch yet, I reckon. But *we* have."

"You bet. Red, that *hombre* will persuade Beryl to go with him—or he'll take her anyway."

"Do you reckon he can persuade her?"

"I hate to think so—but I do."

Red's voice sank to a whisper. "Hey—I see someone comin'!" He peered like a nighthawk into the gloom up the riverbank. "Holy mackeli, Talk about the devil! It's Beryl an' Ormiston. Let's hide. Heah, this way!"

In another moment Red had himself and comrades under the bank, where a ledge ran out a few feet, and some long plumed grasses obscured it from sight above.

A rustle of weeds above, a footfall, and then Beryl's rich voice: "Here, Ash, this is far enough. I'd like to hear the corroboree."

"Yes, you like those damned niggers. I smell cigarette smoke! Somebody has been here," came in Ormiston's voice, guarded and low.

"Well, they're gone. And all I smell is cooking meat."

"Hazelton has been here with that damned little baggage," growled Ormiston.

"Hazelton is no good. Like as not he's one of those American gunmen. A killer! Jack saw six notches cut on his revolver. That means the blighter has killed six men, at least. I'd be a fool to provoke him further."

"Indeed you—would be, Ash," she said. "He has made himself valuable. Dad has come to rely upon him."

"The Yankee is a help, I'm bound to admit that. But, Beryl, I can't stand your praising him. I see him watching you. He is as fascinated by your beauty as that redheaded chum of his. Their eyes just gloat over you. Beryl, you are so lovely! I'm mad over you. I love you beyond reason!"

"Oh, Ash!—do you, darling?" she murmured. "Ash!—you—must not . . ." she remonstrated, but it was the remonstrance of love, that invites rather than repels. That next tense moment, with its murmurings, must have been a dreadful ordeal for Red Krehl. Sterl's heart was heavy for his comrade.

"Ash, darling, we came away to talk seriously," said Beryl, evidently regaining composure. "I must not stay much longer. Tell me."

"Yes, we must settle it," he rejoined, in a deep low voice, without a trace of hesitation. "Beryl, I'm leaving this trek at the forks of this river, not many days from here."

"Ashley! Not going?—Oh!"

"No. We can't get along. Your father will never cross the Never-never! He will be lost."

"We dared that risk," replied the girl. "Somehow father has imbued me with his wonderful faith. We'll win through."

"I doubt it. I almost know it. This interior out-back grows impossible west of the Warburton. I'm no pioneer—no empire builder."

"Ash, I promised to marry you. I will. But come with us to the Kimberleys. Make a home there."

"No. You come with me. Stanley Dann will go on that interior trek without his brother and Hathaway and me. Beryl, come!"

"Oh-h Ash! How I would love to! But I will not betray my father. I will go on, even if they *all* desert him."

"They all will, sooner or later."

"Never! Not Hazelton! Not that droll Red Krehl! Not Leslie, or her family. They will go. And *I* will go, Ash!"

Her voice had begun low and rich with emotion, then gathering power and passion, ended with the ring of a bell.

"But Beryl—you love me!" he cried, huskily.

"Yes, I do. I do! But Ash, I beseech you—give up this selfish blind purpose of yours. For my sake, Ash, reconsider!"

"Darling, I will, despite my better judgment," Ormiston made haste to reply. Presently she was whispering brokenly, won over anew, if not to complaisance then surely to belief. They moved away from the log.

Red sat with drooping head. He heaved a long sigh.

"Pard, in the pinch heah she saved me my belief in her honor," he said, his voice trembling.

"She did, Red, she did, and I feel like a coyote— like a low-down greaser, spying on her.

"Me, too. But my hunch was true. Sterl, Leslie,

if it wasn't for you both, an' a hell-bent somethin', I'd walk right in this heah river!"

But Leslie was in no condition to answer. She clung to Sterl, weeping convulsively.

ON THE morning of December twenty-fourth, the day before Christmas, Stanley Dann's trek toiled and limped into camp at the forks of the Diamantina, there to be stranded until after the rainy season.

Owing to waterholes lying in deep cuts almost inaccessible to the cattle, dragging sand and terrific heat, the last fifty miles of that trek turned out to be all but insurmountable. Smoke signals still preceded the drovers and aborigines still followed them.

Dan selected his permanent camp site on the west side of the main river, above the junction of the several branches, which were steep-banked, deep, dry beds of rock and sand, with waterholes dispersed at widely separated points. The heat was fast absorbing the water. Animals and birds ringed the pools in incredible numbers. They would be dry in a few weeks. But below this junction the main waterhole was a mile-long, narrow, partly shaded pool that would last until the next rainy season. Except in sandy patches, grass grew abundantly. Dann was assured of the cardinal necessities for man and beast for as long a spell as they were compelled to wait there.

Dann picked a camp site on the left bank in a eucalyptus grove, standing far apart in stately aloofness. The pitching of this camp registered for the trekkers an immense relief and joy. Ormiston, however, refused to camp on that side of the river. He drove his cattle and Hathaway's, which together constituted a mob of about three thousand head, across the dry stream beds. As a bird flew, the distance between the two camps was scarcely a quarter of a mile.

Sterl and Red pitched their tent in a circle of pandanus trees whose tops commingled, forming a dense canopy. The great seeds, somewhat resembling small pineapples, clustered aloft amid the foliage. Leaves covered with a ground canvas, furnished a thick and soft carpet for the tent. Their nets promised protection from mosquitoes and flies. But nothing could save them from the heat. They worked naked to the waist. Friday built himself a bark shack back of the tent, Slyter's wagon, some fifty rods or more distant, was sheltered by the largest gum. Near at hand Bill established a comfortable cooking unit. The camps of the Danns were lower down, nearer the riverbank, and most picturesquely located among the gums.

Not until late in the afternoon did Sterl feel free to wash up and change his wet and dirty garments. Then he turned to the never failing black, who was always there when wanted. "Come, Friday. Let's go look-see."

Théy crossed the grassy flat back of camp, and climbed a low ridge. From this point Sterl expected to get in his mind's eye the lay of this upper Diamantina land. But the blazing sunset and the appalling grandeur of that country drove from his mind at first any thought of topography.

"Good camp place, Friday?" he asked.

"Plenty wood, plenty water, plenty meat. All same bad," replied the black.

"Why all same bad?"

"Plenty black fella, plenty lubra, plenty fly. Eatum up alive. No rain long time. Big water bimeby."

"One thing at a time, Friday. Why plenty black fella bad?"

"Some black fella good. No good alonga here. Eat—steal. More come all time. Eat—steal. White fella like lubra. That bad."

"What black fella do about lubra?"

"Mebbe stickum white fella spear."

"Not so good. But I hope our friend Ormiston runs true to type, and gets speared," muttered Sterl, half to himself.

"Friday spearum imm bimeby."

The black had said that once before, months back. Gazing up at him, Sterl thought his native ally was not one to forget.

"Friday, what you mean, no rain long time?"

"Black fella tell all about," replied Friday, making one of his eloquent gestures. It seemed to include the sun, the land, the growths, the living things within its compass. "Why bad when rain comes bimeby?"

"Big water. All alonga. Cattle stuck."

Sterl shaded his eyes and feasted them. A sheen of gold illumined the sky and enveloped the land. The three forks of the Diamantina, dry watercourses, white and glaring by day, now wound away like rivers of golden fire. That afterglow of sunset left the league-wide areas of green grass faintly suffused with its hue, but the river beds of rock and sand took on a phenomenal and supernatural intensity of color. There was a deeper tinge of gold on the canvas wagon tops, the tents; and a flock of white cockatoos, covering the branches of a dead gum tree, appeared transformed birds of paradise. Below camp to the right, where the water of the river gleamed through the trees, there was a flickering, twinkling myriad of golden facets.

"Never-never Land!" said Friday.

Red sat with his back against a tree, his hands spread listlessly. The cowboy was too tired to care about anything.

"Pard, I seen you up there, like an Apache scout. Pretty nifty, huh?" he drawled, lazily.

"Red, I've no regrets, any more."

"Wal! Not atall?"

"Not atall, old friend."

"Thet's dog-gone good! Neither have I, Sterl. Couldn't we jest be happy but for thet bastard?"

Leslie approached, for once not running nor even showing any of her usual energy. She had changed her rider's ragged garb for a light cotton dress. "Do you boys know what day tomorrow is?" she asked wistfully.

Sterl knew, but he remained thoughtfully silent.

"It's Christmas. I'm going over to see the Danns. Mum is there. Won't you come?"

"Les, I'm too dog-gone daid tired even to see Beryl, or to care whether it's Christmas or the Fourth, days thet used to be red letters in my life."

"Me, too, Leslie. You see, we've let down. I did have the strength to climb the hill back here. And that was all!"

When Leslie left, Sterl sat down heavily beside his comrade.

"Red, you remember that day in Brisbane when we spent so much money?"

"Hell, yes. But it seems years ago."

"Well, I flatter myself I'm a pretty wise *hombre*, if I do say it myself. I bought Christmas presents for you and myself. And as we heard there were to be ladies with us, I took a chance and bought some for them."

"Aw, pard!" wailed Red. "I never thought of thet. What a pore muddlehaided cowboy I am!"

"Umpumm, Red, you haven't missed it. I bought

enough for you to give too."

"What kind of presents?" ejaculated Red, elated.

"Candy, for one thing."

"Naw, not candy! Why, pard, you're loco. Heah we been trekkin' a thousand miles under this hot sun! Candy would melt."

"No, it's hard candy packed in tin boxes. Then I bought some pretty handkerchiefs and sewing kits. Lastly, two leather cases full of toilet articles—you know the kind of things girls like. Imported from England, mind you! Tomorrow morning we'll unpack the stuff and plan our surprise."

Breakfast was called at sunrise. "Dann wants us all present after breakfast," announced Slyter. Sterl and Red went to their tent and reappeared, mysteriously, each carrying a canvas knapsack on his shoulder. They were the last to arrive at the Dann encampment. All of the trekking party were present except Ormiston's drovers and several of Dann's. Stanley Dann stood up, bareheaded to read a passage from the Bible. After that he offered up a general prayer, commemorating the meaning of Christmas, of peace on earth and good will to man, and ended with a specific thanksgiving to God for their good fortune.

Beryl, looking lovely in a blue gown that had evidently been donned for this occasion was holding a little court all her own in the shade of a tree near her wagon.

"Tip off your mother an' Dad to rustle over heah pronto," whispered Red to Leslie.

They approached Beryl. Cedric, Larry and the younger drovers were offering felicitations of the day. Ormiston, shaven and in clean garb, occupied what looked like a privileged place close to Beryl.

Suddenly Beryl espied Sterl and Red. Her eyes sparkled with delight and anticipation when the cowboys unlimbered their knapsacks, to set them down dwith a flourish.

"Folks, me an' Sterl heah air playin' Santa Claus," drawled Red, with the smile that made him boyishly good to look at. "But he is a modest gazabo, so I have to do the honors."

Beryl let out a shriek of delight. Leslie, blind to the issue until that moment, flushed with amaze and rapture. The Danns and their company looked on, smiling.

Then Red and Sterl reached into the knapsack with the air of magicians, to fish out a small box of • cigars for Dann and his partners, some brightly wrapped gifts for Miss Dann and Mrs. Slyter.

"My word!" boomed Stanley Dann, "I haven't had a good smoke for months. Well, well, to think these Yankees could outdo English people in memory of Christmas!"

The donors gave Beryl and Leslie handy little sewing kits which were received with deep appreciation. Then came the two handsome leather cases which evoked cries of delight.

"Out here in the Never-never!" exclaimed Beryl, incredulously.

"Sterl Hazelton," cried Leslie, with glad eyes

upon him, "when all my things are gone or worn out—Aladdin!"

"Girls, thet ain't nothin' atall," beamed Red. "Come on, pard, all together."

Then in slow deliberation, purposely tantalizing to the quivering girls, each cowboy produced two boxes, one of goodly size, the other small, both wrapped in shiny paper and tied with colored ribbons.

"What in the world?" cried Beryl, her eyes shining in purple eagerness.

"Oh! Oh! Oh!" burst out Leslie, reaching brown hands for her boxes. "What? Oh, what?"

"Candy!" shouted Sterl, triumphantly.

"Red Krehl! You mean *sweets*? Not ever!" whispered Beryl. "You could not guess how I've missed that. But—but lollies would be too much!"

Evidently Leslie had been rendered mute, but she bestowed upon Sterl's cheek a kiss that left no doubt of her unspoken delight.

Beryl scrambled up, holding all her presents in her arms.

"Leslie, you shall not outdo me in thanks," she cried, with spirit. "Red Krehl, come here! I would knight you if I were a queen. I am glad *somebody* remembered me on Christmas Day!" And as the awkward cowboy, impelled beyond his will, stumbled to his knees before the girl, she lifted a lovely rosy face and kissed him.

Sterl, glancing at Ormiston, saw his face grow ashy and a glare of jealous hate light his prominent eyes. Then Ormiston turned on his heel and strode away, an erect, violent, forbidding figure.

He did not return the next day or the next. Beryl palpably chafed and worried at this evidence of his resentment, but so far as Sterl could see, her pride upheld her. His conviction was now that Ormiston, having arrived at the scene of his intended split with Dann, had an arrow to his bow besides persuasion.

A different kind of fight had begun for Stanley Dann's trekkers; a fight not against distance and time, rough land, treacherous water, but against heat and flies and, what was worst of all, the peril of idleness, of waiting, and of their effect on the mind. Each day— between the blazing sun and the thirst of thousands of cattle—saw the water in the long waterhole recede inches down the sand and rock. One night from Ormiston's side of the river gunshots and shrill yells of aborigines startled the campers on Dann's side. There was no corroboree that night.

Next morning a drover reported to Dann that Ormiston's men had shot five blacks. No reason was given. Stanley Dann was overheard to express the opinion that his surly partner had sought to drive thieving natives away from camp. But Sterl, after talking with Friday, came to the conclusion that Ormiston wanted to drive the aborigines across the river. At any rate that was what had happened. The several hundred blacks had congregated in a grove at the lower end of the long waterhole.

By way of reparation and kindness Dann ordered crippled cattle shot and dragged down to the aborigine camp. Blacks, lubras, gins, pickanninies deserted their camp while this restitution took place. But later, after Friday had visited them, they gradually approached nearer and nearer to Dann's camp. Dann argued for pursuing any course that would keep the blacks friendly and Slyter agreed with him. Friday, Sterl thought, might have influenced Dann toward this attitude, but their leader, in any case, would be generous and kind. When Sterl asked Friday what he had told Dann and Slyter the black replied:

"Plenty black fella good. Mebbe steal bimeby. No fightum."

"Wal, I'd rather stand for thet," asserted Red, "then rile them into slitherin' spears around."

Beryl weakened in the end, and sent a note by one of the drovers across the way to Ormiston, who came to see her that evening. Thereafter he appeared at Dann's camp every evening. Beryl Dann would need a terrible lesson before she began to react from her infatuation and then it might come too late.

The trekkers settled down to suffer and to wait. The second hour after sunset usually brought a night breeze that gave a little welcome respite from the torrid heat of the day, but the hours from daylight until an hour or more after breakfast were the most supportable. Sterl made use of this time, often with Leslie or Friday. The middle of the day was intolerable in the sun and just endurable in the shade. The cattle, needing no watch then, sought the shade of the trees where they lay down or stood resting. In these hours, the ever-increasing flies made existence well-nigh unbearable and all the trekkers kept under cover of tents and mosquito nets. The constant humming and buzzing outside, like that of a great hive of bees, made this protection so welcome that the stifling heat was endurable.

So the days wore on endlessly, each one hotter than the last. The small waterholes dried up and living creatures were dependent upon the long one. No cloud appeared in the sky. At midday rocks were so hot that they blistered a naked hand, the cattle ceased to bawl, the birds to scream, the aborigines to move about. Sterl had always thriven on hot weather; likewise Red. They could sleep, but they would wake wringing wet with sweat. However, when the mercury rose to a hundred and ten degrees, even the cowboys were hard put to endure it.

When Friday was asked if the rains were ever coming he would reply:

"Might be, bimeby."

But the bearable hours always renewed interest in things of the moment and hope for the future.

Sterl never tired of the aborigines nor of his efforts to observe and understand them. These blacks seemed far below Friday in development. Friday could not name their tribe, but he understood their language well enough to interpret, and it was through him that the overtures of Stanley Dann and Sterl counteracted the fright and hostility for which Ormiston and his drovers were responsible.

Sterl learned that when a death occurred in a

camp of theirs, they moved away at once. They went
stark naked except for a breechcloth of woven grass
or hair. The men were tall, lean though muscular,
black as coal, with broad faces and large heads covered by a mop of tangled black hair. The troops of
pot-bellied youngsters, upon being approached, at
first scattered like a flock of frightened quail. The
mature women, or gins were such monstrosities that
Sterl had to force himself to glance at them. For the
most part the lubras were not good to look at. A few
of them, however, were prepossessing and far from
averse to making eyes at the younger drovers.

The problem of the aboriginal was to eat, and
he ate everything from dirt and grass and seeds and
fruit to all living creatures, including ants—and his
own species. He was a hunter. He made his own
weapons, very few in number, and these he carried.
Friday told Sterl that these people caught live fish
under water with their hands. Sterl saw some of them,
at Dann's camp, swim under water, drag ducks down
beneath the surface. He saw them eat every last vestige of a bullock, meat, entrails, and even the
smashed-up horns. He found lubras and children out
on the plain, digging for roots, herbs, lizards, eggs,
and one of their reptile luxuries, the goanna.

One morning Red accompanied Sterl and Leslie,
with the inseparable Friday, on a visit to the aborigines. They came upon two blacks, both mature men,
tall and lean, who fastened ghoulish eyes upon Leslie's supple and brown bare legs, and then shifted
their black gaze to the cowboy's red head. One of

them held a most striking posture. He stood on one long leg, leaning on his spear, while his other leg was bent at right angles, with his foot flat against the inside of his thigh. Yet he stood at ease.

"What'n'll is the matter with this gazabo?" inquired Red.

"Nothing. He's just resting. I see a good many blacks stand like that," replied Sterl.

The abo, evidently impressed by Red, spoke to him in his native jargon.

"Yeah?" drawled Red, and then added sonorously: "Holy Mackeli—Kalamazoo—Ras pa tas—Mugg's Landin'—You one-laiged black giraffe!"

Whereupon the aborigine, tremendously impressed, let out a flow of speech that in volume certainly matched Red's.

"Ahuh? Thet didn't sound so good to me. Friday, what he say?"

Friday indicated Krehl's red head and replied: "Makeum fun alonga you."

"Hell he did?" roared Red. "Hey, you! I'm from Texas, an' I'm liable to shoot thet one laig out from under you."

Upon their return to the Dann encampment Slyter called Red and Sterl to him, and informed them that Stanley Dann wanted to see them promptly.

"Now, what's up?" queried Sterl, impatiently, quick to catch Slyter's sober mood.

"I'd rather Dann told you," returned the drover. "There's been a fight, and the drovers are upset."

"Yeah? Wal, if you ask me thet ain't nothin' new

these days," drawled Red, with a bite in his tone.

Slyter accompanied them the few rods under the trees to the bright campfire, where Stanley stalked to and fro. He was bareheaded, in his shirt sleeves, a deep-eyed giant standing erect under obvious burdens. Beryl was in the background, with her aunt and Mrs. Slyter. A group of men, just visible near one of the tents, stood conversing in low tones.

"You sent for us, sir," spoke up Sterl, quickly.

"Yes, I regret to say. Harry Spence has been shot. The drovers just fetched him in. He died without regaining consciousness."

"Spence? That is regrettable, sir. But it can hardly have anything to do with us," returned Sterl. He had not thought much of Spence, and several other of the rougher element among Dann's drovers.

"Only indirectly," rejoined Dann, hastily.

"Boss, who shot Spence?" interposed Red, coolly.

"Ormiston's drover, Bedford. Tom Bedford. He was badly wounded in the fight, but should recover."

"Wal, beggin' yore pardon, boss, an' if you ask me, there ain't much love lost in Spence's case, an' if Bedford croaked, it'd be a damn good night's job," replied Red, in cold deliberation.

"I'm not asking for your judgments, Krehl," said the leader, tersely.

"I'm sorry, boss, but you gotta take them jest the same."

Sterl put a placating and persuasive hand on Red's shoulder. But he was glad that the cowboy had spoken out. He, too, was sick of subterfuge and concealment.

"Sir, why did you send for us?" repeated Sterl, quietly.

"Boys, it is only that I preferred to tell you myself, rather than have you hear it from others. I want to persuade you to see it my way. I have come to rely upon you both. I have come to have a personal regard for you. Can I exact a promise from you both—not to shed blood, except in some drastic necessity of self-defense?"

"Yes, sir, you can from me," declared Sterl, instantly rallying to his sympathy for this great and trouble-besieged man. "Red, you'll promise, too, won't you?"

"Boss," said Red, "you ain't goin' to ask me to make a promise like thet, an' keep it forever?"

"Krehl, don't misunderstand me," returned Dann, in haste. "I would not presume to have you deny your creed, your honor. I beg this promise only for the present, because I still hope we can go through this trek without more bloodshed."

"Wal, boss, as I see it, you won't," flashed Red. "It wouldn't be natural. You've got some lown-down *hombres* mixed up with you on this trek. All the same, I'll give you my promise thet I won't raise a hand against Ormiston, or anyone, except in self-defense—or to save somebody's life."

"Thank you, Krehl," replied Dann. "Now, for the detail that will be as offensive to you as it was to me. This morning a new contingent of blacks arrived.

It seems there were some unusually comely lubras among them. Ormiston propitiated them with gifts—an action Slyter and I are strongly opposed to. But Ormiston did it, and took several to work around his camp. Spence and Bedford quarreled over one of them. It was obvious that all the drovers had been drinking. The two men fought, with the result I told you. Ormiston sent the report to me. And I at once ordered him here. I took him to task. We had bitter words, that might have led to worse but for Beryl. She came between us; and in part, when Ormiston maligned you boys, she took his side. She believes him. I do not."

"Thanks, boss. But spill it. What has Ormiston said now?" retorted Sterl, harshly.

"He ridiculed my offense at the idea of his drovers making up to the lubras. And the part applicable to you is this, in his own words: 'Look at your Yankee cowboys—Hazelton, posing as a gentleman, and Krehl as a comedian—to please the ladies! They go from their soft speeches to Beryl and Leslie to the embraces of these nigger lubras!'"

If Stanley Dann expected the cowboys to arise in rage to disclaim against their traducer, he reckoned without his host. Nothing Ormiston might do or say could surprise them any more.

As fate would have it Leslie had followed them over, and Beryl with the two older women, evidently wishing to intercept her, had all come within range of Dann's stern voice. Sterl threw up his hands. What was the use?

Red did not fortify himself with knowledge and bitterness, as Sterl had done. But his innate chivalry permitted of no intimation that these girls could believe such vile slander.

"Beryl, you needn't look so orful bad," he said, gently. "Leastways not on my account. I jest promised yore Dad I wouldn't throw a gun on Ormiston for what he said."

"You don't deny it, Red Krehl?" cried Beryl, passionately, beside herself.

"What you mean—I don't deny?"

"Ormiston's accusation that you cowboys go from me and Leslie—to—to those nigger lubras," rang out the outraged girl. She was pale under her tan and her big eyes strained with horror.

Red twitched as if he were about to draw a gun. His visage lost its ruddiness then. "Me deny thet? Hell no! I'm a Texan, Miss Dann. You English never heahed of Texas, let alone know what a Texan stands for in regard to women. What you've got in yore mind, Beryl Dann, what you think of *me*, is what's true of yore rotten lover. An' by Gawd, some day you'll go on yore knees to me for thet!"

The girl recoiled. She gasped. Her eyes dilated. But she could not cope with passion and jealousy and hate—those primitive emotions that this trek had increased by leaps and bounds. She let Red stalk away without another word.

"Sterl!—Sterl!" burst out Leslie, wildly. "*You* deny—that—that—or I'll hate you!"

"Leslie, it is a matter of supreme indifference to

me what you believe," returned Sterl, cold and aloof. Then he addressed the parents of the girls. "Dann, Slyter, and you, Mrs. Slyter, you all can't fail to see what your wilderness outback has done to your precious offspring. Next, they'll condone, in Ormiston and his bunch, the very thing they insult us with now!"

CHAPTER
16

*L*ESLIE met Sterl next morning at breakfast
as if awakening from a nightmare; she appeared stunned to bewilderment that he did
not notice her. Sterl felt that she, the same as Beryl,
must learn her bitter lesson. Until that time she
would not exist for him, so far as intimacy and
friendly contact were concerned. He was deeply hurt,
but not resentful. She was only a sentimental young
girl, placed in a terrible situation. Sterl felt sorry for
her. Little by little his love had grown until it had
almost made him forget that he was an outlaw, who,
if he considered marriage, must find himself in a
grave plight. Sterl had been hurt before by love. He
could not kill this new love but he put it aside. Krehl's
love affair with Beryl, however, had a fair chance to

survive, if the girl herself proved strong enough to survive. Sterl seemed to feel something deep and latent in this Dann girl. She was blindly in love with this dark-browed bushranger. But when she learned the truth about Ormiston, as must inevitably happen, it was Sterl's opinion that the girl would hate him more than she had loved him.

January blazed to its end, but the rains did not come. They might skip a year. The heat and the flies had become insupportable. Yet human life lived on, though in each and every person there were signs, even in himself, revealing to Sterl's keen eyes that white people could not live there for long. The days were terrible; the sky a vast copper dome close to the earth; the night hot even till dawn. Work and meals were undertaken before sunrise and after sunset. The mob of cattle grazed slowly by night and rested by day. The flies were harder on them than the sun. Hundreds of calves were born. Stanley Dann had now more cattle than when he had left Downsville.

Bedford, being a tough and phlegmatic man, recovered from his serious wound. Hathaway came down with some kind of a fever which neither Ormiston nor Dann could alleviate. Stanley Dann's sister was a woman along in years, unused to life in the open, and despite what had appeared at first a certain robustness she began to fail. It was mental, Sterl thought, more than physical. She simply dried up into a shadow of her former self, and met death with a wan and pathetic gladness.

Eric Dann presented a problem to Sterl. The man had something on his mind, either a cowardice he could not beat, a gnawing indecision about splitting with his brother, or something secret. Sterl had seen criminals not big enough to stand up under the adversity that tried men's souls; and it seemed to him there was a furtive similarity between their moods and Eric's. Ormiston has turned gaunt of visage, hollow-eyed. But for that matter, all the drovers lost flesh, hardened, tanned almost as black as Friday, and if they ever smiled, Sterl did not see it. It was in Ormiston's eyes, however, that the difference lay. He never met Sterl's scornful gaze. He ceased to eat at Dann's table, but at sunset and dusk he haunted Beryl, and kept her up late. Beryl Dann could not lose her grace of form or beauty of profile, but she grew thin, and her large violet eyes had a wild look.

Leslie bore up surprisingly well. She lost but little weight. The sun burned her very dark. She grew quieter, less cheerful, more considerate and helpful. She approached Sterl endlessly with subterfuges, innocent advances, unthinking expectations which were never realized, and which left her pondering and sad.

Stanley Dann proved to be the great physical and spiritual leader Sterl had imagined he would be. He remained imperturbable, cheerful, confident. But he seldom talked to his brother, he never voluntarily addressed Ormiston, though he often came to Slyter's camp to smoke and talk.

Always when Sterl watched these people he

ended by going back to study Friday, the aborigine, who day by day loomed greater in his sight. Here was a man. His color mattered little. He was always on night guard with Sterl and Red. He had made their lives his life. He asked nothing for his allegiance. Separated from them by inestimable ages, by aboriginal mystery and darkness of mind, he yet felt for them, for their trials and sorrows and terrors.

"Bimeby rains come. All good," he said, on several nights. And once, as if the question of rain was not altogether the trenchant thing, he wagged his black head, and gazed at Sterl, his great black eyes unfathomable, "Ormiston tinkit he get cattle, Missy Dann, eberyting. But no, boss Hazel, nebber!"

On Friday, February thirteenth, the limit of heat was reached—a hundred and twenty-five in the shade. It had to be the limit because Dann's thermometer burst as if the mercury had boiled. Red said it was a good thing. They all had been asking how hot it was, watching the instrument, wondering how much hotter it would get. But now there would be no way to learn. The noonday sun would have burned the eyeballs sightless. Sterl and Red waded into the river a dozen times without bothering to remove their garments. The birds and beasts and reptiles Sterl encountered in his early morning walk did not trouble to move out of the way. Almost he could pet the gray old kangaroos; the wild fowl pecked at him, but did not fly.

*   *   *

Hathaway's death, coming one night when he was unattended, shocked everyone, even the cowboys, out of their abnormal unfeeling states. For days he had been delirious and burning up with fever. They buried him beside Emily Dann, and erected another cross. Stanley Dann, in his faltering prayer, committed his soul to rest and freedom from the plague of unsatisfied life.

Sterl wondered if the leader was breaking. But that very night, when Ormiston, who had not attended the funeral, presented himself at Dann's camp, professing grief for the loss of his friend, the leader delivered himself of a significant speech.

"Ormiston," he boomed in his sonorous voice, "you need not demean yourself to tell me that you won *Hathaway's* cattle at cards, or that he otherwise owed you money."

That staggered the bushranger for a moment, perhaps because both the cowboys and Beryl were present. His dark gaze, scarcely veiling malignance, would have warned a man less noble than Stanley Dann. He dropped his head and went his way.

"Dad!" exclaimed Beryl, petulantly, "anyone would think you doubted Hathaway owed Ash money. I knew it ages ago."

"Yes, daughter, *anyone* who hadn't a mind would think that," returned her father, and left her. The cowboys sat staring into the fire, enduring its smoke to insure a relief from the pest of mosquitoes that had been recently added to the tribulations of the forks.

Sterl revolved Dann's caustic speech in his mind.
Their leader was not so guileless after all. He was
merely greater than most men! When would this
giant stamp upon the viper?

Some time during that night Sterl opened his
eyes, wide awake intstantly. It was pitch dark, stifling
hot, still as the grave, yet in a flash his consciousness
told him that he had been awakened by something
unusual. Despite the heat and his own burning sweat,
a queer little chill ran over him.

Suddenly the painful silence broke in a long low
rolling rumble. *Thunder!* Was he dreaming? It
sounded again, like the distant roar of stampeding
buffalo. Yes , it was thunder!

Sterl sat up. His heart thumped audibly. He had
a dry mouth and a constriction in his throat.

"Red—Red!" he panted, huskily.

"Hell, pard. I heahed it!"

There came Friday's voice.

"Boss, bimeby rain!"

They pulled on their boots, crawled from under
their mosquito nets, and out of the tent. There was
starlight enough to see Friday's tall black image, the
pale wagons, the spectral trees. The air was sultry,
oppressive, heavy, yet strangely different. Then a
flare of lightning ran along the eastern horizon. How
exceedingly beautiful, beneficent, overwhelming!
With bated breath Sterl waited for the thunder, to
assure himself, to enable him to judge how far distant. Would it never come? That storm was far away.

"How far—when?" Sterl asked Friday.

"Rain mebbe soon—mebbe no!"

Slyter came stamping from the direction of his wagon. Leslie's rich, glad voice rang out. Stanley Dann boomed to his brother. The drovers were calling one to another. Across the river lights flashed at Ormiston's camp. They had all heard. They were all astir.

Slyter's thought was for his horsees. Dann boomed to his drovers that thunder and lightning, after so long a dry spell, might stampede the mob. In short order all were mounted and on guard.

But that storm passed by to the southward. Soon, however, the disappointed trekkers thrilled to more thunder. In due course that storm, too, passed by the forks, but closer, heavier, longer.

But just the same the sun rose fiery red—molten steel. The birds and wild fowl came in to water. The slopes and flats were black with kangaroos and wallabies. Again the heat blazed down; again the infernal horde of whirling, humming, biting, bloodsucking flies settled down around man and beast.

After breakfast Stanley Dann called all his trekkers to his camp.

"Friends, countrymen, my brother, my daughter," he boomed, "my prayers have been answered. The wet season is at hand. We are saved, and we lift up our voices in thanksgiving to Him, in Whom we have never lost faith. When the rains cease, or when it has rained enough to fill the rivers and creeks, we shall proceed on our trek. But with this change: we will go by the Gulf route, and on to Darwin, and from there to the Kimberleys. A year longer—but that is better than to divide our party, our cattle, our strength, our harmony. Ormiston, you who have been even more stubborn than my brother in refusal to cross the Never-never, you can rejoice now that I have changed my mind."

A loud hurrah from a half dozen lusty-throated drovers broke up the silence following Dann's address. The leader waited, naturally anticipating a response from Ormiston. But none came. The drover turned away his dark face. Beryl dropped her head as if stupefied and made for her wagon. Eric Dann, however, received the news with a blank visage, then a gradually breaking expression which Sterl interpreted as consternation.

Leslie, in the stress of the hour, forgot the estrangement she had caused between herself and Sterl and met him with eyes darkly excited, to grasp his arm with the old familiar intimacy.

"Oh, Sterl! I'm glad—glad in a way. But I did want to cross the Never-never. Didn't you?"

The answer that sprang to Sterl's lips was both cruel and insulting, but somehow he could not hold back the words: "Yes," he said caustically, "I sure hate the idea of having to spend a year longer in the society of two shallow, mindless girls like you and Beryl."

Her face burned red, her eyes blazed, and there was little doubt that but for Red's intervention she would have struck him. He went on his way, deeply disturbed by the encounter. Red caught up with him.

"Say, pard, the kid would have smacked the day-lights out of you but for me," he said.

"That didn't escape me, Red."

"I left her cryin'. That was a mean kind of speech you gave her, Sterl."

"Agree with you," Sterl snapped. Then after a pause, "Did you look at Beryl?"

"Shore. Beryl was surprised. Mebbe she's not so strong for them noble idees of bein' true to her Dad. Mebbe she's been talked into elopin' with Ormiston."

"Ah, I had that thought, too. I hoped I was wrong. Red, Eric Dann was sunk at his brother's decision. Sunk!"

"He oughta be overjoyed. If he ain't—why ain't he? He always struck me as kinda phony—weak or somethin'. Gosh, ain't it hot again? Thet false alarm last night made us expect this goshawful sun wouldn't shine no more."

"But the air feels different."

There was an infinitesimal humidity in the atmosphere that morning. That afternoon white clouds, like ships at sea, sailed over the ranges to the north-east. They were good to see. Before they crossed the zenith the heat had dissipated them. The sunset was ruddy, dusky, smoky. The cattle lowed. There was an uneasy activity among the birds and kangaroos. Friday talked to the old men among the aborigines, and returned uncommunicative.

After supper, Sterl was reading by firelight when

Red nudged him. In the gloaming distance—Ormiston and Beryl!

"Watch awhile, pard. It won't be long now!" said Red, getting up to glide off like an Indian.

Out of the corner of his eye Sterl watched Leslie, and knew she would approach him. At last she did.

"Red has followed them—Ormiston and Beryl. What's he going to do? Kill that blighter?"

Sterl did not answer.

"Eric Dann has got the willies, whatever Red means by them," went on Leslie, restlessly, edging closer. "And he was drinking whisky. In this heat!"

"How do you know?"

"I saw him. I smelled it. Sterl, the rains will come?"

"Friday says bimeby. Mebbe soon. Mebbe no."

"I thought I'd die last night, hoping, waiting. It'll never rain. We'll all dry up and blow away."

Leslie came closer, and suddenly, desperate, sat down beside Sterl.

"You hateful, callous, unforgiving cowboy!" she whispered, huskily.

"Leslie, how very unflattering!" he rejoined, mildly.

"I hate you!" she burst out.

"That is only natural, Leslie. You are a headstrong child."

"Headstrong, yes, but I'm not even a girl any more. I'm old. I'll be like these gins, presently."

"Very well, then, you're old. What of it?"

"Oh, I don't care. Nobody cares. You don't. I—

I wish I'd thrown myself away on Ormiston."

"Yeah? Is it too late?"

"Don't be a damn fool," she flashed. "It's bad enough for you to be a monster of indifference. A man of rock! I'm sick. I'm wild. I'm scared. I'm full of—of—"

"You must be full of tea, darling," interposed Sterl, lightly.

"Sterl Hazelton, don't you dare call me that—that—when you're making fun of me. I'm so miserable. And it's not all about myself."

"Who then?"

"Beryl. She's strange. She was lovely to me for a while. Now she's changed. She's—numb. Sterl, you must do something, or she'll go away with him!"

"Les, hadn't you better go to bed?" he queried, gently.

"Yes. I'm weak as a cat and wet as water. But before I go I want to tell you something I heard Mum say to Dad. Mum said: 'I see Hazelton doesn't go to the lubras any more'. And Dad replied: 'I hadn't noticed. But it's none of your business, woman.' Then Mum snapped: 'Bingham Slyter, I didn't hold it against Sterl. I'd do it myself, if I were a man! In this horrible hole, where God only knows what keeps us from going mad!'"

"Well, well!" ejaculated Sterl, taken aback, and flustered. "Then what did your dad say?"

"He swore terribly at Mum."

Sterl relaxed into the flimsy protection of silence. All these good people might be forgiven for anything. It was a diabolical maelstrom—this trek.

"That—distressed me—Sterl," went on Leslie, falteringly. "I'm as crazy as Mum, or any of them. I— I lied when I said I hated you. It hurt me—that about you—and the lubras. But I forgive you. I—I don't care. There! I've told you. Maybe now I can sleep."

She ran off sobbing. It was well, he reflected, that she did. A kind word, a tender touch from him at that crucial moment would have brought the distracted girl into his arms. There could never be anything between them. He could keep the secret that had made him a man without a country.

Sterl sat there a long time. The fire died down and Friday crossed a couple of sticks over the ashes. Mosquitoes began to snarl. Red returned, dragged his feet, his gait like that of a whipped cur. A furious flame of passion waved over Sterl. That this cowboy, as keen as flint, a man who had laughed and drawled in the very face of death—that he should crawl back to the firelight, ashamed and abased, crushed at the weakness or perfidy of a girl, was too revolting to withstand. Sterl leaped up muttering, "I won't endure it!" Then a deep low roll of thunder brought him to himself.

CHAPTER

17

*T*HUNDER! Deep, detonating, long-rolling! Krehl approached the burned-out campfire, his head lifting like that of a listening deer. Again the heart-shaking rumble!

"You heah, pard?" he queried.

"You bet. Deeper, heavier tonight, Red."

Friday loomed out of nowhere, soft-stepping, black as the night. He replenished the fire with two sticks laid crosswise, squatted down, rested his weapons, and became a statue like black marble. Friday could sleep in any position, at any time. Sterl had caught him asleep standing on one leg, like a sandhill crane.

Back inside the tent, pulling off his boots, Sterl said, "What kicked you in the middle, pard?"

Red heaved a sigh. "Somethin' wuss tonight, Sterl. I had my gun out to kill Ormiston when that first clap of thunder fetched me to my senses."

Sterl cursed his friend lustily. It silenced Red and relieved his own overwrought feelings. Then he stretched out on the hot blankets to rest if not to sleep. As on the night before, this thundering fore-runner of the season's storms passed by the forks, booming on, rolling on to rumble and mutter and die away in the distance. Day broke. And when the sun rose, fire again possessed the sky and earth.

At breakfast Larry told how three thunderstorms had passed by about midnight; the last had gone to the west of the forks.

"We'll get socked right in the eye tonight," he said, cheerfully.

"Folks, am I gettin' balmy or is it hot sooner an' wusser than yestiddy mawnin'?" inquired Red.

Slyter interposed to inform them that the last day of a hot spell was the hottest. The temperature this day would top one hundred and thirty degrees. If the forks had been a dusty place, with hot gales blowing, life would have been impossible.

"As long as your face is wet, you're all right," he said. "But if it gets dry and hot, look out. Keep in the shade with a pail of water and bathe your head."

When Sterl followed Red to their tent, Friday pointed to Eric Dann crossing the main fork of the dry river bed toward Ormiston's camp. Sterl got his field glass from under a flap of the tent.

"From what I heard last night," said Red, "he's

carryin' a message from the big boss. He's gonna persuade Ormiston to drive his herd back on this side, before the river rises. Haw! Haw! Like hell—"

"Here by this log," interrupted Sterl. "Nobody can see us." He adjusted the glass. At first glance he saw that Ormiston's camp was a busy place considering the torrid heat. Drovers naked to the waist were carrying things from one wagon to another. Ormiston paced under a shelter of palm and pandanus leaves. His right-hand man, Bedford, sat on the ground mending harness. They saw Eric Dann plodding up the sand of the river slope, and their remarks must surely have fitted their malevolent looks. But in a moment more the drover was again the smiling Ormiston, greeting his visitor agreeably. They talked, and Sterl did not need to hear them to know that Eric Dann never delivered his brother's message.

"Lemme have a look, you hawg," spoke up Red. He glued his eyes to the glass and remained rigid for a long time.

"Wal, thet's over, whatever it was," he said, presently. "Dann is comin' back. He's carryin' the world on his shoulders, if I know a sucker when I see one. He doesn't know Ormiston is goin' to double-cross him, any more than does Stanley Dann. Gosh, I can hardly wait to bore thet beady-eyed bastard! There he goes, back to thet wagon they're packin'."

His ice-blue eyes glinted as he faced Sterl.

"All over but the rain—an' the shootin', pard," he rang out.

"Well, dammit, suppose we go over there and

do the shooting before it rains," snapped Sterl.

"Now! There ain't no good motive yet thet'd go far with Stanley Dann. We gotta have thet. What we been waitin' for all these months? Use yore haid, pard."

"Red, oughtn't we tell Stanley?"

"Hell no! Not before, an' ruin our chanct to bore that *hombre*. Afterward we won't have to talk. Ormiston will raid the boss's mob an' *remuda*, shore as you're born."

"Okay then. But where does Beryl come in?"

"Pard, thet stumps me, too. Beryl thinks Ormiston will take the Gulf road, now thet Stanley has given in. But Ormiston isn't takin' it, as we know. An' I'm about shore there's no hope of Ormiston persuadin' Beryl to elope. He ain't the kind of a man who'd risk much for a woman. Shore you've seen how Beryl has failed lately. She'd be a burden. What he wants air hosses an' cattle."

"Red, you're overshooting here," declared Sterl. "Beryl's physical condition wouldn't deter him one single whit, if he *wants* her. He has to travel with wagons. She can be packed like a bag of flour. If she dies on the way, what the hell?"

"Wal," cut in Red, wearily, "let's wait for the showdown. It's a cinch Ormiston will try to steal some of Dann's hosses an' cattle. Mebbe some of Slyter's, too. But if he's as pore a bushranger as he is everythin' else, why, hell, it'll make us laugh!"

Stanley Dann sent orders by Cedric for all to lie quiet that day, protected from the direct rays of the sun. Before that, the cattle had strung out in the shade of trees along the riverbanks. Kangaroos kept to the brush. The whirling hordes of flies were out early, but they soon vanished. The sun was too hot for them. The younger blacks stayed in or by the water; the older ones did not move from their shelters.

Sterl and Red found the inside of the tent unendurable. Almost naked they lay under their wagon on the grass. Friday lay in the shade of the big gum tree. That was the only time Sterl ever saw him incapacitated. He, too, although as perfect an engine to resist the elements as evolution had ever turned out, had to fight for his life.

The sun set at last. That awful odor of the blast furnace closed. In the west colossal thunderhead clouds loomed halfway to the zenith. Low down over the horizon their base was a dusky purple, but as they billowed and mushroomed upward, the darker hues changed to rose and gold, and their rounded tops were pearl white.

Friday appeared stalking under the gum trees. He came directly to them.

"Howdy," he said, using the cowboy greeting Sterl had taught him. And accompanying it was a transfiguration in the black visage that Sterl recognized as Friday's exceedingly rare smile.

"Boss, rain come," he said, as if he were a chief addressing a multitude of aborigines.

"Bimeby?" asked Sterl, huskily.

"Alonga soon night. Rain like hell."

A call to supper disrupted this conversation. While the cowboys forced themselves to partake of the eternal damper, meat and tea, the magnificent panorama of pillared cloud pageant lifted perceptibly higher. The bases closed the gaps between and turned to inky black. The purple deepened and encroached upon the gold, blotting it out until the sculptured, scalloped crowns lost their pearl and white. Slyter heard the good news and ran across the way to tell the Danns. Red whooped and hobbled after him, evidently to inform Beryl.

"I'm going to ride herd tonight," announced Leslie, brightly, approaching Sterl.

Her face showed the havoc of these torrid weeks less than that of anyone else, Sterl observed, but the change was enough to give him a pang.

"Yeah? You look like it," he rejoined, dubiously.

"How do I look?" she retorted, hastily.

"Terrible."

"So do you. If I look terrible you should see Beryl! What do you mean by terrible?"

"Eyes hollow, lines you didn't use to have."

"Oh, Sterl! Am I pretty no longer?"

"You couldn't help being pretty, Leslie!" replied Sterl, yielding as always to the appeal which destroyed his relentlessness.

"Then I'm not to ride herd with you tonight?"

"I didn't say so."

"But you're my boss."

"Long ago, Leslie, before this trek had made me

old and you a little savage—then I called myself your boss. But no more!"

"What if I *am* a little savage?" she asked, wistfully.

Red and Slyter returned from the Dann camp, and Slyter said: "Saddle up, all hands. Stanley wants the mob driven into that basin out there, and surrounded."

Sterl went on with Red. The afterglow of sunset shone over the land. The vast mass of merging clouds shut out the northeast. The two seemed to be in conflict.

"I seen Beryl," Red was saying, his voice deep with pain. "She lay on her bed under the wagon. When I called she didn't answer. I stepped up on the wheel, so I could look down at her. I spoke an' she whispered, 'Bury me out on—the lone prairiee!' You know I used to sing thet to her—before Ormiston. . . . Sterl, *could* Beryl Dann look at me like thet, smile like thet, say thet to me if she meant to run off with this black-faced rustler?"

"Red, give me something easy," replied Sterl, grimly. "Back home I'd swear to God she couldn't. But out here, after what we've gone through, I say hell yes, she could! Take your pick."

"Pard, if you was me, would you watch Beryl's wagon tonight, instead of guardin' herd?"

"No!—Red, you might kill Ormiston, and kill him too soon. Let these Danns find out what we know. Then you can break loose an' I'll be with you. Man alive, *she* can't get away—Ormiston can't get away—

not with her or his stolen cattle or his life. If he took Beryl on horseback we'd run him down. Red, old man, come to your senses!"

"Thanks, pard. Reckon I—I was kinda queer. Mebbe the heat—Heah's the hosses."

"What'll you ride?" asked Sterl, as he looked the *remuda* over. King whinnied and thudded toward him.

"Leslie's Duke. He's a big water dog. An' mebbe there'll be a flood. Them clouds all same Red River color, pard."

Mounted, the cowboys headed for the grassy basin already half covered with cattle. Slyter, pounding along to join the cowboys, expressed anxiety for his horses. Red said he was sure that they would stand, unless run down by a frightened mob. The peril lay with the cattle.

Stanley Dann rode around the mob, hauling up last where Sterl and Red had been joined by Larry and Roland. "Station yourselves at regular intervals. Concentrate on the river and camp sides," said Dann. "Probably the mob won't rush. If they do, keep out of their way. They won't run far. From the looks of it we are in for a real storm."

"Let's stick pretty close together," suggested Sterl to Red.

"You can't lose me, pard!"

"The air's stirring. Smells dusty!"

"But it's them low clouds thet holds the storm. Gosh, but they're black!"

Then the first deep, detonating thunder rolled

toward the waiting drovers. The tired, heat-dulled cattle gave no sign of uneasiness.

"Bet you they won't stampede," called Red, some yards to Sterl's right.

"They're English cattle. They cain't be scared, maybe," returned Sterl, jocularly.

Thunder boomed over the battlements of the ranges north and east. Flashes of lightning flared from behind them. Puffs of moving air struck Sterl in the face, hot like the breath of fire. The lacy foliage of the eucalyptus trees began to toss against a sky still clear. Heavy thunderclaps turned Sterl's gaze back to the storm. The front of it had rolled over the ranges.

"Whoopee!" yelled Red. "She's acomin', an' a humdinger!"

A hot gale struck Sterl. He turned his back, and felt that he was shriveling up like leather in a flame. The gum trees bent away from its force; streaks of dusty light sped along the ground; the afterglow faded into a gloaming that was a moving curtain before the wind. Leaves and grass and bits of bark whipped by, and King's mane and tail stood straight out.

All at once Sterl's senses awoke to a startling fact. The hot furnace blast had gone on the wind! The air was cool—damp! Red's wild yell came, splitting Sterl's ear. And with it a roar, steady, gaining, tremendous—the roar of rain.

The pall bore down upon them, steel-gray in the blazes of white fire, to swallow up earth and night

and lightning and thunder. He could not see a hand
before his face. But how he reveled in that drenching!

It swallowed up time, too, and he almost forgot
the great mob of cattle. But to think of them was
futile. Sterl shut his eyes, bent his head, and thanked
heaven for every drop of that endless torrent. Stanley
Dann's faith and prayers were justified; the trek was
saved! Then a rough hand on his shoulder roused
him. He opened his eyes. The lightning flashes were
far to the west, and the thunder rolled with them.
The rain was pouring down, but not in a solid sheet.
He could see indistinctly.

"Pard!" yelled Red, close to his ear. "Stampede!
Feel the ground shakin'!"

*L*ET'S find the break!" shouted Red. "You ride back. I'll ride ahaid."

Turned away from the pelting rain, Sterl could distinguish the darker line of cattle against the white grass. They were not moving on this side. He rode forward and checked King to listen again. There was a decided roar of hoofs, but it was lessening in volume.

He pulled King to a walk. Perhaps a spur of cattle had broken out of the main mob. Then, in a lull of the heavy downpour he caught gunshots! Turning to peer back he saw dim flashes far across the herd. Dann's drovers on that side were trying to hold the mob.

Presently Sterl made out the dark shape of a

horseman. Riding close he shouted and got an answer. It was Roland.

"They're quiet here," yelled the drover. "They'll hold now. If they were going to rush over there, it's strange they didn't when the storm was worst."

"Strange at that," replied Sterl. "Where's your next guard?"

"Not far along. Drake. He told me Slyter was fussing about his horses."

"Small wonder. I'll ride back to Red."

The rain still poured down, with intermittent heavier bursts. He had sent Friday back to the camp before the break of the storm, and he did not feel sure just where he and Red had parted. He halted and on the last stop found the cattle jostling and pressing one another. The roar seemed to have grown louder. In the gray gloom the mob moved and swayed as if from irresistible pressure at its center.

Sterl trotted King a hundred yards farther round the herd. Two riders emerged from the impenetrable black.

"Heah you air," shouted Red, as the three met.

"All jake down the line on this side." reported Sterl.

"Wal, it shore ain't round on the other. Tell him, Larry."

Larry told him that Dann's drovers on that side of the herd were all gone.

"Cattle rarin' to slope around there," interposed Red. "It ain't safe, but we might stop a stampede."

"But those guards will be back unless..."

Red interrupted: "Like hell they will! Pard, we had it figgered. Some of them drovers, in cahoots with Ormiston, have cut out a bunch of cattle. It wasn't no stampede. But there will be one if we don't watch out. Let's mosey."

The three riders loped their mounts through the driving rain and lashing grass.

"Ride up an' down heah," shouted Red. "Blaze away with yore guns. If there's a break anywhere, run for yore lives."

They separated. Sterl rode back firing, along the way they had come. Close to the herd he felt their unrest and heard their bawling. Along Sterl's line of progress the restive cattle finally settled down and stood. But in the other direction Red and Larry were encountering extreme difficulty. Sterl joined them at the crucial point. For a few moments it seemed vain to attempt blocking the cattle. But the intrepid riders, at the expense of practically all their ammunition, finally held the animals in check. The excited fringe of the mob quieted down.

"Jest luck!" panted Red, as the three reined in together.

"Boys," said Larry, "I'll tell the Danns who saved their mob. New work to me, and my heart was in my throat half the time... Where are those drovers?"

"Haw! Haw! Yes, shore, where in the hell air they? *Heah*! Listen ... What's thet roar?"

"My God, they're on the rampage again!"

"No, boys," yelled Red. "Thet's not cattle! I know thet noise! It's the river!"

Sterl marveled that he had not been as quick as Red to recognize that steady, increasing roar. All in a flash he was back along the Cimarron, the Purgatory, the Red, the Brazos—all those western rivers that he had known and battled in flood.

"Fellers, thet big dry wash has been raisin' all the time. This is a flood!"

"Red, we'd better pull leather out of here."

"I should smile. It's good the camp is on thet high bench.... Gosh, do you heah her comin'?"

A seething, crashing, bumping roar bore down from the black night. The riders loped their horses toward higher ground. They encountered a two-foot wall of water rushing in at that end. Somewhere above the basin an overflow from a tributary had met the main flood head on. They waded their horses through to the rising slope.

Gray dawn broke. The rain had ceased except for a drizzle, but the overcast sky predicted continuous downpour. The mob of cattle stood heads down, knee-deep in the overflow. The stream that had half filled the basin had dwindled to a ribbon. Across the basin and the flat beyond, the main stream raced full from bank to bank. Green trees and logs floated swiftly by. In the middle of the river huge waves curled up to break back upon themselves.

"Red, give us a count," said Sterl, grimly.

"Wal, I was jest about to," replied the cowboy. "About four thousand haid there now. Ormiston an' his bushrangers have sloped with half of our cattle!"

"Bushrangers!" yelled Larry. "Good grief!"

"Shore, bushrangers! Let's go to camp. All the rest of the drovers have rid in for tea, or they're drowned—or gone."

Friday met them and took Sterl's horse. The aborigine's blank visage and his silence were ominous. Bill had a fire going, with tea brewing. No womenfolk were in sight. Over at Dann's camp there was less activity, but a group of drovers stood as if stunned.

Slyter paced to and fro like a maniac confined in a cell. Some of Leslie's race horses were gone, including Lady Jane and Jester.

"What the hell you beefin' about, boss?" queried Red, curtly. "Thet ain't nothin' atall. Wait till you get the load."

Sterl, still silent, hurried to change into dry clothes, refill his belt with cartridges, and get out his rifle. He made sure that the oilskin cover was tight. Red cursed Slyter through his teeth. "What you think, Sterl? Thet hoss-mad geezer doesn't even know about the loss of the cattle. An' damn little he'd care if he did. It's a cinch Ormiston stole those race hosses."

"Rustle!" rasped Sterl. "We've got a job. And my God, am I ready for it!"

They hurried out to the fire and ate standing, eyes alert, thinking hard. Larry came running awkwardly on his bowlegs. His face was gray, and his eyes popped.

"Hey, wait a minnit, you!" ordered Red, sharply. "Get yore breath. Slyter, come heah."

The drover, gloomy-faced and disheveled, stamped to the fire, almost belligerently.

"How many hosses missin?" asked Red.

"Five! Leslie's! We can't track those racers, not after this deluge. And I'll lose them. It'll about kill Leslie."

"Yore hosses were stole, Slyter."

"Who—Who?" gasped Slyter, staggered.

"By thet bushranger you an' Dann have been harborin'."

Sterl broke his silence. "Keep it from Leslie, boss, if you can. Bill, rustle me some meat and bread."

"Wal, Larry, if you can talk now come out with it," said Red.

"Two thousand head and five drovers gone! Eric Dann gone! *Beryl gone!*"

"Ahuh. How about Ormiston's wagons?"

"Gone too, so Drake said. Mob not in sight."

"Come, Friday," called Sterl.

They hurried toward Dann's camp, followed by the others. The leader turned from the group of drovers.

"Bad doing, boss," said Sterl. "What's your angle?"

"There was a rush during the storm. My drovers followed, but they are not in sight. Eric and Beryl must have crossed to Ormiston's camp last night and been stormbound."

"How do you account for five of Slyter's thoroughbreds being gone?"

"That is more news to me. They must have run away in the storm."

"Mr. Dann, it is our opinion that they were stolen," returned Sterl, bluntly.

Dann took that as Sterl imagined he would have taken a blow in the face—without the bat of an eyelash. "Stolen? Preposterous! What black would steal horses when there are cattle to eat?"

Red Krehl had listened attentively to this interview, while his blue eyes, clear and piercing, covered the camp. They flashed back to fix upon the leader.

"Dann, I'm orful sorry I have to hurt yore feelin's," he bit out, cool and bitter. "You been too friendly with a bushranger who turns out to be a slicker *hombre* than we savvied. Name of Ormiston, which I reckon ain't his real name by a damn sight. He stole Slyter's racers. He corrupted yore drovers an' raided yore mob. He made a sucker out of yore weak-minded brother. He . . ."

"You blasphemous Yankee lout—to whom not even blood relationship is sacred!" boomed the leader.

"Save yore wind, boss," snapped Red. "I'm pretty— —riled myself! Mebbe it might help for you to see thet your brother's wagon is gone."

It was indeed. Only his dray was there, its cover dripping with rain. But that discovery did not by any means convince Stanley Dann.

"Dann, there's a lot to tell when I got time," went on Red. "I heahed Ormiston say he was a bushranger. An' Jack an' thet hombre Bedford were his right-hand men. I knowed they all was rustlers before I'd been a month on this trek. Sterl, heah, knowed it, too."

"Suspicion I don't listen to," thundered Dann. "If you had facts why didn't you produce them?"

"Hellsfire, Dann! No man could tell you some things! But you gotta heah this. Ormiston is gone! An' yore daughter went with him,—an' so help me Gawd I still reckon it was by force!"

"Proofs, man, proofs!" raged the giant.

"Come on out along the river," retorted Krehl. He mounted in one long step. "Come, pard, fetch the black man. Drake, Slyter, all of you get in on this."

Across the river, under the trees, Sterl espied one wagon, from the blackened and dismantled top of which thin smoke rose aloft in spite of the drizzle. Pieces of canvas flapping from branches, boxes and bales littered around attested to a hastily abandoned camp. Sterl did not even look for cattle.

A mile up the river Red halted his horse to wait for the others to come up. At this point there was a break in the border of trees. Above, a constriction in the river bed marked the rough center of the current.

As Sterl and the others reined in to line up back of the cowboy, he swept a fierce hand at a deep, miry trough newly cut in the bank. It extended fully a hundred yards up the river. A big herd of cattle, densely packed, had been run along this course, to go over the bank. Across the flood the opposite bank was sloping, and the center of its sandy incline showed a deep, broad trail of tracks. A novice at the cowboy game could have read that tale. Someone had seized a timely period during the storm to cut out a couple of thousand head, and cross them before the flood rose.

"Mr. Dann," spoke up Drake, hollow-voiced. "I never trusted Ormiston and his drovers. They weren't friendly with us. They had a set plan, and it must have worked out as they plotted it."

All eyes turned to Stanley Dann. "It could have been a rush," he boomed, "a rush in the storm! My drovers are with them."

"You shore die hard," drawled Red, halfway between admiration and contempt. "I gotta hand it to you for thet! Only look theah—down the track aways. There's a daid hoss, an' a daid drover. I've a hunch it's Cedric."

Red dismounted beside the prone drover. He did not recognize the horse, but he knew that wavy, tawny hair, even though it was sodden with blood and sand.

"Pard, it's Cedric, all right, pore brave devil," said Red, as he knelt beside the prone figure. "Herd ran him down. Trampled to a pulp, all except his haid. Look aheah!—So help me Gawd!—Sterl, heah's a bullet hole!"

Sterl knelt to verify Red's diagnosis. He saw plainly the hole in the back of the young drover's head. His passion burned out the nausea caused by the ghastly remains of the fine boy. Then he espied the butt of a revolver almost concealed under Cedric's side. He pulled it out, shook off the sand, opened the chamber. Six empty cartridge shells dropped out.

At this juncture the others, surrounding Dann, arrived.

"Aye, Cedric it is, poor boy!" burst out Dann, his sonorous voice full of grief. "The mob rushed over him. He died on guard!"

"Dann, a blind man could see thet," drawled Red, whose habit was to grow cooler and deadlier as a hard situation tensely worked to its close. "It's a cinch Cedric died on guard. But he was shot in the back of his haid—murdered—before the herd run over him."

"Dann, it's true," put in Sterl, sternly. "There's the bullet hole."

"Larry, you examine thet hole," suggested Red, as he arose, drew out a scarf and wiped his gory hands. "I don't want no one heah to take my word. Nor Sterl's."

Larry, Drake and Slyter in turn minutely studied the wound in Cedric's skull, and solemnly agreed. Stanley Dann, with corded brow and clouded eyes, listened to them; but he maintained that it must have been an accident, that Cedric and the other drovers had been firing to hold the cattle back, that in the blackness of the storm anything could have happened.

Red Krehl eyed the leader with amazing tolerance and respect for that hard cowboy to exhibit at a hard time.

"Dann, from yore side of thet fence thet is good figgerin'," he said. "But I *know* Ormiston either shot Cedric or put somebody up to it. Let's don't argue any more. We're wastin' time, an' we'll know for shore pronto."

"Men, fetch shovels and a ground-cloth," ordered Dann. "We'll bury poor Cedric here on the spot of his brave stand. Keep it from the women!"

A shrill aboriginal yell startled the group. Friday appeared on the highest part of the bank, gesticulating violently.

"What the hell?" muttered Red. Then he mounted a fraction of a second behind Sterl. They raced for the black man, the drovers pounding behind.

With a long arm and a spear Friday pointed across the river. Sterl located an object crawling down a slight sandy slope.

"Man! White fella! Boss's brudder!" called Friday, dramatically.

Sterl wiped his eyes with steady hand.

"Look, pard. Make sure," he said, coolly. His faculties were swiftly settling for action.

"Friday's right," declared Red. "It's Eric Dann. Bad hurt from the way he moves!"

The man across the river flopped down a sandy slope, crawled, got to his knees to wave weakly.

"Ormiston has done for him," said Red.

"Red, strip King's saddle," flashed Sterl, leaping down to sit flat, and tear off spurs and boots. "I can land here, somewhere, if you rope me."

"I could rope yore cigarette. Rustle."

"Hazelton, what do you intend doing?" boomed Stanley Dann.

Sterl had no time for the leader then. Leaping

upon King he seized the bridle and wheeled the black
up the river. At a hard gallop he covered the few
hundred yards of open bank and hauled up. The flood
here came swirling to the edge of the bank. The
muddy torrent appeared crisscrossed with debris,
logs and brush.

King champed his bit and snorted. He knew what
he was in for and wanted to go at it. The drovers,
led by Red, arrived at this juncture.

Stanley Dann thundered, "Hazelton, don't throw
your life away. This is suicide!"

"Now!" pealed out Red Krehl, who had been
watching the current for a favorable moment.

Sterl released his strain on the bridle and
thumped King hard in the flanks. The black sprang
into action and took off in three jumps. As they hit
the current Sterl turned King downstream, quartering
for a point far down on the opposite shore. Again
and again, the backlash of the waves crashed over
the heads of horse and rider. They were strangled,
submerged, tossed. Logs grazed them, a huge piece
of drift rolled over them, a great gum tree bore down
on them, upending now its blunt trunk and now its
roots. But just as it was about to fall, the root caught
momentarily on the river bottom and the stout-
hearted King swam on. Two hundred yards of this,
and King struck the bottom. With a tremendous
heave and snort, he waded out.

When King emerged from the river to shake himself like a huge dog, Sterl did not at once see the
wounded man. Red's piercing yell and outstretched

arm gave him a clue, and presently he saw Dann sprawled upon the sand. Sterl dismounted and ran to him.

Eric Dann lay flat on his back, arms wide, eyes open. That part of his face not covered with dirt and blood was ashen white and clammy. His hair, matted with blood, failed to hide a wound—probably from a blow with the barrel of a gun, Sterl reflected.

"Dann, you've been beaten up," cried Sterl, anxiously. "Have you been shot, too?"

"Not that—I know of," replied Dann, in faint, hoarse tones. "Must have—been unconscious some time."

"Ormiston's work?"

"Yes. Bedford, too—set upon me."

"When?"

"About daylight."

Lifting the drover to his feet, Sterl found that he could not walk even when supported. So Sterl heaved him up to straddle the horse, and holding him there urged King up the river. The bed of this fork of the river widened up stream, with a correspondingly flatter bank. Sterl turned to look across. Red sat his horse in the middle of the open space where the cattle had run. He waved his lasso. Surveying the scene, Sterl knew that King could cross again, if there was no accident. He waded the black into the shallow water up to his haunches.

"Slide off, Eric. I don't want double weight on the horse. I'll drag you."

"Can you?"

"If you drown, so will I," said Sterl. "But we'll make it. All in the day's work."

He helped Eric to slide off feet first, then took hold of his shirt high up in front. He had to keep Dann's head out of the water when that was possible. Even with good fortune and management it would be submerged to the suffocating limit. Then he watched the river for a slatch, and urged King into deep water. Resting Dann's head on his leg he floated him along on the downstream side of the horse. King breasted the flood, held his black nose high, parted the mass of debris, and striking the current broadside on, sheered into the crested waves, magnificently powerful. The last of the heavy driftwood, in front of the open space, caught him and bore him on, submerged him, almost rolled him over. Then they were in the thick of the crashing turmoil, as wave on wave curled back to bury Sterl beneath its yellow crest. For the first time he hauled on the bridle. King responded and swam out of the rough water. Eric Dann hung limp, like a sack, in Sterl's grasp.

A ringing yell—Red was riding Duke at the water's edge, swinging a loop of the lasso round his head. They were fifty feet from the shore, drifting swiftly toward the lower end of a bare place.

"He's founderin', Sterl," yelled Red, at the top of his lungs. "Beat him on! Only a little farther!"

King had spent himself. Sterl knew he never needed to beat that horse. But he bent low and screamed, "You can make it! Only a little farther! *Oh, King!*"

The gallant horse responded. A last violent spurt, a last plunge, his head rose high—then the lasso whipped out and spread, to hiss and tighten with a crack round horse and rider. Red and the drovers dragged them ashore. Strong hands pulled Sterl and his burden up on the bank. Red released Sterl from the noose.

Dann had almost drowned. But rubbing and manipulation brought him to. Then a drover put a black bottle to his lips.

"Boss, he's been beaten on the head—with a gun," said Sterl, panting for breath. "Told me Ormiston and Bedford did it—about daylight. Then they left."

"Boss, get his story," cut in Red, cool and hard. "Let him talk before he croaks or goes out of his haid."

"But now that his life is saved—" remonstrated the leader.

"Hellsfire!" flashed the cowboy. "We're goin' after Ormiston. Hurry. Let him talk. Help us thet much."

"Eric, tell me," interposed Sterl. "It may help. When did you drive your wagon across to Ormiston's camp?"

"Last night—at dusk—before the storm broke," whispered Dann.

"What for?"

"I wanted to be—on that side—to go with Ormiston."

"Did you know he didn't want you?"

"Not till daylight. Then I realized—what he was. Bushranger!—Ash Pell! That's his real name. Notorious Queensland bushranger! We've heard of him. I heard Jack and Bedford call him by his name. I found out they had rushed—our mob—stolen our horses. I confronted him—then they hit me!"

"Did you know he had Beryl there?"

"He told me. She had come willingly.—When I came to—my senses—they were gone. I crawled down—to the bank."

Stanley Dann swayed like a great tree uprooted.

"God forgive my ignorance—my stubbornness! God forgive me for all except my faith in man! Shall that fail because some men are evil? Oh, my little Beryl!"

"Dann, we'll fetch her back," said Sterl. "Red, see if King's all right."

"Me go alonga you," said Friday, simply.

"Good.—Red, we've got some meat and bread. Dried fruit, too. They'll get wet, but no matter. Dan how many of your drovers carry rifles on their saddles?"

"Not one of those drovers who—who deserted me—turned bushrangers—perverted by that villain's promises."

"Red, I remember Ormiston had rifles in his wagon."

"Yes. Small bore. An' he couldn't hit a barn door!"

"Sterl, let me go," entreated Larry. "They murdered my friend—Let me go."

"You bet," retorted Sterl. Larry might never have ridden on a deadly chase, but he had a light in his hawk eyes that was sufficient for Sterl.

Drake addressed himself to their leader. "Mr. Dann, I couldn't let these boys go alone. What Hazelton does we can do—or try."

"Drake, you're on," rang out Sterl. "One more man. Rollie, are you game? There'll be some hard riding—and a little gunplay."

"Hazelton, I was about to ask you," returned Roland, pale and resolute.

"Here, fellows!" ejaculated Sterl, as the other drovers chimed in eagerly. "Three men are plenty. Thanks though. You're real pards. Mr. Dann, I'd advise packing your brother back to camp."

Dann gave the order to his drovers. Then he addressed the cowboys, not with his usual direct assurance.

"If you come up with Ormiston and his drovers then—there will be violence?" went on Dann, swallowing hard. He was on strange ground here.

"For cripe's sake boss!" burst out the cowboy, "Ormiston has damn near croaked yore brother! He has killed one of our drovers and corrupted a lot of yours an' raided yore cattle! An' as for Beryl—I swear to you it's wuss than if she *did* elope with him. Hell no! There won't be any violence! We'll pay our respects, drink some tea with him, an'..." Here Red lost his voice.

"What will you do?" thundered Dann, roused by the cowboy's stinging irony.

Sterl, having got his boots and spurs on, rose to face their leader. He was as cool as Red had been hot.

"Dann, we will hang Ormiston if possible. But *kill* him in any event! And his right-hand men! Your drovers will make a run for it—which may save them. With Beryl to care for we can't chase a lot of white-livered suckers all over the place. You may expect us back with Beryl by nightfall, or tomorrow at the latest."

"My God! You petrify me, Hazelton. But you have never failed me. Nor has Krehl. Go! Bring back Beryl. I leave the decision to you!"

He stalked away, leading his horse.

19

*T*HE five white avengers, picking a relatively calm stretch, swam their horses across the river. Friday crossed by holding onto King's tail and floating behind. Ormiston, Sterl reflected, had probably assumed that the flooded river was an insurmountable barrier to pursuit. There came a slight change in the temperature, the cool air moderating, and the drizzle increasing to rain. The gray overcast sky darkened The water level had risen another foot. Owing to the rain, Dann's wagon had not burned up completely, but the canvas cover was partly destroyed, and some of the contents. Half of the load had evidently been carried away. There was no sign of team or harness.

"Ormiston was kinda rarin' to go, huh?" drawled Red.

They rode out of the timber. Broad wheel tracks curved away to the east.

"Three wagons," said Red, thinking aloud. "All loaded heavy. Ten or twelve miles a day over this ground is about all they could do. Three drivers, which I reckon will be Ormiston, Jack, an' Bedford. They'll drive ahaid of the cattle."

"Righto, Red. Say they left camp an hour or so after daybreak," rejoined Sterl. "Anybody got the time?"

"Half after nine," replied Drake.

Sterl and his riders set off at a lope, with the aborigine running along easily. He had a marvelous stride and he covered ground as smoothly as an Indian. Red followed the wheel tracks for a mile, until they disappeared under the trampling hoofmarks of the cattle. Presently the broad, heavy track of the herd that had been raided across the river joined the main mob.

"One of them there little ridges ahaid will.... Look heah!" Red leaped out of his saddle and bent to pick up something. It was one of the handkerchiefs Red had given Beryl for Christmas. When he carefully stowed the handkerchief away inside his leather coat Sterl thought he would not have been in that bushranger's boots for anything in the whole world.

They rode on to where the mob track curved to the left away from the first ridge. Once beyond that, the country was open bushland, grassy plains, patches of scrub, scattered gum trees with rolling country beyond.

Sterl took note of their three Australian companions. Drake was the only one who was not overexcited. Being a mature man, he had probably seen some hard days. But Larry and Rollie, stalwart young outdoor men though they were, had certainly never shot at a man in their lives. Sterl know how they felt. Red Krehl was always one to be cool and provocative in the face of a fight, but now he looked fierce and relentless.

The rain had let up to a fine mist when the posse climbed another rocky edge. Distance, heights, lowlands preserved their gray-green monotony, but all were magnified. And in the center of a long valley the mob of cattle stood out strikingly clear for so dark a day. The pursuers gazed in silence, each occupied with his own thoughts, until Red spoke:

"Four or five miles, mebbe. I figger they're pushin, the herd—not grazin' atall."

"I can't see any wagons," added Larry "Too far."

Friday touched Sterl's arm. He extended his bundle of long spears.

"Wagons. Alonga dere," and he pointed.

"Ahuh! How far, pard?" And Sterl thought surely that was the only instance in Red Krehl's life when the Texan had called a black man his partner.

"Close up," replied the black.

"Red, the wagons are in front of the cattle," interposed Sterl.

"Jest too bad. Mister Bushranger Ormiston shore

figgers things good for us," returned the cowboy. Then he bent a keen calculating gaze upon the herd of cattle in its relation to landmarks on each side. "Reckon there's plenty of cover all along heah to the left. Come on, fellers. It's gettin' kinda hot."

They descended the ridge on its steep side. Here Red told Friday to get up behind Sterl. The black understood, but he shook his head.

"Come, Friday," called Sterl, and extended his hand. "Look out!—For cripe's sake don't stick me with your spears!" He helped the aborigine to a place astride King behind the saddle. "Hang on to me," he concluded.

Red led off, heading due west from that ridge. They crossed the flat to find a pass between two low ridges, then turned east again. It was thicker bush-land, through which the cowboy led in a zigzag course. Five miles, more or less, of this; then he halted to the left of another ridge.

"Reckon this heah is ahaid of the herd an' drovers. You can all wait heah while I take a look-see."

He took a slanting course up the ridge. Friday had slid off King at once, and if his dark visage could have expressed distaste it would have done so then.

"Me tinkit hoss no good," he said.

Sterl's grimness broke at this, but the perturbed drovers did not even crack a smile.

"What will we do next?" asked Larry, his voice not quite natural.

"I don't know what Red will advise. Depends on the lay of the land. But if there's any chance for a fight he'll have us in it pronto."

"We—we'll attack them?" queried Rollie.

"I rather think so!"

Red appeared, riding back. As he reined Duke in, as was characteristic of him, he lighted a cigarette before he spoke.

"Jest couldn't be better. Herd about a couple miles below us, close to this side of the valley. Bunch of hosses behind. All the six drovers ridin' behind, bunched close, as if they had lots to talk about, an' they're goin' to pass less'n a hundred yards from a patch of brush right around this corner of the ridge."

He paused, puffed clouds of smoke that obscured his lean, red face and fire-blue eyes, and presently resumed, this time cooler and sharper.

"Heah's the deal. This setup will be duck soup. Sterl an' me, with Friday, will ride ahaid, hell-bent for election, an' get in front of the wagons. Drake, you take Larry an' Rollie, ride around this corner, then lead yore hosses back to the thicket you'll see. Keep out of sight. Crawl through thet brush to the edge, wait for the herd to pass by, an' the drovers to come up even with you. I reckon thet's about all."

"All right, Krehl. We'll do it," declared Drake, firmly. "Looks a good deal luckier than I hoped for."

"You'll have to give us the time it takes for the herd an' drovers to come up. We gotta rustle. Let's don't argue. Sterl, what say?"

"Made to order for us," returned Sterl, darkly.

Larry burst out: "Let's not waste time. We'll do it, Krehl!" This young man had never shot at more than a kangaroo. Now he realized that he was going out to shoot at his fellow men, and be shot at. He was trembling but courageous.

"Wait!" ejaculated Rollie, hoarsely. "*What* will we do?"

Red eyed the big drover in supreme disdain. Then he spoke with a deadly softness. "Wal, Rollie, you might wave yore scarf an' call, Woo-hoo!"

"Don't cast aspersions upon me, you cowboy blighter!" retorted Rollie, angrily.

"Hellsfire, then! Come out of yore trance. This is a man hunt. These drovers you've hobnobbed with, mebbe, air murderin' traitors—cattle an' hoss thieves! I've had to help hang more'n one cowboy friend thet I reckoned was a clean honest chap, when he'd come to be a low-down rustler. Same, mebbe, between you boys an' Dann's drovers. It'll be tough. But it's gotta be done."

"Krehl, I can take orders. Stop ranting in your lingo, and give them."

"Short an' sweet. Think of yore pard Cedric. Think of Beryl Dann, who's in Ormiston's hands. Cut loose with yore rifles an' *kill* them drovers. If you cain't down 'em pronto, fork yore hosses an' ride them down."

"Thanks. I understand you a little better," returned Rollie, gray of face.

"Sterl, I had to rake them, but I reckon now they'll give a good account of themselves," said Red, as he watched the three Australians ride away. "Rustle now. Get Friday up an' hang onto him."

Unwilling or not the black had to get up behind Sterl. "Hold those spears low, like that," shouted Sterl, and he reached around with right arm to clasp Friday. "Okay, pard, see if you can run away from King."

The cowboy led off, and Sterl knew what he had suspected would be a fact—that he and Friday were in for a ride. Another hard downpour, right in their faces, made accurate vision difficult. Red Krehl ran Duke on the open stretches, loped him through the brush, jumped him over logs. Friday had a bear clutch on Sterl, yet the black all but fell off several times. The slapping of wet branches and the crackling of saplings added to the pain and discomfort, if no more. Then Red pulled Duke to a slower gait and headed to the right. They had come into bushland again. Red did not halt until he got to the edge of the timber. The three wagons were in plain sight out upon the open, the first about a mile distant, and the other two farther out, but still separated.

"Haidin' almost straight for us," soliloquized Red.

Friday fell off from behind Sterl, undoubtedly pretty much mauled. He rubbed his lean wet legs.

"Tinkit hoss bad!" he remarked.

Then, straightening up, he took a long look at the three wagons and pointed.

"Ormiston wagon dere farder. Hosses alonga 'imm," he said.

"Thet *hombre* last, huh? Come on, Sterl."

Red turned back into the bush, somewhat away

from the course he decided the first wagon driver would take. The rain lessened again. Perhaps two miles back from the open, Red halted.

"Far enough, I reckon, pard," he said, "now... Say, where in the hell did Friday go to?"

"I never noticed. But he won't cramp us, Red. Don't worry."

"All I'm worryin' about is thet he'll get to Ormiston before I do," ground out Red.

"Hurry. What's your plan?"

"I'll ride back aways. Let the first wagon go by me, onless it should happen to be Ormiston. You wait about heah someplace. An' when thet wagon comes up introduce yoreself either to Jack or Bedford.... Then you better rustle back after me."

"You'll time it to meet that second wagon just about when the first one gets up to me?"

"I reckon. But it's all over 'cept the fireworks."

Red rode off under the dripping gums, keeping to the left of the expected wagon line, and soon disappeared in the gray-green bush. Sterl chose as cover some gum saplings, close together and leafy enough to make a comparatively safe hiding place. He dismounted, and drawing his rifle from its saddle sheath removed the oilskin cover and put it in his pocket. Then he leaned the rifle against the largest sapling, and with a quieting hand on King peered back through the drenched bushland.

With a tense wait like this, it was almost impossible not to think. He had, he reflected, no dislike for this job and no compunction. He would not shoot from ambush, although he had retaliated upon red-skins by that very act. But here, he wanted to face Jack or Bedford.

Naturally, however, he had concern for his comrade. Sterl would have preferred to be with Red, for more than one reason. Beryl's life might be at stake. Because of that, Red could be capable of any rash act, even to a sacrifice of himself. Then again, Sterl wanted powerfully to see Ormiston meet the cowboy.

King suddenly vibrated slightly and shot up his ears. He had heard something.

"Quiet!" whispered Sterl, and patted the wet neck. "Want to spoil the party?"

More moments passed before Sterl's alert ear caught a creaking of wheels. King threw up his head. He had been well trained, but not to stand still and keep silent. Sterl stepped to his head and held him. A thud of hoofs sounded through the silent bush. At last a sight of four horses plodding along, then a canvas-topped wagon, then a burly driver, reins and whip in hands. It was Jack. A slight cold chill quivered over Sterl. But he thought fast. He would wait until the team had come almost opposite him, then step out, confront Jack and force him to draw.

A distant gunshot rang out, spiteful, ripping asunder the bushland silence. Red's .45 Colt speaking. Almost at once a duller heavier shot.

The drover Jack hauled his four horses to a dead stop, and dropped the reins. He was in the clear, with the wagon on level and bare ground. Sterl saw the man sweep out a hand to grasp a rifle, then peer all around.

At this instant King let out a loud neigh, and the other horses answered. Jack's gaze fixed upon King. Quick as thought he leaped out of the wagon. As Sterl plunged to get low down behind a log the drover fired from behind the left front wheel. The bullet whistled closer to King than it did to Sterl. Fearful that Jack might kill the horse, Sterl took a snapshot at the only part of the wheel he could see—the under rim and a section of spokes. His bullet struck with a thud, to spang away into the bush. It must have stung the drover's foot, or come too close, for he leaped away to the rear end of the wagon. His boots were in plain sight down between the two right wheels. And Sterl's second shot hit one of them. The drover flopped down like a crippled chicken, bawling frightfully, and crawled behind the only gum tree near. The trunk was not broad enough wholly to protect his body. But he knelt low, risking that. He had Sterl marked but could not see him. Sterl tried a ruse as old as wars. He stuck up his sombrero. Jack fired, once and again. His second shot knocked Sterl's sombrero flat. Then the drover rashly stood up and stuck his rifle, his shoulder, and half of his head out from behind the tree. Sterl drew a careful bead on the one baleful eye visible, like a hole in a mask, and fired. Jack pitched to one side of the tree and his rifle flew to the other.

Sterl worked the lever of his rifle, waited a moment, then snatched up his sombrero and leaped on

King. The excited horse was hard to hold. Sterl rode by the wagon. A glance at the drover lying on his back, one eye blank and the other set hideously, and Sterl took up the wheel tracks and raced through the bushland.

It grew more open. In less than half a mile he sighted another wagon, standing still, the foremost team of horses plunging. Sterl drew closer and was pulling King to a slower gait when again he heard gunshots, and not far away. Two revolvers of different caliber! No rifle shot! Throwing caution to the winds he struck the steel into King's flanks. As the black tore on at top speed, and reached the leading wagon, Sterl saw the drover Bedford hanging head first over the right wheel. His feet had caught somewhere. In the middle of his broad back his gray shirt showed a huge bloody patch. Red had shot him through from front to back.

The third and last wagon! It had been pulled half broadside across the line of wheel tracks. Horses tethered to the rear were plunging. Even at that distance and through a drizzling rain, Sterl recognized Jester.

The driver's seat was vacant. No one in sight! But another shot cracked. The cowboy was alive! Sterl drove King down upon the wagon with tremendous speed.

Suddenly to Sterl's right and ahead, he caught the gleam of something white, something red, something black. There was a bare glade close ahead—a huge gum towering over the wagon—a low branch sweeping down. Through the thin foliage that white thing moved. And a woman's scream, high-pitched, piercing, rent the air.

Sterl lay back with all his might upon the bridle. King plunged to slide on his haunches into the glade.

Red, his temple bloody, was lying in the middle of the bare spot, raised on his left elbow, his gun extended, his posture unnatural. In a flash Sterl was out of his saddle.

The white thing was Beryl Dann, half nude, in the grasp of Ormiston. A black blanket had slipped to her knees. Ormiston crouched behind her, left arm around her middle. In his right he had a gun leveled at Red. As he fired, the girl threw up his arm. She shrieked in terror, in fury. And she fought the drover like a panther. The red thing near them was Leslie's horse Sorrel, saddled and bridled. Ormiston had tried to get away on that horse.

"Kill him—Red—Don't mind me!" panted the girl, wildly.

STERL leveled a cocked gun, but dared not risk firing. Only a portion of Ormiston's body projected from behind the desperately struggling girl.

She hung onto Ormiston's rigid arm as he lifted her in his effort to align his gun upon Krehl. He fired. Dust and gravel flew up into the cowboy's face. Red rolled convulsively over and over, as if struck. Sterl just barely held himself back from a rash onslaught at the drover. But Red came out of that roll to lie flat with his gun forward.

"Hurry, St— erll!" shrieked the girl, frantically.

Then the drover espied Sterl, and struggled to aim at him. Sterl leaped to dive behind a rock. On his knees he thrust his gun over the top.

He had time to see Beryl's last frenzied struggle to destroy the bushranger's aim. Then she collapsed, arms, head and shoulders hanging down, supported by Ormiston's clutching clasp. Ormiston's stooping caused him to bend his left leg, and his knee became exposed. Red's gun cracked. Sterl heard the bullet thud into flesh. That shot of Red's had broken his aim. Cursing savagely the bushranger gathered his forces for another attempt.

Sterl's finger quivered on the trigger, in the act of imperiling Beryl's life to save Red's. Then behind him a strange, tussling sound checked his firing. *Whizz!* A dark streak flashed across his line of vision. *Chuck!* Sterl's taut senses registered the sickening thud of something rending flesh.

Ormiston uttered a strangling, inhuman yell and sprang up as if galvanized. His gun went flying to the ground. Beryl dropped from his hold like an empty sack. His hands went up, clutching as a drowning man might at straws. An aborgine spear stuck out two feet beyond his throat. Its long end still quivered. Ormiston's hands tore at it, broke the shaft square off.

"Friday!" yelled Sterl, as he leaped from behind the rock. "Look, Red, look! Friday has done for him!"

Red got up, bloody-faced and grim as death. Blood flowed from a shot in his head and his left shoulder. But he showed no weakness. As he strode toward the whirling Ormiston, swift footfalls thudded behind Sterl, and Friday came leaping into the open. He held a long spear low down.

"Hold on, Friday!" yelled Red, blocking the aborigine. "No go with thet. You're gonna help me with a little necktie party!"

Sterl could not turn his sight from the spectacle of the doomed Ormiston. He reeled and swayed like a drunken man, his hands still tearing at the spearhead. A red-tinged froth issued from his mouth. He fell, to bound up again with marvelous vitality. Sterl ran over and kicked Ormiston's gun into the grass. And again his trigger finger pressed quiveringly as the bushranger made ghastly inarticulate sounds and plunged like a wounded bull.

Red's jangling footfalls sounded behind Sterl, just as Ormiston's protruding eyes fell upon Beryl. She was on her knees trying to pluck up the blanket over her bare shoulders. He made at her, insane to drag even her to perdition. But before Sterl could shoot, a hissing lasso shot out. The noose fell over Ormiston's head. Red gave the rope a tremendous pull. Ormiston lunged backward, to fall face upward, his arms upflung, and that queer vociferation ended abruptly.

"Lend a hand, Friday," shouted the cowboy. "Don't forget how this white trash treated you!"

The black leaped to Red's assistance. They dragged the bushranger under the spreading arm of the huge gum tree. The cowboy paused there to gaze down at his victim.

"Rustler, you swing! Jest the same as any cattle thief in my country! But bad as they came, I never seen one as low down as you!"

Red threw the free end of his lasso up over a low branch and caught it as it fell.

"Git in an' help me, Friday! Pull, you black man who's shore no nigger! All my life I'll love you for this day's work. Ha! There you air, Ormiston! Swing an' kick!"

Sterl wrenched his gaze from the gruesome spectacle and wheeled to Beryl. She was on her knees, the blanket slack in her nerveless hands, her big blue eyes fixed in horror.

"Beryl! Don't look!" cried Sterl, sheathing his gun and rushing to her. "Shut your eyes, Beryl. It's—all over. You're saved. And he...It's justice, no matter...."

But he realized that she had fainted. He carried her to the wagon, laid her up in the seat out of the rain and tucked the blanket around her bare feet. Her eyes fluttered open. "Okay now?" inquired Sterl. She nodded. "Then lie here awhile until you get yourself together. No more danger." And he drew away.

A jingling step, and he turned to see Red approaching. Beyond, Friday appeared, gazing fixedly up at the limp figure in dark relief against the gray sky.

"Close shave, pard," said Red, just a little huskily, as he wiped his bloody hands with his scarf, and glanced up to see Beryl's pale, quiet face. Sterl indicated by a gesture that the cowboy should leave her alone.

"Gosh! I don't recall a closer shave!" ejaculated, Red. "But wasn't Beryl the game kid? She kept him from borin' me a second time. She fainted! I'm glad she didn't see the end of it."

"But she did, Red. She did! She saw it all, believe me!"

"Aw, thet's too bad. But, pard, did you get it? Beryl had on only her nightgown. Thet *hombre* stole her from her bed. She didn't run off with him!"

"Yes, I savvied that, Red, and I never was any gladder in my life.... But you're all shot up. Let me see!"

"They'd have to be a hell of a lot wuss than they air to croak me *now*. Let me tell you. When I ran down on Bedford he saw me comin', an' he was ready for me. I bored him, but damn if he didn't hit me heah in this shoulder. Ormiston was trying to get away with Beryl on the sorrel there when I run in on him. Beryl was fightin' him. But for her I'd shore have bored him before he got in thet first shot. It knocked me flat. Better look these bullet holes over an' tie them up. This one on my haid hurts like hell."

Examination disclosed in Red's head, a groove that cut through the scalp, but had not touched the skull, and another in his left shoulder, high up. The bullet had lodged just under the skin on the far side. It would have to be cut out, but Sterl left that operation for camp, and bound his scarf tightly around the wound.

"We'd better leave the other one open," he said. "Hello, what's that?"

Red rose up to listen. "Fag end of a stampede,

I'd say. Look out for Beryl. I'll wrangle the horses. Come, Friday."

The black ran off under the gums to get Duke, while Sterl drew King and the sorrel back away from the open. A bobbing line of cattle hove in sight down through the brush, loping along wearily.

"Wal, they might have started wild, but they're bein' chased now," said Red. "Get the rifles heah pard, an' if it happens to be any of Ormiston's outfit, they'll never get nowhere."

On a front so wide that Sterl could just make out the far end, a herd of cattle came loping past, scattered and bawling, almost ready to drop.

"Coupla of thousand haid, shore as you're born," said Red when they had passed. "Thet's sort of queer. I recognized that bull. Pard, thet was the bunch raided out of Dann's last night!"

"Might be."

"Heah comes some riders. Two! Thet's Larry's hoss. An' Rollie's too. But Drake ain't with them."

From some hundred paces away the riders espied the bushranger swinging with horrible significance, and this brought them to a quick halt. Then they rode slowly up, their eyes gleaming, their lips tight.

"Beryl?" queried Larry, hopefully.

"She's up theah, on the seat, comin' out of a daid faint."

Larry slumped out of his saddle to sit down like a man whose legs were wobbly. Sterl did not like the looks of either of the drovers.

"Where's Drake?"

"He wouldn't shoot barefaced from ambush," replied Larry, tragically. "Rol and I didn't know it though, till right at the last, he ran out, yelled at Anderson and Henley. They drew their revolvers and he shot them both off their horses. I—I killed Buckley. Herdman and Smith had begun to shoot. It was Herdman, I think, who hit Drake and did for him. Rol's horse was shot from under him. The mob rushed, ran us back into the brush. Herdman and Smith had to ride hard. But they got around them and headed off to the east. We couldn't chase them until the cattle had run by. Then it was too late."

"Ahuh. Too bad about Drake. Air you shore he was daid?"

"There was no doubt of that."

"It's orful tough, Larry. I reckon Sterl an' me feel for you. But the fact is, we got off lucky."

"Jack and—Bedford?"

"They beat Ormiston to hell pretty considerable."

"There's only one thing to do now," said Sterl. "Take Beryl back to camp pronto. You're all shot up, too. We've got to cross that infernal river before dark."

Stanley Dann, the Slyters, with Heald and Monkton, and one of Dann's drovers stood on the east bank, awaited their landing, visibly laboring under extreme excitement and fear.

"My—daughter?" asked Dann, almost voiceless.

"Safe," replied Sterl, not looking at him, and leaped to the ground. He waved his sombrero to Red and Larry. Then as they waded in, Sterl untied his lasso.

"Get your rope ready," he said to Rollie.

Sterl had been aware of Leslie's presence close beside him and a little behind. Once she touched him with a timid hand, as though to see if he were really back in the flesh. They were all talking except Leslie. Finally she spoke in her deep contralto: "Sterl! ... Sterl? ..."

Then he looked around and down upon her, meaning to be kind, trying to smile as he said: "Hello, kid!" but she instinctively recoiled from his face. Sterl did not marvel at that. It had happened before to girls who approached him after a hard job. But how could he help it? Men had to kill other men! The wonder in him was that it made any difference in his face and look.

Sterl turned to watch the swimming horses as they entered the current. Sorrel, and Leslie's other horses, hesitated but finally followed. "Rollie, go below me.... Everybody get back so I can swing this rope."

Red and Larry were ten feet apart, heading evenly into the current. The lean noses came on abreast, and the shoulders of the riders rose into plain sight. The onlookers watched, tense and breathless, while the horses swept down with the current, at last to forge out of it, and come straight for the bank. A cheer of released emotions rent the air. Duke, as powerful as if he had not already performed miracles that day, waded out in King's tracks. To make

sure, Sterl roped him and hauled lustily to help him
pound up the bank. Rollie helped Larry. No one
thought of Leslie's four horses, now making for shore.

Stanley Dann crowded close, his bearded jaw
wobbling, his great arms outstretched. With one
shaking hand, Red unfolded the dripping slicker over
Beryl and let it fall away from her white face. If her
eyes had not been wide open, she would have looked
like a drowned girl.

Red lifted her and bent down to yield her to her
father's eager arms.

"Dann, heah's yore girl—safe—an' sound," said
Red, in a queer voice Sterl had never heard before.
"An' thet lets me out!"

What did the fool cowboy mean by that speech,
wondered Sterl? Red had settled some debt to himself, not to anyone else.

"Ormiston?" boomed the drover.

"Wal, the last we seen of thet bushranger, he
was dancin'. Yep, dancin' on thin air!" And with that,
passion appeared to have spent its force as well as
Red's strength. "Where the hell air—you—pard?" he
went on, in a strangely altered tone. "I—cain't—see
you. . . . Aw, I—get it. . . . Heah's where—I cash!"

His staring blue eyes, as blank as dead furnaces,
told their own story. He swayed and fell into Sterl's
arms.

*L*ARRY helped Sterl carry Red across to Slyter's camp, and into their tent. For Sterl all
this slow walk was fraught with icy panic. It
might well be that Red had been more severely
wounded than a superficial examination had shown.
How like Red Krehl to have such a finish! The fool
cowboy would have died at Beryl's feet, to give the
vain beauty everlasting remorse and grief.

"Get hot water—Larry," he ordered. They undressed Red, rubbed him dry, forced whisky between
his teeth. Then Sterl unbound the wounds, washed
them thoroughly, ruthlessly cut open the one on his
back, and extracted the heavy bullet. It hàd gone
under his collarbone, to stop just beneath the surface. Sterl dressed the shoulder injury, bandaged it,

and went on with steadying hands to that bullet groove in Red's scalp. Sterl could not be fearful over either wound. He had seen the cowboy laugh at scratches like this. But Sterl found evidence that Red had bled freely all during the ride back to the river. The water had washed him clean, but one of his boots was half full of diluted blood. There lay the danger!

Sterl took a long pull at the flask Larry offered. It burned the coldness out of his vitals. Then he rubbed himself thoroughly and got into dry clothes.

"I'd feel all right, if only Red . . ." he choked over the hope. He went out. It was almost dark and the rain still fell steadily. Under Bill's shelter, a bright blaze gleamed with shining rays through the rain. Bill had steaming vessels upon the gridiron.

"Eat and drink, lad," said Slyter. "We have to go on, you know. . . . How is Red?"

"Bad. Bled almost to death. . . . But I hope—I—I believe he'll recover. . . . How did the kid take the return of her horses?"

"Sterl, you wouldn't believe it—the way that girl cried over them. . . . But it was a breakdown, after all this day's strain, and the tremendous relief of your return."

"Of course! Leslie is not one to crack easily."

"My son, I very much fear Leslie is in love with you."

"Slyter, I fear that, too," replied Sterl, ponderingly, a little bitterly. "I hope, though, that it isn't quite so bad as what happened to Beryl."

"My wife says it's good. We have trusted you, Hazelton."

"Thanks, my friend. That'll help some."

The return of Slyter's womenfolk put an end to that intimate talk, much to Sterl's relief. They threw off wet coats and stood before the fire, Leslie with her back turned and her head down.

"Leslie, how is Beryl?" asked Sterl.

"I don't know. She—she frightened me," replied the girl, strangely.

"How is your friend Red? He looked terribly the worse for this day's work," interrupted Mrs. Slyter.

Sterl briefly told them his hopes for Red, omitting his fears. But that sharp-eyed psychic, Leslie, did not believe him. When Sterl looked at her she averted her piercing gaze.

"Who shot him?" rang out Leslie, suddenly.

"Yes, you'll have to be told about it all, I suppose," returned Sterl, in sober thoughtfulness. "Bedford shot Red first in the shoulder—and then Ormiston nicked his head. Not serious wounds for a cowboy. But Red lost so much blood!"

"I heard Red say to Mr. Dann—that about Ormiston dancing on thin air. I know....But Bedford?"

Slyter interposed: "Leslie, wait until tomorrow. Sterl is worn to a frazzle."

Sterl wanted to get part of it over with and he bluntly told Leslie that Red had killed Bedford.

"What did *you* do?" queried this incorrigible young woman, unflinchingly.

"Well, I was there when it happened." That

seemed to be all the satisfaction Sterl could accord the girl at the time.

"Thanks, Sterl. Please forgive my curiosity. But I must tell you that I asked Friday."

"Oh, no. . . . Leslie!" exclaimed Sterl, taken aback.

"Yes. I asked him what happened to Ormiston. He said: 'Friday spearum. Red shootum. Me alonga Red hangum neck. . . . Ormiston kick like hellum. . . . Then imm die!'"

It was not so much Friday's graphic and raw words that shocked Sterl as the girl's betrayal of the element.

"Retribution!" added Mrs. Slyter, in a moment. "He stole Beryl from her bed. I'll never forgive myself for believing she ran off with him!"

"Neither will I, Mrs. Slyter," said Sterl, in poignant regret.

"I was afraid of it," put in the girl, frankly.

"Sterl, Dann will want to see you. Let us go now, before Les and Mum loosen up," suggested Slyter.

Glad to escape, though with a feeling for Leslie that he did not wish to analyze, Sterl accompanied the drover through the dark and rain. They found Dann at his table under a lighted shelter. Before him lay papers, watches, guns, money and money belts.

"Hazelton, do I need to thank you?" asked Dann, his rich voice thick.

"No, boss. All I pray for is Red's recovery."

"Please God, that wonderful cowboy lives! Slyter, our erstwhile partner had thousands of pounds, some of which I recognize as belonging to Woolcott and Hathaway and put aside for their heirs. I appropriated from Ormiston's money what I consider fair for my loss. Do you agree that the rest should go to the cowboys, and Larry, and Roland?"

"I do, most heartily," rang out Slyter.

"Not any for me, friends," interposed Sterl. "But I'll take it for Red. He deserves it. He uncovered this bushranger. He made our plan today, saved Beryl—and hanged Ormiston."

"Terrible, yet—yet. . . . I'll want your story presently. I've heard that of Larry and Roland. Poor Drake! Too brave, too rash! You may not know that Drake was friendly with both Anderson and Henley. That may account—what a pity he had to find them unworthy—to see them seduced by a notorious bushranger—and kill them! Yet how magnificent!"

"Boss, if you don't mind, I'd like to have Ormiston's gun," said Sterl, restrainedly.

"You're welcome to it. Now for your story, Sterl."

Sterl told it as briefly as possible. Dann took the narrative as one who at last understood the villainy of evil men and the righteous and terrible wrath of hard avengers.

"I'm not one to rail at the dispensation of Providence," said the leader, at length. "How singularly fortunate we have been! I've a mind to let well enough alone, except to try to save the mob that rushed to its old grazing ground across the river."

"That can be done, Dann, as soon as the river drops. But I think you're wise not to attempt mustering the cattle that stampeded by us up there.

Those two drovers will escape with one wagon and some of Ormiston's horses. Let them go, Dann. We have more cattle now than we can handle. And fewer drovers!"

"Righto, Hazelton. But I'll send Larry and four men up there tomorrow, to fetch back the other two wagons. Later, we'll gather in that mob which obligingly rushed back to us. They won't leave that fine grazing over there."

Sterl and Slyter left the chief, to return to their camp. "He was hit below the belt, Hazelton," said Slyter, "but never a word! I wonder what will happen next?"

"All our troubles are not over, boss. Red would say, 'Wal, the wurst is yet to come!' By the way, how is Eric Dann?"

"He'll be around in a few days. Good night. It has been a day. Never mind guard duty while Krehl needs attention."

Friday loomed up in the dark.

"Has he been quiet, Friday?"

"All same imm like dead. But imm strong, like black fella. No die."

Sterl struck a match in the darkness of his tent, and lighted his candle. Indeed Red looked like a corpse, but he was breathing and his heart beat steadily. "If he only hangs on till tomorrow!" whispered Sterl, fervently, and that was indeed a prayer. Sterl undressed, which was a luxury that had been difficult of late; and when he stretched out he felt as if he would never move again. His last act was to reach for the candle and blow it out.

Stress of emotion, no doubt, had more to do with his prostration than the sleepless night and strenuous day. He caught himself listening for Red's breathing. But sleepy as he was, he could not arrive at the point of oblivion. That speech of the cowboy's, when he delivered Beryl into her father's arms, haunted Sterl. It meant, he deduced, that Red had withstood love and shame and insult and humiliation and torture for willful and vain Beryl Dann; in the face of opposition and antagonism he had killed Ormiston to save the girl. And that had let Red out! Yet Red was tenderhearted to a fault, and never had Sterl, in their twelve years of trail driving, seen him so terribly in love before.... Outworn nature conquered at last.

When Sterl awakened day had broken and the rain had ceased temporarily. In the gloom he saw Red lying exactly as he had seen him hours ago. He crawled out of bed to bend over his friend, and his acute sensibilities registered a stronger heartbeat. But now pneumonia must be reckoned with—a disease likely to fasten upon a man so wounded and exposed.

Sterl got out in time to see five horsemen across the river riding at a brisk trot to the east—the drovers Dann had sent after the wagons and horses, of course.

While he ate breakfast with Slyter, Mrs. Slyter approached from Beryl's wagon. Her usual brightness was lacking.

"Mum, you don't look reassuring," said Slyter, anxiously. "At midnight, Leslie said Beryl was sleeping."

"Beryl has been shocked beyond her strength—any sensitive woman's strength," returned Mrs. Slyter, gravely. "She's violently delirious. I fear she'll go insane or die."

Leslie, pale but composed, arrived in time to hear this.

"What do you think, Sterl?" she asked.

"Well, it's the cold gray dawn after two terrible nights with an awful day between. We can at least think clearly. Of course I don't know what Beryl had to endure before we appeared on the scene, but what happened afterward was enough to tax any girl's strength." Here Sterl described, sparing no detail, Beryl's fight with the bushranger, to keep him from killing Red, and the gruesome aftermath.

"Beryl was game and she went the limit," he added. "If she had fainted when Friday speared Ormiston, it would not have been so bad for her. But she saw Ormiston plunge around, like a crazy bull. ...She saw—all the rest. I ran to shut out that sight. And it was only then that she fainted."

"Mercy!" gasped Mrs. Slyter.

"I'd like to have been there," declared Leslie Slyter, with an unnatural calm that was belied by the piercing glint in her hazel eyes.

"Talk sense, you wild creature!" returned her mother.

Sterl had not at all intended such a disclosure,

and felt at a loss to understand why he had yielded to the impulse. If it was to see Leslie's reaction, however, he had been strangely justified.

Toward what would have been sunset if there had been any sun, Sterl admitted Dann to the tent. The leader bent over the cowboy, listened to his breathing and heart, studied his stone-cold face. Then he said: "I've played many parts in my time, including both Wesleyan clergyman and amateur physician. Be at peace, Sterl. He will live."

They went out, to be followed by Friday. Rain had set in again, and the air was muggy. Sterl sighted a large wagon, which he recognized as Ormiston's, rolling into the timber toward the old camp across the river. Four riders were driving a bunch of horses down to the shore. Larry led off into the river, with the four drovers behind urging and whipping the loose horses ahead of them. The flood had dropped, and neither riders nor unsaddled horses required any help at the landing.

"Well done, Larry," said Dann, as the young drover rode up to make his report.

"We got them all, I think," was the reply. "The—the two who got away—took four teams, but only one wagon. They either buried Jack and Bedford or took them away. Ormiston's wagon had been fired, but its load was so wet that it wouldn't burn.... We erected a cross over Drake's grave."

"That was well," replied Dann, as Larry hesitated. "But what about Ormiston?"

"They left him hanging. So did we."

There was flint in Larry's eyes and words. Stanley Dann, seldom at a loss for words, found none to say here.

That night at supper there was a release of tension as to Red's condition, but not as to Beryl's. She had fallen into a lethargy that preceded the sinking spell Mrs. Slyter feared. Eric Dann, too, according to Slyter, was either a very sick man or pretended to be.

At daybreak, Red came out of his stupor and whispered almost inaudibly for whisky.

"You son-of-a-gun!" cried Sterl in delight, as he dove for a flask. "Easy, now, old-timer!"

Red did not heed Sterl's advice. A tinge of color showed in his gray cheeks.

"How—long?" he asked, in a husky whisper.

"This is the third day."

"Get anythin'—back from? ..."

"One wagon, Ormiston's, twenty odd horses—and this." Here Sterl picked up Ormiston's bulky belt to shove it in front of Red. "He sure was heeled, pard. Dann took out what was due him, with Woolcott's and Hathaway's money and shares for the boys. The rest is yours. Wages justly earned, the boss said."

"Hell—he did....How much?"

"I only took a peep. But plenty mazuma, pard."

"I'm gonna—get drunk. Never be sober—again."

"Is that so?"

"Gimme a cigarette."

"No. But I'll see what Mrs. Slyter advises in the way of grub."

Still the sky stayed drab and gloomy, shedding copious rains at slowly widening intervals. On the fifth day there came a break in Red's fever and a lessening of his pain. The river had fallen low enough for the drovers to pack Ormiston's supplies and wagon across, piece by piece. And in the next day or so the cattle on that side were to be swum across. Eric Dann was up and about, moody and strange. That day, however, showed no improvement in Beryl's condition. Red continued to mend. He was as tough as wire, young and resilient, and as soon as his depleted blood began to renew itself, his complete recovery was only a matter of days. But not even of the persistent and sentimental Leslie did he ever ask about Beryl.

During the last few days of this period, it still rained, but far less frequently. The flat, dull sky broke at intervals, showing the first rifts of blue sky for over weeks. Bird life with its color and melody predicted a return of good weather; kangaroos and wallabies, emus and aboriginals appeared in increasing numbers. The last, Friday asserted, were different black fellas from those who had crowded at the forks before the flood. The great triangle of grassland, which had its apex at the junction of the river forks, waved away incredibly rich with new grass. Larry and Sterl reported that the trek could be resumed, rain or shine. But the patient Dann stroked his golden beard and said: "We'll wait for the sun. Eric is not sure about the road. He thinks it'd be more difficult to find in wet weather."

"Then you'll keep to this Gulf road, if we find it?" queried Sterl, quietly.

"Yes. I shall not change my mind because Ormiston is gone."

"Mr. Dann," ventured Larry, with hesitation, "the creeks, waterholes, springs will be full for months."

"I am aware of that. But Eric has importuned me and I have decided."

Dann might have been actuated to delay because that would be better for Beryl. She had come to herself, and only time and care were necessary to build up the flesh and strength she had lost.

When one night the stars came out, Dann said, "That rainbow today is God's promise. The wet season is over. Tomorrow the sun will shine. We go on and on again with our trek!"

CHAPTER

22

SUNRISE next morning was a glorious burst of golden light.

    The joyous welcome accorded this one-time daily event seemed in proportion to that of the Laplanders after their six months of midnight. Even Beryl Dann, from under the uprolled cover of her wagon, gazed out with sad eyes gladdened. Breakfast was almost a festival. The drovers whistled while they hitched up the teams to the packed wagons; they sang as they mustered the mob for the trek.

    Sterl, mounted on King, and as eager as the horse, waited with Friday for the wagons to get under way. But Slyter was detained by Leslie's pets. At the last moment Cocky had betrayed that his freedom at this long camp was too much for him. Leslie had not even clipped his wings. And when he flew up to join a flock of screeching white cockatoos he became one of many. Laughing Jack, the tame kookaburra, also turned traitor. He sat on the branch of a dead gum with three of his kind, bobbed up and down, ruffled his feathers, and laughed hoarsely at the mistress who had been so kind to him. Both had tasted the sweetness of freedom.

"I—I always lose everything I love," wailed Leslie, and mounting Lady Jane she rode out under the trees and did not look back.

Sterl was the last to leave the forks. He was glad to go, because that was imperative, yet he felt a strong regret as he rode over the grazed and trampled grass to his old position at the left of the mob. Many cattle and horses, several wagons, fourteen dead men and one dead woman had been left behind. Only Slyter's five drovers, not including him and Red, and four of Dann's, remained to get the mob, three hundred horses and six heavily laden wagons across the endless leagues.

The sky was deep azure, floating a few silver-white clouds. The sun appeared no relation to that molten copper disk of a few weeks past. King's mane and smooth hide were a dead black, yet somehow they shone. Friday, stalking beside Sterl with his spears and wommera, naked except for his loincloth, presented another kind of black, a glistening ebony. The mob of cattle appeared to consist of a hundred hues, yet there were really only very few. It was the variation of them that gave the living mosaic effect.

They looked as clean and bright as if they had been freshly scrubbed.

Compared to one of the trail driver's herds in Texas, these long-horned, moss-backed, red-eyed devils that were the bane of cowboys' lives, this herd of five thousand bulls and steers and cows and calves were tame, lazy, fat pets. The slow trek, the frightening situations and the kindness of the drovers accounted for this.

Ahead of the leisurely moving mob, the grass resembled that of the Great Plains in thickness and height, but in its richness of color and multitude of flowers it could have no comparison. In the distance all around loomed purple, bush-crowned hills, and to the north, far beyond, lilac ranges hung to the fleecy clouds like mirages right side up. If there could be enchantment on earth, here Sterl rode amidst it. That he seemed not the only one under its spell he proved by glancing at his companions on the trek. Every one of them rode alone, except Friday, who stalked lost in his own lonely, impenetrable thought. The drovers sat their horses and gazed, no doubt, at things that were only true in dreams. Red Krehl had forgotten his cigarette. Leslie rode far behind, lost in her world.

At the wattle-bordered stream beside which they camped, Stanley Dann inaugurated a new arrangement whereby everything was consolidated into one camp. The exhilaration of the morning had carried through to evening.

"Pard, it's kinda good to be alive at thet," drawled Red.

"Red, you've never fooled me about your indifference to beautiful places any more than to girls," replied Sterl, satirically.

"Yeah? Wal, mebbe Les was right when she said onct thet I wore my heart on my sleeve."

"Red Krehl," spoke up Leslie, "if you *have* a heart it's an old burlap bag stuffed with grass, and what not."

Leslie had come over to where Sterl sat writing in the journal—he had long ago relieved her of that duty—and Red was smoking. Friday, as usual, had made a little fire.

"Gosh, am I thet bad?" rejoined Red, mildly.

"Why wouldn't you come with me to see Beryl when I asked you before supper?"

"Wal, I reckon I didn't want to see Beryl."

"But she begged to see you. And I was embarrassed. I lied to her."

"Shore, you always was a turrible liar."

"I was not. Red, you're so queer. You never were hard before. Why, you've stood positive cruelty from that girl! Now, she needs to be cheered, fussed over—loved."

"Would you mind shettin' up, onless you want me to go out an' commune with the kangaroos?"

"You mean the abos, Red Krehl," returned Leslie, spitefully.

"Wal, I would at thet if there was any about."

Leslie plumped down beside Sterl and pretended

to peep at the journal, which he believed was only a ruse to get near to him.

"I'm busy, Leslie. Way behind. Will you slope off to bed, or somewhere?"

"No, I won't slope off to bed—or to hell, as you hint so courteously," she retorted petulantly, but she left them.

"Pard, what'd she mean by that crack about abos?" asked Red.

"I think it was a dirty crack. But don't ever overlook this, old pard. Every dirty crack a woman makes, every terrible blunder, like Beryl's for instance, can be blamed on some man."

"Aw hell! You've said thet before. It ain't so. What did *you* ever say or do to make Nan Halbert doublecross you, an' send us off to this turrible Australia?"

That blunt query pierced like a blade in Sterl's heart. The sudden opening of a healed wound flayed him. Still it drove him to be honest.

"Red, I flirted with Nan's best friend—that damned little black-eyed hussy who wouldn't let any man alone."

"Hell you say! You mean Flo, of course. Wal, so did I! Thet ain't nothin' atall."

"Well, it was enough to make Nan furious. Then to hurt me she went hotfoot after Ross Haight. And there she made her terrible blunder. It was my fault."

"But, you locoed two-faced Romeo, you never told me thet. You swore Nan liked Ross best."

"I lied, Red," returned Sterl, somberly, closing the journal.

"Wal, I'm a son of a sea cook! ... If you'd told me thet back home, Ross Haight could have gone to jail for his little gunplay. An' we wouldn't be heah!"

"For me, Red, it is better so. Only I grieve for what I led you into."

"Funny how things come about. But you needn't grieve too hard. I'm not sorry."

"Honest, Red?" appealed Sterl, earnestly.

"Honest to Gawd. This trek is right down my grub-line trail. 'Course I've had an orful blow in the gizzard. But if I get over it, an' we get through ..."

"Red, Leslie's hurt that you wouldn't go with her to see Beryl. You used to be kind to anyone sick, even a horse."

"Mebbe I was. Mebbe I've changed a lot," rejoined Red, bitterly. "I wouldn't want to see Beryl if she was like she used to be before thet hot spell, but let alone now, after ..."

"Red! You're hard," exclaimed Sterl, sharply.

"Shore. Harder than the hinges on the gates of hell. But if you cain't see thet I've had aplenty to make me hard, wal, you're as blind as a bat!"

"Red Krehl," flashed Sterl, "Are you keeping something secret from me?"

"Hellsfire, man, you can think, cain't you?" cut out Red, with that icy edge in his voice. "An' let's change the subject."

The trek fell back into its old, leisurely, time-effacing stride. One day was like another, though every league of that lonely land had infinite variety as well as endless monotony. Sterl had his surfeit of loveliness. It had passed into his being. At last seas of green and golden grass, islands of flowers, kangaroo-dotted plains, flamboyant bushland, myrids of birds, flocks of emus, mile-wide ponds where the mob splashed across, scattering the flocks of waterfowl, winding tiny brooks and still reed-bordered streams, and always, every hour of the long day, that illusive beckoning haunting purple mountain range—at last Sterl Hazelton's soul was everlastingly filled to the brim with these physical things which he divined were rewards in themselves.

Seventeen days, to where the headwaters of the middle fork sprang from the tropic verdure of the foothills. "Camp here two days," boomed Stanley Dann. "We will rest the stock, make repairs, and scout for this Gulf road. Eric has not found it yet." Leslie named the place Wellspring. It was felicitous, because the splendid volume of water spring as from a well, deep under the shadow of a bold, dark green foothill. Bill, with Scotty, the other cook, prepared the best meal they could devise, in honor of Beryl Dann's first attendance at supper for many weeks.

While they waited at their tent, Sterl had had some words with his friend.

"Pard, you will be decent to Beryl? You have not spoken to her since—since that mess!"

"Umpumm," drawled Red.

"Say, do you see that?" rang out Sterl, extending a big fist.

"Shore, I ain't blind."

"You know where it used to hurt you to be hit?"

"Ahuh. My belly. An' I ain't recovered yet, either."

"That's dinkum. If you don't swear to be nice to Beryl, I'll lam into you right now. And I'm not fooling."

"Yeah? Wal, I choose the wusser of two evils. I'll speak to Beryl an' be as—as nice as I can. It's gotta be done sometime, jest for appearances. An' after all what the hell do I care?"

Then Leslie arrived; once again, after so long an interval, clad in feminine apparel, a flowered gown in which she looked extremely pretty.

"Red, you'll—come?" she asked, falteringly.

"No, Les," he said, contriving to wink at Sterl. "Umpumm, nix come the weasel!"

That he could jest at such a moment, certainly poignant and important to Leslie, called to all that was spirited in her.

"You ornery, bullheaded, low-down..." she burst out, choking over the last two words, which, like those preceding, were from Red's vocabulary. Then as quickly as the flare-up of her temper, she broke into sobs.

"Aw now, Leslie, don't bawl, please," begged the cowboy, who could not bear to see a girl cry. "Don't you see I'm all spruced up. I'll go with you an' do the elegant."

"Hon-nest, Red? You're such a—a brute. You might be—teasing."

"No, I mean it. Thet is I'll go if you stop cryin'. Why, the idee! Spoilin' thet happy face!"

Beryl rose from her father's knees to greet her visitors. Her blue gown hung loosely upon her slender form, yet not at the expense of grace. Every vestige of the golden tan had vanished from her face, the whiteness of which accentuated the loveliness of her violet eyes and fair hair. Her beauty struck Sterl with great force, and suddenly he understood both Ormiston and Krehl. Leslie ran to Beryl. "Oh, it's dinkum to see you out again!"

Beryl returned her kiss and greeting, then offered her two hands to Sterl. "Now, Mr. Cowboy, what do you think of me, up and well—and rarin' to go?"

"Great!" responded Sterl, heartily, as he took her hands. "Beryl, you just look beautiful!"

But she did not even hear that last. Red had stepped out from behind Sterl, and Sterl saw with a pang what a terrible moment this was for both of them.

"Beryl—I—I'm shore dog-gone glad to see you out again," said Red, huskily, and he was both gallant and self-possessed. One of his long strides bridged the distance between them. Her eyes dilated and turned black.

"Red—*Red*!" she whispered, as she put out quivering hands. They groped, missed his, to clutch his blouse. She fell against him with a gasp, and fainted in his arms.

"She is not so strong as she thought," said Dann. He took her from Krehl and sat her gently down in the one chair. "Mrs. Slyter—Leslie!" he called.

Sterl could not withdraw his gaze from Beryl's

face. Her eyes were closed, long fair lashes on her white cheeks. He turned to Red, and forgot his concern for Beryl in the dumb misery of his friend. Dann's hearty voice attested to the fact that Beryl had regained consciousness.

"I fainted," she said, weakly. "How stupid! I'm all right now. Why, Leslie, you are as white as a sheet."

"No wonder! Beryl, I thought you'd gone to join the angels."

"No such luck for me! Boys, come back. I promise you I won't be such a weakling again."

Sterl, with his arm through Red's dragged the hesitant cowboy to the small circle, of which Beryl was the center. She had color in her cheeks. The cowboys found seats. Mrs. Slyter insisted that Beryl sip a cup of tea. Leslie hovered over her.

"Red, perhaps I fainted because sight of you brought you back—as you looked when I last saw you—how long ago? . . . Ages ago?"

"I forget. It shore was an orful long time," drawled Red. "An' about thet faintin'—I knowed a girl onct who could faint—or let on—whenever she wanted to knock the daylights out of a feller. So you see, Beryl, I been educated."

"Did that girl faint in your arms?" asked Beryl, her speaking eyes on him.

"Wal, thet was one way she had of gettin' into 'em. An' onct she got there, she'd come to orful quick."

Presently Beryl's nurses, despite her protests,

led her away to her wagon and bed. The look she gave Red as she bade him good night was not lost upon Sterl.

At this juncture Eric Dann entered the shelter, greeted the cowboys and drank with Stanley. He had a livid scar on his forehead, a mark that he would carry to his grave.

Sterl took advantage of the opportunity to question him: "Dann, if I remember correctly we lost the Gulf road half way or more down the Diamantina from the forks?"

"Somewhere back there. It didn't concern me then because I expected to come across it any day," returned Eric.

"We haven't crossed it. I've kept a sharp lookout for wheel tracks. On level ground half a dozen wagons would leave a rut that would last for years."

"Surely. We have just missed them, unless, of course, they have washed out."

"Did you take this route on your back track?" went on Sterl.

"Part way. I don't recall just where we made short outs."

"Some of these landmarks along here, if you ever saw them, you couldn't forget."

"Landmarks meant very little to me."

"Hmm, it's unfortunate you did not have an instinct for such things," said Stanley. "You said you knew the way, Eric."

"I've told you a hundred times that I thought I did," replied Eric, impatiently.

Sterl made note of the shifty eyes and of the beads of sweat coming out on Eric's brow, under the livid scar, and his dubious conjectures became definite doubts. Sterl could never swallow his relation to Ormiston.

Red fixed his piercing eyes upon Eric. "Dann, if you don't know this country atall you oughta tell us damn pronto."

"But I do know it, in general. I've recognized a good many places we passed at a distance from this trek. I'd like it understood that I'll not be put on the witness stand by you Americans," declared Dann, with signs of nervousness and heat.

"Wal, we Americans ain't puttin' you on nothin', except yore word," rejoined Red, coolly. Then he asked bluntly, "Have you ever been through this Diamantina country?"

Dann made what appeared to be a powerful effort to control unstable nerves. Nevertheless he did not reply to Red's query.

"Wal, heah's one you *can* answer, Mr. Dann, onless. . . ." Red did not complete his dubious inference. "This heah range we've come to an' have seen for so many days—there's a pass in it thet nobody could miss seein'. If yore trek or any other trek traveled north from Cooper Creek up the Diamantina, you or they'd have to go through this pass. Ain't thet figgerin' reasonable?"

"Yes, it is, Krehl. They'd have to," replied Dann, readily.

"All right. Then what kind of country will we find

on the other side of this range?"

"It will be practically the same as this."

"Thanks, Dann. We'll remember thet," returned Red, caustically. Then he addressed Sterl: "Pard, do you reckon I oughta shet up now or relieve my mind to the boss?"

"By all means, Krehl," boomed Stanley.

"Wal, I wouldn't presume to advise you heah. I'm no Australian. But I've known open wilderness country since I was knee-high to a grasshopper. This heah country has been changin'. It's altogether different from the forks. Grass shorter an' not so rich, trees fewer an' smaller. An' when you cross that range, you'll find plenty trouble. Thet's my hunch, boss. Take it or leave it."

Turning on a jangling heel Red stalked away from the Danns with a mien that left little to the imagination. Dann, so seldom perturbed, was bewildered by what was evidently a new aspect to him.

"Incredible!" he ejaculated. "We should be still hundreds of miles from the watershed that sends its streams into the Gulf. Eric, you substantiate this, do you not?"

"Absolutely," answered Eric Dann. "Northeast of this range, when we pass it, we will reach the headwaters of the Warburton River. That runs westward. Beyond that we will come to the headwaters of rivers emptying into the Gulf."

"That agrees with our map. I am sure Krehl has miscalculated. What do you think, Hazelton?"

"All I say is, I'm sorry we are not trekking west."

"If we should make a blunder now—and go the wrong way...." Sterl heard the leader's voice ring and break but he made it his business to be watching Eric Dann. Either he was prejudiced against this man's vacillation and incompetence, or he saw through him with Red Krehl's lynx eyes!

CHAPTER
23

*A*NOTHER conference of Stanley Dann's. A few
days out of Wellspring camp, they had approached a break in the foothills, apparently leading to the pass through the range. Eric Dann
asserted that he was sure he had been through that
notch, going or coming, and so the mob was driven
into its narrow defiles. Larry had reported dubious
ground ahead; Red Krehl had climbed to a hilltop to
reconnoiter. Upon his return he said to Dann in no
uncertain terms, "Cain't see far. But no country to
drive cattle, let alone wagons!"

"No hurry, friends," Stanley told his associates.
"We'll climb to look the ground over. Krehl should
know where and where not to drove a mob."

But Eric Dann leaped from his wagon-seat to

confront his brother in a terrific fury.

"First it was Hazelton! Now it's Krehl—*Krehl*—KREHL!...I'm tired of having my judgment overruled!"

"Eric, you've lost your temper," replied Stanley, severely. "Calm yourself. These cowboys have been a help to me, not a detriment. As others—and *you*—have been!"

Eric Dann's visage grew purple.

"By God, I'll turn back!" he shouted.

"But that wagon and team are mine," rejoined Stanley Dann, controlling evident heat.

"I don't care. I'll take them. I've earned them on this infernal trek!"

Red Krehl slid off his horse.

"Bah! It's a bluff, boss. He hasn't got the nerve."

"Wait, Krehl," ordered Stanley Dann. "Eric, what is it you want?"

"You brought me on this trek as partner and guide," hoarsely shouted Eric.

"Yes, I did."

"Then hold to that contract or I'll leave you!"

"Eric, I was not aware that I had broken it. Very well, I will hold to it—come what may," returned the leader.

"It's understood that I am the guide?"

"Yes. But you must *guide* us. Once more, for the last time, do you *know* this country?"

"Yes, I do," rasped Eric, passionately, yet he gulped as if something had stuck in his throat. "In a general way, I mean. This is an enormously vast country...."

"Yeah, an' you *know* it?" interrupted Red, with stinging scorn.

"Yes, I know it, you—you—" burst out the goaded drover, foaming at the mouth.

"Dann, you're a — — liar! Go for yore gun—if you got the guts!"

"KREHL!" thundered the leader.

"Too late, boss. Stay where you air. Come on, Mr. Eric Dann, throw yore gun!"

Pale-faced instead of red now, gasping and speechless, Eric Dann turned to spread wide his hands, appealing to the leader.

"Let this end here!" commanded Dann.

"All right, boss, it's ended," replied Red, curtly. "But I'll bet you live to see the day you wish it'd ended my way!"

And they trekked into the hills. Days without end before what seemed to be the pass; Sterl lost track of days. By now, Slyter, beating down the opposition of Eric Dann, had insisted that the wagons go ahead; for in places they had actually to improvise roads. Sometimes three miles a day were good going. The cattle found little grass and took to browsing. Many of them strayed. The drovers rode herd at night in five-hour shifts. Slyter's second wagon, with Roland driving, went over a steep bank. He escaped, but the horses had to be shot. Often at night Sterl and Red could find no level place to pitch their tent. They would drop on the ground, cover their heads against mosquitoes and sleep like logs nevertheless. More and more, Sterl inclined to the truth of Red's caustic forecast.

Ten nightmare days up a V-shaped valley which led to the deceiving pass. And then the trek seemed halted for good. Eric and Larry and Slyter returned in defeat from their scouting. But Friday, last to get back, galvanized their low spirits and energies.

"Go alonga me," he said, and the black had never failed them yet.

They hitched six horses to a wagon, and with a drover on each side, pulling with a lasso, and whipping the teams, hauled over the "saddle" which had blocked them. It took all the rest of that day to get the other wagons over. The mob had to be left behind in the valley until the morrow.

Riding across that saddle, Sterl groaned his disappointment at the apparently impenetrable labyrinth of jungle and rock-ribbed confines ahead. Ten miles or more of incredibly rough going stretched ahead—a distance that might as well have been ten times that—and then a gap and a blue void. And then—another conference.

"We will go on," declared Stanley Dann.

"We can't get through," averred Slyter.

"I've missed the—the way," added Eric Dann, falteringly.

No one paid any attention to him.

"Larry, Bligh, what do you say?" queried the leader.

They replied practically in unison that it looked very bad, well-nigh impassable.

"Hazelton?" he boomed.

"Boss, we can't go back," said Sterl.

"Krehl, what do you think?"

"Me? Wal, I ain't thinkin' atall," drawled the cowboy.

"Don't bandy ridicule with me!" roared Stanley Dann.

"All right, boss. Excoose me. I ain't no mule-haid. I think we must find a way out thet we cain't see from heah."

"Right! Men, look for a place where we can camp."

They camped on the right side of the saddle at the base of a rugged slope. Firewood and water had to be carried up, a job Red and Sterl took upon themselves. There were no idle hands any more. Even Beryl helped Mrs. Slyter and Bill.

"You've only begun to pick up," said Sterl to her that evening. "Please rest."

"Sterl, I'll do my bit," replied Beryl, smiling up at him. She might not have realized that she was telling him she had begun to learn a great lesson of life. How frail she looked, yet her sad face seemed lovelier than ever! She had courage—that thing Sterl respected more than all else in man or woman. If she lived she would come through this fire pure gold.

He went out along the saddle to look for Leslie. He met her climbing the slope on foot, in the track of the wagons, lithe and supple, clear-eyed as a falcon, her drover's garb ragged and soiled.

"Howdy, Sterl. Been worrying about me?" she panted.

"No, Les. Only King and the *remuda*."

"King, Jester, Duke, Lady Jane, all tiptop. Sorrel is lame. Count is fagged out. Sterl, will we ever, ever get through this pass?

"I don't know—and don't care much."

"Sterl!—that's not like you. Oh, dear boy, you're worn out!"

"Les, you and Beryl make me feel a little ashamed," replied Sterl.

"Sterl, you and Red all through this terrible year have filled my heart, and Beryl's, and Mum's with courage to carry on. Small wonder that you lag a little now! But don't fail me, Sterl. And don't let Red fail Beryl. It is he who has saved her—who is changing her very soul. . . . Sterl, would you mind—holding me a bit—as you used to?"

But Sterl evaded that, despite the warmth she stirred in his heart, and made excuses, and talking kindly to her he led her to camp. Darkness fell upon silent trekkers, some going to their beds and others about their jobs, and all with spirits bowed but not broken.

It took all the next morning to drove the mob over the "saddle." Friday had returned from a scout. To Stanley Dann he spread his wonderful, sinewy black hands, fingers wide. "Boss, might be cattle go alonga dere," he said, and manifestly he meant they should separate and streak through various channels to whatever lay at the end of that green maze. So like a great waterfall the mob poured off the "saddle," to roll and clatter down, to disappear almost at will in the jungle.

Then began the feverish and ceaseless labor of fourteen men to chop and build a road for six wagons through ten miles of wilderness jungle.

It dwarfed all their former labors. After five days of digging, chopping, carrying rocks, packing supplies, wading in mud and water and grass, all the toilers except Stanley Dann and Slyter forgot about the cattle and horses. Every day Friday, whose duty it was to report on the mob, would say: "Cattle along dere farder," and that day when he said: "Cattle gone!" not one of the trekkers betrayed anxiety. It was now a battle for their lives.

In daylight, the flies were almost as fierce as at the forks, and at night the mosquitoes were so thick and bloodthirsty that they would have killed an unprotected man. The second cook practically died on his feet, sticking it out with fever and dysentery, and then collapsing. Monkton was bitten by a death adder and for days his life was despaired of.

In the middle of that jungle Eric Dann made a startling proposal.

"We should abandon the wagons and pack out!"

Stanley Dann, soiled and sweaty and bedraggled, gazed at this blood kin of his with great, amber eyes that had not lost their magnificent light.

"What about the women?" he asked.

"They can ride horseback. I asked Beryl. She said

she could," returned Eric, eagerly.

"We are two thousand miles from anywhere. Beryl would die."

"If she gave out—we could carry her!" exclaimed this extraordinary man.

The giant shook his shaggy golden head, wearily, as if it was useless to listen to his brother.

"We can't get through," bawled Eric Dann, his voice rising. "I climbed up to see. We're not halfway! Man, would you sacrifice us all for your worthless daughter?"

Red Krehl leaped upon Dann and felled him. He would have kicked the man, too, but for a sharp cry. Beryl and Leslie had heard and seen. But it could not silence him.

"Dann, I'm gonna kill this brother of yores yet," bitterly predicted the cowboy.

"Red, don't kill Uncle Eric. Not for me!" cried Beryl, passionately. "I'm not worth it. I *was* a fool. I *was* vain, brazen, mad! But Uncle Eric only knows the half. I planned with Ash Ormiston—that he should seem to steal me from my bed. He meant to kill anyone who opposed him—especially to kill Uncle Eric, with whom he had plotted. I agreed to go with him, to save Uncle Eric's life, to save Dad from ruin, if not worse. But Ormiston betrayed me. He stole Dad's cattle. He would have murdered Uncle Eric but for me. He—He...."

She broke down then. Leslie led her away from the stunned group of men. Eric Dann slunk away under the trees. Of all present, Sterl thought, his friend Red seemed the most staggered by Beryl's revelation. It was not in his case, as in that of the others, that Beryl's participation in Ormiston's plot had come to light. Red had known that! He had kept it secret even from Sterl. But now he knew why the girl had betrayed him and her father and all of them.

After what seemed a long silence Stanley Dann said: "Men, we are being sorely tried, but let us not lose our faith in God and in each other. Krehl, I thank you, but I disagree with my daughter. She *is* worth— all she declared she was not."

"Wal, boss, if you ask me, I kinda reckon so myself," returned Red Krehl, ponderingly.

"All of you back to work. We are going through!" boomed the leader.

Sterl bent for his shovel and whispered to his friend: "Pard, now my job is to keep you from being shot in the back!"

Before many more hours passed that break in their toil, with its resurgence of lulled passions, was forgotten in sheer physical exhaustion.

But at last, and when the trekkers were sunk to their lowest ebb, Friday found a gateway for them out into the open. They faced vastly different country from that which Eric Dann had pictured to them. A few miles below a gentle green slope, out upon a velvet green down, Stanley Dann's mob of cattle grazed in a great colorful patch. Beyond them spread endless other downs dotted with clumps of pandan- uses and palms, streaked by black fringes of trees, bisected from league to league by shining threads of water, and bordered by limitless purple horizon. They were all so overjoyed to get clear of that awful jungle that no one of them asked audibly where they were. Only Sterl thought of what Eric Dann had sworn—that the country beyond the range would be the same as that at the headwaters of the Diamantina.

CHAPTER 24

DAYS of leisurely and comfortable going now, over level downs with grass and water abundant but firewood so scarce that whenever they found any deadwood Bill collected it for the next camp. But one jarring fact—in a week's trekking they reached a point opposite the flattening out of that range whose crossing had cost them so many supplies, so much toil and life. By a week's detour, they could have gone round it. Six weeks more than lost!

Late one afternoon, the black, ragged line that had gradually grown for days turned out to be a good-sized river. It flowed north. It presented a problem, not only to cross, but because the water, flowing the wrong way, upset their calculations. The Warburton, for which Dann thought he was trekking, would have flowed due west. According to the leader's rude map, when they crossed it they would be headed north to a point between the Never-never Land and the Gulf and would cross the headwaters of all the streams flowing into the Gulf. At Dann's conference, the first for a long time, Eric Dann asserted positively, "This is the Flinders River. Probably we are two or three hundred miles from the Gulf."

"Flinders River? Gulf?" echoed Stanley, aghast. "That means salt water, crocodiles and cannibal abos!"

"Gosh!" ejaculated Red Krehl. "Boss, of course, hunches mean nothin' atall to you. But let's follow mine an' rustle back onto dry land."

Any suggestion of the cowboy's was to Eric Dann like a red flag to a bull.

"Stanley, it's along the fringe of the Never-never that bad blacks are to be encountered," he said, impressively.

"How do you *know* that?" demanded the leader intensely.

"I know it," returned Eric, stubbornly.

"What *is* your objective?"

"Southeast of Port Darwin," answered the brother, glibly, "there are fertile ranges. We can choose to stop there, if you like, and send in to Darwin for supplies. I think you will decide for this site instead of the Kimberleys."

"Yes, true enough," mused the leader. "We have that information from more than one reliable source.

I could always move on to the Kimberleys. Eric, you have made mistakes—this last one, terrible! But in your heart are you speaking honestly?"

Before that stern and just leader, the hawk-eyed cowboys, and the dubious Slyter with his drovers, Eric Dann solemnly asserted his truth. What—Sterl wondered—was his game?

The river, which Leslie called the Muddy, appeared to be fresh water, though it had a weed taste, and the middle channel had to be swum. Neither accident nor injury marked the crossing of the wagons and the herd, though it took four days of persistent labor.

Leslie and Beryl, with Friday, had been left for the last. Stanley Dann sent the cowboys Larry and Rollie back for them.

"Where's a horse for me to ride?" demanded Beryl, as the bedraggled riders waded their horses out to the bank.

"Boss's order is for us to pack you over," replied Larry, uneasily.

To Sterl's surprise, and certainly to Red's, Beryl acquiesced without further remark.

"Red, I'd feel safer with you on Duke. He's so big," said Beryl, casually. "Besides you have carried me already."

Sterl leaped off to help Beryl up in front of Red. Red put his left arm around her, and Beryl put her right arm around his neck. Anyway Sterl looked at the position it was an embrace, reluctant on Red's part, subtly willing on Beryl's. She laid her head back and looked up at him.

"Red, it won't take long," said Sterl, in cheery significance. But he did not mean the trip across.

"I don't care how long it takes—if only...." murmured Beryl, with a hint of her old audacity.

Red's reaction was as natural as his sincerity was hidden. "Slope along, Duke," he drawled. "Pick out that deep hole, fall in, an' never come up!"

Red entered the river with Larry close on one side and Rollie on the other. Leslie waited for Sterl, who watched the trio ahead for a moment before he started. Then he became aware of Leslie's poignant joy at sight of Beryl in the cowboy's arms.

"Oh, Sterl! Isn't love wonderful?" she sighed, dreamily.

"It must be. I can't speak from personal experience, as evidently you can. But real love must be wonderful."

"That's true, you devil!" flashed Leslie, disrupted from her sweet trance, and rode ahead of him, splashing the water in great sheets.

Sterl idled along, reflecting sadly that this little byplay had been the first pleasantry, the first lessening of the raw tension, for many a week

Dann's caravan covered in five days some fifty miles of green downs, not one long or short stretch differing noticeably from any other. Its beauty palled, its sameness irritated the nerves; it monotony grew unbearable.

But on that fifth day darker and apparently higher ground broke the level horizon. Two more days travel proved that it consisted of low ridges and round areas covered with dense but scrubby timber, No blue foothills, however, loomed above the wandering black line of scrub. And the day came when Sterl, gazing backward, could no longer see the shadowy, purple ranges. They kept on to the northwest, traveling by compass.

"Slyter," said Sterl, at Blue Grass camp, "if we are trekking *through* this country to get to the headwaters of the Warburton—it's all right. But if we're trekking *deeper* into these downs...."

"Red says if we follow this four-flushed Eric Dann much farther we'll be lost."

"We're the same as lost now, Sterl. But I won't nag Stanley any more. He's set. We're going through, he swears. Says to remember the bad times before— how we always came out."

Days and days and days! And dark cool dewy nights, when the stars blazed white, the bitterns boomed from the reed-bordered lakes and streams, and the owls hooted dismally in the pandanus scrub! The moon soared in the sky, blanching the endless downs. Solitude reigned. Sterl fought a feeling that they had reached the end of the world. Insupportably slowly the trek went on into this forbidding land of grass.

*   *   *

They came at length into a stranger, blacker, wilder country.

The dense growth of bush denoted a river—a river somewhere beyond the dark fringe of giant ash trees and bloodwoods and enormous trees with multiple trunks grotesque and gnarled. They camped where a huge wide-spreading banyan afforded a thick green canopy for the whole caravan. A boiling spring of sweet water ran away from the bank of bushland, forming a little stream that meandered away toward a pale lake, black and white with waterfowl. Kookaburras flew under the trees, perched on branches to watch the intruders, but they were silent. And that strange feature alone affected the morbid trekkers. The sun slanted in what appeared the wrong direction. Sterl was completely turned around. Red wearily said he did not give a damn and that he wished what was going to happen would come pronto.

Friday appeared at suppertime. There was that in his mien to induce awe. All the trekkers mutely interrogated him, then the leader asked, "What ho, Friday?"

"Plenty bad black fella alonga dere. Big ribber. Plenty croc. Plenty salt."

They were crushed. Stanley Dann sat with his elbows on his knees, his broad hands over his golden beard. The corded veins stood out upon his bronzed brow.

"*Lost!*" he ejaculated, in a hollow voice. "Hundreds of miles out of our way."

"Salt water!" burst out Slyter, appalled.

"It must be the Flinders River," croaked Eric Dann.

"What-at?" roared the giant. "According to you we crossed the Flinders weeks back!"

"But afterward I remembered it was not. This is the Flinders. Near its source. Once across we will find higher ground."

He seemed so fired with inspired certainty that most of his listeners, grasping at straws, felt a renewal of hope. But Red and Sterl eyed him with suspicion.

The sun rose red on the wrong side.

"Spread along the river to find a place to cross," ordered Stanley Dann to his drovers.

Below camp some distance, Sterl, Red and Larry found an opening in the bush where the mob could be driven to the river, and where a road could be opened for the wagons.

"Look dere," called Friday, who strode beside Sterl, and he pointed to smoke signals rising beyond the break in the bush. "Imm black fella know."

They rode through the opening, with Friday in the lead, scaring the tiger snakes out of his path with his long spear, and presently emerged upon the low bank of a wide river. Slopes of yellow mud ran a hundred yards out to meet a turgid channel of about the same width, and the opposite slope ran up to the bush.

"Tide running out. Swift, too," observed Larry.

"Gosh, you mean this heah is tidewater?" queried Red.

"It must be. Friday said it was salt water."

"Friday, go alonga see how deep mud," said Sterl.

Ankle-deep the black waded some rods out, and then began to sink in deeper and deeper until he was over his knees.

"Even with the tide in full the mob would have to wade a bit, at least close to shore," observed Larry, seriously. "And the wagons. What a job to cross them here!"

"Righto. But it can be done," averred Red. "We'd cut poles and brush to make a road. Thet channel buffaloes me, though. What say, Sterl?"

"Boys, without the menace of crocodiles, which Friday mentioned, we'd have a killing job here. Larry, how big do these Gulf crocodiles grow?"

"Up to twenty-five feet, I've heard. They can break a man's leg with one whack of their tails."

"Red, *how* will we get the girls across?"

"Aw, thet's a sticker. I was thinkin' about it. If we only had a boat! Mebbe we could build a raft. In a pinch we might use the bed of our wagon. But I wonder—should we go across?"

They rode back to camp. The other drovers who had ranged still farther up the river reported no practical crossing.

"Boss, there's a ford below. But it looks awful tough," said Sterl.

"Mr. Dann, cain't we get out of tacklin' this heah river?" queried Red, anxiously.

"Krehl," returned the chief, patiently, "as we cannot go back we must cross."

"Hell no! We can go back a ways, an' thet'd save
an orful job, a lot of cattle, an' somebody's life shore
as Gawd made little apples! Dann, yore a cattleman
as big as all this heah outdoors. But a dry land
drover."

But Eric Dann's abnormal and malignant obses-
sion again protruded its hydra head.

"Krehl is afraid," he shouted, hoarsely. "Once
and for all, I demand to be heard! No foreigner is
going to upset my plans—to make me ridiculous."

"Brother," rejoined the leader, "I ask you once
more—do you know what you're doing when you
advise us to cross this river?"

"Yes, I know. I know too, that Krehl is afraid. Ask
him yourself. I'll ask him! See here, cowboy, are you
man enough to confess the truth—that you *are*
afraid?"

Red Krehl gave the drover a long, uncompre-
hending gaze. Dann was indeed a new one for the
Texan. Then he spoke: "Hell yes. I shore am afraid
of this river, the crocs an' the abos. But I reckon I
oughta be more afraid of you, Mr. Dann. Because
you're a queer mixture of fool, liar an' crook."

Sterl restrained himself until this argument
ended, then he addressed the leader.

"Dann, I want you to know—and to remember—
that I strongly advise against the attempt to cross
this river here."

"Sorry, Hazelton. But we cross!"

*   *   *

But the river and the tide had something to say about that, and when they were right, as near as the drovers thought they could be, then the cattle had the last word. This mob had been extraordinarily docile and easily managed, as the cowboys knew cattle. Many of the calves and cows that had distinguishing marks or habits that brought them into the daily notice, had become veritable pets. Toward the end of that day, however, they manifested evidences of a contrary disposition. About midafternoon Friday reported that they stopped grazing and became uneasy. Slyter went out to observe for himself. Upon his return he announced: "For some reason or other they dislike this place."

"Then, we may be in for a night of it. I wouldn't care to try to stop a rush in this bush."

"Might be smellum crocs," said Friday.

Flying foxes had appeared during the afternoon, great, wide-winged grotesque bats, swishing out of the bush over the cattle, and their number increased toward sunset.

"Shore, it's them dinged bats thet have the herd buffaloed, an' they're gonna get us, too," said Red Krehl.

Here was one camp where a fire did not flame brightly, cheerily. The wood burned as if it were wet, and the smoke was acrid. Night settled down black, with the stars obscured by the foliage on three sides.

Supper had been eaten and five drovers had ridden out on guard when all left in camp were startled by a weird, droning sound off in the bush, apparently across the river.

"Black fella corroboree. Imm no good," said Friday, his long black arm aloft.

Suddenly—a trampling roar of hoofs. The cowboys were as quick to leap up as Larry and Rollie. Slyter came thudding from his wagon. Eric Dann lifted a pale and haggard face. *"A rush!"* cried Stanley Dann.

"Aw, I knowed it," said Red, grimly, "Come, Sterl. Let's rustle our hosses."

"Wait, you cowboys," ordered Dann. "Some of us must guard camp. Larry, Roland. Call Benson and join the drovers out there."

Slyter made off with the hurrying drovers, shouting something about his horses. Friday, at the edge of the circle of light, turned to the others and yelled, "Tinkit mob run alonga here!"

"My God!" boomed Stanley Dann. "Stand ready all! If the mob comes this way, take to the trees!"

The increasing roar, the quaking ground, held all those listeners fraught with suspense and panic for an endless moment.

"Stampede'll miss us!" yelled Red Krehl. Then Friday stooped to make violent motions with his right arm, indicating that the herd was rushing in the direction of the river. Gunshots banged faintly above the din.

"All right! We're safe!" yelled Sterl, and then felt himself sag under the release of tension. It had been a few moments of terrible uncertainty.

Then a crashing augmented the trampling roar. The stampede, now evidently pointed up the river, had run into the bush. The noise lasted for minutes before it began to lessen in volume.

"Providence saved us again," rang out Stanley Dann, in immense relief. "But this rush will be bad for the mob."

"Dog-gone bad for the drovers, too, I'd say," declared Red.

"You may well think so. But usually a mob does not rush long. I am hopeful."

"They might stampede into the river," interposed Sterl.

Eric Dann sat down again and bent his gaze upon the ruddy fire embers. It was necessary to sit close to the heat and smoke to be even reasonably safe from mosquitoes. Eric Dann, however, sat back in the shadow. Not improbably he had too much on his mind to feel bites. Presently Slyter returned to camp.

"Horses all right," he was saying to Dann as they approached the fire. "The rush was bad. But half the mob were not affected."

"That was strange. Usually, cattle follow the leaders, like sheep. Uncanny sort of a place."

"Righto. I jolly well wish we were out of it. Hello, Mum. You and Les should be in bed."

"I see ourselves, with the mob threatening to run us down. And Stanley calling us to climb trees!" retorted his good wife. "But we'll go now."

"Beryl, that would be a good idea for you," said her father.

"I'm afraid to go to bed," replied the girl, petulantly.

"Me too," added Leslie. "These sneaky, furry bats give me the creeps. I just found one in our wagon. Ugh!"

"Well, as long as Sterl and Red have to sit up, I suppose it's all right for you girls. But it's not a very cheerful place for courting."

Beryl let out a scornful little laugh. "Courting! Whom on earth with?"

"Sometime back it was royalty condescending. Now it's how the mighty have fallen!" returned Mrs. Slyter, subtly, and left them.

"Leslie, whatever did your mother mean by that cryptic speech?" asked Beryl, annoyed.

"Oh, Mum's got softening of the brain," returned Leslie, and she dropped down on the log very close to Sterl. Red, who sat across the fire from them, looked up at Beryl, who was standing.

"Say, all you women have softenin' of the brain," he drawled.

"Yeah?" queried Leslie.

"Is that so, Mr. Krehl?" added Beryl.

"Yes, it's so. Take that crack of Leslie's mother, for instance. Les's Ma an' you girls air of one mind, I reckon. The idec is to collar a man, any man temporarily, till you meet up with one you aim to corral for keeps."

"That is true, Red. Disgustingly true," admitted Beryl, suddenly frank and earnest. "But Les and I are not to blame for being born women."

"I reckon not, Beryl," returned Red, conciliated by her sincerity.

"Go on, Red. You *were* going to say something," went on Beryl.

"I was," rejoined the cowboy. "It seemed to me kind of far-fetched an' silly —thet sentimental yearnin' of yores, if it *was* thet. Heah we air lost in this Gawd-forsaken land. Aw, I know Eric there swears we ain't lost, but thet doesn't fool me. An' this hole is as spooky an' nasty a place as I ever camped. It's more. It's a darned dangerous one. We jest escaped somethin' tough. An' thet's why I jest wondered at you womenfolks, feelin' thet soft, sweet mushy sentiment in the face of hell."

"Red Krehl, that's the wonder of it—that we *can* feel and need such things at such a time," returned Beryl, eloquently. "I left such things behind, to come with my father. I could have gone to live in Sydney. But I came with Dad. And you've seen something of what I've suffered. This hard experience has not wholly destroyed my sensitiveness, my former habits. I can see why Sterl thinks we're going bush. I can see that we'll turn into abos, if we're stuck here forever. But just now, I'm a dual nature. By day I'm courageous, by night I'm cowardly. I can't sleep. I'm afraid of noises. I lie with the cold chills creeping over me. I can't forget what—what has already happened to me. Red Krehl, you said you wonder at me. But I say it's a wonder you cannot see how I'd welcome any kindness, any attention, any affection, to keep me from thinking!"

It was a long speech, though quickly spoken, one that Sterl took to his heart in shame and self-reproach. He was intensely curious to see how Red would take it, and somehow he had faith in the cowboy's greatness of soul.

"Come heah, girl," said Red, gently, and held out his hand. Beryl stepped to him and leaned, as if compelled. He drew her to a place beside him on the narrow pack, and he put his arm around her to draw her close. "I'm sorry I made all them hard cracks about this place. Only I'm glad, 'cause I understand you better. But Beryl, I reckon you can't figger me out. When all was goin' fine back on this trek you gave me some pretty bad times. So, even if I wanted to be sweet an' soft about you, which I shore don't after the way you treated me, I couldn't be on account of what this damn trek has done to *me*. I've saved yore life a coupla times, an' I reckon I'll have to do thet a heap more. If I wasn't a hard-ridin', hard-shootin' cowboy, a killer, grim an' mean, I couldn't do thet much for you. Thet ought to make you see me clear."

"Oh, Red," Beryl cried, poignantly, "I don't want you any different!"

The thud of hoofs disrupted this scene, and Larry rode up. Friday came running to throw brush upon the blaze.

"Larry, you're all bloody!" exclaimed Sterl.

"No. Just ran—into a snag," panted the drover. "Let me—sit down."

Dann arrived to bend over Larry. "Bad scalp cut.

Girls, fetch water and linen. Larry, are you all right?"

"Yes, sir—except played out."

"Where are the other drovers?"

"Back with what—was left of the mob. That rush got—away, sir."

"How many?"

"Benson said one-third of the mob. They rushed into the bush. They were a crazy lot of cattle. They crashed through the bush—some into the river. So we yelled to come together—then rode back. That mob will work out of the bush by morning."

Meanwhile Dann had unwound the scarf from Larry's head and begun to dress the wound. Slyter told the girls to go to bed, and this time they obeyed. Red was sent off to take Larry's place with the drovers and Sterl ordered to stay in camp.

When toward dawn Red and Rollie came in, relieved by two of Dann's drovers, Sterl lay down beside Red. The sun was up when Friday called them.

"Where black fella, Friday?"

"Alonga dere. No good. Hidum about. Watchum white man."

"Sterl, these abos up heah 'pear to be a different breed. All same Comanche Injuns," said Red.

They found the drovers straggling in. Benson reported two- thirds of the mob intact. Their ragged garb, scratched hands, bruised faces gave evidence of their strenuous effort to head that rush.

"We stopped it, five miles west," reported Bligh, wearily. "They're out in the open, not many on their feet. Dehorned, crippled, snagged—a sorry mess!"

Friday appeared, carrying a kangaroo that he had speared.

"Plenty roo," he said. "Ribber full up. Plenty croc."

"Friday, see any blacks?" asked Sterl.

"Black fella imm alonga bush. Bimeby."

"Men, eat and drink all you can hold," said Stanley Dann, "We'll leave those cattle that started the rush last night until the last. If they scatter, we'll abandon them. Our mob has been too large. We'll break camp now. Move all the wagons and horses to the open break in the bush below. Then drove the main mob closer. Two guards on and off for two hours. We'll ford the river with the wagons, divide our party and camp on both sides until the last job, which will be to drove the mob across."

It was a bold and masterly plan, Sterl conceded. The execution remained to be an inspirition of genius and an heroic job. They mounted and rode away.

The river! The drovers, even their leader, had only to go within sight of that reed-bordered, mud-sloped, yellow swirling tide to be confronted by seeming impossibilities.

"Friday, where are the crocodiles?" boomed Dann.

"Alonga dere," replied the black, his spear indicating the river and the margins of reeds.

"Slyter, do they hide in the grass?"

"Yes, indeed. These big crocs live on animals. This water is brackish. Kangaroos, wild cattle, brumbies would drink it. I've been told how the crocs lie in wait and with one lash of their tails knock a large animal or an aborigine into the water."

"They may not be plentiful. But all of you use your eyes. Have your guns ready. Slyter, you will drive your wagon in first. Send a drover ahead to test the bottom. Make haste, while the tide is in."

They all watched Heald wade his sturdy horse into the river. After perhaps a hundred steps, he returned to say: "Mud bottom. Soft. But not quicksand. If you keep your horse moving you can make it."

"What will a heavy wagon do?" queried Slyter, dubiously.

"It'll stick, but not sink," declared Dann. "We have heavy ropes and strong horses. We can pull out." In a moment more Slyter, accompanied by Dann and six drovers, had driven his big teams into the river.

Slyter had not got quite so far out as Heald had waded when the wheels stuck. Two drovers leaped out of their saddles to unhitch the teams. Bligh and Hood dragged the teams out. Rollie, with a bag in front of him and a cracking stockwhip in hand, kept abreast of the teams. Soon they were swimming. Four drovers followed carrying packs. Slyter stood up in his wagon, rifle in hand, watching vigilantly.

"Crocs over dere all alonga," cried Friday, pointing.

Sterl saw the reeds shake and part, "Grab your rifle, Red," he shouted.

Suddenly on the opposite bank there was a loud

rush in the reeds, then a *zoom*, as a huge reptile leaped off the bank and slid upon the narrow strip of mud. But it was not quick enough to escape Red's shot.

Sterl heard the bullet thud, and then the huge reptile flopped up and flashed into convulsions. Sterl let out a yell as he drew a bead upon it and pulled the trigger. The distance was nothing to a marksman. His bullet, too, found its mark.

Another! Four shots left that reptile rolling in the mud. Its back seemed broken.

"Dere, alonga dere!" shrilled Friday, pointing below.

Slyter was shooting at another one, smaller and nimbler. But there was another rush and zoóm as a big one catapulted off the bank to meet a hail of lead. Crippled and slow, he crawled into the river.

Stanley Dann's horse appeared, wading out. The drovers dragged and yelled at the teams, while Rollie cracked his long whip from behind. They got across at last and climbed the bank to deposit the packs and find a place to land the wagon. Then they piled into the river-pell-mell, keeping close together, some of them with drawn guns held high.

Slyter yelled, "Make all the commotion possible."

They crossed in short order and, loading heavily turned back in haste, crossed again. Suddenly Friday screeched out something aboriginal. Then Slyter roared unintelligibly, and began to pump lead into the water. A thumping splash followed, then a vicious churning of the surface, yellow and red mixing.

"I got him!" shouted Slyter, peering down. "Right on top of me!—Longer than the wagon! Never saw him till he came up!"

When the drovers arrived at the wagon again, Stanley Dann called out lustily: "Boys, that was splendid work. I heard your big bullets hit. It's not so bad having Yankee gunmen with us!"

During nine more trips, while the cowboys, with Slyter, Larry and the black kept vigil from several points, nothing untoward happened. Dann, with three of the drovers, then remained on the far side with the teams backed out into the shallow water, while the other three, dragging tackle and ropes, swam their horses back to make fast to the wagon.

Bligh slid off his horse, and waist-deep groped about with his feet to find the wagon tongue. To watch him thus exposed made the cold sweat ooze out all over Sterl. Bligh found it, and went clear under to lift it up. In a moment more the heavy tackle was fast. He yelled and waved to Dann. The two teams sagged down and dug in; the drovers in front of the wagon laid hold of the thick rope. Slyter lifted his arms on high, swung his rifle, and added his yell to that of the others. A moment of strain and splash— then the empty wagon lurched, moved, half floated. Slyter stood up on the driver's seat, balancing himself, still peering into the water for crocodiles. The two teams and the six single horses did not slow up until the wheels touched bottom. In a very few moments the wagon was safely up on the bank. Despite the crocodiles the achievement augured well for the success of the operation.

CHAPTER
25

*A*LL this time the tide was slowly going out. The channel split wide bare stretches of mud. Sterl observed that a big crocodile which he had thought surely killed had disappeared from the bank opposite. The one Slyter had shot lay on its back, claw-like feet above the shallow water.

Some of Dann's party cut poles and brush to lay lengthwise on the mud over the plowed-up tracks of wheels and horses. Bill set about erecting a canvas shelter to work under; Sterl, Red and Friday hurried at camp tasks the crossing had halted. Presently Slyter and Dann's drovers, all except Roland, who had been left on the far side of the river, arrived muddy and wet, noisy and triumphant, back in camp.

"Volunteer wanted to drive the small dray," called the leader.

They all wanted that job. Dann chose Benson, the eldest. Six men cut brushy trees while two riders snaked these down to the river. Dann and Slyter built the corduroy road. Eric Dann lent a hand, like one in a trance. Friday pointed to aborigine smoke signals far back in the bush, and shook his shaggy head.

Many energetic hands made short work of the road on the camp side of the river. It was significant that Slyter covered his dead crocodile with brush. Then Benson drove the one-team dray off the bank. The brush road upheld both horses and wheels as long as they moved. But it stuck in the channel and, before it crossed, the drovers had to unload it and carry its contents to the far bank. By this time the afternoon was far spent, and Bill had supper ready. Benson volunteered to pack supper across to Roland and Bligh, left on guard, and remain over there with them.

The drovers, bedraggled, slimy from the river mud, ate like wolves, but were too tired to talk. Sterl and Red went out on duty with the mob.

Again the night was silent, except for the bark of dingoes and the silken swish of flying foxes. But the mob appeared to be free from the fears of the night before. Sterl and Red kept together, and after a few hours one of them watched while the other slept. But Sterl, in his wakeful intervals, could not rid himself of misgivings. His mind conjured up fateful events for which there seemed no reason.

At last the dawn came, from gray to daylight, and then a ruddiness in the east. He awakened Red from his hard bed on the grass. They rounded up the *remuda*, and changed their mounts for King and Duke.

"Red, it's dirty business to risk Leslie's horses in that river," said Sterl, as they rode campward.

"Wal, I was thinkin' thet same. We won't do it, 'cept to cross them. We'll fork two of these draft hosses. But, Holy Mackeli, *they* cain't keep one of them crocs away! I swear, pard, I never had my gizzard freeze like it does at thet thought."

"Nerve and luck, Red!"

"Them drovers shore had it yestiddy."

Breakfast was over at sunrise. Friday approached the fire to get his fare.

"Crocs alonga eberywhere," he announced.

That silenced the trekkers like a clap of thunder. Slyter, the cowboys, and the drovers followed the striding Dann out to view the stream. A dead steer floated by in mid-channel, gripped by several crocodiles. Downstream a cow or steer had stranded in the shallow water. Around it ugly snouts and notched tails showed above the muddy water. Upstream on the far side a third cow, stuck in the mud, was surrounded by the reptiles.

Larry explained, "Night before last a number of cattle rushed into the river. We heard them bawling and plunging."

Slyter said, "Blood scent in the river will have every croc for miles down upon us."

330 • Zane Grey

"It may not be so bad as it looks," replied the
leader with his usual optimism. "Let's cross Bill's
dray at once. Tell Bill to keep out food and tea for
today and tomorrow. One of you to put tucker on
the dray for the boys across there. A kettle of hot
tea! Who'll drive Bill's dray?"

Red Krehl elected himself for that job. But Dann
preferred to have the cowboy on shore, rifle in hand,
and selected Heald. He drove in until the water came
almost to the platform of the wagon. Then the pro-
cedure of the day before was carried out with even
more celerity. It struck Sterl that in their hurry the
drovers were forgetting about the crocodiles, which
might have been just as well. This big job done the
drovers took time out for a cup of tea. That inevitable
rite amused Sterl.

"Ormiston's wagon next," shouted Stanley Dann.
"That duty falls to Eric."

The drovers hitched two teams to this wagon,
while others, at the leader's order, unpacked half of
its contents. Flour in special burlap sacks and other
food supplies came to light.

At the take-off the leading team balked, and upon
being urged and whipped they plunged, and Eric laid
on the stockwhip. No doubt a scent of the dead crocodiles came to them. Stanley Dann boomed orders
that Eric did not hear or could not obey. About a
hundred steps out was as far as either of the other
vehicles had been driven. But Eric drove until the
teams balked, with the leaders submerged to their
shoulders. This was extremely bad, because it was

evident that they were sinking in the mud. Half a dozen drovers urged plunging horses to the rescue.

At that critical moment Friday let out a wild yell. Sterl saw a dead steer, surrounded by crocodiles, drifting down upon the teams.

"Back, Heald! Back, Hood!" shouted Sterl, at the top of his lungs. "CROCS!"

Snorting, lunging, the horses wheeled and sent mountains of water flying. They reached the shore just as the dead steer drifted upon the teams and lodged. Stanley Dann was yelling for his brother to climb back over the wagon and leap for his life. Eric might have heard, but his gaze was glued to the melee under him.

The dead steer drifted in between the two teams to lodge against the wagon tongue. And the great reptiles attacked the horses. The snap of huge jaws, the crack of teeth, could be heard amid the roar of water and the clamor of the drovers.

Eric pulled his gun and shot. Not improbably he hit the horses instead of the crocodiles. The left front horse reared high with a crocodile hanging to its nose. Sterl sent a bullet into its head, but it did not let go. It pulled the horse under. The right front horse was in the clutches of two crocodiles. The open jaws of one stuck beyond the neck of the horse. Krehl's rifle cracked. Sterl shot to kill a horse if he missed a crocodile. The second team had been attacked by half a dozen of the leviathans.

And at that awful moment for Eric Dann, horses and wagon were pulled into deep water. The wagon sank above its bed and floated. Eric leaped to the driver's seat and held on. As he turned to those on shore his visage appeared scarcely human. The wagon drifted down the river.

"Fellers, fork yore hosses!" yelled Red. Leaping on Duke, his rifle aloft, he raced into the bush downstream. Sterl was quick to follow, and he heard the thud and crash of the drovers at his heels. When he broke out into the clear, a low bank afforded access to the river, which made a bend there. He came out at the edge of the mud. Red had Duke wading out. The wagon had lodged in shallow water. A horrible fight was going on there. Beyond it several other crocodiles were tearing at a horse that had been cut adrift. Eric Dann still clung to the driver's seat.

Stanley Dann and his followers arrived. For once, the leader's booming voice was silent at a crisis.

Red threw aside his rifle. He held his revolver in his left hand and his lariat in his right. At that moment, a lean, black-jawed crocodile stuck his snout and shoulders out of the water, and, reaching over the wagonbed, snapped at Eric. He missed by more than two feet.

The horses had ceased to struggle. What with the tugging and floundering of the crocodiles the wagon appeared about to tilt over. It would all be over with Eric Dann if the reptiles did not tear the horses free.

Red sent his grand horse plunging into the water. Duke's ears stood up, his piercing snorts made the other horses neigh wildly. Red was taking a chance

that the crocodiles would be too busy to see him.
When Duke was up to his flanks and the curdled,
foamy maelstrom scarcely a lasso's length distant,
Red yelled piercingly: *"Stand up, Eric!"*

The man heard, and tried to obey. But he must
have been paralyzed with horror.

"Stick out yore laig—yore arm!" shrieked Red,
in a fury, and he shot the outside crocodile, sliding
into view.

But Eric was beyond helping himself. Again that
ugly brute lunged out and up, his corrugated jaws
wide, and as they snapped they missed by only a few
inches.

Then the lasso shot out, and the noose cracked
over Eric's head and shoulders. Red whirled the big
horse and spurred him shoreward. Eric was jerked
off the wagon, over the very backs of the threshing
crocodiles. Red dragged him free, through the shallow water, up on the mud. He leaped off, to run and
loosen the noose. Eric's head had been dragged
through the mud. Stanley and two drovers lifted the
half-dead man, and carried him ashore. Sterl sat on
his horse with his throat constricted. He had not
cared much about Eric Dann, but the mad risk that
intrepid cowboy had run! ...

"He ain't—hurt none," Red panted, coiling the
muddy rope. "I was afraid—I'd get the noose—
'round his neck. But it was a damn narrow shave!
Pard, that's one hoss—in a million. By Gawd, I was
scared he—wouldn't do it. But he did—he did!"

They laid Eric Dann on the bank to let him recover. Sterl dismounted, and every time a head or a body lunged up he met it with a bullet. But the angle was bad. Most of the bullets glanced singingly across the river. One by one the horses were torn loose from the traces, and dragged away, until they disappeared under the deep water.

The heavy wagon had remained upright, with the back end and wheels submerged. The tide was falling.

"Miraculous, any way you look at it!" exclaimed Stanley Dann. "Red Krehl, as if my debt to you had not been great enough!"

"Hell, boss. We've all been around yestiddy an' today, when things came off," drawled the cowboy.

At low tide Ormiston's wagon was hauled out and back to camp. The girls clamored for the story. Red laughed at them, but Sterl told it, not wholly without elaboration. He wanted to see Beryl Dann's eyes betray her quick and profound emotions.

"For my uncle! Red—when he hated you!"

"Beryl, all in the day's ride," drawled Red. "Now if you was only like Duke!"

"Red, I am not a horse. I am a woman," she rejoined with no response to his humor.

"Shore, I know thet. I mean a hoss, if he's great like Duke an' cottons to a feller why he'll do anythin' for you." Red also had turned serious. "Beryl, I'd die for him, an' shore he'd die for me."

"I'd like you to feel that way for me, Red Krehl," she returned, vibrantly. "I would die for you!"

"Wal, yore wants, like yore eyes an' yore heart, air too big for you, Beryl."

Leslie let go of Duke's neck to face Red.

"Red, I give Duke to you. And you can return Jester to me," she said.

"Wal! Dog-gone-it, Les, you hit me below the belt!"

"It'll make me happy. And Beryl too."

Stanley Dann broke in upon them with his booming order:

"Cut more poles. We'll relay the road and cross my wagon before this day is done."

While his drovers worked like beavers, he had Beryl's bed and baggage unloaded. Stanley drove his big wagon across. Friday sighted crocodiles, but none came near. Load and wagon were crossed in record time, after which six drovers carried Beryl's belongings across in two trips.

The sun set red and evilly. The trekkers ate, and tried to be oblivious to the abo signals, the uncanny bats, the howls of the dingoes and the unseen menace that hovered over this somber camp. Stanley Dann roused them all in the gray of dawn. It was wet and chill. Dingoes bayed dismally in the bush. The cowboys found two of Dann's drovers mustering horses for the day. The cowboys bridled Duke, King and Lady Jane, and drove the rest of Leslie's horses into camp. Stanley Dann's hearty voice, his spirit, the drab gray dawn lighting ruddily, the hot breakfast—all seemed to work against the gripping, somber spell.

"Men, this is our important day," boomed the

leader. "Roland's wagon first. Unload all the heavy articles. Pack these bags of dried fruit Ormiston had—unknown to me. Slyter, will you drive Roland's wagon?"

"Yes," replied Slyter. "Mum, you ride with me."

"With Beryl and Leslie that will be a load!" said Dann.

"Dad, I won't cross in the wagon," spoke up his daughter decidedly.

Leslie interposed to say, "I'm riding Lady Jane."

The leader gazed at these pioneer daughters with great luminous eyes, and made no further comment. He hurried the unpacking, and the hitching of two big draft horses to Roland's wagon. The sun came up gloriously bright. When Slyter mounted the high wagon seat, shouts from across the river told him that the drovers over there were ready. Roland straddled one of the lead horses of the teams. The tide was on the make, wanting a foot in height and a dozen yards up the mud bank to fill the river bed.

"Friday! Everybody watch the river for crocs," ordered the leader.

Leslie sat her horse, pale and resolute. She knew the peril. At this juncture Beryl emerged from the tent, slim in her rider's garb. She carried a small black bag.

"Red, will you carry me across?" she asked, simply. Her darkly dilated eyes betrayed her terror.

"Shore, Beryl, but why for?" drawled the cowboy.

"I'd feel safer—and—and—"

"Wal, dog-gone! There. Put yore foot on my stirrup. Up you come! No, I cain't hold you that way, Beryl. You've gotta fork Duke. Slip down in front of me. Sterl, how about slopin'?"

"Friday grins good-o," replied Sterl, grimly. "Les, keep above me close. Larry, keep upstream from Red. Idea is to move pronto!"

They plunged in, passed Slyter's teams and the drovers, reached the deeper water, breasted the channel.

"Fellers, get ready for gunplay!" shouted the hawk-eyed Red. "Shet yore eyes, Beryl!"

Across the river from the reedy bank above Roland's position came a crackling rush, a waving of reeds, then a *zoom*, as a big crocodile took to the water. The guns of Roland's group banged; mud splattered all around the reptile.

Farther upstream, muddy-backed crocodiles, as huge as logs, piled into the river. The drovers were clamoring in fright and excitement. Slyter had driven his teams in up to their flanks. One drover was unfastening the traces, while two others were ready to drag the teams into the channel. Sterl spared only a glance for them. Roland and his men came pounding through the shallow water. Halfway across—two-thirds! Bligh's horse was lunging into the channel above Larry, carrying the tackle and rope for the wagon.

Suddenly, almost in line with them, an open-jawed, yellow-fanged monster spread the reeds, and zoomed off the bank. Red, Sterl, Larry, Roland, were shooting. But the crocodile came on, got over his depth, and disappeared.

"Watch for the wake!" called Red. "Thet feller is mean. Heah he comes! See them little knobs. That's his haid!"

Sterl espied them. He regretted having left his rifle in the wagon.

"Drop behind me, Leslie," he called. "Don't weaken. We'll get by him."

Sterl did not fire because he did not want to drive the brute under water again. Evidently Red had the same thought. He headed Duke quarteringly away from the long ripple, and leaned far forward, gun extended. His left arm held the drooping girl. At the right instant he spurred Duke. Just then Duke struck bottom, and lunged. The crocodile was less than six feet distant when Red turned his gun loose. The bullets splashed and thudded, but they did not glance. With a tremendous swirl the reptile lurched partly out of the water, a ghastly spectacle. Sterl sent two leaden slugs into it. Falling back, the monster began to roll over and over, his ten-foot tail beating the water into foam.

Red waded Duke past the teams and waiting drovers, out onto the bank. The drovers cheered. Sterl, with Leslie behind him, followed Red up to the new camp. Red slid off and laid his gun on the grass. Beryl swayed, her eyes tight shut.

"Beryl, come out of it," shouted Red. Her arms fell weakly.

"I won't—faint! I won't," she cried with passion

still left in her weak voice.

"Who said you would?" drawled Red, as he helped her off.

Leslie dismounted and came to Beryl. They clung together—a gesture more eloquent than any words.

"Come, pard. Let's slope out there," called Red.

When they rode out on the mud flat again Sterl was amazed to see Friday dragging what evidently was the monster crocodile into shallow water. A long spear sticking in the reptile spoke for itself. A splashing melee distracted Sterl. The two teams were straining on the ropes, plowing through the mud. Between them and the wagon the drovers were yelling and hauling. Sterl observed that this wagon, the one in which he had calked the seams, floated almost flat. Mrs. Slyter stood behind her husband hanging on to the seat while he made ready for the waiting teams. Once the wagon was in shallow water they unfastened the ropes and tackles, hitched the two teams and gave Slyter the word to drive out.

Sterl and Red followed the muddy procession up the bank.

Friday said to Sterl and Slyter, "Tinkit more better boss wait alonga sun. Crocs bad!"

"We can't stop Dann now," Slyter said, grimly. "Come, all who're going back."

"Wal, if you ask me we oughta load our guns," drawled Red.

FIVE drovers crossed the river with Sterl and Red. Dann met them like a general greeting a victorious army.

"We've time to drove Slyter's horses across, and carry these loose supplies," he said. "Tomorrow we will muster the cattle that rushed and drove the mob."

When next morning the drovers had the big herd lengthened out to perhaps half a mile, at a signal from Dann they opened fire with their guns and charged. The fifty-yard-wide belt of cattle headed for the river and piled over the low bank. Across the river crocodiles basked in the sun, their odor thick on the air. The leading cattle took fright and balked. Then it was too late. The pushing, bawling lines behind forced them on. Some of them were bogged, to be trampled under. But almost miraculously the mob were driven into the mud before they could attempt a rush back.

The point of least resistance lay to the fore. The leaders had to gravitate that way. From the opposite bank crocodiles slid down and shot across the mud into the shallow water. Released from a wall in front, the mass behind piled frantically into the river. As if by a miracle, thousands of horned heads breasted the channel. In several spots swirling, churning battles ensued, almost at once to be overridden by swimming cattle. As the front line struck bottom, the stench of the crocodiles and their furious attack, precipitated a rush that was obscured in flying spray.

"Come on, pard!" yelled Red, from below. "We wanta be close behind that stampede or the crocs will get us!"

All the other drovers were in the mud, some at the heels of the mob, others shooting crippled and smashed cattle. The horse herd, driven in the wake of the mob, excited by the roar, made frantic efforts to get ahead. When they found bottom again, and plunged on into shallow water, Sterl looked up.

A sea of bobbing backs sloped up to a fringe of bobbing horns. The long belt of cattle was moving with amazing speed. Sterl gazed back. Mired cattle dotted the river. Squirming crocodiles attested to the trampling they had received. Only one horse was down, and it appeared to be struggling to rise.

"Laig broke!" yelled Red, close to Sterl's ear.

"Saddled too! By Gawd, pard, that's Eric Dann's hoss! An' if he ain't lyin' there on the mud, my eyes air pore!"

Stanley Dann and two others appeared riding at a gallop. The leader was pointing at the fallen horse and rider. Sterl and Red had already headed in his direction.

"Look!—a croc slipping off into deep water," yelled Sterl.

Stanley Dann reached the prostrate man and horse ahead of Bligh and Heald. Sterl and Red got there as the drovers were dismounting, to sink ankle-deep in the mud.

"It's Eric!" boomed the leader, as he leaned over. "Dead—or—no! He's still alive."

"Horse's front legs broken," reported Bligh, tensely.

"Shoot it! And help me—two of you."

They lifted him across Bligh's saddle. How limp he hung! What a slimy, broken wreck of a man!

"Hazelton, you and Krehl and Heald follow the mob," ordered the leader, harshly. "That rush will end soon."

From the height of bank Sterl looked over bush-land and green downs which led to higher and denser bush. In the foreground, the mob of cattle had halted.

"All the stampede is out of them," said Red.

"Crocodile stampede. New one on us, Red," rejoined Sterl.

"Cost Dann and Slyter plenty. Hundreds of cattle down, daid an' dyin' Sterl, about Dann's drovers—

after this last shuffle, what's the deal gonna be?"

"You mean if Eric Dann holds up the trek?"

"I shore mean that little thing."

"Damn serious, pard."

"Serious? If Bligh an' Hood an' the others stick it out, I'd say it'll be a damn sight more than any Americans would do. 'Cept a couple of dumb-haid, lovesick suckers like us!"

When the cowboys arrived, the cattle had begun to lie down, too exhausted even to bawl. The horses had scattered off to the left toward camp. Sterl and Red helped muster them and drove them within sight of the wagons.

"What held up Stanley Dann?" inquired Bligh, as the drovers collected again. Bligh was a young man, under thirty, gray-eyed and still-faced, a man on whom the other drovers leaned.

"Eric injured. Legs broken I think," replied Sterl.

Bligh exchanged apprehensive glances with his intimates. He turned back to Sterl: "If the boss's brother is unable to travel, it'll precipitate a most serious situation."

"We appreciate that. Let's hope it's not so bad he cannot be moved in a wagon."

"Yes. You hope so, but you don't believe it," said Bligh, brusquely.

"Righto."

"Hazelton, we all think you and Krehl are wonderful drovers, and what is more, right good cobbers," said Bligh, feelingly.

"Thanks, Bligh," returned Sterl, heartily. "Red

and I sure return the compliment."

"For us this trek seems to have run into a forlorn hope."

"Well, Bligh, I'm bound to agree with you. But it's not a lost cause yet."

The drover shook his shaggy head, and ran skinned, dirty fingers through his scant beard. "Friend, it's different with you cowboys, on account of the girls—if you'll excuse my saying so."

Neither Beryl nor Leslie put in an appearance at supper. Dann seemed for once an unapproachable figure. Slyter conversed in low tones with his wife, and once Sterl saw him throw up his hands in a singular gesture for him. Red stayed in the tent. The seven young drovers remained in a group at the other side of camp, where Bligh appeared to be haranguing them.

Suddenly Bligh, leading Derrick, Hod and Heald, rose and started toward Stanley Dann's shelter. Pale despite their tan, resolute despite their fear! It did not seem a coincidence that Beryl and Leslie appeared from nowhere; that Slyter came out, his hair ruffled, his gaze fixed; that Red emerged from his tent, his lean hawklike head poised; that Friday hove in sight, lending to the scene the stark reality of the aborigine.

Under Dann's shelter it was still light. Mrs. Slyter stood beside the stretcher where Eric Dann lay, his head and shoulders propped up on pillows, fully conscious and ghastly pale. His legs were covered with a blanket. Stanley Dann sat with bowed head. The drovers halted just outside of the shelter. Bligh took a further step.

"Mr. Dann, is it true Eric is injured?" burst out Bligh, as if forced.

Dann rose to his full height to stare at his visitors. He stalked out then like a man who faced death.

"Bligh, I grieve to inform you that he is," he said.

"We are—very sorry for him—and you," rejoined Bligh huskily.

"I'm sure of that, Bligh."

"Will it be possible to move him? In a wagon, you know, to carry on our trek?"

"No! Even with proper setting of the bones he may be a cripple for life. To move him now—over rough ground—would be inhuman."

"What do you intend to do?"

"Stay here until he is mended enough to travel."

"That would take weeks, sir. Perhaps more...."

"Yes. Weeks. There is no alternative."

Bligh made a gesture of inexpressible regret. He choked. He cleared his throat. "Mr. Dann, we—we feared this very thing.... We talked it over. We can't—we won't—go on with this wild-goose trek. You started all right. Then Ormiston and your brother.... No sense in crying over spilled milk! We've stuck to the breaking point. We four have decided to trek back home."

"Bligh!—*you too*?" boomed the leader. Sterl saw him change as if he had shriveled up inside.

"Yes *me*!" rang out Bligh. "You ask too much of young men. We built our hopes on your promises.

Hood has a wife and child. Derrick is sick of this. . . . We are going home."

"Bligh, I have exacted too much of you all," returned Dann. "I'm sorry. If I had it to do over again. . . . You are welcome to go, and God speed you. . . . Take two teams for Ormiston's wagon. It is half full of food supplies. Bill will give you a box of tea. And if you can muster the cattle that rushed up the river— you are welcome to them."

"Boss—that is big and fine—of you," returned Bligh, haltingly. "Honestly, sir. . . ."

"Don't thank me, Bligh. I am in your debt."

Eric Dann called piercingly from under the shelter. "Bligh—tell him—*tell him!*"

"No Eric," returned Bligh, sorrowfully. "I've nothing to tell."

"Tell me what?" boomed the leader, like an angry lion aroused. "Bligh, what have you to tell me?"

"Nothing, sir. Eric is out of his head."

"No I'm not," yelled Eric, and his attempt to push himself higher on the stretcher ended in a shriek of pain. But he did sit up, and Mrs. Slyter supported him.

"Eric, what could Bligh tell me?" queried Stanley Dann, hoarsely.

There ensued a silence that seemed insupportable to Sterl. Every moment added to the torment of coming terrible disclosures. Eric Dann must have been wrenched by physical pain and mental anguish to a point beyond resistance. "Stanley—we are lost!" he groaned.

"Lost?" echoed the giant, blankly.

"Yes—yes. *Lost!*" cried Eric wildly. "We've been lost all the way! I didn't know this bushland.... I've never been on a trek through outback Queensland!"

"Merciful heaven!" boomed the leader, his great arms going aloft. "Your plans? Your assurances? Your map!"

"Lies! All lies!" wailed Eric Dann. "I never was inland—from the coast. I met Ormiston. He talked cattle. He inflamed me about a fabulous range in the Northern Territory—west of the Gulf. Gave me the map we've trekked by. I planned with him to persuade you to muster a great mob of cattle.... I didn't know that he was the bushranger Pell. That map is false. I couldn't confess—I couldn't—I kept on blindly.... We're lost—Bligh knows that. Ormiston could not corrupt him. Yet he wouldn't betray me to you. We're lost—irretrievably lost. And I'm damned—to hell!"

Stanley Dann expelled a great breath and sat down on a pack as if his legs had been chopped from under him.

"Lost? Yea, God has forsaken me," he whispered.

Bligh was the first to move after a stricken silence. "Mr. Dann you've got to hear that I didn't know all Eric confessed."

"Bligh, that is easy to believe, thank heaven," said Stanley, presently, his voice gaining timbre. "We'll thresh it all out right now.... Somebody light a fire to dispel this hateful gloom. Let me think a moment." And he paced somberly to and fro outside the shelter. Presently Stanley Dann faced them and the light; once more himself.

"Listen, all of you," he began, and again his voice had that wonderful deep roll. "I cannot desert my brother. Whoever does stay here with me must carry on with the trek when we are able to continue. I have exacted too much of you all. I grieve that I have been wrong, self-centered, dominating. Beryl, my daughter, will you stay?"

"Dad, I'll stay!" There was no hesitation in Beryl's reply, and to Sterl she seemed at last of her father's blood and spirit. "Don't despair, Dad. We shall not *all* betray you!"

A beautiful light warmed his grave visage as he turned to Leslie, "Child, you have been forced into womanhood. I doubt if your parents should influence your decision here."

"I would not go back to marry a royal duke!" replied Leslie.

"Mrs. Slyter, your girl has indeed grown up on this trek," went on Dann. "But she will still need a mother. Will you stay?"

"Need you ask, Stanley? I don't believe whatever lies in store for us could be so bad as what we've lived through," rejoined the woman, calmly.

"Slyter?"

"Stanley, I started the race and I'll make the good fight."

"Hazelton!" demanded Dann, without a trace of doubt. His exclamation was not a query.

"I am keen to go on," answered Sterl.

"Krehl!"

The cowboy was lighting a cigarette, a little clumsily, because Beryl was hanging to his arm. He puffed a cloud of smoke which hid his face.

"Wal, boss," he drawled, "it's shore a great privilege you've given me. Jest a chanct to know an' fight for a man!"

Larry, Rollie, and Benson, almost in unison, hastened to align themselves under Red's banner.

Bill, the cook, stepped forward and unhesitatingly spoke: "Boss, I've had enough. I'm getting old. I'll go home with Bligh."

"Bingham, put it up to our black man Friday," said Dann.

Slyter spoke briefly in that jargon which the black understood.

Friday leaned on his long spear and regarded the speakers with his huge, unfathomable eyes. Then he swerved them to Sterl and Red, to Beryl, to Leslie, and tapped his broad black breast with a slender black hand: "Imm no fadder, no mudder, no brudder, no gin, no lubra," he said, in slow, laborious dignity. "Tinkit go bush alonga white fella cowboy pards!"

At another time Sterl would have shouted his gladness, but here he only hugged the black man. And Red clapped him on the back.

Suddenly a heavy gunshot boomed hollowly under the shelter, paralyzing speech and action. The odor of burnt powder permeated the air. There followed a queer, faint tapping sound—a shuddering quiver of hand or foot of a man in his death throes. Sterl had heard that too often to be deceived. Stanley

Dann broke out of his rigidity to wave a shaking hand. "Go in—somebody—see!" he whispered.

Benson and Bligh went slowly and hesitatingly under the shelter. Sterl saw them over Eric Dann on the stretcher. They straightened up. Bligh drew a blanket up over the man's face. That pale blot vanished under the dark covering. The drovers stalked out. Bligh accosted the leader in hushed voice: "Prepare for a shock, sir."

Benson added gruffly: "He blew out his brains!"

Red Krehl was the first to speak, as he drew Beryl away from that dark shelter. "Pard," he ejaculated, "he's paid! By Gawd, he's shot himself—the only good thing he's done on this trek! Squares him with me!"

N *O MAN* ever again looked upon the face of Eric Dann. The agony of his last moment after the confession of the deceit which plunged his brother and the drovers into tragic catastrophe was cloaked in the blanket thrown over him. An hour after the deed which was great in proportion to his weakness, he lay in his grave. Sterl helped dig it by the light of a torch which Friday held.

They were called to a late supper. Bill, actuated by a strange sentiment at variance with his abandonment of the trek, excelled himself on this last meal. The leader did not attend it.

No orders to guard the mob were issued that night. But Sterl heard Bligh tell his men they would share their last watch. The girls, wide-eyed and sleepless, haunted the bright fire. They did not want to be alone. Sterl and Red sought their own tent.

"Hard lines, pard," said Red, with a sigh, as he lay down. "It's turrible to worry over other people. But mebbe this steel trap on our gizzards will loosen now that Eric at last made a clean job of it. You never can tell about what a man will do.... An' as for a woman—didn't yore heart jest flop over when Beryl answered her dad?"

"Red, it sure did!"

"Bingham, we break camp at once," said Stanley Dann as he met Slyter at breakfast. "What do you say to trekking west along this river?"

"I say good-o," replied the drover. "Why not divide the load on the second dray? There's room on the wagons. That dray is worn out. Leave it here."

"I agree," returned the leader. Already the tremendous incentive of starting a new trek, in the right direction, had seized upon them all.

"My wife can drive my wagon. So can Leslie, where it's not overrough. We'll be shy of drovers, Stanley."

"Plenty bad black fella close up," Friday broke in.

Rollie tramped up to report that the mob was still resting, but that the larger herd of horses had been scattered.

"We found one horse speared and cut up. Abo work," added Rollie.

"Could these savages prefer horseflesh to beef?"

queried Dann, incredulous.

"Some tribes do, I've been told. Bligh heard blacks early this morning," asserted Slyter. "We cannot get away any too soon now."

Bligh and his three dissenters drove a string of horses across the river. Bill, the cook, had slipped down the bank, under cover of the brush, to straddle one of those horses. He did not say good-by nor look back but followed the drovers down the path, and into the river.

"Queer deal that," spoke up the ever vigilant Red, who sat by the fire oiling his rifle. "Bligh was sweet on Beryl at first. You'd reckon he'd say good-by an' good luck to her, if not the old man."

"Red, I'll bet you two-bits Bligh comes back."

"Gosh, I hope he does. I jest feel sorry for him, as I shore do for the *other* geezers who got turribly stuck on Beryl Dann...."

"Uk—oh!" warned Sterl, too late.

Beryl had passed Red, to hear the last of his scornful remark to Sterl.

"You're sorry for whom, Red Krehl?"

"Beryl, I was sorry for Bligh," drawled Red, coolly. "Me an' Sterl air gamblin' on his sayin' good-by to you. I'm bettin' thet if he's smart he won't try. Sterl bets he will."

"And if Bligh's smart *why* won't he try to say good-by to me?" retorted Beryl.

"Wal, he'll get froze for his pains."

"He will indeed—the coward! And now what

about the *other* geezers who're stuck on Beryl Dann?"

"Aw, just natoorally I feel sorry for them."

"Why—*Why*? You-all-of-a-sudden noble per-son!" she flashed, furiously.

"Wal, Miss Dann, it so happens thet I'm one of them unfortunate geezers who got turribly stuck on you," returned the cowboy.

All in one moment, Beryl was transformed from a desperately hurt woman, passionately furious, to one amazed, bluntly told the truth that she had yearned for and ever doubted, robbed at once of all her blaze, to be left pale as pearl.

"Mr. Krehl, it's a pity—you never told me," she cried. "Perhaps the *geezer* who's so terribly *stuck* on me might have found out he's not really so unfor-tunate, after all."

"Come out of it, kids," whispered Sterl. "Here comes Bligh, and I win the bet."

The young drover faced Sterl to remove his som-brero and bow. Water dripped off him from the waist down.

"Beryl, I dislike to go—like this," he said huskily. "But when I came on this trek I had hopes—of—of—of—you know what. I pray your Dad gets safely through—and I wish you happiness. If it is as we—we all guess, then the best man has won!"

"Oh, Bob, how sweet of you!" cried Beryl, ra-diantly, and all the pride and scorn of her were as if they had never been. "I'm sorry for all—that you must go....Kiss me good-by!" And giving him her hands she leaned to him and lifted a scarlet face.

Bligh kissed her heartily, but not on her lips. Then releasing her he turned to Sterl and Red.

"Hazelton, Krehl, it's been dinkum to know you," he said, extending his hand. "Good-by and good luck." Then Bligh espied Dann coming from his wagon, and strode to intercept him. At that instant Red leaped like a panther. *"Injuns!"* he yelled, *"Duck!"*

Sterl ducked, his swift gaze taking the direction of Red's leveling rifle. He was in time to see a naked savage on the ridge in the very action of throwing a spear. Then Red's rifle cracked. The abo fell back out of sight on the ridge.

Sterl heard, too, almost simultaneously, the chucking thud of a spear entering flesh. Wheeling he saw the long shaft quivering in the middle of Bligh's broad back.

"Get down behind something!" yelled Sterl, at the top of his lungs. And he ran for the rifle leaning against a wagon wheel.

"Plenty black fella—close up," panted Friday, and pointed to the low rise of brushy ground just back of camp.

Red's rifle cracked again. There was a hideous screech of agony. Dann and Slyter had taken refuge behind Slyter's wagon. A drover was hurrying the women inside it. "Lie down!" Slyter commanded. "Stanley, here's one of my rifles.... Watch sharp! Along that bit of bush!"

Yells of alarm from the drovers across the river drew from Dann a booming order: "Stay over there! Ride! Abo attack!"

Sterl swept his glance around in search of Red. It passed over Bligh, who was lying on his side, in a last convulsive writhing.

"Pard," shouted Red, from behind the dray a dozen steps away, "they sneaked on us from the left. They'll work back that way. An' I seen Larry an' Ben ridin' hell bent for the river bank. We'll heah them open the ball pronto. . . ."

Red's rifle spoke ringingly. "Ha! These abos ain't so careful as redskins."

"Where's Rollie?"

"To my right heah, back of thet log. But he's only got his six-gun. Pard, put yore hat on somethin' an' stick it up, all same old times."

The ruse drew whistling spears. One struck the wagon seat; the other pierced Sterl's hat and jerked it away.

Again Red shot. "I got that bird, pard. Seen him throw. Aw no, these blacks cain't throw a spear atall!"

Then the drovers across the river entered the engagement, and Larry and Benson began to shoot.

"They must be slopin', pard, but I cain't see any," called Red.

The firing ceased. One of the drovers across the river hailed Dann:

"They broke and ran. A hundred or so."

"Which way?"

"Back over the downs."

"You drovers get on!" yelled Dann. "Clear out! Bligh's done for!"

Friday appeared, darting from tree to tree, and

disappeared. Red came running to join Sterl. "All over most before it started," he said. "Did you bore one, pard?"

"I'm afraid not. But I made one yell."

"Wal, I made up for thet. They was great tall fellers, Sterl, an' not black atall. Kinda a cross between brown an' yaller."

Presently Friday strode back into camp, his arms full of spears and wommeras. The cowboys met him, and Slyter and Dann followed in haste. Rollie was next to arrive.

"Black fella run alonga dere," said Friday. "All afraid guns. Come back bimeby."

Red gazed down at the dead drover: "My gawd, ain't thet tough? Jest a second quicker an' I'd saved him! I saw somethin' out of the corner of my eye. Too late!"

"Bligh stepped in front of me in time to save my life," rolled Dann, tragically. "That black was after me! Friday, will those abos track us?" queried Dann.

"Might be. Pretty cheeky."

"Pack! Hazelton, you and Krehl go with Larry and Benson. Drove the mob up the river. We'll follow behind the horses. Slyter, you and Friday help me bury this poor fellow."

Riding out with the drovers, the cowboys had a look at the dead aborigines. The savage who had murdered Bligh lay in the grass on the open ridge where Red had espied him. The abo did not resemble Friday in any particular. He was taller, more slender, more marvelously formed. The color appeared to be a cast between brown and red. His visage was brutish and wild, scarcely human. Red was wrathful over the fine horse the abos had slaughtered and cut up. "Hoss-meat eaters! When there was live beef an' daid beef for the takin'!"

The mob had moved upriver of its own volition. The drovers caught up in short order. The ground on this side of the river made better going than that on the other. The surface was hard and level, the grass luxuriant, and clumps of brushland widened away to the north. The sky was black with circling, drooping birds of prey. The larger gum trees were white with birds. Ahead of the mob, kangaroos dotted the rippling downs.

Friday, trotting along beside Sterl's horse, spears and wommera in hand, often gazed back over his shoulder. It was not possible to believe they had seen the last of this strange and warlike tribe of aborigines. According to Slyter, a daylight attack was extremely rare. The earliest dawn hour had always been the most favorable for the blacks to attack and perhaps the worst for the drovers, since tired guards are likely to fall asleep.

Toward sundown Slyter left his wife to drive his wagon and mounting a horse rode ahead, obviously to pick a camp site. Besides grass, water and firewood, there was now imperative need of a camp which the aborigines could not approach under cover. Sunset had come when Slyter finally called a halt. Three gum trees marked the spot. Off toward the river a hundred rods grew a dense copse fringed by isolated bushes. The rest was level, grassy downs.

"From now on everyone does two men's work," boomed Dann. "Mrs. Slyter and the girls take charge of rations and cooking. We men will supply firewood, and wash dishes."

"It's important to sleep away from the fire and the wagons," asserted Slyter. "Keep a fire burning all night. Blacks often spear men while they are asleep."

"Old stuff for me an' Sterl, boss," drawled Red. "We're used to sleepin' with one eye open. An' heah—why we can heah a grasshopper scratch his nose!"

But none of the trekkers laughed any more, nor smiled.

The cowboys helped Dann and Slyter carry ground cloths, blankets and nets over to the fringe of brush near the copse. That appeared to be an impenetrable thorny brake, a favorable place, thought Sterl. Beds were laid under the brush. The three women were to sleep between Dann and Slyter. The greedy mosquitoes had become a secondary trial.

The men returned to the fire.

"It will be bright moonlight presently," Dann said. "That's in our favor. Benson, take Larry and Roland on guard. I needn't tell you to be vigilant. Stay off your horses unless there's a rush, or something unusual. Come in after midnight to wake Hazelton and Krehl."

"Hazelton, where will you sleep?" asked Benson.

"What do you say, Red?" returned Sterl.

"Somewhere pretty close to these trees, on the side away from the open. We'll heah you when you call."

When a gentle hand fell on his shoulder and Friday's voice followed, Sterl felt that he had not had his eyes closed longer than a moment.

"All well, Friday?" he asked.

"Eberytink good. But bimeby bad," replied the black.

Red had sat up putting on the coat he had used for a pillow. Everything was wet with dew. The moon had soared beyond the zenith and blazed down with supernatural whiteness. The downs resembled a snowy range. A ghastly stillness reigned over the wilderness. Even the mosquitoes had gone.

At the campfire the three drovers whom they were to relieve sat drinking tea.

"How was tricks, Ben?" asked Red.

"Mob bedded down. Horses quiet. Not a move. Not a sound."

The mob was like a checkerboard on the silvery downs. They passed the two herds of horses, the larger of which, Dann's, were grouped between the cattle and the camp.

Red chose a position near a single tree on that side from which they could see both the mob and the *remuda*. They remained on foot. Friday made off into the ghostly brightness, returned to squat under the tree. His silence seemed encouraging.

"Let's take turns dozin'," suggested Red, and

proceeded to put that idea into execution.

Sterl marked a gradual slanting of the moon and a diminishing of the radiance. He fell into a half slumber. When he awakened the moon was far down and weird. The hour before dawn was close at hand.

"Pard, there's no change in the herd, but Dann's hosses have worked off a bit, an' Slyter's air almost in camp," said Red.

"Ssh!" hissed the black. If he had heard anything he did not indicate what or whence. Rifles in hands, the cowboys stood motionlessly in the shadows of the tree. Several times Friday laid his ear to the ground, an action remarkably similar to that of Indian scouts they had worked with. The gray gloom made the campfire fade into a ghostly flicker.

"Smellum black fella!" whispered Friday suddenly. Like a hound, his keenest sense was in his nose. An aboriginal himself, he smelled the approach of his species on the downs.

"What do?" whispered Sterl, hoarsely, leaning to Friday's ear.

"Tinkit more better along here."

"Pard, I cain't smell a damn thing," whispered Red.

"I'm glad I can't. If we could—these abos would be close....Red, it's far worse to stand than a Comanche stalk."

"*Ssh!*" The black added a hand to his caution. Again the cowboys became statues.

"Obber dere," whispered Friday. And to Sterl's great relief he pointed away from camp. But though

Sterl strained his ears to the extent of pain he could not hear a sound.

Suddenly the speaking and sinister silence broke to a thud of hoofs. Sterl jerked up as if galvanized.

"Skeered hoss. But not bad. Reckon he got a scent, like Friday," whispered Red.

Another little run of hoofs on soft ground!

"I heahed a hoss wicker," whispered Red, intensely. Friday held up his hand. Events were about to break, and Sterl greeted the fact with a release of tension.

Whang! On the still air sped a strange sound, familiar, though Sterl could not identify it. Instantly there followed the peculiar thud of missile entering flesh! It could not have been a bullet, for no report followed. Hard on that sound came the shrill, horrid unearthly scream of a horse in mortal agony. A pounding of hoofs—and a heavy body thudding the ground. The herd took fright, snorting and whistling.

"You savvy wommera?" asked Friday, in a whisper.

"I shore did. An' you bet I shivered in my boots," replied Red.

Then the strange sound, almost a twang, became clear to Sterl's mind.

"Black fella spearum hoss," added Friday.

Red broke into curses. "They're cuttin' up one of our hosses....I can heah the rip of hide! Let's sneak over an' shoot the gizzards out of them!"

CHAPTER
28

S *TERL* gave grim acquiescence to Red's bold suggestion.

But Friday whispered: "More better black fella go alonga bush corroboree."

"Pard, he talks sense," said Red. "It's better we let the abos gorge themselves on horse meat, than for us to run the littlest risk."

"Righto, Red. But it galls me," rejoined Sterl, and lapsed into silence again. New, faint sounds reached their ears—what must have been a rending of bones. Splashing sounds succeeded; and then the keenest listening was in vain. At daylight Red said he would ride out and see what signs the marauding abos might have left. Sterl returned to camp.

All the men were up and Slyter was helping his

wife get breakfast. His eyes questioned Sterl in mute anxiety. But upon hearing Sterl's report he was far from mute. Dann, too, ground his teeth.

"We could spare a bullock, but a good horse—"

"Boss," said Red, as he rode into camp, "I found where them abos had killed an' butchered yore hoss. Nary hide nor hair nor hoof left! Must have been a hundred abos in thet outfit!"

For ten nights that band of aboriginals, reinforced at every camp, hung on the tracks of the trekkers. Nothing was ever seen of them but their haunting smoke magic. The silence, the mystery, the inevitable attack on the horses in the gray dawn, wore increasingly upon the drovers. The savages never killed a beef. The horrible fear they impressed upon the pursued was that when they tired of horseflesh they would try to obtain human flesh. For Slyter averred that they were cannibals. Friday, when anyone mentioned this dire possibility, looked blank.

Now the trekkers approached the end of the downs. The river had diminished to a creek. Day by day the patches and fringes of bush had encroached more upon the green, shining monotony. Vague blue tracery of higher ground hung over the horizon. The waterfowl, except for cranes and egrets, had given way to a variable and colorful parrot life.

"Makes no difference if we do pass the happy huntin' ground of this breed of abos," said Red, one night. "We'll only run into more. This heah bunch has got me buffaloed. You cain't see them. A coupla more hosses butchered will put me on the warpath, boss or no boss! I figger that killin' some of them would stop their doggin' us. Thet used to be the case with the plains redskins."

As the bush encroached more upon the downs, corroborees were held nightly by the aborigines. The wild revels and the weird chantings murdered sleep for the trekkers. Always over them hovered the evil portent of what the cannibals had been known to do in the remote Australian wildernesses.

One gray morning dawned with bad news for the Slyters. Leslie's thoroughbred, a gray roan stallion of great promise, which the girl called Lord Chester, was missing from the band. Red ran across the spot where he had been killed and butchered. Upon their return to camp, Leslie was waiting in distress.

"Les, we cain't find him," confessed Red. "An' I jest reckon he's gone the way of so many of Dann's hosses." She broke down and wept bitterly.

"Say, cain't you take yore medicine?" queried Red, always prone to hide his softer side under a cloak of bitterness or scorn. "This heah trek ain't no circus parade. What's another hoss, even if he is one of yore thoroughbreds?"

"Red Krehl!" she cried in passionate amaze at his apparent callousness. "I've lost horses—But Chester!—It's too much—I loved him—almost as I do—Jane."

"Shore you did. I felt thet way once over a hoss. It's tough. But don't be a baby."

"Baby? I'm no baby, Red Krehl! It's Dann and

Dad—and *you*—all of you who've lost your nerve! If you and Sterl—and Larry and Rol—if you had any man in you—you'd *kill* these abos!"

The girl's passion, her rich voice stinging with scorn, appeared to lash the cowboy.

"By gosh, Leslie," he replied. "I shore deserved thet. No excuse for me, or any of us, onless we're jest plain worn to a frazzle."

"Red Krehl, what do you mean by that speech?" demanded Beryl.

"Never mind what I meant. Leslie hit me one below the belt."

"That is no reason for you to concoct some blood reprisal of revenge. Leslie is a grand girl. She has proved that to me. But she's like you—a savage. She forgets."

"Yeah? Forgets what?" drawled the cowboy.

"That her loss was only a horse. If you and Sterl and Larry and Rollie should be killed or badly wounded—our trek is doomed."

"Beryl," returned Red, "you're smarter than any of us. But Leslie's ravin' is more sense than yore intelligence. It's a hard nut to crack...."

A hundred times that day Sterl saw Red turn in his saddle to look for the smoke signals of the ab-originals rising above the bush horizon to the north. Toward noon of that day they vanished. But that night in camp, when Larry, Rollie and Benson were about to go out on guard, Friday held up his hand: "Corroboree!" They listened. From the darkness wailed a chant as of lost souls.

"How far away, Friday?" asked Red, tersely.

"Close up."

"How many?"

"Plenty black fella. No gin. No lubra."

Red swept a blue-fire glance all around to see that he would not be overheard by the women. "Fellers, it's a hunch. Grab yore rifles an' extra cartridges. We'll give these abos a mess of lead."

Friday led the way beyond camp. As they neared the bush the chant swelled to a pitch indicating many voices. Soon, dark, dancing forms grotesquely crossed the firelight. Friday led a zigzag way through the bush and brush.

They were halted by a stream or pond.

"About as far as we can get," whispered Red. "Let's take a peep. Careful now!"

Silently the five rose from behind the fringe of brush, to peer over the top. Sterl was surprised to see a wide stretch of water, mirroring three fires and fantastic figures of abos dancing in strange gyrations. The distance was about a hundred yards.

"Plenty black fella," whispered Friday, in tense excitement. "Big corroboree! Full debbil along hoss meat! Bimeby bad!"

"I should snicker to snort," whispered Red. "Mebbe he means thet hossflesh has gone stale. They want long-pig! Let's frame it thet way."

"It's a cinch they'll roast us next!" said Sterl.

"All right," whispered Red, tensely. "Make shore

of yore first shot. Then empty yore rifles pronto, re-load, an' slope. Pard Sterl, forget yore Injun-lovin' weakness, an' shoot like you could if one of us was in there roastin' on the coals."

They cocked and raised their rifles. Sterl drew down upon a dense group of dark figures, huddled together, swaying in unison.

"One—two—three—*shoot!*" hissed Red.

The rifles cracked. Pandemonium broke loose. The abos knocked against each other in their mad rush. And a merciless fired poured into them. When Sterl paused to reload he peered through the smoke. Red was still shooting. From the circle of light, gliding black forms vanished. But around the fires lay prone abos, and many writhing, and shrieking.

"Slope—fellers," ordered Red, huskily, and then turned away on the run. At length the cowboy halted from exhaustion.

"Reckon we're out of—reach of—them spears," he gasped. "I ain't used—to runnin'—Wal, did it work?"

"Work? It was a—massacre," declared Benson, in hoarse, broken accents.

"Let's rustle—for camp," added Red. "They'll all be—scared stiff."

His premonition had ample vindication. When Red called out, they all appeared from under the wagon.

"What the hell?" boomed Dann, as he stalked out, rifle in hand.

"Were you attacked?" queried Slyter, sharply.

Beryl ran straight into Red, to throw her arms round him, then sink limply upon his breast. She was beyond thinking of what her actions betrayed.

"Boss," he said, "we went after them. It jest had to be done."

"Well—what happened?" demanded the leader, his breath whistling.

"We blasted hell out of them," declared Benson. "And it was a good thing."

"Hazelton, are you dumb?" queried Slyter, testily.

"Wholesale murder, boss," replied Sterl. "But justifiable. Friday intimated that we might be roasting next on their spits."

"Oh, Red!" cried Beryl. "I thought you had—broken your promise—that you might be—"

"Umpumm, Beryl," returned Red, visibly moved, as he released himself and steadied her on her feet. "We was shore crazy, but took no chances. Beryl, you an' Leslie can feel shore thet bunch of abos won't hound us again."

Red's prediction turned out to be true. There were no more raids on the horses—no more smoke signals on the horizon. But days had to pass before the drovers believed in their deliverance.

They trekked off the downs into mulga and spinifex country, covered with good grass, fairly well watered and dotted with dwarf gums and fig and pandanus trees. The ground was gradually rising. They came next into a region of anthills. Many a field of these queer earthen habitations had they passed through. But this one gave unparalleled and remarkable evidence of the fecundity and energy of the wood and leaf-eating ants. Gray and yellow in the sunlight, the anthills were of every size, up to the height of three tall men. At night they shone ghostly in the starlight. Sterl found that every dead log he cut into was only a shell—that the interior had been eaten away. And from every dead branch or tree poured forth an army of ants, furious at the invasion of their homes.

At last Sterl understood the reason for Australia's magnificent eucalyptus trees. In the ages past, nature had developed the gum tree with its many variations, all secreting eucalyptus oil, as defensive a characteristic as the spines on a cactus.

Then they camped on a range of low hills, with a watercourse which gave them an easy grade. Followed to its source, that stream led to a divide. Water here ran toward the west. That was such a tremendous circumstance, so significant in its power to stir almost dead hopes, that Dann called a halt to rest, to recuperate, to make much needed repairs.

"It is that unknown country beyond outback Australia!" exclaimed Slyter.

Friday made a slow gesture which seemed symbolic of the infinite. Indeed this abyss resembled the void of the sky. The early morning was hot, clear, windless. Beneath and beyond him rolled what seemed a thousand leagues of green-patched, white-striped slope, leading down, down to a nothingness that seemed to flaunt a changeless inhospitality in the face of man. It was the other half of the world. It dreamed and brooded under the hot sun. On and on forever it spread and sloped and waved away into infinitude.

"Never-never Land!" gasped Slyter.

"White fella go alonga dere nebber come back!" said Friday.

Turning away from that spectacle, the men returned down the hill. At camp Slyter reported simply and truthfully that the trek had passed on to the border of the Never-never Land. No need to repeat the aborigine's warning.

"Good-o!" boomed Stanley Dann. "The Promised Land at last! Roll along, you trekkers!"

Midsummer caught Dann's trek out in the arid interior. They knew it was midsummer by the heat and drought, but in no other way, for Dann and Sterl had long since tired of recording labor, misery, fight and death.

They had followed a stream bed for weeks. Here and there, miles apart, they found clear pools in rocky places. The bleached grass had grown scant, but it was nutritious. If the cattle could drink every day or two they would survive. But many of the weak dropped by the wayside. Cows with newly born calves had been driven from the waterholes; and when the calves failed the mothers refused to leave them. Some mornings the trek would be held up because of strayed horses. Some were lost. Dann would not spare the time to track them. The heat was growing intense.

The trek had become almost chaotic when the drovers reached a zone where rock formations held a succession of pools of clear water including one that amounted to a pond.

"Manna in the wilderness!" sang out Stanley Dann, joyfully. "We will camp here until the rains come again!"

To the girls that meant survival. To the drovers it was exceedingly joyous news. The water was a saving factor, just in the nick of time. For everywhere were evidences of a long cessation of rain in these parts. In good seasons the stream must have been a fair little river, and during flood time it had spread all over the flat. Birds and animals had apparently deserted the locality. The grass was bleached white; plants had been burned sere by the sun; trees appeared to be withering.

Dann said philosophically to Slyter: "We have water enough and meat and salt enough to exist here for five years." That showed his trend of thought. Sterl heard Slyter reply that the supply of water would not last half as long as that. "We'll have to build a strong brush roof over that pond, in case the dust storms begin," he added.

The most welcome feature of this camp was the cessation of haste. For days and weeks and months the drovers had been working beyond their strength. Here they could make up for that. The horses and cattle, after a long dry trek, would not leave this sweet water. Very little guarding would they need.

Sterl and Red, helped by Friday, leisurely set about selecting a site, pitching their tent, making things comfortable for a long stay. Working at these tasks took up the whole first day. Everyone else had been busy likewise. At supper Sterl gazed around to appreciate a homelike camp. But if, or when, it grew windy in this open desert, he imagined, they would have more to endure than even the scorching heat of the camp at the forks.

Mrs. Slyter laid out the same old food and drink, but almost unrecognizable because of her skill in cooking and serving. As for Beryl and Leslie, Red summed it up: "Wal, dog-gone it, I reckon a cowboy could stand a grubline forever with two such pretty waitresses.... Heah you air, girls, thin as bean poles an' burned brown as autumn leaves."

"We're not as thin as bean poles!" asserted Leslie. This epithet of Red's was not wholly true—yet how slim and frail Beryl was, and how slender the once sturdy Leslie!

The womenfolk, having served the supper, joined the drovers at the table. Afterward Larry and Rollie cleared away and washed the dishes. The drovers sat and smoked awhile, conversing desultorily.

"No flies or mosquitoes here," said Dann.

"Flies will come bye and bye," replied Slyter.

"There'll be a good few calves dropped here."

"And colts foaled, too. But we have lost so many!"

"Boss, where do you figger we air?" asked Red.

"Somewhere out in the Never-never Land. Five hundred miles outback, more or less."

"Dann, I'll catch up with my journal now," interposed Sterl. "I can recall main events, but not dates."

"Small matter now. Keep on with your journal, if you choose. But I—I don't care to recall things. No one would ever believe we endured so much. And I would not want to discourage future drovers."

Red puffed a cloud of smoke to hide his face, while he drawled: "Girls, you're gonna be old maids shore as shore can be, if we ever get out alive."

"You bet we are, Red Krehl, if help for such calamity ever depended on Yankee blighters we know," cried Leslie, with spirit.

Beryl's response was surprising and significant. "We are old maids now, Leslie dear," she murmured, dreamily. "I remember how I used to wonder about that. And to—to pine for a husband.... But it doesn't seem to matter now."

"But it would be well if we could!"

Stanley Dann said: "God gave us thoughts and vocal powers but we use them, often, uselessly and foolishly. You young people express too many silly ideas.... You girls are not going to be old maids, nor are you cowboys ever going to be old bachelors. We are going through."

"Shore we air, boss," flashed Red. "But if we all could forget—an' face this hell like you—an' also be silly an' funny onct in a while, we'd go through a damn sight better!"

Dann slapped his knee with a great broad hand. "Righto! I deserve the rebuke—I am too obsessed— too self-centered. But I do appreciate what I owe you all. Relax, if you can. Forget! Play jokes! Have fun! Make love, God bless you!"

As Dann stamped away, Sterl remarked that there was gray in the gold over his temples—that his frame was not so upright and magnificent as it had once been. And that saddened Sterl. How all the dead must haunt him!

The abrupt change from excessive labor, from sleeplessness and fear to rest, ease, and a sense of safety, reacted on all the trekkers. They had one brief spell of exquisite tranquillity before the void shut down on them with its limitless horizon lines, its invisible confines, its heat by day, its appalling sol- itude by night, its sense that this raw nature had to be fought.

Nothing happened, however, that for the time being justified such fortification of soul and body. If the sun grew imperceptibly hotter, that could be gauged only by the touch of bare flesh upon metal. The scarcity of living creatures of the wild grew to be an absolute barrenness, so far as the trekkers knew. A gum tree blossomed all scarlet one morning, and the girls announced that to be Christmas Day. Sterl and Red found the last of the gifts they had brought on the trek. At supper presentations fol- lowed. The result was not in Sterl's or Red's calcu- lations. From vociferous delight Beryl fell to hysterical weeping, which even Red could not assuage. And Leslie ate so much of the stale candy that she grew ill.

One day Friday sighted smoke signals on the horizon. "Black fella close up!" he said.

At once the camp was plunged into despair. Dann ordered fortifications thrown up on two sides. Then Friday called the leader's attention to a strange procession filing in from the desert. Human beings that did not appear human! They came on, halted, edged closer and closer, halted again, paralyzed with fear yet driven by a stronger impulse. First came a score or less of males, excessively thin, gaunt, black as ebony and practically naked. They all carried spears, but appeared the opposite of formidable. The gins were monstrosities. There were only a few lubras, scarcely less hideous than the gins. A troop of naked children hung back behind them, wild as wild beasts, ragged of head, pot-bellied.

Friday advanced to meet them. Sterl heard his voice, as well as low replies. But sign language predominated in that brief conference. The black came running back.

"Black fella starbbin deff," he announced. "Plenty sit down die. Tinkit good feedum."

"Oh, good indeed Friday," boomed Dann, gladly. "Go tell them white men friends."

"By jove!" ejaculated Slyter. "Poor starved wretches! We have crippled cattle that it will be just as well to slaughter."

Benson had butchered a steer that day, only a

haunch had been brought to camp. The rest hung on a branch of a tree a little way from camp down the river course. Head, entrails, hide and legs still lay on the rocks, ready to burned or buried. Dann instructed Friday to lead the aborigines to the meat. They gave the camp a wide, fearful berth. Slyter brought a small bag of salt. Larry and Rollie built a line of fires. Sterl and Red, with the girls, went close enough to see distinctly. The abos watched the drovers with ravenous eyes. Larry pointed to a knife and cleaver on a log. All of them expected a corroboree. But this tribe of abos had passed beyond ceremony. They did not, however, act like a pack of wolves. One tall black, possibly a leader, began to hack up the beef into pieces and, pass them out. The abos sat down to devour the beef, raw. When, presently the blacks attacked the entrails, Beryl and Leslie fled.

When darkness fell the little campfires flickered under the trees, and dark forms crossed them, but there was no sound, no chant. Next day discovered the fact that the abos had devoured the entire carcass, and lay around under the trees asleep. More abos arrived that morning as famished as the first ones.

Friday had some information to impart that night. These aborigines had for two years of drought been a vanishing race. The birds and beasts, the snakes and lizards, had all departed beyond the hills to a lake where this weak tribe dared not go because they would be eaten by giant men of their own color. Friday said that the old abos expected the rains to come after a season of wind and dust storms.

The drovers took that last information with dismay, and appealed to their black man for some grain of hope.

"Blow dust like hellum bimeby!" he ejaculated, solemnly.

Days passed, growing uncomfortably hot during the noon hours, when the trekkers kept to their shelters.

The aborigines turned out to be good people. Day after day the men went out to hunt game, and the gins to dig weeds and roots. Dann supplied them with meat and the scraps from the camp table. Presently it became manifest that they had recovered and were faring well. The suspicion of the drovers that they might reward good deeds with evil thefts had so far been wholly unjustified. They never came into the encampment.

One night the sharp-eyed Leslie called attention to a dim circle around the moon. Next morning the sun arose overcast, with a peculiar red haze.

A light wind, the very first at that camp which had been named *Rock Pools* by Leslie, sprang up to fan the hot faces of the anxious watchers, and presently came laden with fine invisible particles and a dry, pungent odor of dust.

CHAPTER
29

ANY of you folks ever been in a dust or sand storm?" asked Red Krehl, at breakfast.

The general experience in that line had been negative, and information meager. "Bushwhackers have told me that duststorms in the outback were uncomfortable," vouchsafed Slyter.

"Wal, I'd say they'd be hell on wheels. This heah country is open, flat an' dry for a thousand miles."

"Are they frequent on your western ranges?" queried Dann.

From the cowboys there followed a long dissertation, with anecdotes, on the dust and sandstorms which, in season, were the bane of cattle drives in their own American Southwest.

"Boys, I've never heard that we had anything

similar to your storms here in Australia," said Dann, when they had finished.

"Wal boss, I'll bet you two-bits—one bob—you have wuss than ours," drawled Red.

"Very well. We are forewarned. By all means let us fortify ourselves. We have already roofed the rock pool. What else?"

Without more ado Sterl and Red put into execution a plan they had previously decided upon. They emptied their tent and repitched it on the lee side of Slyter's big wagon. Then while they were covering the wheels as a windbreak, Beryl and Leslie approached, very curious.

"Red, why this noble look on your sweaty brow?" asked Beryl.

"Don't be funny, Beryl Dann. This heah is one hell of a sacrifice. Dig up all yore belongin's an' yore beds, an' put them in this tent."

"Why?" queried Beryl, incredulously.

" 'Cause you're gonna bunk in heah an' stay in heah till this comin' dust storm is over."

"Yeah? Who says so?"

"I do. An', young woman, when I'm mad I'm quite capable of usin' force."

"I'll just love that. But it's one of your bluffs."

Beryl stood before Red in her slim boy's garb, hands on her hips, her fair head to one side, her purple eyes full of defiance and something else, fascinating as it was unfathomable.

"I'll muss yore nice clothes all up," insisted Red. "But they gotta go in this tent an' so do you."

"Red Krehl, you are a tyrant. I'm trained to be meek and submissive, but I'm not your slave *yet*!"

"You bet you're not an' you never will be," said Red, hot instead of cool. "You meek an' submissive?—My Gawd!"

"Red, I could be both," she returned, sweetly.

"Yeah? Wal, it jest wouldn't be natural. Beryl, listen heah." Red evidently had reacted to this situation with an inspiration. "I'm doin' this for yore sake. Yore face, Beryl—thet lovely gold skin of yores, smooth as satin, an' jest lovely. A dry dust storm will shrivel it up into wrinkles! You girls will have to stay in heah while the dust blows. All day long! At night it usually quiets down—at least where I come from. ...Please now, Beryl."

"All for my good looks!" murmured Beryl, with great, dubious eyes upon him. "Red, I'm afraid I don't care so much about them as I used to."

"But I care," rejoined Red.

"Then I'll obey you," she said. "You are very sweet to me. And I'm a cat!"

The cowboys helped the girls move their beds, blankets, and heavy pieces into the tent. For their own protection they packed their belongings under the wagon, then folded and tied canvas all around it, and weighted down the edges. They advised the drovers to do likewise which advice was followed. Sterl, going to the rock pool for water, saw that the abos were erecting little windbreaks and shelters.

There seemed to be fine invisible fire embers in a wind that had perceptibly strengthened. Transparent smoke appeared to be rising up over the sun. A dry, acrid odor, a fragrance of eucalyptus and a pungence of dust, seemed to stick in the nostrils.

"There she comes, pard, rollin' along," drawled the Texan, pointing northeast, over the low ground where the bleached stream bed meandered.

At first, Sterl saw a rolling, tumbling, mushrooming cloud, rather white than gray in color, moving toward them over the land. With incredible speed it blotted out the sun, spread gloom over the earth, bore down in convolutions. Like smoke expelled with tremendous force the front bellied and bulged and billowed, whirling upon itself and threw out great rounded masses of white streaked by yellow, like colossal roses.

They ran back to camp, aware of thick streams of dust racing ahead of them. They wet two sheets and fastened one over the door of the girls' tent.

"Air you in there, girls?" shouted Red.

"Yes, our lords and masters, we're here. What's that roar?" replied Beryl.

"It's the storm, an' a humdinger. Don't forget when the dust seeps in bad to breathe through wet silk handkerchiefs. If you haven't handkerchiefs use some of them folderol silk things of Beryl's thet I seen once."

"Well! You hear that, Leslie? Red Krehl, I'll wager you have seen a good deal that you shouldn't have."

"Shore, Beryl. Turrible bad for me, too. Adios now, for I have no idee how long."

Sterl's last glimpse, as he crawled under the wagon, was the striated, bulging front of the dust cloud, almost upon them.

"And now to wait it out," he said, with a sigh as he lay down on his bed. "We have a lot to be thankful for. Suppose we were out in it?"

"Suppose thet mob rushes? There wouldn't be no sense in goin' out to stop them."

They settled down to endure. It was pretty hot inside. After awhile invisible dust penetrated the pores and cracks in the canvas. Red had covered his face with a wet scarf, and Sterl followed suit. After sunset the wind lulled. The cowboys went out. An opaque gloom cloaked the scene. The dust was settling. The drovers were astir; the Slyters getting supper.

By evening the air had cleared a good deal and cooled off. After supper, Sterl and Red went out with the drovers to look for the horses and cattle. They had not strayed, but Dann ordered guard duty that night in three shifts. When they returned, Friday sat by the fire with a meat bone in one hand and a piece of damper in the other.

"How long storm last?" asked Red.

"Old black fella say bery long."

"Friday, I wish the hell you'd be wrong once in awhile," complained Red.

"Bimeby," said the black.

Sterl kept a smooth-barked piece of eucalyptus in his tent, and for every day that the dust blew and the heat grew more intense he cut a notch. And then one day he forgot, and another he did not care, and after that he thought it was no use to keep track of anything because everybody was going to be smothered.

Yet they still carried on. Just when one of the trekkers was going to give up trying to breathe the wind would lull for a night. Every morsel they ate gritted on the teeth. The drovers nightly circled the mob and horses; and butchered a bullock now and then for themselves and the abos. Fortunately their drinking water remained pure and cool, which was the one factor that kept them from utter despair.

Leslie, being the youngest, and singularly resistant in spirit, stood the ordeal longest before beginning to go downhill. But Beryl seemed to be dying. On clear nights they carried her out of the tent, and laid her on a stretcher. At last only Red could get her to eat. Sterl considered it marvelous that she had not passed away long ago. But how tenaciously she had clung to love and life! Red had become silent, grim, in his grief over Beryl.

One night, after a scorching day that had been only intermittently windy, the air cleared enough to let a wan spectral moon shine down upon the camp. There was a difference in the atmosphere which Sterl imagined to be only another lying mirage of his brain. Friday pointed up at the strange moon with its almost indistinguishable ring, and said: "Bimeby!"

In the pale moonlight Beryl lay on her stretcher, a shadow of her old self, her dark little face lighted by luminous lovely eyes that must have seen into the infinite. She was conscious. Dann, in his indestructible faith, knelt beside her to pray. Red sat at her head while the others moved to and fro, silently, like ghosts.

"Red!—don't take it—so hard," whispered Beryl, almost inaudibly.

"Beryl—don't give up—don't fade away!" implored Red, huskily.

"Red — you'd never — marry me — because of...."

"No! But not because of thet....I'm not good enough to wipe yore feet!"

"You are as great—as my Dad."

Sterl led the weeping Leslie away. He could endure no more himself. Red would keep vigil beside Beryl until she breathed her last. He had no feeling left when he put the clinging Leslie from him and slunk back to his prison under the wagon, to crawl in like an animal that hid in the thicket to die. And he fell asleep.

He awoke in the night. The moan of wind, the rustle of leaves, the swish of branches were strangely absent. The stillness, the blackness, were like death.

Then he heard a faint almost imperceptible pattering upon the canvas. Oh! That lying trick of his fantasy! That phantom memory of trail nights on the home ranges, when he lay snug under canvas to hear the patter of sleet, of snow, of rain! He had dreamed of it, here in this accursed Never-never Land!

But he heard the jingle of spurs outside, and the soft pad of Friday's bare feet.

Pard!—Pard! Wake—up!"

That was Red's voice, broken, sobbing.

"I'm awake, old-timer," replied Sterl.

"It's rainin'—pard!—Beryl's gonna live!"

For nineteen days it rained—at first, steadily. Before half that time was over the dry stream bed was a little river running swiftly. After the steadiest downpour had ceased, the rains continued part of every day and every night. On the morning of the twentieth day since the dust storm, the drovers arose to greet the sun again, and a gloriously changed land.

"On with the trek!" boomed Stanley Dann.

He gave the aborigines a bullock, and steel implements that could be spared. When the trek moved out of Rock Pools these black people, no longer scarecrows, lined up stolidly to watch the white men pass out of their lives. But it was impossible not to believe them grateful.

The grass waved green and abundant, knee-high to a horse; flowers born of the rain bloomed everywhere; gum trees burst into scarlet flame, and the wattles turned gold; kangaroos and emus appeared in troops upon the plains. Water lay in league-wide lakes, with the luxuriant grass standing fresh and succulent out of it. Streams ran bank-full and clear, with flowers and flags bending over the water.

The Never-never Land stretched out on all sides, boundlessly. It was level bushland, barren in dry seasons, rich now after the rains. Eternal spring might have dwelt there.

O *NLY* the black man Friday could tell how the trekkers ever reached the oasis from the camp where Beryl came so near dying in the dust storm and his limited vocabulary did not permit of detailed description.

"Many moons," repeated the black perplexedly. "Come alonga dere." And he pointed east and drew a line on the ground, very long, very irregular. "No black fella, no kangaroo, no goanna. This fella country no good. Plenty sun. Hot like hell. White fella tinkit he die. Boss an' Redhead fightum. Cattle no drink, fall down. Plenty hosses go. White fella sit down. No water. Friday find water. One day two day alonga dis. Imm waterbag. Go back. Makeum come."

That was a long dissertation for the black. Sterl

pieced it together and filled in the interstices. His mind seemed to be a labyrinthine maze of vague pictures and sensations made up of hot sun and arid wastes, of wheels rolling, rolling, rolling on, of camps all the same, of ghostly mirages, the infernal monotony of distances, and finally fading faces, fading voices, fading images, a horrible burning thirst and a mania for water.

He had come to his senses in a stream of clear, cool running water. Gray stone ledges towered to the blue sky. There were green grass, full-foliaged trees blossoming gold, and birds in noisy flocks. Once more the melodious cur-ra-wong of the magpie pealed in his dulled ears.

"God and our black man have delivered us once more. Let us pray instead of think what has passed," said Stanley Dann, through thick, split lips from which the blood ran. All seemed said in that.

As great a miracle as the lucky star that had guided the trekkers here was their recovery through sweet fresh cool water. Even its music seemed healing. It gurgled and bubbled from under the ledges to unite and form a goodly stream that sang away through the trees to the west. That was the birth of a river which ran toward the Indian Ocean. For Sterl, and surely all of them, it was the rebirth of hope, of life, of the sense of beauty. On the second morning Leslie staggered up to gaze about, thin as a wafer. She cried: "Oh, how lovely! Paradise Oasis!"

Beryl could not walk unaided, but she shared Leslie's joy. How frail a body now housed this chastened soul! Hammocks were strung for them in the shade, and they lay back on pillows, wide-eyed.

Wild berries and fruit, fresh meat and fish, bread from the last sack of flour, added their wholesome nourishment to the magic of the sweet crystal water.

"Let me stay here forever," pleaded Beryl.

And Leslie added: "Oh, Sterl, let us never leave!"

One morning Friday sought out Sterl. "Boss, come alonga me."

"What see, Friday?" queried Sterl.

The black tapped his broad breast with his virile hand. "Black fella tinkit see Kimberleys!"

"My—God!" gasped Sterl, suddenly pierced through with vibrating thrills. "Take me!"

They scaled a gray escarpment. Far across a warm and colorful plain an upflung purple range rolled and billowed along the western horizon.

Turning toward camp and looking down, Sterl cupped his hands and loosed a stentorian yell that pealed in echo from hill to hill. He waved his sombrero. The girls waved something white in return. Then Sterl ran down the hill, distancing the barefooted black.

Leslie ran to meet him, her heart in her eyes. But Sterl saved his speech for that gaunt, golden-bearded leader. The moment was so great that he heard his voice as a whisper.

"Sir—I report—I sighted—the Kimberleys!"

Ten days down the stream from that unforgettable Paradise Oasis the trek came out of a bushland into more open plains where rocks and trees and washes were remarkable for their scarcity. The trekkers had been reduced to a ration of meat and salt with one cup of tea, and one of stewed dried fruit each day. They throve and gathered strength upon it, but Sterl felt certain that the reaction came as much from the looming purple range, beckoning them on. Twenty-two-hundred strong, the mob had improved since they struck good water, and every day calves were born, as well as colts. No smoke signals on the horizon!

One day Sterl rested a lame foot by leaving his saddle for Slyter's driver seat. Slyter's good wife lay asleep back under the canvas, her worn face betraying the trouble that her will and spirit had hidden while she was awake. Sterl talked to Slyter about the Kimberleys, the finding of suitable stations, the settling, all of which led up to what was in his mind— the future.

"Slyter, would it interest you to learn something about me?" asked Sterl.

"Indeed it would, if you wish to tell," returned the drover.

"Thanks, boss. It's only that I'd feel freer—and happier if you knew," rejoined Sterl, and told Slyter why he and Red had come to Australia.

"And we'll never go back," he concluded.

"After this awful trek, you can't still like Australia!"

"I'm mad about it, Slyter!"

"You tell me your story because of Leslie?"

"Yes, mostly. But if there had been no Leslie, probably I'd have told you anyhow."

"She loves you."

"Yes. And I love her, too. Only I have never told her that—nor the story you've just heard."

"Sterl, I could ask little more of the future than to give my daughter to such a man as you, or Krehl. We have been through the fire together. . . . As for you, young man, Australia will take you to its heart, and the past will be as if it had never been."

"I'm happy and fortunate to be able to cast my lot with you!"

"Righto! And here comes sharp-eyed Leslie. Sterl, I think I'll get off and straddle a horse for awhile. You drive and talk to Leslie."

Almost before the heavy-footed drover was on the ground, Leslie was out of her saddle to throw him her bridle reins.

"How jolly!" she cried in gay voice, as she leaped to a seat beside Sterl. "Months, isn't it, Sterl, since I rode beside you like this?"

"Years, I think."

"Oh, that long long agony!—But I'm forgetting it. Sterl, *what* were you talking to Dad about? Both of you so serious!"

"I was telling him what made me an outcast—drove me to Australia."

"*Outcast?* Oh, Sterl! I always wondered. Red, too, was so strange. But I don't care what you've ever been in the past. It's what you are that—that made me. . . ."

When she choked up, Sterl repeated the story of his life and its fatality.

"How terrible! Sterl, was—was Nan very pretty? Did you love her very much?"

"I'm afraid so."

"Love is a terrible thing!"

"Les, that gives me an idea, as Red says. Let's get the best of this old terrible love."

"Sterl, it can't be done. I know."

"Les, it can. Listen. You get hold of Red the very first chance—tonight in camp. Tell him that Beryl is dying of love of him—that she dreams of him—babbles in her sleep—that she can't live without him. ...And anything more you can make up!"

"Sterl Hazelton, I wouldn't have to lie. That is all absolutely true," returned Leslie.

"You don't say? That bad? Then all the better. Leslie, I'll tell Beryl what a state Red is in over her."

"Is it true? Does Red care that much?" queried Leslie.

"Yes. I don't think it's possible to exaggerate Red's love for that girl. But he feels he is a no-good cowboy, as he calls it."

"You bet I'll help!" she flashed. "But—but who is going to—to tell *you*—about *me*?"

"Oh, that? Well, darling, if you think it's necessary you can tell me yourself."

She fell against him, quivering, her eyelids closed. He wrapped his arm round her and drew her close. At this juncture Mrs. Slyter's voice came to them wildly.

"I've been listening to some very interesting conversation."

"Oh—Mum!" faltered Leslie, aghast, starting up.

But Sterl held her all the closer. Presently he said: "Well, then—Mum—we have your blessing, or you would have interrupted long ago."

Sterl had contrived to get Red and the girls for a walk along the stream, and there at a murmuring waterfall, he led Beryl away from their companions.

"I'm terrribly fond of you, Beryl."

"I am of you, too, Sterl. But you—and Red will be leaving us to become wanderers again—seeking adventure. I wish I were a man."

"Who told you we'd be doing that?"

"Red."

They paused beside a rock, upon which Sterl lifted Beryl to a seat, and he leaned against it to face her.

"So that geezer has been hurting you again? Doggone him! Beryl, I'm going to double-cross him, give him away."

"You mean betray him?—Don't Sterl!"

"Ummpumm. We're not—leaving," he said. "I wouldn't leave Leslie and..."

"Oh, Sterl! Then—then—"

"Yes, then! And Red would never leave me. For why?" Here Sterl related for the third time that day the story of his exile.

"How very wonderful of Red! Sterl, this Aussie lass will make up for all you've lost."

"Beryl, I'd be happier than I ever was if you and Red..."

"If only he could see!" she interrupted, passionately. "If only he could forgive and forget Ormiston—what I—what—he..."

Sterl grasped her slim shoulders and drew her down until her face was close.

"Hush! Don't say *that*—don't ever think of that again!" he said, sternly. "That is absolutely the only obstacle between you. The jealous fool in his bad hours thinks you regret.... I won't say it, Beryl Dann. And for Red's sake and yours and ours, Les's and mine, forget. *Forget!* Because Red Krehl worships you. Don't grieve another single hour. Don't believe in his indifference. Break down his armor. Oh, child, a woman can, you know. Why—why Beryl..."

She slid off the rock into his arms, blind, weeping, torn asunder, her slender hands clutching him. "No—more," she sobbed. "You break—my heart—with joy. I—I had—despaired. Twice I have—nearly died. I knew—the next time.... But this—this will save me."

Day after day the purple range loomed closer. The scouts saw at last that the stream they had followed for so long was presently going to join a river. That green and gold line disappeared round the northern end of the range. And the next day the leader of the drovers, for once actuated by haste, made for the junction. Blue smoke rose about the big trees. It must come from aboriginals, but it was not hostile.

"Boss, I ben tinkit no black fella," said Friday to Sterl.

Sterl rode ahead to tell Dann.

"Aye, my boy, I guessed that," he cried. "We have fought the good fight. With His guidance! Look around you, Sterl—richest, finest land I ever saw! Ha! A road—a ford!" and Dann pointed. He had indeed come to a road that sloped down under the giant trees to the shallow stream. His followers all saw, but none could believe his eyes.

Three white men came out into the open, halting to stare. They pointed. They gesticulated. They saw Dann's wagons, the women on the drivers' seats, the mounted drovers, the big band of horses, the great mob and ran to meet the trekkers. Dann halted his four horses, and Slyter stopped beside him. The mounted drovers lined up, a lean ragged crew, with Leslie conspicuous among them, unmistakably a girl, bronzed and beautiful.

"Good day, cobbers!" called Dann.

"Who may you be?" replied one of the three, a stalwart man with clean-shaven, rugged face and keen, intelligent eyes.

"Are those mountains the Kimberleys?" asked Dann, intensely.

"Yes. The eastern Kimberleys. Drover, you can't be Stanley Dann?"

"It really seems I can't be. But I am!" declared Dann.

"Great Scott! Dann was lost two years and more ago, according to reports at Darwin. It has taken you two years and five months to get here!"

"But death visited and dogged our trek, alas!" said Dann. "We trekked almost to the Gulf and then across the Never-never Land. And we lost several drovers, five thousand head of cattle, and a hundred horses on the way."

"My word! What great news for western Australia! I see you have a mob of cattle left. I'm glad to be the first to tell you good news."

"Good news?" boomed Dann, in echo.

"Well, rather. Dann, cattle are worth unheard of prices. Horses the same. Reason is that gold has been discovered in the Kimberleys!"

"GOLD!"

"Yes, gold! There's been a rush-in for months. Mines south of here. Trekkers coming in from Perth and Fremantle. Settlers by ship to Darwin and Wyndham. I have been freighting supplies in to the gold fields. My name is Horton."

"Do you hear, all?" boomed Dann. "The beginning of the empire I envisioned."

"We all hear, Stanley, and our hearts are full," replied Slyter.

"What river is this?" queried Dann, shaking off his bedazzlement, to point to the shining water through the trees.

"That is the Ord. You have come down the Elivre," replied Horton. "Dennison Plains are in sight to the south. The finest country, the finest grazing for stock in the world!"

"Aye, friend. It looks so. But this road? Where

does it lead and how far?"

"Follows the Ord to the seaport, Wyndham, a good few miles less than two hundred. You are in the nick of time, Dann. The government will sell this land to you so cheap it is unbelievable!"

"Ha! This land?" called Dann, his voice rolling. "*Dann's Station!* This will be our range!"

"Stanley, we must send at once for supplies," said Slyter, rousing.

"Horton, do we look like starving trekkers?"

"Indeed you do. I never saw such a peak-faced, ragamuffin lot of drovers. Or ladies so charming despite all!"

"They have lived for days now wholly on meat."

"Forgive me, Dann, for not thinking of that! Sam, run and boil the billy. Dann, I can let you have tea, fruit, sugar, tinned milk ..."

"Enough, man! Do not overwhelm us! Slyter, what shall we do next—that is, after that cup of tea?"

"Stanley, we should thank heaven, pitch camp, and plan to send both wagons to Wyndham for supplies."

"Wal, air you gonna ask *us* to get down an' come in?" drawled Red. "I reckon I can stand tea."

"American!" called out Horton, with twinkling eyes.

"Savvied again. The name is Krehl. An' heah's my pard, Hazelton."

After supper, Beryl and Leslie went into conference over the innumerable things they wanted bought. Sterl and Red sat beside a box and racked their brains to think of necessities to purchase from town.

"Strange, Red, just think!" ejaculated Sterl. "We don't really *need* anything. We have lost the sense of need."

"Yeah! How about toothbrushes, powder, soap, towels, iodine, glycerine, combs, shears to cut hair—an' socks?"

"On account of the girls we must get over all these savage habits, I suppose. . . . Have you made up your mind about Beryl?" Sterl asked, averting his eyes.

"Pard, she cared more about me than I deserve—than I ever had a girl care for me before. An' lately, I don't know for how long, she's been different. All that misery gone! She's forgot Ormiston an' every damn bit of thet—thet. . . . An' she's been happy. Jest the sweetest, softest, lovingest, most unselfish creature under the sun! An' I'd be loco if I didn't see it's because of me—that she takes it for granted. . . ."

"I should think you'd be the happiest man in the world," declared Sterl, feelingly. "I am."

"I reckon I'd be too, if I'd jest give up."

"Red! Then right this minute—do it!"

"Holy Mackell! Don't knock me down. All right, old pard, I knuckle, I show yellow! But there's a queer twist in my mind. She always got the best of me. If I could jest think up one more way to get the best of *her* before, or mebbe better *when* I tell her how I want her—then I'd match you for who's the luckiest an' happiest man." He changed the subject abruptly. "Have you looked over this range? Grandest I ever seen! Wal, think! I've got more money in my kick than I ever earned in my life. An' you had a small fortune when I seen yore belt last."

"I have it all, packed in my bag."

"Good! Wal, bright prospect, huh?"

By the eighth day, on which Benson and Roland were expected to return with the wagons and supplies, Sterl and Red had progressed well with their cabin building. The site was the Ord River side of the wooded point, high up on a grassy, flower-spangled bank, shaded by great trees from the morning sun, and facing the Kimberleys.

The cabin was to have thatched roof and walls, for which Friday scouted out a wide-leaved palm, perhaps a species of pandapus. Slyter designed the framework, which consisted of long round poles carefully fitted. Larry, who was a good carpenter, often lent a helping hand. The girls, enthusiastic over its beauty, visited the site several times a day. Red, who was now unusually mild and sweet, made one characteristic remark.

"Say, anybody would think you girls expected to live over heah with us fellers!"

That sally precipitated blushes, a rout, and from a little distance, very audible giggles.

"Red, that was a dig," remonstrated Sterl. "You are a mean cuss. If you would only take a tumble to yourself the girls *could* come over here to live."

"Hell! I've shore tumbled. What do you want for

two-bits? Canary birds? An' why don't you figger out thet trick for me to play on Beryl? I cain't last much longer. Why, when she comes near me I go plumb loco."

"Whoopee! That's talking! I've got the deal planned!"

"Yeah?"

"It's clever. Even Dann thought so. He agreed. And he was tickled!"

"You double-crossin' two-faced, Arizonie geezer!"ejaculated Red. "You told Dann before you told me?"

"Sure. I had to get his consent. Listen, pard...."

Excited cries broke in upon their colloquy. The girls appeared off at the edge of the grove. Leslie cupped her hands to her lips and shrieked: "Boys, wagon's back! Come!"

They raced like boys, to draw up abreast and panting before two bulging, canvas-covered wagons, and their excited comrades.

"Mr. Dann," Benson was saying. "Ten days going and coming. Fair to middling road. One wagon loaded with food supplies, milk, sugar, vegetables, fruit, everything. Other full of personal articles.... Four freight wagons following us with lumber, galvanized iron roofing, tools, utensils, hardware, harness, mattresses, staples—the biggest order ever filled in Wyndham!"

While the big wagons were being unpacked, while the cowboys whooped and the girls squealed, a steady, voluminous stream of questions poured into the bewildered ears of Benson and Roland, who had been to town, to a seaport, who had heard news of the world, and of the old home.

Gold had indeed been discovered in the south and west of the Kimberleys. Ships and prospectors, sheepmen and drovers, trekkers and adventurers were coming north from Perth and Fremantle and points far to the south. Ships plied regularly to Darwin. Stanley Dann's trek across the Never-never Land was the wonder of two busy seaports.

There were letters for all the company except Sterl and Red. Somehow that silenced the drawling Red and struck a pang to Sterl's heart. Stanley Dann read aloud in his booming voice a communication from Heald. He had got out safely with his comrades and the mob of cattle Dann had given them. They worked out toward the coast into fine grazing country where he and his partners established a station. Ormiston's three escaping bushrangers had been murdered by aborigines. A rumor that Dann's trekkers had perished on the Never-never had preceded Heald's return to Queensland. But he never credited it and chanced a letter. The government had offered to sell hundred-mile-square tracts of land in the outback for what seemed little money.

"Gosh! A hundred-mile-square ranch!" drawled Red. "I reckon I gotta buy myself a couple of them."

They settled themselves in the pleasant shade. Mrs. Slyter and Leslie served tea. Beryl sat pensive and abstracted. On that auspicious morning, when all had been gay, Red had not deigned to give her even a smile. What a capital actor Dann was! To all save Sterl and Red he appeared only the great leader, glad and beaming.

Presently Dann produced a little black book, worn of back and yellow of leaf. He opened it meditatively.

"Beryl, will you please come here," he said, casually. "In this new and unsettled country I think I may be useful in other ways besides being a cattleman. I shall need practice to acquire a seemly dignity, and a clarity of voice."

He continued to mull over the yellow pages. Sterl saw the big fingers quiver ever so slightly. Beryl, used to her father's moods, came obediently to stand before him.

"What, Dad?" she inquired, curiously.

"Sterl, come here and stand up with Beryl," he called. "No, let Krehl come. He might be more fitting."

Red strolled forward, his spurs jingling, his demeanor as cool and nonchalant as it ever had been.

"I've observed you holding my daughter's hand a good few times on this trek," Dann said, mildly. "Please take her hand now."

As Red reached for Beryl's hand she looked up at him with a wondering smile and her color deepened. Then Dann stood up to lift his head and expose his bronze-gold face, which appeared a profound mask, except for the golden lightning in his amber eyes.

"What's the idea, boss?" drawled Red.

"Yes, Dad, what is—all this?" faltered Beryl, confused.

"Listen, child and you Krehl," replied Dann. "This should be fun for you, and surely for the others. Please watch me. Criticize my ministerial manner and voice. Trekking does not improve even the civilized and necessary graces. Well, here we are...."

And in a swift resonant voice he ran over the opening passages of the marriage service. Then, more slowly and impressively, he addressed Red.

"James Krehl, do you take this woman to be your lawful wedded wife...to have and to hold...to love and to cherish...until death do you part?"

"I do!" replied Red, ringingly.

The leader turned to his daughter. "Beryl Dann, do you take this man to be your lawful wedded husband...to have and to hold...to love, cherish and obey until death do you part?"

"I- -I—I do!" gasped Beryl, faintly.

Dann added sonorously: "I pronounce you man and wife. Whom God has joined together let no man put asunder!"

Beryl stared up at him, visibly a prey to conflicting tides of emotions. It had been a play, of course, but the mere recital of the vows, the counterfeit solemnity, had torn her serenity asunder. When her father embraced her, thick-voiced and loving, she appeared further bewildered.

"Daddy, what a—a strange thing—for you to practice *that*—on me!"

"Beryl, it is the most beautiful thing of the ages.

...Krehl, I congratulate you with all my heart. I feel that she is safe at last."

Sterl dragged the astounded and backward Leslie up to the couple. "Red, old pard, put it there!" he cried, wringing Red's free hand. "Beryl, let me be the first to kiss the bride!" Leslie could only stare, her lips wide.

"But—but it was only a play!" flashed Beryl. Then Red kissed her lips with a passion of tenderness and violence commingled.

"Wal, wife, it was about time," drawled Red.

That word unstrung Beryl. "Wife?" she echoed, almost inaudibly. "Red! You—you *married* me— really? Father! Have I been made a—fool of?" cried Beryl, tragically.

"My daughter, compose yourself," returned Dann. "We thought to have a little fun at your expense. I am still an ordained clergyman. But you are Mrs. Krehl! I'll have marriage certificates somewhere in my luggage!"

She swayed back to Red. She could not stand without support. She lifted frail brown hands that could not cling to Red's sleeves.

"Red!—You never *asked* me!"

"Wal, honey, the fact was I didn't have the nerve. So Sterl an' I went to yore Dad an' fixed it up. Beryl, he's one grand guy." He snatched the swaying girl to his breast. Her eyelids had fallen.

"Beryl!" he shouted, in fear and remorse. "Don't you dare faint! Not heah an' now of all times in our lives! I did it thet way because I've always been dyin' of love for you. Since thet—thet orful time I've been shore you cared for me, but I never risked you out-wittin' me. I swore I'd fool you onct an' go on my knees to you the rest of my life!"

Suddenly she was shot through and through with revivified life. She did not see any others there. And when she lifted her lips to Red's, it was something—the look of both of them then—that dimmed Sterl's eyes.

"Come Sterl and Leslie," boomed Dann. "I require more practice. Here, before me, and join hands. Our bride and groom there may stand as witnesses." And almost before Sterl was sensible of anything ex-cept the shy and bedazzled girl beside him, clutching his hand, he was married!

Friday wrung Sterl's hand. No intelligence could have exaggerated what shone in his eyes.

"Me stopum alonga you an' missy. Me be good black fella. No home, no fadder, no mudder, no brud-der, no lubra. Imm stay alonga you, boss."

Sterl and Red walked by the river alone.

"Pard, it's done," said Red. "We're Australians. Who would ever have thunk it? But it's great. All this for two no-good gun-slingin' cowboys!"

"Red, it is almost too wonderful to be true!"

It was as Stanley Dann had said of them all: "We have fought the good fight." In that moment Sterl saw with marvelous clarity. It had taken a far country and an incomparable adventure with hardy souls to make men out of two wild cowboys.

Zane Grey, author of over 80 books, was born in Ohio in 1872. His writing career spanned over 35 years until his death in 1939. Estimates of Zane Grey's audience exceed 250 million readers.

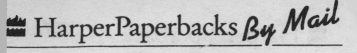

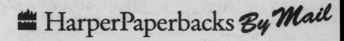

ZANE GREY CLASSICS

THE DUDE RANGER
0-06-100055-8 $3.50

THE LOST WAGON TRAIN
0-06-100064-7 $3.99

WILDFIRE
0-06-100081-7 $3.50

THE MAN OF THE FOREST
0-06-100082-5 $3.95

THE BORDER LEGION
0-06-100083-3 $3.95

SUNSET PASS
0-06-100084-1 $3.50

30,000 ON HOOF
0-06-100085-X $3.50

THE WANDERER OF THE WASTELAND
0-06-100092-2 $3.50

TWIN SOMBREROS
0-06-100101-5 $3.50

BOULDER DAM
0-06-100111-2 $3.50

THE TRAIL DRIVER
0-06-100154-6 $3.50

TO THE LAST MAN
0-06-100218-6 $3.50

THUNDER MOUNTAIN
0-06-100216-X $3.50

THE CODE OF THE WEST
0-06-100173-2 $3.50

ARIZONA AMES
0-06-100171-6 $3.50

ROGUE RIVER FEUD
0-06-100214-3 $3.95

THE THUNDERING HERD
0-06-100217-8 $3.95

HORSE HEAVEN HILL
0-06-100210-0 $3.95

VALLEY OF WILD HORSES
0-06-100221-6 $3.95

WILDERNESS TREK
0-06-100260-7 $3.99

THE VANISHING AMERICAN
0-06-100295-X $3.99

CAPTIVES OF THE DESERT
0-06-100292-5 $3.99

THE SPIRIT OF THE BORDER
0-06-100293-3 $3.99

BLACK MESA
0-06-100291-7 $3.99

ROBBERS' ROOST
0-06-100280-1 $3.99

UNDER THE TONTO RIM
0-06-100294-1 $3.99

Saddle-up to these

THE REGULATOR *by Dale Colter*
Sam Slater, blood brother of the Apache and a cunning bounty-hunter, is out to collect the big price on the heads of the murderous Pauley gang. He'll give them a single choice: surrender and live, or go for your sixgun.

THE REGULATOR—Diablo At Daybreak *by Dale Colter*
The Governor wants the blood of the Apache murderers who ravaged his daughter. He gives Sam Slater a choice: work for him, or face a noose. Now Slater must hunt down the deadly renegade Chacon...Slater's Apache brother.

THE JUDGE *by Hank Edwards*
Federal Judge Clay Torn is more than a judge—sometimes he has to be the jury *and* the executioner. Torn pits himself against the most violent and ruthless man in Kansas, a battle whose final verdict will judge one man right...and one man dead.

THE JUDGE—War Clouds *by Hank Edwards*
Judge Clay Torn rides into Dakota where the Cheyenne are painting for war and the army is shining steel and loading lead. If war breaks out, someone is going to make a pile of money on a river of blood.